Running the Gauntlet

by

Edmund Yates

The Echo Library 2019

Published by

The Echo Library

Echo Library
Unit 22
Horcott Industrial Estate
Horcott Road
Fairford
Glos. GL7 4BX

www.echo-library.com

Please report serious faults in the text to complaints@echo-library.com

ISBN 978-1-40689-513-1

RUNNING THE GAUNTLET.

A Novel,

BY

EDMUND YATES,

AUTHOR OF
"BLACK SHEEP," "KISSING THE ROD,"
ETC.

FORTITER—FIDELITER—FELICITER.

New Edition.

LONDON:
GEORGE ROUTLEDGE AND SONS,
THE BROADWAY, LUDGATE.
NEW YORK: 416, BROOME STREET.

1867.

TO
NICHOLAS HERBERT HARRINGTON,
OLD COMRADE AND TRIED FRIEND.

CONTENTS.

RUNNING THE GAUNTLET.

CHAPTER I.

NEWS.

Throughout the length and breadth of this London of ours there were few legal firms, no matter of how old standing, doing a better, larger ready-money business than that of Moss and Moss of Cursitor Street, Chancery Lane. Looked down upon? Well, one could hardly say that. Old Mr. Trivett, of the firm of Trivett, Coverdale, and Trivett of Bedford Row, who had the secrets of half the first families in England locked up in his dusty japanned boxes; young Mr. Markham, who, besides being nominally a solicitor, was a high-bailiff somewhere, and had chambers in the Albany, and rode a very maney and taily light chestnut cob in the Row; and a few others,—might shrug their shoulders when the names of Moss and Moss were mentioned; but that did no harm to Moss and Moss, who, on the whole, were very well respected throughout the profession. At Mrs. Edward Moss's Sunday-evening parties in the Regent's Park were to be met many people whose names were pleasantly familiar to the public. Mr. Smee, Q. C., known as "Alibi Smee" from his great success in proving that his clients never had been within fifty miles of the spot where the crime with which they were charged was committed; Mr. Sergeant Orson; Mr. Tocsin, who bullied a witness admirably, but who gave more trouble to Edward Moss than any other man at the bar, wanting perpetual cramming and suggestions, and having the face of brass and the lungs of steel and the head of wool; Mr. Replevin, the most rising junior at the O.B.; and others, amongst them. Gilks, the marine painter, some of whose choicest bits adorned Mrs. Moss's walls; Kreese, the editor of the great sporting, literary, and theatrical Sunday print, *The Scourge*; O'Meara of the Stock Exchange; and actors, actresses, and singers too numerous to mention. These last were invited through Mr. Marshall Moss, Edward's brother and junior partner, who was a bachelor, and who, though he gave occasional excellent Greenwich and Richmond dinners, yet had no house of his own to entertain in. Marshall Moss attended to the more convivial portion of the clients; the actors who had differed from their managers; the ladies who wanted certain settlements arranged; the sporting publicans who wanted "the screw put upon certain parties;" the fast young gents requiring defence from civil process,—were shown up to Marshall's room on the first-floor, a comfortable room with several armchairs, and a cupboard never without sherry and soda-water; a room where some of the best stories in London were from time to time told, and which was fenced off with thick double doors, to prevent the laughter caused by them penetrating to Edward's sanctum downstairs.

For Edward attended to the real clients of the house—those for whom it was originally established—those by whom its fame had been made. And these were—thieves. Yes, there is no blinking the word. If a burglar were "in trouble," if a forger had been apprehended, if some very heavy turf-robbery had come to light, Edward Moss's busy brain was at work, and Edward Moss's hours of sleep were ruthlessly curtailed. He did not care about the heaviest kind of business, though two or three murderers unquestionably owed their necks to his skill and forethought; and he refused all petty cases of magsmen, skittle-sharps, and card-swindlers. They would have longed to have him; but they knew it was impossible. He did not like their style of business, and, above all things fatal to a chance of their engaging him, he never did anything on spec. When a man was "in trouble" he knew that it was no use sending for Mr. Moss without being able to tell him that at such-and-such a tavern or lodging-house he would find a landlord willing and ready to advance the fee for the prisoner's defence. Then Mr. Moss would step into the first hansom outside the station, and hie away to St. Luke's, Cripplegate, Drury Lane, or any other locality indicated, and returning with the money in his pocket, would hear all that the prisoner had to say, and straightway—determine on the line of defence. A wonderful little man, Edward Moss! wonderful to look at! without the smallest sign of colour in his shrunken, baggy, parchmenty face, with small gray eyes under overhanging bristly brows, with a short stubbly head of gray hair, a restless twitching mouth, thin wiry figure, and dirty hands with close-bitten dubby nails. In these respects a very different man from his brother Marshall, who was a by-no-means bad-looking Hebrew, with a handsome beard and moustache, full scarlet lips, prominent brown eyes, and in face and figure showing a general liking for the flesh-pots and other good things of this life. Where Edward Moss wore dirt, Marshall Moss sported jewelry, and each brother was sufficiently vain of his display. Each knew his business perfectly, and neither interfered with the other. Marshall's clients drove up in broughams or rattled in hansoms to the front-door, went up the broad staircase to the first-floor, and either passed straight into the presence, or beguiled the necessary interval in the perusal of the daily papers handed to them by obsequious clerks. Edward's clients sneaked in through a narrow door up a side-court; had their names and business wrung from them by the most precocious and most truculent of Jew boys; were left to rub their greasy shoulders up and down the whitewashed walls of a ghastly waiting-room until "Mithter Edward" chose to listen to the recital of their distress and wishes.

Occasionally, however, visitors to Mr. Edward Moss came in at the large front-door, and afterwards made the best of their way to his sanctum. They were generally people who would not have been regarded with much favour by the greasy-shouldered clients in the court. This was one of them who entered Cursitor Street on a warm June afternoon, and made straight for the front-door blazing with the door-plate of "Moss and Moss." A middle-sized fattish man, ill-dressed in an ill-fitting blue frock-coat and gray trousers, and a very innocent-looking small hat with a black mourning-band; a sodden-faced sleepy-looking man with mild blue eyes and an undecided mouth; a man like a not very prosperous publican; a man, who, with a fresher complexion, and at another time of year, might have been taken for a visitor to the Cattle Show; who looked, in fact, anything but what he was—chief officer of the City detectives and the terror of all the evil-doers of the East-end. He walked through the hall, and, leaving the staircase leading to Mr. Marshall Moss's rooms on his right, passed to the end of the passage and tapped at a door on which was inscribed the word "Private" in large letters. It must have been a peculiar knock which he gave, for the door was immediately opened merely wide enough to admit him, and closed as he passed through.

"Ah, ah!" said a little man in an enormous pair of spectacles; "ah, ah! 'ith you, inthpector! The governor'th been athkin' after you to-day. Let'th have a look," he continued, lifting a corner of a green-baize curtain; "ah! he'th jutht shakin' off that troublethome perjury. Now I'll give him your name."

This was Mr. Amedroz, Edward Moss's right-hand man, who knew all his master's secrets, and who was so reticent that he never opened his mouth where he could convey as much by writing. So Mr. Amedroz inscribed "Stellfox" in large round-text on a slip of paper, laid it before his principal, and, receiving an affirmative nod, ushered the inspector into the presence.

"Morning, Stellfox," said Mr. Edward, glancing up from a mass of papers in front of him; "report?"

Inspector Stellfox, unbuttoning his blue frock-coat, produced from his breast-pocket a thick notebook, and commenced:

"Sorry to say, nothing new about Captain Congreve, sir. We've tried—"

"Now look here, Stellfox," interrupted Mr. Moss; "you've had that business in hand a fortnight. If you don't report by Wednesday, I'll give that to Scotland Yard. Your men are getting lazy, and I'll try what Sir Richard Mayne's people can do. What next?"

Crestfallen, Inspector Stellfox continued,—"Slimy William, sir."

"Well," said Mr. Moss keenly, "what of him?"

"I think that's all right, sir. We've found out where his mother lives,—Shad's Row, Wapping, No. 3; bill up in the window, 'a room to let.' If you've no objection, one of my men shall take that room, sir, and try and work it that way."

"No," said Mr. Moss; "must put a woman in there. Don't you know a woman up to that sort of thing?"

"There's Hodder's wife, sir, as helped us in Charlton's case; she'd do."

"I recollect; she'll do well. Furnished or unfurnished?"

"Unfurnished room, sir."

"All right; hire some furniture of the broker. Tell Mrs. Hodder to get in at once. Widow; or husband employed on railway in the country. Must keep a gin-bottle always open, and be generous with it. Old lady will talk over her drink; and Mrs. Hodder must find out where Slimy William is, what name he's going under, and must notice what letters old lady receives. Tell her to take a child with her. Has she got a child?"

"Not of her own, sir."

"Never mind; must get one of some one else's. Must see you, or one of your men, every morning. Child will want air—excuse for her taking him out. If Slimy William is coming home on the sudden, child must be taken ill in the middle of the night; she can take it to the doctor, and come down to you."

"Right, sir. Now about Coping Crossman."

"Well?"

"Markham will have him to-night, sir. That girl 'Liza Burdon blew his gaff for him last night. He's a comic singer, he is. Goes by the name of Munmorency, and sings at the Cambridge Music-hall."

"Good! What of Mitford?"

"Well, nothing yet, sir. You're hard upon me, Mr. Moss, and that you are. We've only had that case three days, and you're expecting information already."

"Stellfox," said Mr. Moss rising, and taking a sonorous pinch of snuff, "you detectives are mere shams. You've been spoilt by the penny press, and the shilling books, and all that. You think you're wonderful fellows, and you know nothing—literally nothing. If I didn't do your work as well as my own, where should we be? Don't answer; listen! Mitford has been three times within the last week to the Crown coffee-house in Doctors' Commons. There's very little doubt that he'll go there again; for it's a quiet house, and he seems to like it. You've got his description; be off at once."

Inspector Stellfox had transacted too much business with Mr. Edward Moss to expect any further converse, so he took up the child's hat and quietly bowed and departed.

To say that of all the intensely-quiet and respectable houses in that strange portion of the City of London known as Doctors' Commons the Crown coffee-house is the most quiet and respectable, is making a strong assertion, but one which could yet be borne out by facts. It is a sleepy, dreamy neighbourhood still, although its original intense dulness has been somewhat enlivened by the pedestrians who make Paul's Chain a passage to the steamboats calling at Paul's Wharf; and the hansom cabs which find a short cut down Great St. Andrew's Hill to the South-Western Railway. But it is still the resort of abnormal individuals,—ticket-porters, to wit; plethoric individuals in half-dirty white aprons and big badges like gigantic opera-checks, men whose only use seems to be to warn approaching vehicles of the blocking-up of the narrow streets; and sable-clad mottled-faced proctors and their clerks. There are real green trees in Doctors' Commons; and flies and butterflies—by no means bad imitations of the real country insect—are seen there on the wing in the sultry summer days, buzzing round the heads of the ticket-porters, and of the strong men who load the Bottle Company's heavy carts, and who are always flinging huge fragments of rusty iron into the capacious hold of the Mary Anne of Goole, stuck high and dry in the mud off Paul's Wharf before mentioned. Life is rampant in the immediate vicinity,—in enormous Manchester warehouses, perpetually inhaling the contents of enormous Pickford's vans; in huge blocks of offices where the representatives of vast provincial firms take orders and transact business; in corn-stores and iron-companies; in mansions filled from basement to roof with Dresden china and Bohemian glass in insurance-offices and banks; and in the office of the great journal, where the engines for six days out of the seven, are unceasingly throbbing. But in the Commons life gives way to mere existence and vegetation. The organ-man plays unmolested on Addle Hill, and the children's shuttlecocks flutter in Wardrobe Place; no Pickford's vans disturb the calm serenity of Great Knightrider Street; and instead of warehouses and offices, there are quaint old dumpy congregationless churches, big rambling old halls of City Companies, the forgotten old Heralds' College with its purposeless traditions, a few apparently nothing-doing shops, a number of proctors' offices into which man is never seen to enter, and two or three refreshment-rooms. Of these the Crown is the oldest and the dirtiest. It was established—if you may trust the half-effaced legend over its door—in 1790, and it has ever since been doing the same quiet sleepy trade. It cannot understand what Kammerer's means by it. Kammerer's is the refreshment-house at the corner, which has long since escaped from the chrysalis state of coffee-shop, and now, resplendent with plate-glass and mahogany bar, cooks joints, and draws the celebrated "Crm Grw" Llangollen ale, and is filled with a perpetual stream of clattering junior clerks from the adjacent warehouses. The Crown— according to its proprietor, in whose family its lease has been vested since its establishment—don't do nothin' of this sort, and don't want to. It still regards chops and steaks as the most delicious of human food, and tea and coffee as the only beverages by which their consumption should be accompanied. Across its window still stretches an illuminated blind representing an Italian gentleman putting off in a boat with apparently nothing more serviceable for navigation purposes than a blue banjo; and it still makes a gorgeous display of two large coffee-cups and saucers, with one egg in a blue egg-cup between them. Its interior is still cut up into brown boxes with hard narrow seats, on which you must either sit bolt upright, or fall off at once; its narrow old tables are scarred and notched and worm-eaten; and it holds yet by its sawdusted floor.

About seven o'clock in the evening of the same day on which Inspector Stellfox had consulted Mr. Moss, the green-baize door of the Crown was gently swung open, and a man slinking in dived into the nearest box then vacant. He was a young fellow of not more than three-and-twenty, with well-cut regular features, and who would have been handsome had not his complexion been so sallow and his cheeks so pinched. His gaunt attenuated frame, thin hands, and eyes of unnatural brightness and restlessness, all told of recent illness; and though it was summer time his threadbare coat was tightly buttoned round his throat, and he shivered as he seated himself, and looked hungrily at the cooking-fire burning in the kitchen at the other end of the shop. After furtively glancing round him he beckoned the proprietor, gave him an order for some small refreshment, and then taking down an old volume of the

Gentleman's Magazine from a neighbouring shelf, began to turn over its pages in a listless, purposeless manner. While he was thus engaged, the green-baize door swung open again, admitting a portly man with a child's hat perched on the top of his round head, who, walking into the middle of the shop, ordered from that post of vantage "a large cup of coffee and a rasher," then looked round the different boxes, and finally settled himself with his back to the light in that box where the last arrival was seated. The portly man made the other visitor a very polite bow, which was scarcely returned, and the first comer bent more earnestly over his book and shrouded his face with his hand. But the portly man, who was no other than Inspector Stellfox, had been too long in his profession not to know his business thoroughly, and so he hung up the child's hat on a peg immediately over his friend's head, and he took hold of a newspaper which lay directly under his friend's elbow; and taking advantage of each opportunity to look his friend over and over, saw that he was on the right track, and thoroughly made up his mind what to do when the chance arrived. The chance arrived simultaneously with the refreshment ordered by the haggard man: he had to put down his hand to reach the tray, and in so doing his eyes met those of the inspector, who at once winked and laid his finger on his lip.

"Mr. Mitford?" said he in a fat voice; "ah! I thought so. No, you don't, sir," he continued, pushing back the man, who had attempted to start up; "it's all right; that little matter at Canterbury's been squared up long since. I wanted to see you about something else. Look here, sir;" and the inspector took from his pocketbook a printed slip of paper, and handed it across the table to his companion, who read as follows:

"FATAL AND APPALLING ACCIDENT.

"We (*Bridgewater Mercury*) deeply regret to hear that a telegram has been received from Malta stating that Sir Percy Mitford of Redmoor near this town, and his two sons, aged twelve and nine, were drowned by the upsetting of a little boat in which they were proceeding to Sir Percy's well-known yacht Enchantress, then anchored off Valetta. By this dreadful accident the title and estates pass into another branch of the family; the heir being Sir Percy's nephew, Mr. Charles Wentworth Mitford, now studying abroad."

"There, sir! there's news for you!" said Inspector Stellfox; "we know what studying abroad means, don't we? We knows—" but Inspector Stellfox stopped suddenly; for his companion, after glaring at him vacantly for an instant with the paper outstretched in his rigid hand, fell forward in a fit.

CHAPTER II.

MORE NEWS.

Twenty years ago the Maecenas Club, which is now so immensely popular, and admission to which is so difficult, was a very quiet unpretending little place, rather looked down upon and despised by the denizens of the marble palaces in Pall Mall and the old fogies in St. James's Street. The great gaunt stuccoed mansion, with the bust of Maecenas in the big hall, then was not; the Club was held at a modest little house, only differing from a private residence in the size of its fanlight, in the fact of its having a double flight of steps (delicious steeple-chase ground for the youth of the neighbourhood), and from its hall-door being always open, typical of the hospitality and good-fellowship which reigned within. Ah! a glorious place in those days, the Maecenas! which, as it stated in its prospectus, was established "for the patronage of literature and the drama, and the bringing together of gentlemen eminent in their respective circles;" but which wisely left literature, the drama, and the eminent gentlemen to take care of themselves, and simply brought together the best and most clubbable fellows it could get hold of. There was something in the little M., as the members fondly abbreviated its name, which was indescribably comfortable and unlike any other club. The waiters were small men, which perhaps had something to do with it; there was no billiard-room, with noisy raffish frequenters; no card-room, with solemn one-idea'd fogies; no drawing-room for great hulking men to lounge about, and put up their dirty boots on yellow satin sofas. There was a capital coffee-room, strangers'-room, writing-room, reading-room, and the best smoking-room in London; a smoking-room whence came three-fourths of the best stories which permeated society, and whither was brought every bit of news and scandal so soon as it was hatched. There was a capital *chef* who was too true an artist to confine himself to made-dishes, but who looked after the joints and toothsome steaks, for which the M. had such a reputation; and there was a capital cellar. Furthermore, the members believed in all this, and believed intensely in one another.

That a dislike to clubs is strongly rooted in the female breast is not a mere aphorism of the comic writer, but is a serious fact. This feeling would be much mitigated, if not entirely eradicated, one would think, if women could only know the real arcana of those much-loathed establishments. Life wants something more than good *entrées* and wine, easy-chairs, big waiters, and a place to smoke in: it wants companionship and geniality—two qualities which are very rare in the club-world. You scowl at the man at the next table, and he scowls at you in return; the man who wants the magazine retained by your elbow growls out something, and you, raising your arm, growl in reply. In the smoking-room there is indeed an attempt at conversation, which is confined to maligning human nature in general, and the acquaintance of the talkers in particular; and as each man leaves the room his character is wrested from him at the door, and torn to shreds by those who remain.

It was its very difference from all these that made the Maecenas so pleasant. Everybody liked everybody else, and nobody objected to anybody. It was not too pleasant to hear little Mr. Tocsin, Q.C., shrieking some legal question across the coffee-room to a brother barrister; to have your mackerel breathed over by Tom O'Blather, as he narrated to you a Foreign-Office scandal, in which you had not the smallest interest; to have to listen to Dr. M'Gollop's French jokes told in a broad-Scotch accent, or to Tim Dwyer's hunting exploits with his "slash'n meer;" but one bore these things at the M., and bore them patiently. How proud they were of their notable members in those days; not swells, but men who had distinguished themselves by something more than length of whisker and shortness of head—the very "gentlemen eminent in their respective circles" of the prospectus! They were proud, and justly so, of Mr. Justice Ion, whose kindly beaming face, bright eye, and short-cropped gray hair would often be seen amongst them; of Smielding and Follett, the two great novelists of the day, each of whom had his band of sworn retainers and worshippers; of Tatterer, the great tragedian, who would leave King Lear's robes and be the delight of the Maecenas smoke-room; of Gilks the marine-painter; of Clobber, who was so great in cathedral interiors; and Markham, afterwards the great social caricaturist, then just commencing his career as a wood-draughtsman. The very reciprocity of regard was charming for the few swells who at that time cared for membership; they were immensely popular; and amongst them none so popular as Colonel Laurence Alsager, late of the Coldstream Guards.

By the time that Laurence Alsager was gazetted as captain and lieutenant-colonel, he had had quite enough of regimental duty, quite enough of transition from Portman Barracks to Wellington Barracks, from Winchester to Windsor; quite enough of trooping the guard at St. James's and watching over the treasures hidden away in the Bank-cellars; of leaning out of the little window in the old Guards Club in St. James's Street; quite enough of Derby drags and *ballet* balls, and Ryde pier and Cowes regatta, and Scotch moor and Norway fishery, and Leamington steeple-chase and Limmer's, and all those things which make up the life of a properly-regulated guardsman. The younger men in the Household Brigade could not understand this "having had quite enough." They thought him the most enviable fellow in the world. They dressed at him, they walked like him, they grew their whiskers as nearly like his as they could (mutton-chop whiskers were then the fashion, and beards and moustaches were only worn by foreign fiddlers and cavalry regiments), they bragged of him in every possible way, and one of them having heard him spoken of, from the variety of his accomplishments, as the Admirable Crichton, declared that he was infinitely better than Crichton, or any other admiral that had ever been in the sister service. The *deux-temps* valse had just been imported in those days, and Alsager danced it with a long, quick, swinging step which no one else could accomplish; he played the cornet almost as well as Koenig; while at Windsor he went into training and beat the Hammersmith Flyer, a professional brought down by the envious to degrade him, in a half-mile race with twelve flights of hurdles; he was a splendid amateur actor; and had covered the rough walls of the barrack-room at Windsor with capital caricatures of all his brother officers. He knew all the mysteries of "battalion drill" too, and had been adjutant of the regiment. When, therefore, he threw up his commission and sold out, everybody was utterly astonished, and all sorts of rumours were at once put into circulation. He had had a quarrel with his governor, old Sir Peregrine Alsager, some said, and left the army to spite him. He was bitten with a theatrical mania, and going to turn actor ("Was he, by G—!" said Ledger, the light comedian, hitherto his warmest admirer; "we want none of your imitation mock-turtle on the boards!"); he had got a religious craze, and was going to become a Trappist monk; he had taken to drinking; he had lost his head, and was with a keeper in a villa in St. John's Wood. All these things were said about him by his kind friends; but it is probable that none of them were so near the mark as honest Jock M'Laren, of the Scots Fusiliers, a great gaunt Scotchman, but the very best ferret in the world in certain matters; who said, "Ye may depen' upon it there's a wummin in it. Awlsager's a deevil among the sax; and there's a wummin in it, I'll bet a croon." This was a heavy stake for Jock, and showed that he was in earnest.

Be this as it may, how that Laurence Alsager sold out from her Majesty's regiment of Coldstream Guards, and that he was succeeded by Peregrine Wilks (whose grandfather, *par parenthèse*, kept a ham-and-beef shop in St. Martin's Court), is it not written in the chronicles of the *London Gazette*? Immediately after the business had been settled, Colonel Alsager left England for the Continent. He was heard of at Munich, at Berlin, at Vienna (where he remained for some considerable time), and at Trieste, where all absolute trace of him was lost, though it was believed he had gone off in an Austrian Lloyds' steamer to the Piraeus, and that he intended travelling through Greece, the Holy Land, and Egypt, before he returned home. These were rumours in which only a very few people interested themselves; society has too much to do to take account of the proceedings of its absent members; and after two years had elapsed Laurence Alsager's name was almost forgotten, when, on a dull January morning, two letters from him arrived in Loudon,—one addressed to the steward of the Maecenas ordering a good dinner for two for the next Saturday night at six; the other to the Honourable George Bertram of the Foreign Office, requesting that distinguished public servant to meet his old friend L. A. at the Maecenas, dine with him, and go with him afterwards to the Parthenium Theatre, where a new piece was announced.

Honest Mr. Turquand, the club steward, by nature a reticent man, and one immersed in perpetual calculation as to ways and means, gave his orders to the cook, but said never a word to any one else as to the contents of his letter. George Bertram, known among his colleagues at the Foreign Office as "Blab Bertram," from the fact that he never spoke to anybody unless spoken to, and even then seldom answered, was equally silent; so that Colonel Alsager's arrival at the Maecenas was thoroughly unexpected by the members. The trimly-shaved old gentlemen at the various tables stared with wonder, not unmixed with horror, at the long black beard which Alsager had grown during his absence. They thought he was some stranger who had entered the sacred precincts by mistake; some even had a horrible suspicion that it might be a newly-elected man, whose beard had never been mentioned to the committee; and it was not until they heard Laurence's clear ringing voice, and saw his eye light up with the old fire, that they recognized their long-absent friend. Then they crowded round him, and wanted to hear all his two-years' adventures and wanderings told in a breath; but he laughingly shook them off, promising full particulars at a later period; and went over to a small corner-table, which he had been accustomed to select before he went away, and which Mr. Turquand had retained for him, where he was shortly joined by George Bertram.

It is probable that no man on earth had a greater love for another than had George Bertram for Laurence Alsager. When he saw his old friend seated at the table, his heart leapt within him, and a great knot rose in his throat; but he was a thorough Englishman, so he mastered his feelings, and, as he gripped Laurence's outstretched hand, merely said, "How do?"

"My dear old George," said Laurence heartily, "what an age since we met! How splendidly well you seem to be! A little stouter, perhaps, but not aged a day. Well, I've a thousand questions to ask, and a thousand things to tell you. What the deuce are you staring at?"

"Beard!" said Mr. Bertram, who had never taken his eyes off Laurence's chin since he sat down opposite to him.

"O, ah, yes!" said Laurence. "That's a relic of savage life which I shall get rid of in a few days; but I didn't like to have him off suddenly, on account of the change of climate. I suppose it shocks the old gentlemen here; but I can't help it. Well, now, you've got oceans of news to tell me. It's full a twelvemonth since I had letters from England; not a line since I left Jerusalem; and—ah, by Jove! I've never told you how I happened to come in such a hurry. It's horribly absurd and ridiculous, you know; I hadn't the least idea of returning for at least another year. But one sultry evening, far up the Nile, as I was lying back in my kandjia,—boat, you know,—being towed up by three naked chaps, pulling away like grim death, we met another kandjia coming down. In it were two unmistakable Englishmen; fellows in all-round collars and stiff wideawakes, with puggerees put on all the wrong way. They were chattering to each other; and I thought, under that burning sky and solemn stillness, and surrounded by all the memorials of the past, they would probably be quoting Herodotus, or Gardner Wilkinson, or, better than all, Eothen; but, just as they passed me, what do you think I heard one of them say to the other? 'No, no, Jack,' said he, 'you're wrong there: it was Buckstone that played Box!' He did, by Jove! Under the shadow of the Pyramids, and close by the Sphinx, and the vocal Memnon, and Cheops and Cephrenes, and all the rest of it, to hear of Buckstone and *Box and Cox*! You can't tell the singular effect it had on me. I began to feel an awful longing for home; what the Germans call *Heimweh* came upon me at once. I longed to get back once more, and see the clubs and the theatres, and all the old life, which I had fled from so willingly; and I ordered the Arabs to turn the boat round and get me back to Cairo as quickly as possible. When we got to Cairo, I went to Shepherd's, and found the house full of a lot of cadets and fellows going out; and one of them had a *Times*, and in it I saw the announcement of the new piece at the Parthenium; and, I don't know why,—I fixed upon that as a sort of date-mark, and I said, I'll be back in England to see that first night;' and the next day I started for Alexandria. And on board the P.-and-O. boat I made the acquaintance of the post-office courier in charge of the Indian mail, a very good fellow, who, when he found my anxiety to get on, took me with him in his *fourgon*, brought me through from Marseilles to Calais without an instant's delay; let me come on board the special boat waiting for him, and landed me at London Bridge last night, having got through my journey wonderfully. And I'm in time for the first night at the Parthenium; and—now tell me all your news."

"Blab" Bertram had been dreading the command, which he knew involved his talking more in twenty minutes than he was in the habit of doing in a month. He had been delighted to hear Laurence rattling on about his own adventures, and fondly hoped that he should avoid any revelations for that night at least. But the dread edict had been issued, and George knew his friend too well not to obey. So he said with a sigh, drawing out a small notebook, "Yes, I knew you'd be naturally anxious to hear about people, and what had happened since you've been away; and so, as I'm not much good at telling things, I got Alick Geddes of our office—you know him, Lord M'Mull's brother—to put down some notes, and I'll read them to you."

"That'll do, George," said Laurence, laughing; "like the police, 'from information you have received,' eh? Never mind, so long as I hear it.—Mr. Turquand, they've not finished that bin of Thompson and Crofts' 20 during my absence? No. Then bring us a bottle, please. —And now, George, fire away!"

For the purposes of this story it would be needless to recount all the bits of scandal and chit-chat, interesting and amusing to those acquainted with the various actors in the drama, but utterly vapid to every one else, which the combined memories of Messrs. Alexander Geddes and George Bertram, clerks in the Foreign Office, and gentlemen going a great deal into all kinds of society, had furbished up and put together for the delectation of Colonel Alsager. It was the old, old story of London life, known to every one, and, *mutatis nominibus*, narrated of so many people. Tom's marriage, Dick's divorce, and Harry's going to the bad. Jack Considine left the service, and become sheep-farmer in Australia. Little Tim Stratum, of the Treasury, son of old Dr. Stratum the geologist, marrying that big Indian widow woman, and becoming a heavy swell, with a house in Grosvenor Square. Ned Walters dead,—fit of heart disease, or some infernal thing,—dead, by Jove; and that pretty wife of his, and all those nice little children, gone—God knows where! Lady Cecilia married? Oh, yes; and she and Townshend get on very well, they say; but that Italian chap, Di Varese, with the black beard and the tenor voice, always hanging about the house. Gertrude Netherby rapidly becoming an old woman, thin as a whipping-post, by George! and general notion of nose-and-chinniness. Florence Sackville, as lovely and as jolly as ever, was asking after you only last night. These and a hundred other little bits of gossip about men in his old regiment, and women, reputable and disreputable, formerly of his acquaintance, of turf matters and club scandals, interspersed with such anecdotes, seasoned with *gros sel*, as circulate when the ladies have left the dinner-table, did Laurence Alsager listen to; and when George Bertram stopped speaking and shut up his notebook, he found himself warmly complimented on his capital budget of news by his recently-arrived friend.

"You've done admirably, old fellow," said Laurence. "'Pon my oath I don't think there's hardly any one we know that you haven't had something pleasantly unpleasant to say about. Now," taking out his watch, "we must be off to the theatre, and we've just time to smoke a cigarette as we walk down there. You took the two stalls?"

"Well—no," replied George Bertram, hesitating rather suspiciously; "I only took one for you; I—I'm going-that is—I've got a seat in a box."

"George, you old vagabond, you don't mean to say you're going to desert me the first night I come back?"

"Well, I couldn't help it. You see I was engaged to go with these people before you wrote; and—"

"All right; what people are they?"

"The Mitfords."

"Mitfords? *Connais pas.*"

"Oh, yes; you know them fast enough; Oh, I forgot—all since you left; only just happened."

"Look here, George: I've had quite enough of the Sphinx during the last six months, and I don't want any of the enigma business. *What* has only just happened?"

"Mitford—and all that. You'll give me no peace till I tell you. You recollect Mitford? with us at Oxford—Brasenose man, not Christ Church."

"Mitford, Mitford! Oh, I recollect; big, fair man, goodish-looking. His father failed and smashed up; didn't he? and our man went into a line regiment. Oh, by Jove, yes! and came to grief about mistaking somebody else's name for his own, and backing a bill with it; didn't he? at Canterbury, or somewhere where he was quartered?"

"Same man. Had to leave service, and came to awful grief. Ran away, and nothing heard of him. His uncle, Sir Percy, and two little boys drowned off Malta, and title came to our man. Couldn't find him anywhere; at last some Jew lawyer was employed, put detectives on, and hunted up Mitford, nearly starved, in some public in Wapping, or somewhere in the East-end. When he heard what a swell he'd become, he had a fit, and they thought he'd die. But he's been all square ever since; acted like a gentleman; went down to the place in Devonshire where his people lived before the smash; married the clergyman's daughter to whom he had been engaged in the old days; and they've just come up to town for the winter."

"Married the clergyman's daughter to whom he had been engaged in the old days, eh? George Bertram, I saw a blush mantle on your ingenuous cheek, sir, when you alluded to the lady. What is she like?"

"Stuff, Laurence! you did nothing of the kind. Lady Mitford is a very delightful woman."

"*Caramba*, Master George! If I were Sir Mitford, and heard you speak of my lady in that earnest manner, I should keep a sharp eye upon you. So you've not improved in that respect."

George Bertram, whose *amourettes* were of the most innocent description, but to accuse whom of the wildest profligacy was a favourite joke with his friends, deeper than ever, and only uttered an indignant "Too bad, too bad!"

"Come along, sir," said Laurence: "I'll sit in the silent solitude of the stalls while you are basking in beauty in a box."

"But you'll come up and be introduced, Laurence?"

"Not I. thank you; I'll leave the field clear for you."

"But Sir Charles Mitford would be so glad to renew his old acquaintance with you."

"Would he? Then Sir Charles Mitford must reserve that delight for another occasion. I shall be here after the play, and we can have a further talk if you can descend to mundane matters after your felicity. Now come along." And they strolled out together.

CHAPTER III.

AT THE PARTHENIUM.

The Parthenium Theatre at the time I write of was a thing by itself. Since then there have been a score of imitations of it, none of them coming up to the great original, but sufficiently like to have dimmed the halo surrounding the first attempt, and to have left the British public undecided as to whom belonged the laurels due to those who first attempted to transform a wretched, dirty, hot building into an elegant, well-ventilated, comfortable *salon*. It was at the Parthenium that stalls were first introduced. Up to that time they had been only known at the Opera; and it was the triumph of the true British playgoer,—the man who had seen Jack Bannister, sir, and Munden and Dowton, and all those true performers who have never had any successor, sir,—that he always sat in the front row of the pit, the only place in the house whence the performance could be properly seen. When Mr. Frank Likely undertook the lesseeship of the Parthenium, he thought he saw his way to a very excellent improvement founded on this basis. He hated the true British playgoer with all his heart. In the style of entertainment about to be produced at the Parthenium, he had not the smallest intention of pandering to, or even propitiating, the great historic character; but he had perfect readiness to see that the space immediately behind the orchestra was the most valuable in the theatre; and so he set carpenters at once to work, and uprooted the hard black deal pit-benches, and erected in their stead rows of delicious *fauteuils* in crimson velvet, broad soft padded-backed lounges with seats which turned upon hinges, and left a space underneath for your hat and coat; charming nests where you could loll at your ease, and see and hear to perfection. The true British playgoer was thus relegated to a dark and dismal space underneath the dress-circle, where he could see little save the parting of the back-hair of the swells in the stalls, and the legs, from the knee downward, and feet of the people on the stage; where the ceiling seemed momentarily descending on him, as on the prisoner in the story of the "Iron Shroud;" and where the knees of the orange-sellers dug him in the back, while their baskets banged him in front. It is needless to say that on the Saturday after the opening of the Parthenium under the new regime, the columns of the *Curtain*, the *Thespian Waggoner*, and the *Scourge* were found brimming over with stinging letters from the true British playgoer, all complaining of his treatment, and all commencing, "By what right, sir, I should like to know." But Mr. Frank Likely cared little enough for this, or for anything else indeed, so long as he could keep up his villa at Roehampton, have his Sunday parties, let his wife dress like a duchess, have two or three carriages, and never be compelled to pay anybody anything. Not to pay was a perfect mania with him. Not that he had not the money. Mr. Humphreys, the treasurer, used to come round about half-past ten with bags of gold and silver, which were duly deposited in Mr. Likely's dressing-room, and thence transferred to his carriage by his dresser, a man whose pound-a-week wages had been due for a month; but if ever he were to ask for a settlement Mr. Likely would look at him with a comic surprise, give a short laugh, say, "He, he! you don't mean it, Evans; I haven't a fourpenny-piece;" and step into the brougham to be bowled away through the summer night to lamb-cutlets and peas and Sillery Mousseux at the Rochampton villa, with a prime cigar on the lawn or under the conservatory afterwards. He took the money, though he never paid any one, and no one knew what became of it; but when he went through the Court the Commissioner complimented him publicly, as he gave him his certificate, and told him in his private room that he, the Commissioner, had experienced such pleasure from Mr. and Mrs. Likely's charming talent, that he, the Commissioner, was really glad it lay in his power to make him, Mr. Likely, some little return.

It is, however, only in his position as lessee of the Parthenium Theatre that we have to do with Mr. Frank Likely, and therein he certainly was admirable. A man of common-sense and education, he saw plainly enough that if he wished to amuse the public, he must show them something with which they were perfectly familiar. They yawned over the rage of Lear, and slept through Belvidera's recital of her woes; the mere fact of Captain Absolute's wearing powder and breeches precluded their taking any interest in his love affairs; but as soon as they were shown people such as they were accustomed to see, doing things which they themselves were accustomed to do, ordinarily dressed, and moving amongst ordinary surroundings, they were delighted, and flocked in crowds to the Parthenium. Mr. Likely gave such an entertainment as suited the taste of his special visitors. The performances commenced at eight with some trifle, during the acting of which the box-doors were perpetually banging, and early visitors to the stalls were carefully stamped upon and ground against by the club-diners steadily pushing their way to their seats. The piece of the evening commenced about nine and lasted till half-past ten; and then there came forty minutes of a brilliant burlesque, with crowds of pretty coryphées, volleys of rattling puns and parodies, crackling allusions to popular topics, and resplendent scenery by Mr. Coverflats, the great scenic artist of the day. When it is recollected that though only two or three of the actors were really first-rate, yet that all were far above the average, being dressed under Mr. Likely's eye, and taught every atom of their "business;" that the theatre was thoroughly elegant, and unlike any other London house in its light-blue-and-gold decorations and airy muslin curtains, and that its *foyer* and lobbies were happy meeting-grounds for wits and men of fashion,-no wonder that "first-nights" at the Parthenium were looked forward to with special delight.

On the occasion on which Colonel Alsager and Mr. Bertram were about to be present, a more than ordinary amount of curiosity prevailed. For some weeks it had been vaguely rumoured that the new comedy, *Tried in the Furnace*, about to be produced, was written by Spofforth, that marvellous fellow who combined the author with the man of fashion, who was seen everywhere, at the Premieress's receptions, at the first clubs, always associating with the best people, and who flavoured his novels and his plays in the most piquante manner with reproductions of characters and stories well known in the London world. It was rumoured that in *Tried in the Furnace* the plot strongly resembled the details of a great scandal in high life, which had formed the *plat de résistance* of the gossips of the previous season; and it was also said that the hero, an officer in the Guards, would be played by Dacre Pontifex, who at that time had turned all women's heads who went regularly into society, and who, to a handsome face and figure and a thoroughly gentlemanly bearing, seemed to add great natural histrionic genius.

All these reports, duly set afloat in the various theatrical journals, and amongst the particular people who think and talk of nothing else but the drama and its professors,—a set permeating every class of society,—had whetted the public appetite to an unparalleled amount of keenness; and long before its representation, all the retainable stalls, boxes, and seats generally, for the first night of *Tried in, the Furnace* had been secured. The gallery-people were certain to come in, because Mugger, the low comedian, had an exceedingly humorous part, and the gallery worshipped Mugger; and the diminished area of the pit would probably be thronged, as it had been whispered in the columns of the *Scourge* that the new play was reported to contain several hits at the aristocracy, invariably a sure "draw" with the pittites. It was only of the upper boxes that the manager felt doubtful; and for this region he accordingly sent out several sheaves of orders, which were duly presented on the night by wild weird-looking women, with singular head-dresses of scraps of lace and shells, dresses neither high nor low, grimy gloves too long in the fingers, and bonnets to be left with the custodian.

It was a great night; there could be no doubt of that; Humphreys had said so, and when Humphreys so far committed himself, he was generally right. Humphreys was Mr. Likely's treasurer, confidential man, factotum. He stood at the front of the theatre to receive the important people,—notably the press,—to settle discord, to hint what was the real strength of the forthcoming piece, to beg a little indulgence for Miss Satterthwaite's hoarseness, or for the last scene of the second act, which poor Coverflats, worn off his legs, had scarcely had time to finish. He knew exactly to whom to bow, with whom to shake hands. He knew exactly where to plant the different representatives of the press, keeping up a proper graduation, yet never permitting any critic to think that he was not sufficiently honoured. He knew when to start the applause, when to hush the house into silence. Better than all, he knew where to take Mr. Likely's acceptances to get them discounted; kept an account of the dates, and paid the renewal fees out of the previous night's receipts. An invaluable man Humphreys; a really wonderful fellow!

When Laurence Alsager flung away the end of his cigarette under the Parthenium portico, and strolled leisurely into the house, he found Humphreys standing in exactly the same position in which he had last seen him two years since; and he almost quailed as, delivering up his ticket, he returned the treasurer's bow, and thanked him for his welcome. "Glad to see you back, Colonel. Something worth showing to you to-night!" and then Laurence laughed outright. He had been away for two years; he had seen the Sphinx and the Pyramids, and all the wonders of the East, to say nothing of the European continent; and here was a man congratulating himself that in a three-act tinpot play they had something worthy of his observation. So he nodded and laughed, and passed on into the theatre. Well, if there were no change in Humphreys, there was little enough in any one else. There they were, all the old set: half-a-dozen newspaper critics dotted over the front rows of the stalls; two or three attached to the more important journals in private boxes; celebrated author surrounded by his family in private box; other celebrated author scowling by himself in orchestra stall; two celebrated artists who always came to first-nights amusing themselves by talking about art before the curtain goes up; fat man with vulgar wife with wreath of roses in her head,—alderman, wholesale stationer, said to be Mr. Frank Likely's backer, in best stage-box; opposite stage-box being reserved by Jewish old party, landlord of the theatre, and now occupied by the same, asleep and choking. Lady Ospringe of course, with (equally of course) the latest lion of the day by her side—on this occasion a very little man, with long fair hair, who, as Laurence afterwards learned, had written a poem all about blood and slaughter. The Duke and Duchess of Tantallan, who are mad about private theatricals, who have turned the old northern feudal castle into an uncomfortable theatre, and whose most constant guests are little Hyams (the costumier) and Jubber ('heavy old man') of the Cracksideum Theatre, who 'gets up' the duke's plays. Sir Gerald Spoonbill and Lord Otho Faulconbridge, jolly old boys, flushed with hastily-eaten dinner at Foodle's, but delighting in the drama; the latter especially having inherited taste for it, his mother having been—well, you know all about that. That white waistcoat which glistens in the stalls could belong to no one but Mr. Marshall Moss, next to whom sit on either side Mr. Gompertz, the stockjobber, and Mr. Sergeant Orson, the last-named having entertained the other gentlemen at a very snug little dinner at the Haresfoot Club. Nor was pipe-clay wanting. The story of the plot, the intended character to be assumed by Mr. Pontifex, had been talked over at Woolwich, at Brompton,—where the sucking Indian heroes, men whose names long afterwards were household words during the Mutiny campaigns, were learning soldiering,—at the Senior and the Junior, and at the Rag, the members of which, awaiting the completion of their present palatial residence, then occupied a modest tenement in St. James's Square. There was a boxful of Plungers, big, solemn, heavy men, with huge curling moustaches, conspicuous among whom were Algy Forrester and Cis Hetherington of the Blues; Markham Bowers of the Life Guards, who shot the militia-surgeon behind the windmill at Wimbledon; and Dick Edie of the 4th Dragoon Guards—Dick Edie, the solicitor's son, who afterwards ran away with Lady Florence Ormolu, third daughter of the house of Porphyry; and on being reconciled and introduced to whom on a future occasion, the Dowager Countess of Porphyry was good enough to make the remark that she "had no idea the lower orders were so clean."

Where are ye now, lustrous counts, envied dandies of that bygone time? Algy Forrester, thirty-four inches round the girth, has a son at Oxford, breeds fat sheep, and is only seen in London at cattle-show time. Cis Hetherington, duly heralded at every outlawry proclamation, lies *perdu* in some one of the barren islands forming the

Hebrides cluster. Markham Bowers fell in the Balaklava charge, pierced through and through by Cossack spearmen; and Major-general Richard Edie, M.P., is the chief adviser and the trusted agent of his mother-in-law, the Dowager Countess of Porphyry. In the next box, hiding behind the muslin curtains, and endeavouring to hide her convulsions of laughter behind her fan, sat little Pauline Désirée, *première danseuse* at the Opera Comique, with Harry Lindon of the Coldstreams, and Prothero of the Foreign Office, and Tom Hodgson the comic writer; none of them one atom changed, all of them wonder-struck at the man in the big beard, all of them delighted at suddenly recognizing in him an old friend, not much thought of perhaps during his absence, as is the way of the world, but certainly to be welcomed now that he was once more among them.

Not one atom changed; all of them just the same. What were his two years of absence, his wanderings in burning solitudes, or amongst nomadic tribes? His sudden rushing away had been undertaken with a purpose; and whether that purpose had been fulfilled was known to himself alone. He rather thought it had, as, without an extra heart-beat, he looked into a box on the pit-tier, and his grave face flashed into a sardonic grin as his eyes lit on the bald forehead and plaited shirt-frill of an elderly gentleman, instead of the light-chestnut bands and brilliant bust which once reigned dominant there on every "first night." But all the others were just the same; even the people he did not know were exactly like those whom he had left, and precisely answered to those whom he should have expected to find there. No, not all. The door of a box on the grand tier next the dress-circle opened with a clang, and a lady whom he had never seen before, coming to the front, settled herself opposite the corner in the stage. The noise of the door attracted the attention of the house; and Ventus, then playing his celebrated cornet-solo in the overture, cursed the interruption; a whisper ran round the stalls; the arrival was telegraphed to the Guards' box: this must be some star that had risen on the horizon since Laurence's absence. Ah, there is Blab Bertram at the back of the box! This, then, must be Lady Mitford!

She was apparently about twenty, and, so far as could be judged from her sitting position, tall and slight. Her complexion was red and white, beautifully clear,—the white transparent, the red scarlet,—and her features regular; small forehead, straight Grecian nose, very short upper-lip, and mouth small, with lips rather thin than pouting. Her dark-brown hair (fortunately at that time it was not considered necessary for beauty to have a red head), taken off behind the ears in two tight bands, showed the exquisite shape of her head, which was very small, and admirably fitted on the neck, the only fault of which was its excess in length. She was dressed entirely in white, with a green necklace, and a tiny wreath of green ivy-leaves was intertwined among the braids into which her hair was fastened at the back of her head. She took her seat gracefully, but looked round, as Laurence noticed, with a certain air of strangeness, as though unaccustomed to such scenes; then immediately turned her eyes, not on the other occupants of the theatre, not on the stage, nor on George Bertram, who, after some apparent demur, took the front seat opposite to her, but towards a tall man, who relieved her of her cloak, and handed her a fan, and in whom

Alsager recognized the Charles Mitford of his Oxford days. A good realization of Tennyson's Sir Walter Vivian,—

"No little lily-handed baronet he;
A stout broad-shouldered genial Englishman,"—

was Sir Charles Mitford, with strongly-marked, well-cut features, bright blue eyes, curling reddish-brown hair, large light breezy whiskers, and a large mouth gleaming with sound white teeth. The sort of man who, you could tell at a glance, would have a very loud hearty laugh, would grip your hand until your fingers ached, would be rather awkward in a room, but who would never flinch across country, and never grow tired among the turnips or over the stubble. An unmistakable gentleman, but one to whom a shooting-coat and gaiters would be more becoming than the evening-dress be then wore, and who evidently felt the moral and physical restraint of his white choker, from the way in which he occasionally tugged at that evidence of civilization. Shortly after they had settled themselves, the curtain went up, and all eyes were turned to the stage; but Laurence noticed that Lady Mitford was seated so as to partly lean against her husband, while his left hand, resting on her chair-back, occasionally touched the braids of her hair. George Bertram seemed to be entirely overlooked by his companions, and was able to enjoy his negative pleasure of holding his tongue to the fullest extent.

They were right who had said that Spofforth had put forth all his power in the new piece, and had been even more than usually personal. The characters represented were, an old peer, wigged, rouged, and snuff-box bearing, one of those wonderful creations which have never been seen on the English stage since Farren left it; his young wife, a dashing countess, more frequently in a riding-habit than anything else, with a light jewel-handled whip, with which she cut her male friends over the shoulders or poked them in the ribs,—as is, we know, the way of countesses in real life; a dashing young cavalry-officer very much smitten with the countess, excellently played by Dacre Pontifex, who admirably contrived to do two things at the same time—to satisfy the swells by his representation of one of their class,—"Doosid good thing; not like usual dam cawickachaw," they said,—and simultaneously to use certain words, phrases, and tones, to fall into certain attitudes and use certain gestures, all of which were considered by the pittites as a mockery of the aristocracy, and were delighted in accordingly. It being an established fact that no play at the Parthenium could go down without Mugger the low comedian, and there being in the "scandal in high life," which Spofforth had taken for his plot, no possible character which Mugger could have portrayed, people were wondering what would be done for him. The distribution of the other characters had been apparent to all ever since it was known that Spofforth had the story in hand: of course Farren would be the marquis, and Miss Amabel the marchioness (Spofforth had lowered his characters one step in rank, and removed the captain from the Guards to the cavalry—a great stroke of genius), and

Pontifex the military lover. But what could be done for Mugger? The only other character in the real story, the man by whom the intrigue was found out, and all the mischief accidentally caused, was a simple old clergyman, vicar of the parish close by my lord's country estate, and of course they could not have introduced a clergyman on to the stage, even if Mugger could have played the part. This was a poser. At first Mugger proposed that the clergyman should be turned into a Quaker, when he could appear in broad-brim and drab, call everybody "thee," and snuffle through his nose; but this was overruled. At last Spofforth hit upon a happy idea: the simple old clergyman should be turned into a garrulous mischief-making physician; and when Mugger appeared at the back of the stage, wonderfully "made up" in a fluffy white hat, and a large shirt-frill protruding from his waistcoat, exactly like a celebrated London doctor of the day, whose appearance was familiar to all, the shouts of delight rose from every part of the house. This, with one exception, was the hit of the evening; the exception was when the captain, in a letter to his beloved, writes, "Fly, fly with me! These arms once locked round you, no blacksmith shall break them asunder." Now this was an expression which had actually been used by the lover in the "scandal in high life," and had been made immense fun of by the counsel in the trial which ensued, and by the Sunday newspapers in commenting on that trial. When, therefore, the phrase was spoken by Pontifex in his most telling manner, it created first a thrill of astonishment at the author's daring, then a titter, then a tremendous roar of laughter and applause. Mr. Frank Likely, who was standing at the wing when he heard this, nodded comfortably at Spofforth, who was in the opposite stage-box anxiously watching the effect of every line; and the latter shut up his glass, like the Duke of Wellington at Waterloo, and felt that the battle was won. "It was touch-and-go, my boy," Likely said to the author afterwards; "one single hitch in that speech, and the whole thing would have been goosed off the stage."

There were, however, a few people in the theatre who were not so intensely delighted with Mr. Spofforth's ingenuity and boldness. Laurence Alsager, whose absence from England had prevented his hearing the original story, thought the whole play dreary enough, though he appreciated the art of Pontifex and the buffoonery of Mugger; but the great roar of delight caught him in the middle of a yawn, and he looked round with astonishment to see how a very silly phrase could occasion such an amount of laughter. Glancing round the house, his eyes fell upon Lady Mitford, and he saw that her cheeks were flushed, her looks downcast, and her lips compressed. She had been in the greatest wonderment, poor child, during the whole of the piece: the manners of the people represented were to her as strange as those of the Ashantees; she heard her own language and did not understand it; she saw men and women, apparently intended to be of her own nation and station, conducting themselves towards each other in a manner she had never heard of, much less seen; she fancied there had been a laxity of speech and morals pervading the play, but she only knew it when the roar of welcome to Mr. Pontifex's hint about the blacksmith fell upon her ear. She had never heard the origin of the phrase, but her natural instinct told her it was coarse and gross; she knew it from the manner in which her husband, unable to restrain a loud guffaw, ended with "Too bad, too bad, by Jove!" She knew it by the manner in which Mr. Bertram studiously turned his face away from her to the stage; from the manner in which the ladies all round endeavoured to hide their laughter behind their fans, oblivious of the betrayal afforded by their shaking shoulders; she knew it from the look of intense disgust in the face of that curious-looking bearded man in the stalls, whose glances her eyes met as she looked down.

Yes, Laurence Alsager was as thoroughly disgusted as he looked, and that was saving much; for he had the power of throwing great savageness of expression into his bright eyes and thin lips. Here had a sudden home-sickness, an indescribable longing, come upon him, and he had hurried back after two years' absence; and now within half-a-dozen hours of his arrival he had sickened at the change. He hated the theatre, and the grinning fools who laughed at the immodest rubbish, and the grinning fools who uttered it; he hated the conventionality of dress and living; he could not stand going in with a regular ruck of people again, and having to conform to all their ways. He would cut it at once; go down to Knockholt to-morrow, and stay a couple of days with Sir Peregrine just to see the old governor, and then be off again to South America, to do prairies and bisons and that sort of thing.

As he made this resolution, the curtain fell amidst a storm of applause, and rose again to show the actors in a row, bowing delightedly with their hands on their waistcoats; Spofforth "bowed his acknowledgments from a private box," and kissed his hand to Alsager, who returned the salute with a very curt nod, then rose and left the theatre. In the lobby he met the Mitford party, and was quietly slipping by when Sir Charles, after whispering to Bertram, touched his shoulder, saying, "Colonel Alsager, let me renew our old acquaintance." There was no escape from this big man's cheery manner and outstretched hand, so Laurence, after an instant's admirably-feigned forgetfulness, returned the grasp, saying, "Ah, Mitford, I think? of Brasenose in the old days?"

"Yes, yes, to be sure! All sorts of things happened since then, you know."

"O yes, of course; though I've only been in England six hours, I've heard of your luck and the baronetcy. George Bertram here is such a terrific talker, he couldn't rest until he had told me all the news."

This set Sir Charles Mitford off into one of his great roars again, at the finish of which he said, "Let me introduce you to my wife; she's just here with Bertram.—Here, Georgie darling, this is Colonel Alsager, an old acquaintance of mine."

Of any one else Mitford would have said "an old friend;" but as he spoke he glanced at Laurence's stern, grave expression, and changed the word. Perhaps the same feeling influenced Lady Mitford, as her bow was constrained, and her spirits, already depressed by the performance, were by no means raised by the introduction to this sombre stranger.

Sir Charles tried to rally. "Hope we shall see something of you, Alsager, now you're back. You'll find us in Eaton Place, and—"

"You're very good; but I shall leave town to-morrow, and probably England next week."

Probably no man had ever been more astonished than was George Bertram as he stood by and heard this; but, true to his creed, he said never a word.

"Leave England!" said Sir Charles. "Why, you've only just come back. You're only just—All right; we're coming!" This last in answer to roars of "Lady Mitford's carriage!" surging up the stairs. "Thank you if you'll give my wife your arm."

Lady Mitford accepted this courtesy very frigidly, just touching Laurence's arm with the tips of her fingers. After she had entered the brougham, Alsager stood back for Sir Charles to follow; but the latter shut the door, saying, "Goodnight, Georgie dear; I shan't be late."

"Oh, Charley, are you not coming with me?" she said.

"No, dear, not just yet. Don't put on such a frightened face, Georgie, or Colonel Alsager will think I'm a perfect Blue-beard. I'm going to sup with Bligh and Winton; to be introduced to that fellow who acted so well,—Pontifex, you know. Shan't be late, dear.—Home, Daniell's."

And as the carriage drove off, Sir Charles Mitford, forgetting to finish his civil speeches to Laurence, shook hands with him and Bertram, and wishing them goodnight, walked off with his companions.

"Chaff or earnest," said Mr. Bertram, when they were left alone, "going away again?"

"I don't know yet; I can't tell; I've half a mind to—How horribly disappointed that little woman looked when that lout said he was going out to supper! He is a lout, your friend, George."

"Cubbish; don't know things yet; wants training," jerked out Mr. Bertram.

"Wants training, does he? He'll get it soon enough if be consorts much with Bligh and Winton, and that set. They'll sharpen him."

"Like Lady Mitford?" said Bertram, interrogatively.

"I think not; I don't know. She seems a little rustic and missish at present. Let's come to the Club; I want a smoke."

But as they walked along, Laurence wrung some further particulars about Lady Mitford from his friend; and as they ascended the club-steps, he said, "I don't think, if I had a pretty wife like that, I should leave her for the sake of passing my evening with Winton and Bligh, or even of being introduced to Mr. Pontifex. Would you, George?"

"Can't say. Never had one," was Mr. Bertram's succinct reply.

CHAPTER IV.

IN THE SMOKING-ROOM.

Among the advantages upon which I have not sufficiently dilated, the Maecenas Club had a smoking-room, of which the members were justly proud. Great improvements have been lately made; but in those days the smoking-room was a novel ingredient in club-comfort, and its necessity was not sufficiently recognized. Old gentlemen, generally predominant in clubs, were violently opposed to tobacco, save in the shape of the club snuff; regarded smoking as a sure sign of dissipation, if not of entirely perverted morality, and combined together in committee and out of committee to worry, harass, and annoy the devotees of the cigar. Consequently these last were in most clubs relegated to a big gaunt room at the top of the house, which had palpably been formed by the removal of the partition between two servants' attics, a room with bare walls, an oil-cloth-covered floor, like a hair-dresser's cutting-room, a few imitation-marble-topped tables, some windsor chairs, and a slippery black-leather ottoman stuck against the wall. Thither, to that tremendous height, the waiter, humorously supposed to be devoted to the room, seldom penetrated; and you sat and smoked your cigar, and sipped your gin-and-seltzer when you were lucky enough to get it, and watched your neighbour looming through a fog of his own manufacture in solemn silence. It required a bold man to penetrate to such howling wildernesses as the smoking-rooms of the Retrenchment, the True Blue, and the No Surrender in those days; nor were they much better off at the Rag, save in summer, when they rigged up a tent in the back-yard, and held their *tabagie* under canvas. At the Minerva they had no smoking-room; the bishops, and other old women in power there, distinctly refusing to sanction a place for any such orgies. But at the Maecenas the smoking-room was *the* room in the house. None of your attics or cock-lofts, none of your stair-climbing, to get into a bare garret at the end of your toil. At the Maecenas you went straight through the hall, past all the busts of the eminent gentlemen, through a well-lit stone passage, where, if you were lucky, you might see, in a little room on the right, honest Mr. Turquand the steward brewing a jorum of that gin-punch for which the Club was so renowned; past the housekeeper's room, where Mrs. Norris sat breast-high in clean table-linen, and surrounded by garlands of lemons and groves of spices; past the big refrigerator, into which Tom Custance threatened to dip little Captain Rodney one night, when that peppery light-weight had had too much of the Club claret; and then, built over what should have been the garden, you found the pride of the little M. A big square room, lit by a skylight in summer, or sun-burner in winter, with so much wall paper as could be seen of a light-green colour, but with the walls nearly covered with sketches in oil, crayon, and water-colour, contributed by members of the Club. From mantel-shelf to ceiling had been covered by Gilks, in distemper, with "Against Wind and Tide"—a lovely bit of seascape, to look at which kept you cool on the hottest night; opposite hung Sandy Clobber's hot staring "Sphinx and Pyramids;" Jack Long's crayon caricature of "King Jamie inditing the Counterblast" faced a charming sketch of a charming actress by Acton, R.A.; and there were a score of other gems of art. Such cosy chairs and luxurious lounges; such ventilation, watched over specially by Fairfax, the oldest and perhaps the jolliest member of the Club; such prime cigars and glorious drinks, and pungent anecdote and cheerful conversation, were to be had nowhere else.

The room was full when Laurence and Bertram entered, and the former was immediately received with what dramatic critics call "an ovation;" that is, the men generally shook hands with him, and expressed themselves glad to see him back.

"And I see by your dress that you've no sooner arrived than you've plunged into the vortex of society, Colonel," said old Fairfax from his post of honour in the chimney-corner.

"Not I, Mr. Fairfax," replied Laurence, laughing; "I've only been to the play."

"What! not to Spofforth's,—not to the Parthenium?"

"Why not? is there any harm? is it a riddle? what is it? Let me know at once, because, whatever it is, I've been there."

"No, no; only there's been a difference of opinion about the new piece. Billy Gomon thinks it capital, and gave us a flaming account of it; but since then Captain Hetherington has come in and spoken very strongly against it. Now, Colonel, you can act as umpire between these two referees."

"Not at all, not at all," said Mr. Gomon, a mild baldheaded little gentleman who did Boswell to Spofforth, and was rewarded for perpetually blowing his idol's trumpet by opera-ivories and first-night private boxes, and occasional dinners with pleasant theatrical people. "I merely said that there was—ah, an originality,—a cleverness,— and—a—above all a gentlemanly tone in the piece such as you never find in any one's writings but Spofforth's."

Most of the men sitting round laughed heartily as Billy Gomon uttered his sentiments in the mildest, most deprecatory manner, and with the pleasantest smile.

"Well, that's not bad to begin with; and now, Cis, what have you got to say?"

A big man, half sitting, half lolling on an ottoman at the other side of the room, wholly occupied in smoking a very large cigar, staring at the ceiling and pulling his long tawny moustaches, looked up at the mention of his name and said:

"Well, look here, Alsager I'm not clever, and all that sort of thing, you know; I'm not particularly sweet on my own opinion; of course, being a Plunger, I can't spell or write, or pronounce my r's 'cordin' to *Punch* and the other funny dogs, and so I've no doubt Billy Gomon's right; and it's doosid clever of Mr. Spofforth, a gentleman whose acquaintance I've not the pleasure of possessing—and don't want, by Jove, that's more!-doosid clever of Mr. Spofforth to rake up a dunghill story out of the newspapers when it had been forgotten, and to put the unfortunate devils who were concerned in it on to the stage, and bring back all the old scandal. I've no doubt it's doosid clever;

and I'm sure it's a very gentlemanly thing of Mr. Spofforth to do; so gentlemanly that, if any of my people had been mixed up in it, I'd have tried the strength of my hunting-crop over Mr. Spofforth's shoulders!" And having concluded, Cis Hetherington leant back lazily, and resumed his contemplation of the ceiling.

There was a pause for a moment, and then Bertram said:

"Quite right, Hetherington; horrible piece, dreary and dirty. D—d unpleasant to think that one can't go to the theatre with a modest woman without having innuendoes and *doubles entendres* thrown at you."

"By Jove, a second edition of the miraculous gift of tongues!" said a man seated on Laurence's right. "I never heard the Blab so charmingly eloquent. You were with him at the theatre, Alsager; who was the lady whom he so deliciously described as a 'modest woman' that he escorted?" The speaker was Lord Dollamore, a man of good abilities and position, but a confirmed Sybarite and a renowned roué.

"Bertram escorted no one; he merely had a seat in a box with Lady Mitford and her husband," said Laurence coldly. He hated Lord Dollamore. As he himself said, he "didn't go in to be strait-laced; but Dollamore was a cold-blooded ruffian about women, and, worse still, a boaster."

"Ah, with Lady Mitford!" said Lord Dollamore, slowly expelling a mouthful of smoke; "I have the pleasure of her acquaintance. She's very nice, Alsager!"

There was a succulence in the tone in which these last words were spoken that sounded unpleasantly on Laurence's ear; so he said shortly, "I saw Lady Mitford for the first time to-night."

"Oh, she's very nice; a little too classical and statuesque and Clite-like for my taste, which leans more to the *beauté-du-diable* order; but still Lady Mitford's charming. Poor little woman! she's like the young bears, with all her troubles before her."

"Her troubles won't be many, one would think," said Laurence, who was growing irritated under his companion's half-patronizing, half-familiar tone in speaking of Lady Mitford.

"Won't they?" said Lord Dollamore, with another slow expulsion of smoke; this time in the shape of rings, which he dexterously shot one through the other.

"I can't see how they should. She has beauty, wealth, and position; a young husband who dotes on her,—Oh, you needn't grin; I saw him with her in the box."

"Yes, and I saw him without her, but with Bligh and Winton, the two Clarks, who are *coryphées* at Drury Lane, and Mdlle. Carambola from the cirque at Leicester Square, turning in to supper at Dubourg's. Now, then, what do you say to that?"

"Nothing. Mitford told his wife he was going to supper with Bligh and Winton. I heard him."

"Very likely; but you didn't hear him mention the female element. No, of course not."

"Sir Charles Mitford being, I presume, a gentleman, that suggestion is simply absurd."

"Pardon me, my dear Colonel Alsager, I never make any suggestion that can be called 'simply absurd.' The fact is, Alsager, that though I'm only, I suppose, five or six years older than you, I've seen a deal more of life."

"Of which side of it?"

"Well, the most interesting,—the worst, of course. While you've been mounting guard and saluting colours, and teaching bullet-headed recruits to form square, and all that kind of thing, I've been studying human nature."

"How delightful for human nature!"

"That may or may not be," said Lord Dollamore calmly, and without the smallest sign of irritation; "but this I know, that all boy-and-girl marriages invariably come to grief. A man must have his fling some time or other; if he does not have it before his marriage, he will after. And between ourselves, Alsager, this Mitford is a devilish bad egg. I've known of him all his life. He had a fast turn when he was a mere boy, and didn't stick at trifles to raise money, as you may have heard."

"I know all about that; but—"

"And do you think that, now that he has plenty of money and health and position, he won't go in for that style of pleasure which he formerly risked everything to obtain? Nonsense, my dear Alsager; *cela va sans dire.* Lady Mitford will have to run the gauntlet of society, as do most married women with loose husbands; and will certainly be more successful than most of her competitors."

Laurence put down his cigar, and looking steadily at his companion, said, "I don't envy the man who could be blackguard enough to attempt to throw a shadow on such a woman's life."

"Don't you?" said Lord Dollamore, as steadily returning the glance; "of course not." Then, in a somewhat lighter tone, he added, "By the way, have you seen the Hammonds lately?"

A flush, noticeable even through the red bronze, rose on Laurence's cheeks; but before he could speak, a man who was sitting on the other side of Lord Dollamore cut into the conversation by saying, "Oh, by the way, there was a brother of Percy Hammond's dining here last week; Prothero asked me to meet him. He's a sporting parson, and a tremendous character. He told us he always knew when woodcock came in by the lesson for the day."

"I know him," said Cis Hetherington, who had lounged up and joined the party; "Tom Hammond, a thundering big fellow. His vicarage, or rectory, or whatever it is, is close by Dursley; and at the last election Tom seconded my brother—Westonhanger, you know—for the county. The Rads brought over a lot of roughs, navvies and fellows who were working at the railway close by; and whenever Tom spoke these fellows kept yelling out all sorts of blackguard language. Tom roared to them to stop it; and when they wouldn't, he quietly let himself drop over the front of the hustings, right into the middle of 'em. He's a splendid bruiser, you know; and he let out—one two, one two—right and left, and sent half-a-dozen of 'em flying like skittles. Then he asked if any more was wanted, carefully settled his clerical white choker, and went back to the hustings again."

"He owed your brother a good turn after the way in which he astonished your governor a year or two ago, Cis," said Lord Dollamore.

"What was that? Did he pull the Duke up for coming late to the church, or for not hunting the county? The last most likely, I should think."

"Not at all. You all know what a tremendous swell Cis's brother, the Duke, is,—you know it, Cis, as well as anybody,—wants all the pavement to himself in St. James's Street, and finds the arch on Constitution Hill not quite high enough for his head. Well, a year or two ago Tom Hammond had a splendid roan horse which he used to drive in a light Whitechapel to cover. The Duke saw this animal, and thought it would make a splendid match for a roan of his; so he sent his coachman over to Tom's little place to ask if he'd sell. Tom saw the coachman, heard what he had to say, and then told him he never spoke to grooms, except to give them orders; if the Duke wanted the horse, he must come himself. I can't think what message the man can have given to his master; but two days after, the Duke's phaeton pulled up at the parsonage door, and the Duke himself bowed to Tom, who ran to the window with his mouth full of lunch. Tom's account of the interview was delicious. He imitates the Duke's haw-haw manner to perfection,—you don't mind, Cis? He asked him in, and told him that the Stilton was in prime cut; but the Duke declined, and said, I understand you wish to sell your roan, Mr. Hammond.' 'Then your grace understands a good deal more than I gave you credit for,' said Tom. 'Then you don't want to sell the horse? I want him particularly for a match-horse.' 'No,' said Tom, 'I won't sell him. I'm a poor parson, and I wouldn't take three hundred for him; but I'll tell you what I'll do, your grace. I'm always open to a bit of sporting; and I'll *toss your grace for the pair*; or, if that's not exciting enough, I'll get my curate to come in—he's only next door—and we'll go the odd man, the best of three. That's what I'll do.' Tom says he thought the Duke would have had a fit. He never spoke a word, but drove straight away, and has never looked at Tom since."

After the laugh which this story raised had ceased, Lord Dollamore said, "Did Tom say anything about his brother Percy the day he dined here?"

"O yes," said the man who had first spoken; "they're coming back at once. Mrs. Hammond finds Florence disagrees with her."

"Perhaps she'd find Laurence agree with her better," said Dollamore sotto voce; then aloud, "Ah! and so of course poor Percy is to be trotted back again. By Jove, how that woman rules him! She has only to whistle, and he comes to her at once. I should like to see a woman try that on me,—a woman that I was married to, I mean.—By the way, you haven't seen Mrs. Hammond since her marriage, have you, Alsager?"

"No; I left England just previously."

"Ah! she's as pretty as ever, and infinitely more wicked—I beg your pardon, though; I forgot we had turned purist since our Oriental experience."

"At all events we have learned one thing in our Oriental experience, Lord Dollamore."

"And that is—?"

"To keep our temper and—hold our tongue. Goodnight."

And as he said these words, Laurence Alsager rose from his seat and left the room; Bertram had previously taken his departure; so that Laurence walked off alone to his hotel, pondering on all he had seen and heard.

"So she's coming back," he said to himself as he strolled along; "coming back to bring back to me, whenever I may happen to meet her, all the sickening recollections of the old times, the heart-burnings, the heart-breaking, to escape from which I rushed away two years ago. She won the day then, and she'll be as insolent as she can be on the strength of her victory now, though she knows well enough that I did not shoot my best bolt then, but keep it in my quiver yet. It's impossible to fight with a woman; they can descend to so many dodges and meannesses where no man worthy of the name could follow them. No; I'll seek safety in flight. I'll be off again as soon as I've seen the governor; and then—And yet what a strange interest I seem to take in that girl I saw to-night! Poor little child! I wonder if Dollamore's right about her husband. Well, I'll wait a few days, and see what turns up."

While these thoughts were passing through Laurence Alsager's mind, Sir Charles Mitford was leaning against the jambs of the door leading from his dressing-room into his wife's bed-room. He had one boot off, and was vainly endeavouring to discover the hole in the bootjack in which to insert the other foot. The noise which he made in this operation awoke Lady Mitford, who called out, "Oh, Charley, is that you?"

"Course, my dear," said Sir Charles in a thick voice; "who should it be this time o' night? not that it's late, though," he said, correcting himself after a moment's reflection; then looking vacantly at her, added in a high-falsetto key, "quite early."

"You are not ill, Charley?" she asked, looking anxiously at him.

"Not I, my darling; never berrer.—Off at last, are you?" this last observation addressed to the conquered boot. "But you, what's marrer with you? Look all flushed and frightened like."

"I've had a horrid confused dream about the theatre, and people we saw there, and snakes, oh so dreadful! and that grave man, Colonel Somebody, that you introduced me to, was just going to rescue me. Oh, Charley, I feel so low and depressed, and as though something were going to happen. I'm sure we shan't be happy in London. Let's go away again."

"Nonsense, Georgie;—nonsense, my love! Very jolly place for—good supper,— Colonel Snakes;" and with these intelligible murmurings Sir Charles Mitford slipped into the land of dreams.

CHAPTER V

GEORGIE.

If, twelve months before the production of Mr. Spofforth's play (which necessarily forms a kind of Hegira in this story), you had told Georgie Stanfield that she was destined to be the wife of a baronet, the mistress of a house in one of the best parts of London, the possessor of horses and carriages, and all the happiness which a very large yearly income can command, your assertions would have been met, not with ridicule—for Georgie was too gentle and too well-bred for that—but with utter disbelief. Her whole life had been passed in the little Devonshire village of which her father was vicar, and it seemed to her impossible that she could ever live anywhere else. To potter about in the garden during the summer in a large flapping straw hat and a cotton gown, to tie up drooping flowers and snip off dead leaves; to stand on the little terrace dreamily gazing over the outspread sea, watching the red sails of the fishing-smacks skimming away to the horizon, or the trim yachts lying off the little port—the yachts whose fine-lady passengers, and gallant swells all blue broad-cloth and club-button, seen at a distance,—were Georgie's sole links with the fashionable world; to visit and read to the bed-ridden old women and the snuffling, coughing old men; to superintend the preparation of charitably-dispensed gruel and soup; to traverse Mavor's Spelling-book up and down, up and down, over and over again, in the company of the stupid girls of the village-school; to read the *Cullompton Chronicle* to her father on Thursdays, and to copy out his sermon on the Saturday evenings,—these had been the occupations of Georgie Stanfield's uneventful life.

She had not had even the excitement of flirtations, a few of which fall to the lot of nearly every girl, be she pretty or plain, rich or poor, town or country-bred. The military depots are now so numerous that it is hard, indeed, if at least a couple of subalterns cannot be found to come over any distance in the rumbling dog-cart hired from the inn in the provincial town where they are quartered; and though in Georgie's days there was no croquet,—that best of excuses for social gathering and mild flirtation,—yet there were archery-meetings, horticultural shows, and picnics. Failing the absence of the military, even the most-out-of-the-way country village can produce a curate; and an intending flirt has merely to tone-down certain notions and expand others, to modify her scarlets and work-up her grays, and she will have, if not a very exciting, at all events a very interesting, time in playing her fish. But there were no barracks within miles of Fishbourne, nor any temptations there to have attracted officers from them, if there had been. There were no resident gentry in the place, and the nearest house of any importance—Weston Tower, the seat of old Lady Majoribanks—was twenty miles off, and old Lady Majoribanks kept no company As for the curates, there was one, certainly; but Mr. Lucas had "assisted" Georgie's father for the last eighteen years, was fifty years old, and had a little wife as slow and as gray as the old pony which he used to ride to outlying parts of the parish.

Besides, if there had been eligible men in scores, what had they to do with Georgie Stanfield, or she with them? Was she not engaged to Charles Mitford?—at least, had she not been so affianced until that dreadful business about something wrong that brought poor Charley into disgrace? and was that sufficient to permit her to break her plighted word? Mr. Mitford, Charles's father, had been a banker and brewer at Cullompton, and had had a country cottage at Fishbourne, a charming little place for his family to come to in the summer; and Mr. Stanfield had been Charley's tutor; and when the family were away at Cullompton in the winter, Charley had remained at the vicarage; and what so likely as that Charley should fall in love with Georgie, then a tall slip of a girl in short petticoats and frilled trousers and very thin legs, with her hair in a net; or that Georgie should have reciprocated the attachment? Both the fathers were delighted at the arrangement; and there was no mother on either side to talk of extreme youth, the chance of change, or to interpose other womanly objections. There came a time when Charley, then a tall handsome fellow, was to go up to Oxford; and then Georgie, to whom the outward and visible frill period was long past, and who was a lovely budding girl of sweet seventeen, laid her head on his breast on the night before he went away, and promised never to forget him, but to be his and his alone.

Ah, those promises never to forget—those whispered words of love breathed by lips trembling under the thick cigar-scented moustache into delicate little ears trellised by braids fresh from the fingers of the lady's-maid! They are not much to the Corydons of St. James's Street, or the Phyllises of Belgravia. By how many different lips, and into how many different ears, are the words whispered and the vows breathed in the course of one London season! I declare I never pass through any of the great squares and streets, and see the men enclosing the balconies with striped calico, that I do not wonder to myself whether, amongst all the nonsense that has been talked beneath that well-worn awning-stuff, there has been any that has laid the foundation for, or given the crowning touch to, an honest simple love-match, a marriage undertaken by two people out of sheer regard for each other, and permitted by relatives and friends, without a single thought of money or position to be gained on either side. If there be any, they must be very few in number; and this, be it observed, not on account of that supposed favourite pastime of parents—the disposal of their daughters' hands and happiness to the highest bidder, the outcry against which has been so general, and is really, I believe, so undeserved. The circumstance is, I take it, entirely ascribable to the lax morality of the age, under which a girl engages herself to a man without the slightest forethought, often without the least intention of holding to her word, not unfrequently from the increased opportunities such a state of things affords her for flirting with some other man, and under which she can break her engagement and jilt her lover without compromising herself in the least in the eyes of society. Besides, in the course of a London life these vows and pledges are tendered so often as to be worn almost threadbare from the number of times they have been pledged; and as excess of familiarity always breeds contempt, the repetition of solemn phrases gradually takes from us the due appreciation of their meaning, and we repeat them parrot-wise, without the smallest care for what we are saying.

But that promise of love and truth and remembrance uttered by Georgie Stanfield on the sands at Fishbourne, under the yellow harvest-moon, with her head pillowed on Charles Mitford's breast and her arms clasped round his neck, came from a young heart which had known no guile, and was kept as religiously as was Sir Galahad's vow of chastity. Within a year after Charley's departure for Oxford, his father's affairs, which, as it afterwards appeared, had long been in hopeless confusion, became irretrievably involved. The bank stopped payment, and the old man, unable to face the storm of ignominy by which he imagined he should be assailed, committed suicide. The smash was complete; Charles had to leave the University, and became entirely dependent on his uncle, Sir Percy Mitford, who declined to see him, but offered to purchase for him a commission in a marching regiment, and to allow him fifty pounds a year. The young man accepted the offer; and by the same post wrote to Georgie, telling her all, and giving her the option of freeing herself from the engagement. It Was a gentlemanly act; but a cheap bit of generosity, after all. He might have staked the fifty pounds a year his uncle had promised him, on the fidelity of such a girl as Georgie Stanfield, more especially in the time of trouble. Her father, too, with his old disregard of the future, entirely approved of his daughter's standing by her lover under the circumstances of his altered fortune; and two letters—one breathing a renewal of love and trust, the other full of encouragement and hope—went away from Fishbourne parsonage, and brought tears into the eyes of their recipient, as he sat on the edge of a truckle-bed in a whitewashed room in Canterbury Barracks.

The vow of constancy and its renewal were two little epochs in Georgie's quiet life. Then, not very long after the occurrence of the last,—some six months,—there came a third, destined never to be forgotten. There had been no letter from Charley for some days, and Georgie had been in the habit of walking across the lawn to meet the postman and question him over the garden-wall.

One heavy dun August morning, when the clouds were solemnly gathering up together, the air dead and still, the trees hushed and motionless, Georgie had seen the old man with a letter in his hand, and had hastened, even more eagerly than usual, across the lawn, to be proportionately disappointed when the postman shook his head, and pointing to the letter, said, "For the master, miss." The next minute she heard the sharp clang of the gate-bell, and saw her father take the letter from the postman's hand at his little study-window. Some inward prompting—she knew not what—kept Georgie's eyes on her father. She saw him take out his spectacles, wipe then, and carefully adjust them; then take the letter, and holding it at nearly arm's length, examine its address; then comfortably settling himself in his armchair at the window, prepare to read it. Then Georgie saw the old man fall backward in his chair, his hand dropping powerless by his side, and the letter fluttering from it to the ground. Without uttering a cry, Georgie ran quickly to the house; but when she reached the study, Mr. Stanfield was sitting upright in his chair, and had picked the letter from the floor.

"Papa dearest," said Georgie, "you gave me such a fright. I was watching you from the garden, and I thought I saw you faint. O papa, you *are* ill! How white and scared you look! What is it, papa darling?—tell me."

But to all this Mr. Stanfield only murmured, gazing up into his daughter's face, "My poor child! my poor darling child!"

"What is it, papa? Oh, I know—it's about Charley! He's not—" and then she blanched dead-white, and said in a scarcely audible voice, "He's not dead, papa?"

"No, Georgie, no. It might be better if he were,—be better if he were."

"He's very ill, then?"

"No, darling,—at least—there; perhaps you'd better read it for yourself; here, read it for yourself;" and the old man, after giving her the letter, covered his face with his hands and sobbed aloud.

Then Georgie read in Sir Percy Mitford's roundest hand and stiffest style, how his nephew Charles, utterly ungrateful for the kindness which he, Sir Percy, had showered upon him, and regardless of the fact that he had no resources of his own nor expectations of any, had plunged into "every kind of vice and debauchery, notably gambling"—(Sir Percy was chairman of Quarter-Sessions, and you might trace the effect of act-of-parliament reading in his style)-how he had lost large sums at cards; and how, with the double object of paying his debts and retrieving his losses, lie had at length forged Sir Percy's signature to a bill for £200; and when the document became due had absconded, no one knew where. Sir Percy need scarcely say that all communication between him and this unworthy member of—he grieved to say—his family was at an end for ever; and he took that opportunity, while informing Mr. Stanfield of the circumstance, of congratulating him on having been lucky enough to escape any matrimonial connection with such a rogue and a vagabond.

Mr. Stanfield watched her perusal of the letter; and when she had finished it, and returned it to him calmly, he said:

"Well, my dear! it's a severe blow, is it not?"

"Yes, papa, it is indeed a severe blow. Poor Charley!"

"Poor Charley, my dear! You surely don't feel the least compassion for Charles Mitford; a man who has—who has outraged the laws of his country!"

"Not feel compassion for him, papa? Who could help it? Poor Charley, what a bitter degradation for him!"

"For him! degradation for him! Bless my soul, I can't understand; for us, Georgina,—degradation for us, you mean! However, there's an end of it. We've washed our hands of him from this time forth, and never—"

"Papa, do you know what you're saying? Washed our hands of Charles Mitford! Do you recollect that I have promised to be his wife?"

"Promised to be his wife! Why, the girl's going mad! Promised to be his wife! Do you know that the man has committed forgery?"

"Well, papa."

"Well, papa! Good God! I shall go mad myself! You know he's committed forgery, and you still hold to your engagement to him?"

"Unquestionably. Is it for me, his betrothed wife, to desert him now that he is in misery and disgrace? Is it for you, a Christian clergyman, to turn your back on an old friend who has fallen, and who needs your sympathy and counsel now really for the first time in his life? Would you wish me to give up this engagement, which, perhaps, may be the very means of bringing Charles back to the right?"

"Yes, my dear, yes; that's all very well," said the old gentleman,—"all very—well from a woman's point of view. But you see, for ourselves—"

"Well, papa, what then?"

"Well, my dear, of course we ought not to think so much for ourselves; but still, as your father, I've a right to say that I should not wish to see you married to a—a felon."

"And as a clergyman, papa?-what have you a right to say as a clergyman?"

"I—I: decline to pursue the subject, Georgina; so I'll only say this—that you're my daughter, and you're not of age yet; and I command you to break off this engagement with this—this criminal! That's all."

Georgie simply said, "You know my determination, papa." And there the matter ended.

This was the first quarrel that there had ever been between father and daughter, and both felt it very much indeed. Mr. Stanfield, who had about as much acquaintance with human nature, and as much power of reading character, as if he had been blind and deaf, thought Georgie would certainly give way, and laid all sorts of palpable traps, and gave all sorts of available opportunities for her to throw herself into his arms, confess how wrong she had been, and promise never to think of Charles Mitford again. But Georgie fell in with none of these ways; she kissed her father's forehead on coming down in the morning, and repeated the process on retiring at night; but she never spoke to him at meal-times, and kept away from home as much as possible during the day, roaming over the country on her chestnut mare Polly, a tremendous favourite, which had been bought and broken for her by Charley in the old days.

During the whole of this time Mr. Stanfield was eminently uncomfortable. He had acted upon the ridiculous principle vulgarly rendered by the phrase, cutting off his nose to spite his face. He had deprived himself of a great many personal comforts without doing one bit of good. For a fortnight the *Cullompton Chronicle* had remained uncut and unread, though he knew there was an account of a bishop's visitation to the neighbouring diocese which would have interested him highly. For two consecutive Sundays the parishioners of Fishbourne had been regaled with old sermons in consequence of there being no one to transcribe the vicar's notes, which, save to Georgie, were unintelligible to—the world in general and to their writer in particular. He missed Georgie's form in the garden as he was accustomed to see it when looking up from his books or his writing; he missed her sweet voice carolling bird-like through the house, and always reminding him of that dead wife whose memory he so tenderly loved; and notwithstanding the constant horse-exercise, he thought, from sly glances which he had stolen across the table at her during dinner, that she was looking pale and careworn. Worst of all, he was not at all sure that the position he had taken up was entirely defensible on moral grounds. He was differently placed from that celebrated character in the *Critic*, who "as a father softened, but as a governor was fixed." As a father he might object to the continuance of an engagement between his child and a man who had proved himself a sinner not merely against religious ordinances, but against the laws of his country; but he was very doubtful whether, as a Christian and a clergyman, he was not bound to stretch out the hand of forgiveness, and endeavour to reclaim the penitent. If Mr. Stanfield had lived in these days, and been sufficiently before the world, he would probably have had "ten thousand college councils" to "thunder anathema" at him for daring to promulgate the doctrine that "God is love;" but in the little retired parish where he lived, he taught it because he believed it; and he felt that he had rather fallen away from his standard in endeavouring to coerce his daughter into giving up Charles Mitford.

So one morning, when Georgie came down to breakfast looking flushed and worried, and very little refreshed by her night's sleep, instead of calmly receiving the frontal kiss, as had been his wont during the preceding fortnight, the old man's arms were wound round her, his lips were pressed to hers, while he murmured, "Oh, Georgie! ah, my darling! ah, my child!" and there was a display of *grandes eaux* on both sides, and the reconciliation was complete. At a later period of that day Mr. Stanfield entered fully upon the subject of Charles Mitford, told Georgie that if the scapegrace could be found, he should be willingly received at the parsonage; and then the old gentleman concocted a mysterious advertisement, to the effect that if C. M., formerly of Fishbourne, Devon, would call on Mr. Stevens of Furnival's Inn, Holborn, London, he would hear something to his advantage, and be received with hearty welcome by friends who had forgiven, but not forgotten, him.

This advertisement, duly inserted through the medium of Mr. Stevens, the lawyer therein named, in the mystic second column of the *Times* Supplement, appeared regularly every other day during the space of a month; and good old Mr. Stanfield wrote twice a week to Mr. Stevens. inquiring whether "nothing had come of it;" and Mr. Stevens duly replied (at three shillings and sixpence a letter) that nothing had. It must have been two months after the concoction of the advertisement, and one after its last appearance in the columns of the *Times*, that there came a letter for Georgie, written in the well-known hand, and signed with the well-known initials. It was very short, merely saying that for the second time the writer felt it due to her to leave her unfettered by any past engagement existing between them; that he knew how he had disgraced and placed himself beyond the pale of society; but that he would always cherish her memory, and think of her as some pure and bright star which he might look up to, but to the possession of which he could never aspire.

Poor little Georgie was dreadfully touched by this epistle, and so was Mr. Stanfield, regarding it as a work of art; but as a practical man he thought he saw a chance for again working the disruption of the engagement-question—this time as suggested by Charles himself; and there was little doubt that he would have enunciated these sentiments at length, had he not been abruptly stopped by Georgie on his first giving a hint about it. Despairing of this mode of attack, the old gentleman became diplomatic and Machiavellian; and I am inclined to think that it was owing to some secret conspiracy on his part, that young Frank Majoribanks, staying on a desperately-dreary three-weeks' visit with his aunt and patroness, Lady Majoribanks, took occasion to drive one of the old lady's old carriage-horses over to Fishbourne in a ramshackle springless cart belonging to the gardener, and to accept the vicar's offer of luncheon. He had not been five minutes in the house before Georgie found he had been at Oxford with Charley Mitford; and as he had nothing but laudatory remarks to make of his old chum (he had heard nothing of him since he left college), Georgie was very polite to him. But when, after his second or third visit, he completely threw aside Charley as his stalking-horse, and began to make running on his own account, Georgie saw through the whole thing in an instant, and treated him with such marked coldness that, being a man of the world, he took the hint readily, and never came near the place again. And Mr. Stanfield saw with dismay that his diplomacy succeeded no better than his threats, and that his daughter was as much devoted to Charles Mitford as ever.

So the two dwellers in the parsonage fell back into their ordinary course of life, and time went on, and Mr. Stanfield's hair grew gradually more gray, and his shoulders gradually more rounded, and the sweet girl of seventeen became the budding woman of twenty. Then one Thursday evening, in the discharge of her weekly task of reading to her father the *Cullompton Chronicle*, Georgie suddenly stopped, and although not in the least given to fainting or "nerves," was obliged to put her hand to her side and wait for breath. Then when a little recovered she read out to the wondering old gentleman the paragraph announcing the fatal accident to Sir Percy Mitford and his sons, and the accession of Charles to the title and estates. Like Paolo and Francesca,—though from a very different reason,—"that night they read no more," the newspaper was laid by, and each sat immersed in thought. The old man's simple faith led him to believe that at length the long-wished-for result had arrived, and that all his daughter's patience, long-suffering, and courage would be rewarded. But Georgie, though she smiled at her father's babble, knew that throughout her acquaintance with Charley he had gone through no such trial as that to which the acquisition of wealth and position would now subject him; and she prayed earnestly with all her soul and strength that in this time of temptation her lover might not fall away.

A fortnight passed, and Mr. Stanfield, finding not merely that he had not heard from the new baronet, but that no intelligence of him had been received at Redmoor, at the town house, or by the family lawyers, determined upon renewing his advertisement in the *Times*. By its side presently appeared another far less reticent, boldly calling on "Charles Mitford, formerly of Cullompton, Devon; then of Brasenose College, Oxford; then of the 26th regiment of the line;" to communicate with Messrs. Moss and Moss, Solicitors, Cursitor Street, Chancery Lane, and hear something to his advantage. To this advertisement a line was added, which sent a thrill through the little household at the parsonage: "As the said Charles Mitford has not been heard of for some months, any one capable of legally proving his death should communicate with Messrs. M. and M. above named." Capable of legally proving his death! Could that be the end of all poor Georgie's life-dream? Could he have died without ever learning all her love for him, her truth to him? No! it was not so bad as that; though, but for the shrewdness of Edward Moss and the promptitude of Inspector Stellfox, it might have been. A very few hours more would have done it. As it was, little Dr. Prater, who happened to be dining with Marshal Moss at the Hummums when Mitford was brought there by the inspector, and who immediately undertook the case, scarcely thought he should pull his patient through. When the fierce stage of the disorder was past, there remained a horrible weakness and languor, which the clever little physician attacked in vain. "Nature, my dear sir,—nature and your native air, they must do the rest for you; the virtues of the pharmacopoeia are exhausted."

So one autumn evening, as Mr. Stanfield sat poring over his book, and Georgie, her hope day by day dying away within her, was looking out over the darkening landscape, the noise of wheels was heard at the gate; a grave man in black descended from the box of a postchaise, a worn, thin, haggard face peered out of the window; and the next instant, before Mr. Stanfield at all comprehended what had happened, the carriage door was thrown open, and Georgie was hanging round the neck of the carriage occupant; and kiss, kiss, and bless, bless! and thank God! and safe once more! was all the explanation audible.

Dr. Prater was quite right; nature and the patient's native air effected a complete cure. By the end of a month—such a happy month for Georgie!—Sir Charles was able to drive to Redmoor to see the men of business from London; by the end of two months he stood at the altar of the little Fishbourne church, and received his darling from the hands of her father; the ceremony being performed by the old curate, who had learned to love Georgie as his own child, and who wept plentifully as he bestowed on her his blessing.

CHAPTER VI.

THE GRAYS.

When Laurence Alsager awoke the next morning, he did not regard life with such weariness, nor London with such detestation, as when he went to bed. He had slept splendidly, as would naturally fall to the lot of a man who for two years had been deprived of that greatest of earthly comforts—an English bed. Laurence had bounded on French spring-mattresses; had sweltered beneath German feather-lined coverlets; had cramped himself up in berths; had swung restlessly in hammocks; had stifled behind mosquito curtains; and had passed many nights with his cloak for his bed, and his saddle-bags for his pillow, with the half-naked forms of dirty Arabs dimly visible in the flickering firelight, and the howls of distant jackals ringing in his ears. He had undergone every description of bed-discomfort; and it is not to be wondered at that he lingered long in that glorious nest of cleanliness and rest provided for him at his hotel. As he lay there at his ease, thoroughly awake, but utterly averse to getting up, he began to think over all that had happened during the previous evening; and first he thought what a charming-looking woman Lady Mitford was.

The Scotch gentleman who had remarked that Colonel Alsager was "a deevil among the sax" had some foundation for his observation; for it was a fact that, from the days when Laurence left Eton and was gazetted to the Coldstreams, until he sold his commission and left England in disgust, his name had always been coupled by the gossips with that of some lady well known either in or out of society. He was a mere boy, slim and whiskerless, when the intense admiration which he excited in the breast of Mdlle. Valentine, combined with what she afterwards termed the "coldly insular" manner in which he treated her, gave that charming danseuse such a *migraine* as rendered her unable to appear in public for a week, and very nearly caused Mr. Lumley to be favoured with a row equal to the celebrated Tamburini riot in the days of M. Laporte. He was not more than twenty when "Punter" Blair told him that his goings-on with Lady Mary Blair, the Punter's sister-in-law, were the talk of the town; and that if her husband, the Admiral, was blind, he, the Punter, wasn't, as he'd let Alsager pretty soon know. Laurence replied that the Punter had better mind his own business,—which was "legging" young boys at *écarté* and blind-hookey,—and leave his brother's wife alone; upon which Punter Blair sent O'Dwyer of the 18th with a message; and there must inevitably have been a meeting, had not Blair's colonel got a hint of it, and caused it to be intimated to Mr. Blair that unless this matter with Mr. Alsager were arranged, he, the colonel, should have to take such notice of "other matters" affecting Mr. Blair as would compel that gentleman to send in his papers.

So in a score of cases differing very slightly from each other. It was the old story which was lyrically rendered by Dr. Watts, of Satan being always ready to provide congenial occupation for gentlemen with nothing to do. There is not, I believe, very much martial ardour in the Household Brigade just now. That born of the Crimean war has died out and faded away, and the officers have taken to drive off *ennui*, some by becoming district visitors, and others by enjoying the honest beer and improving conversation of the firemen in Watling Street. But even now there is infinitely more enthusiasm, more belief in the profession as a profession, more study of strategy as a thing which a military man should know something of, than there was before the Crimean expedition. The metropolitan inhabitants had little care for their gallant defenders in those days. Their acquaintance with them was limited to the knowledge that large red men were perpetually discovered in the kitchens, and on discovery were presented as relatives of the servants; or that serious, and in some cases fatal, brawls occurred in the streets, when the pleasant fellows laid about them with their belts, or ran amuck amongst a crowd with their bayonets. An occasional review took place in the Park, or a field-day at Woolwich; but no cordial relations existed between the majority of the Londoners and the household troops until the news came of the battle of the Alma. Then the public learned that the Guards' officers were to be heard of in other places than ball-rooms and divorce-courts, and that guardsmen could fight with as much untiring energy as they had already displayed in feeding on householders and flirting with cooks.

Not much worse, certainly not much better, than his compeers was Laurence Alsager in those days, always having "something on" in the way of feminine worship, until the great "something" happened, which, according to Jock M'Laren and one or two others, had occasioned the great change in his life, and caused his prolonged absence from England. But in all his experience he had only known women of a certain kind; women of the world, ready to give and take; women, in his relations with whom there had been no spice of romance save that spurious romance of the French-novel school, so attractive at first, so hollow, and bad, and disgusting, when proceeded with. It is not too much to say that, varied as his "affaires" had been, he had not known one quiet, pure-minded, virtuous woman; and that during his long foreign sojourn he had thought over this, and often wondered whether he should ever have a wife of his own, or, failing this, whether he should ever have a female friend whom at the same time he could love and respect.

Yes, that was the sort of woman, he thought to himself as he lay calmly reflecting. What a good face she had! so quiet and calm and self-possessed. Naturally self-possessed; not that firm disgusting imperturbability which your hardened London coquette has, he thought; like that horrible M'Alister, who puts her double eye-glass up to her eyes and coolly surveys women and men alike, as though they were slaves in the Constantinople market, and she the buyer for the Sultan. There certainly was a wonderful charm about Lady Mitford, and, good heavens! think of a man having such a wife as that, and going off to sup with Bligh and Winton, who were simply two empty-headed *roué* jackasses, and Pontifex, who—Well, it was very lucky that people didn't think alike. Yes, that man Mitford was a lout, a great overgrown-schoolboy sort of fellow, who might be led into any sort of scrapes by—By Jove! that's what

Dollamore had said with that horribly cynical grin. And Lady Mitford would have to run the gauntlet of society, as did most women whose husbands went to the bad.

Laurence Alsager was a very different man from the Laurence Alsager of two years ago. He wanted something to fill up his leisure time, and he thought he saw his way to it. Dollamore never spoke at random. From his quietly succulent manner Alsager knew that his lordship meant mischief, probably in his own person, at all events hinted plainly enough that—Ah! he would stop all that. He would pit himself against Dollamore, or any of them, and it would be at least a novelty to have a virtuous instead of a vicious end in view. Mitford might be a fool, his wife weak and silly; but there should be no disastrous consequences. Dollamore's prophecy should be unfulfilled, and he, Laurence Alsager, should be the active agent in the matter.

Simultaneously with this determination he decided upon deferring his visit to his father, and settling himself in London for a time. He would be on the spot; he would cultivate the acquaintance which Mitford so readily held out to him; he would have the garrison well under surveillance in order carefully to observe the enemy's approach; and—The shower-bath cut short his reflections at this point.

He dressed and breakfasted; despatched his servant to see if his old rooms in Jermyn Street were vacant; lit a cigar and strolled out. He had at first determined to brave public opinion in every shape and form, to retain his beard, to wear the curious light coats and elaborately puckered trousers which a Vienna Schneider had a year before turned out as prime specimens of the sartorial art. But even to this determination the night's reflection brought a change, and he found himself turning into Poole's, and suffering himself to be suited to the very latest cut and colour. Then he must get a hack or two from Saunderson in Piccadilly; and as the nearest way from Poole's in Saville Row to Saunderson's in Piccadilly is, as every one knows, down Grosvenor Place and through Eaton Place, that was the way that Laurence Alsager walked.

Eaton Place is not a very cheerful thoroughfare at the best of times. Even in the season, when all the houses are full of the domesticity of parliament-members, furnished at the hebdomadal rate of twenty guineas, there is a stuccoey and leading-to-not-much thoroughfares depression about it; but on a January morn, as Laurence saw it, it was specially dull. Sir Charles Mitford had mentioned no number, so that Laurence took a critical survey of each house as he passed, considering whether the lady in whom he had suddenly taken so paternal an interest resided there. He had, however, passed a very few doors when at the other end of the street he saw a low pony-carriage with a pair of iron-gray ponies standing at a door; and just as he noted them, a slight figure, which he recognized in an instant, came down the steps and took up its position in the phaeton. It was Lady Mitford, dressed in velvet edged with sable, with a very little black-velvet bonnet just covering the back of her head (it was before the days of hats), and pretty dogskin driving-gloves. She cast a timid glance at the ponies before she got in (she had always had horsy tastes down at Fishbourne, though without much opportunity of gratifying them), and was so occupied in gathering up the reins, and speaking to the groom at the ponies' head, as scarcely to notice Laurence's bow. Then with a view to retrieve her rudeness, she put out her hand, and said cordially:

"How do you do, Colonel Alsager? I beg your pardon; I was taking such interest in the ponies that I never saw you coming up. They're a new toy, a present from my husband; and that must be my excuse."

"There is no excuse needed, Lady Mitford. The ponies are charming. Are you going to drive them?"

"O yes; why not? Saunderson's people say they are perfectly quiet; and, indeed, we are going to take them out to the farm at Acton, just to show Mr. Grieve the stud-groom how nicely they look in our new phaeton."

"You're sure of your own powers? They look a little fresh."

"Oh, I have not the least fear. Besides, my husband will be with me; I'm only waiting for him to come down, and he drives splendidly, you know."

"I've a recollection of his prowess as a tandem-whip at Oxford, when the Dean once sent to him with a request that he'd 'take the leader off.' Well, *au plaisir*, Lady Mitford. I wish you and the two ponies all possible enjoyment." And he took off his hat and went on his way. Oh, he was perfectly right; she was charming. He wasn't sure whether she hadn't looked better even this morning than last night, so fresh and wholesome. And her manner, without the slightest suspicion of an *arrière pensée*, free, frank, and ingenuous; how nicely she spoke about her husband and his driving! There could be no mistake about a woman like that. No warping or twisting could torture her conduct into anything assailable. He'd been slightly Quixotic when he thought to give himself work by watching over and defending her; he—"Good morning, Mr. Spurrier. Recollect me? Mr. Saunderson in?" Revolving all these things in his mind, he had walked so quickly that he found himself in Piccadilly, and in Mr. Saunderson's yard, before he knew where he was.

"Delighted to see you back, Colonel. Thought I caught a glimpse of you at the theatre last night, but was doubtful, because of your beard. No; Mr. Saunderson's gone up to the farm to meet a lady on business; but anything I can do I shall be delighted." Mr. Spurrier was Mr. Saunderson's partner, a very handsome, fresh-coloured, cheery man, who had been in a light-cavalry regiment, and coming into money on the death of a relation, had turned his bequest and his horsy talents to account. There were few such judges of horseflesh; no better rider across country than he. "Thought you'd be giving us a call, Colonel, unless you'd imported a few Arabs; and gave you credit for better judgment than that. Your Arab's a weedy beast, and utterly unfit for hacking."

"No, Spurrier, I didn't carry my orientalism to that extent. I might have brought back a clever camel or two, or a dromedary, 'well suited for an elderly or nervous rider,' as they say in the advertisements; but I didn't. I suppose you can suit me with a hack."

Mr. Spurrier duly laughed at the first part of this speech, and replied in the affirmative, of course, to the second. "You haven't lost much flesh in the East,

Colonel," said he, running him over with his eye,—"I should say you pull off twelve stone still." Then Mr. Spurrier, as was his wont, made a great show of throwing himself into a fit of abstraction, during the occurrence of which he was supposed by customers to be mentally going through the resources of his establishment; and roused himself by calling the head-groom, and bidding him tell them to bring out the Baby.

The Baby was a bright bay with black points, small clean head, short well-cut ears, and a bright eye, arching neck, and, as she showed when trotted up the yard with the groom at her head, splendid action. When she was pulled up and stood in the usual position after the "show" had been given, Laurence stepped up, eyed her critically all over, and passed his hand down her legs. Spurrier laughed.

"All right there, Colonel. Fine as silk; not a sign of a puff, I'll guarantee, and strong as steel. Perfect animal., I call her, for a park-hack." A horse was never a "horse," but always an "animal" with Mr. Spurrier, as with the rest of his fraternity. "Will you get on her, Colonel? Just give her a turn in the Park.—Here, take this mare in, and put a saddle and bridle on her for Colonel Alsager."

It was a bright sunny winter's day, and the few people in town were taking their constitutional in the Row. As Alsager rode round by the Achilles statue he heard ringing laughter and saw fluttering habits, which, associated with the place in his mind with his last London experiences, brought up some apparently unpleasant recollection as he touched the mare with his heel, and she after two or three capricious bounds, settled down into that long swinging gallop which is such perfect luxury. He brought her back as quietly as she would come, though a little excited and restless at the unaccustomed exercise, and growled a good deal to himself as he rode. "Just the same; a little more sun, and some leaves on the trees then, and a few more people about; that's all. Gad! I can see her now, sitting square, as she always used, and as easy on that chestnut brute that pulled so infernally, as though she were in an armchair. Ah! enough has happened since I was last in this place." And then he rode the Baby into the yard, asked Mr. Spurrier her price agreed, to take her, told Spurrier he wanted a groom and a groom's horse, and was sauntering away when Mr. Spurrier said, "You'll want something to carry you to hounds, Colonel?"

"I think not; at all events not this season."

"Sorry for that, as I've got something up at the farm that would suit You exactly."

"No, thank you; where did you say?"

"At our farm at Acton. You've been there, you know."

"The farm at Acton,"—that was where Lady Mitford said she was going to drive. She must be the lady whom Mr. Saunderson had gone to meet. Spurrier saw the irresolution in his customer's face and acted promptly.

"Let me take you out there; we sha'n't be twenty minutes going and this is really something you ought not to miss. He's so good, that I give you my word I wouldn't sell him to any but a workman. You will? All right!—Put the horses to."

Within three minutes Laurence Alsager was seated by Mr. Spurrier's side in a mail-phaeton, spinning along to Mr. Saunderson's farm and his own fate.

There were few whips in London who drove so well or so fast as Mr. Spurrier, and there were none who had better horses, as may be imagined; but Laurence did not find the pace a whit too fast. He had asked Mr. Spurrier on the road, and ascertained from him that it was Lady Mitford who was expected. "And a charming lady too, sir; so gentle and kind with every one. Speaks to the men here as polite as possible, and they're not over-used to that; for, you see, in business one's obliged to speak sharp, or you'd never get attended to. Don't think she knows much of our line, though she's dreadfully anxious to learn all about it; for Sir Charles is partial to horseflesh, and is a good judge of an animal. He's been a good customer to us, and will be better, I expect, though he hasn't hunted this season, being just married, you see. That's the regular thing, I find. 'You'll give up hunting, dear? I should be so terrified when you were out.' 'Very well, dear; anything for you;' and away go the animals to Tattersall's; and within six months my gentleman will come to me and say, 'Got anything that will carry me next season, Spurrier?' and at it he goes again as hard as ever."

"I saw the ponies at the door this morning," said Laurence, for the sake of something to say; "they're a handsome pair."

"Ye-es," replied Mr. Spurrier; "I don't know very much of them; they're Mr. Saunderson's buying. I drove 'em once, and thought they wanted making; but Sir Charles is a good whip, and he'll do that.—Ga-a-te!" And at this prolonged shout the lodge-gates flew open, and they drove into the stable-yard.

Mr. Saunderson was there, but no Lady Mitford. Mr. Saunderson had his watch in his hand, and even the look of gratification which he threw into his face when he greeted Colonel Alsager on his return was very fleeting. There was scarcely a man in London whose time was more valuable, and he shook his head as he said, "I'll give her five minutes more, and then I'm off.—What are you going to show the Colonel, Spurrier?"

"I told them to bring out Launcelot first."

Mr. Saunderson shook his head "Too bad, Spurrier, too bad! I told you how the Duke fancied that animal, and how I'd given his Grace the refusal of him."

"Well, we can't keep our business at a standstill for dukes or any one else. Besides, we've known the Colonel much longer than the Duke."

"That's true," said Mr. Saunderson with a courteous bow to Laurence. "Well, if Colonel Alsager fancies the animal, I must get out of it with his Grace in the best way I can."

It was a curious thing, but no one ever bought a horse of Mr. Saunderson that had not been immensely admired by, and generally promised to, some anonymous member of the peerage.

"Easy with him, Martin, easy! Bring him over here.—So, Launcelot, so, boy."

Launcelot was a big chestnut horse, over sixteen hands high, high crest, long lean head, enormous quarters, powerful legs, and large broad feet. He looked every inch a weight-carrying hunter, and a scar or two here and there about him by no means detracted from his beauty in the eyes of the knowing ones. Martin was the rough-rider to the establishment, bullet-headed, high-cheek-boned, sunken-eyed, with limbs of steel, and pluck which would have made him ram a horse at the Victoria Tower if he had had instructions. As Mr. Spurrier patted the horse's neck, Martin leant over him and whispered, "I've told one o' them to come out on Black Jack, sir. This is a 'oss that wants a lead, this 'oss does. Give 'im a lead, and he'll face anythink."

"All right," said Spurrier, as another man and horse came out; "here they are. Go down to the gate in the tan-gallop, will you? put up the hurdles first.—Now, Colonel, this way, please; the grass is rather wet even now."

They walked across a large meadow, along one side of which from end to end a tan-gallop had been made. Midway across this some hurdles with furze on the top had been stuck up between two gate-posts, and at these the boy on Black Jack rode his horse. A steady-goer, Black Jack; up to his work, and knowing exactly what was expected of him; comes easily up to the hurdles, rises, and is over like a bird. Not so Launcelot, who frets at starting; but moves under Martin's knees and Martin's spurs, gives two or three bounds, throws up his head, and is off like a flash of lightning. Martin steadies him a bit as they approach the leap, and Jack's rider brings his horse round, meets Martin half-way, and at it they go together. Jack jumps again, exactly in his old easy way, but Launcelot tears away with a snort and a rush, and jumps, as Mr. Spurrier says, "as though he would jump into the next county."

"Now the gate!" says Mr. Spurrier; and the hurdles were removed, and a massive five-barred gate put up between the posts.

"You go first, boy," said Spurrier; and Black Jack's rider, who was but a boy, looked very white in the gills, and very tight in the mouth, and galloped off. But Jack was not meant for a country which grew such gates as that, and when he reached it, turned short round, palpably refusing. Knowing he should get slanged by his master, the boy was bringing him up again, when he heard a warning shout, and looking round, cleared out of the way to let Launcelot pass. Launcelot's mettle was up; he wanted no lead this time. Martin, with his face impassably set, brought his whip down heavily on him as he lifted him; but Launcelot did not need the blow; he sprang three or four inches clear of the leap in splendid style.

"By George, that's a fine creature!" said Laurence, who had all a sportsman's admiration for the feat. "I think I must have him, Spurrier, if his figure's not very awful. But I should first like to take him over that gate myself."

"All right, Colonel; I thought he'd, take your fancy.—Get down, Martin, and let down those stirrups a couple of holes for the Colonel, will you?—And you, boy, tumble off there. I'll see whether that old vagabond will refuse with me.—Ah, you're a sly old scoundrel, Jack; but I think we'll clear the gate, old boy!"

Alsager was already in the saddle, and Spurrier was tightening the girths, when the former heard a low rumbling sound gradually growing more distinct.

"What's that?" he asked his companion.

"What?" asked Spurrier, with his head still under the saddle-flap; but when he stood upright and listened, he said, "That's a runaway! I know the sound too well; and—and a pair! By the Lord, the grays!"

They were standing close by the hedge which separated the meadow from the road. It was a high quickset hedge, with thick post-and-rail fence running through it, and it grew on the top of a high bank with a six-foot drop into the road. Standing in his stirrups and craning over the hedge, Laurence saw a sight which made his blood run cold.

Just having breasted the railway-bridge, and tearing down the incline at their maddest pace, came the grays, and in the phaeton, which swung frightfully from side to side, sat Lady Mitford—alone! A dust-stained form gathering itself up out of the road in the distance looked like a groom; but Sir Charles was not to be seen. Lady Mitford still held the reins, and appeared to be endeavouring to regain command over the ponies; but her efforts were evidently utterly useless.

Mr. Spurrier, who had mounted, comprehended the whole scene in a second, and roared out, "Run, Martin! run, you boy! get out into the lane, and stop these devils! Hoi!" this to the grooms in the distance, to whom he telegraphed with his whip. "They don't understand, the brutes! and she'll be killed. Here, Colonel, to the right-about! Five hundred yards off there's a gate, and we can get through and head them. What are you at? you're never going at the hedge. By G—, you'll break your neck, man!"

All too late to have any effect were his last words; before they were uttered, Laurence had turned Sir Launcelot's head, taken a short sharp circling gallop to get him into pace, and then crammed him straight at the hedge. Spurrier says that to his dying day he shall never forget that jump; and he often talks about it now when he is giving a gentleman a glass of sherry, after a "show" just previous to the hunting season. Pale as death, with his hat over his brows, and his hands down on the horse's withers, sat Laurence; and just as Sir Launcelot rose at the leap, he dealt him a cut with a heavy whip which he had snatched out of Spurrier's hand The gallant animal rose splendidly, cleared posts and rails, crashed through the quickset, and came thundering into the lane below. Neither rider nor horse were prepared for the deep drop; the latter on grounding bungled awkwardly on to his knees; but Laurence had him up in an instant, and left him blown and panting, when at the moment the grays came in sight. Lady Mitford was still in the carriage, but had apparently fainted, for she lay back motionless, while the reins were dragging in the road.

Laurence thought there was yet a chance of stopping the ponies, upon whom the pace was evidently beginning to tell severely, but, as they neared a gate leading to a portion of the outbuildings, where on their first purchase by Mr. Saunderson they had been stabled, the grays, recollecting the landmarks, wheeled suddenly to the left and made for the gate. The carriage ran up an embankment and instantly overturned; one of the ponies fell, and commenced lashing out in all directions; the other, pulled across the pole, was plunging and struggling in wild attempts to free itself. The men who had been signalled to by Spurrier were by this time issuing from the lodge-gates, and making towards the spot; but long before they reached it, a tall man with a flowing black beard had sprung in among the *débris*, regardless of hoofs flying in all directions, and had dragged therefrom the senseless form of Lady Mitford.

"What is the matter? Where am I?"

"You're at my farm, Lady Mitford," said Mr. Saunderson, advancing with that old-fashioned courtesy which he always assumed when dealing with ladies; "and there's nothing the matter, thank God! though you've had a bad accident with the ponies, which seem to have run away; and I may say you owe your life to Colonel Alsager, who rescued you at the peril of his own."

She looked round with a faint smile at Laurence, who was standing at the foot of the sofa on which she lay, and was about to speak, when Laurence lifted his hand deprecatingly:

"Not a word, please, Lady Mitford; not a single word. What I did was simply nothing, and our friend Mr. Saunderson exaggerates horribly. Yes, one word—what of Sir Charles?"

"He has not heard of it? He must not be told."

"No, of course not. What we want to know is whether he started for the drive with you."

"Oh no; he could not come,—he was prevented, thank God! And the groom?"

"Oh, he's all right; a little shaken, that's all."

Laurence did not say that the groom had been *not* a little shaken by Mr. Spurrier, who caught the wretched lad by the collar, and holding his whip over him told him mildly that he had a great mind to "cut his life out" for his cowardice in throwing himself out of the trap, and leaving his mistress to her fate.

Then it was arranged that Mr. Saunderson should take Lady Mitford home, and explain all that had happened to Sir Charles. She took Laurence's arm to the carriage, and when she was seated, gave him her hand, saying frankly and earnestly, "I shall never forget that, under Providence, I owe my life to you, Colonel Alsager."

As they drove back to town together, Mr. Spurrier said to his companion "I shall have to book Sir Launcelot to you, Colonel. I've looked at his knees, and though they're all right, only the slightest skin-wound, still—"

"Don't say another word, Spurrier," interrupted Laurence; "I wouldn't let any one else have him, after to-day's work, for all the money in the world."

Laurence spoke innocently enough; but he noticed that during the rest of the drive back to town Mr. Spurrier was eyeing him with great curiosity.

CHAPTER VII.

WHAT HAD DETAINED SIR CHARLES.

The arrangement for the trial of the ponies had been one of some standing between Sir Charles and his wife, and one to which he fully intended to adhere. It is true that on waking after the supper with Messrs. Bligh, Winton, Pontifex, and their companions, he did not feel quite so fresh as he might have wished, and would very much have liked a couple of hours' additional sleep; yet so soon as he remembered the appointment, he determined that Georgie should not be disappointed; and by not having the "chill" taken off his shower-bath as usual, he was soon braced up to his ordinary good condition. Nevertheless, with all his good intentions, he was nearly an hour later than usual; and Georgie had gone up to dress for the drive when Sir Charles descended to the breakfast-room to discuss the second relay of broiled bone and devilled kidney which had been served up to tempt his sluggish appetite. He was making a not very successful attempt to eat, and between each mouthful was reading in the newspaper Mr. Rose's laudatory notice of Mr. Spofforth's play, when his servant, entering, told him that a "person" wanted to speak to him. There is no sharper appreciator of worldly position than your well-trained London servant, and Banks was a treasure.

"What is it, Banks?" asked Sir Charles, looking up.

"A person wishing to see you, Sir Charles," replied Banks.

"A person! is it a man or a woman?"

"The party," said Banks, varying his word, but not altering the generic appellation,—"the party is a man, sir."

"Do I know him?"

"I should say certainly not, Sir Charles," replied Banks in a tone which intimated that if his master did know the stranger, he ought to be ashamed of himself.

"Did he give no name?"

"I ast him for his name, Sir Charles, and he only says, 'Tell your master,' he says, 'that a gentleman,' he says, 'wants to see him.'"

"Oh, tell him that he must call some other time and send in his business. I can't see him now; I'm just going out for a drive with Lady Mitford. Tell him to call again."

"There was a time, and not very long ago either," said Sir Charles, taking up the paper as Banks retired, "that if I'd been told that a man who wouldn't give his name wanted to speak to me, I should have slipped out the back-way and run for my life. But, thank God, that's all over now.—Well, Banks, what now?"

"The party is very arbitrary, Sir Charles; he won't take 'no' for an answer; and when I told him you must know his business, he bust out larfin' and told me to say he was an old messmate of yours, and had sailed with you on board the Albatross."

A red spot burned on Sir Charles Mitford's cheek as he laid the newspaper aside and said, "Show this person into the library, and deny me to every one while he remains. Let your mistress be told I am prevented by business from driving with her to-day. Look sharp!"

Mr. Banks was not accustomed to be told to "look sharp!" and during his three-months' experience of his master he had never heard him speak in so petulant a tone. "I'd no idea he'd been a seafarin' gent," he said downstairs, "or I'd a never undertook the place. The tempers of those ship-captains is awful."

When Banks had left the room Sir Charles walked to the sideboard, and leant heavily against it while he poured out and drank a liqueur-glass of brandy.

"The Albatross!" he muttered with white lips; "which of them can it be? I thought I had heard the last of that cursed name. Banks said a man; it's not the worst of them, then. That's lucky."

He went into the library and seated himself in an armchair facing the door. He had scarcely done so when Banks gloomily ushered in the stranger.

He was a middle-sized dark man, dressed in what seemed to be a seedy caricature of the then prevailing fashion. His coat had once been a bright-claret colour, but was now dull, threadbare, and frayed round the edges of the breast-pocket, out of which peeped the end of a flashy silk handkerchief. He had no shirt-collar apparent; but wore round his neck a dirty blue-satin scarf with two pins, one large and one small, fastened together by a little chain. His trousers were of a staring green shawl-pattern, cut so as to hide nearly all the boot and tightly strapped down, as was the fashion of those days; and the little of his boots visible was broken and shabby. Sir Charles looked at him hard and steadily, then gave a sigh of relief. He had never seen the man before. He pointed to a chair, into which his visitor dropped with an easy swagger; then crossed his legs, and looking at Sir Charles, said familiarly, "And how are you?"

"You have the advantage of me," said Sir Charles.

"I think I have," said the man grinning; "and what's more, I mean to keep it too. Lord, what a precious dance you have led me, to be sure!"

"Look here, sir," said Mitford "be good enough to tell me your business, and go. I'm engaged."

"Go! Oh, you're on the high jeff, are you? And engaged too! Going to drive your missis out in that pretty little trap I saw at the door? Well, I'm sorry to stop you; but you must."

"Must!"

"Yes, must. 'Tain't a nice word; but it's the word I want. Must; and I'll tell you why. You recollect Tony Butler?"

Sir Charles Mitford's colour, which had returned when he saw that his visitor was a stranger to him, and which had even increased under the insolence of the man's manner, fled at the mention of this name. His face and lips were quite white as he said, "I do indeed."

"Yes, I knew you would. Well, he's dead, Tony is."

"Thank God!" said Sir Charles; "he was a horrible villain."

"Yes," said the man pleasantly; "I think I'm with you in both those remarks. It's a good job he's dead; and he *was* a bad 'un, was Tony, though he was my brother."

"Your brother!"

"Ah! that's just it. We never met before, because I was in America when you and Tony were so thick together. You see I'm not such a swell as Tony was; and they—him and father, I mean—were glad to get me out of the country for fear I should spoil any of their little games. When I came back, you had given Tony a licking, so far as I could make out, though he'd never tell exactly, and your friendship was all bust up, and he was dreadfully mad with you. And that's how we never came to meet before."

"And why have we met now, pray?" said Sir Charles. "What is your business with me?"

"I'm coming to that in good time. Tony's last words to me were, 'If you want to do a good thing for yourself, Dick,' he says, 'find out a fellow named Charles Mitford. He's safe to turn up trumps some day,' says Tony, 'he's so uncommonly sharp; and whenever you get to speak to him, before you say who you are, tell him you sailed in the Albatross.' Lord bless you! I knew the lot of 'em-Crockett, and Dunks, and Lizzie Ponsford; they said you and she used to be very sweet on each other, and—"

The door opened suddenly, and Lady Mitford hurried into the room; but seeing a stranger, she drew back. Sir Charles went to the door.

"What do you want, Georgie?" said he sharply.

"I had no idea you had any one here, Charles, or I wouldn't have disturbed you. Oh, Charley, send that horrid man away, and come and drive me out."

She looked so pretty and spoke so winningly that he patted her cheek with his hand, and said in a much softer voice, "I can't come now, child. This man is here on special business, and I must go through it with him. So goodbye, pet, and enjoy yourself."

She made a little moue of entreaty, and put her hands before his face in a comic appeal; but he shook his head, kissed her cheek, and shut the door.

"Pretty creechur, that!" said his companion; "looks as well in her bonnet as out of it; and there's few of 'em does, I think."

"When did you ever see Lady Mitford before, sir?" asked Sir Charles haughtily.

"Ah! that's just it," replied Mr. Butler with a sniggering laugh. "I told you you'd led me a precious dance to find you, and so you had. Tony told me that you had regularly come to grief since you parted with him, and I had a regular hunt after you, in all sorts of lodging-houses and places. There are lots of my pals on the lookout for you now."

"Upon my soul, you're devilish kind to take all this trouble about me, Mr.—Butler. What your motive was I can't imagine."

"You'll know all in good time; I'm coming to that; and not 'Butler,' please: Mr. Effingham is my name just now; I'll tell you why by and by. Well, I couldn't get hold of you anyhow, and I thought you'd gone dead or something, when last night, as I was standing waiting to come out of the Parthenium, I heard the linkmen outside hollering 'Lady Mitford's carriage!' like mad. The name strikes on my ears, and I thought I'd wait and see her ladyship. Presently down came the lady we've just seen, leaning on the arm of a cove in a big black beard like a foreigner. 'No go,' says I, 'that's not my man;' and I says to a flunkey who was standing next to me, 'He's a rum 'un to look at, is her husband.' 'That's not her husband,' he says; 'this is Sir Charles coming now.' The name Charles and the figure being like struck me at once; so I took the flunkey into the public next door, and we had a glass, and he told me all about the old gent and his kids being drowned, and your coming in for the title. 'That's my man,' says I to myself; and I found out where you lived, and came straight on here this morning."

"And now that your prying and sneaking has been successful and you have found me, what do you want?"

"Ah! I thought you'd lose your temper; Tony always said you was hotheaded. What do I want! Well, to be very short and come to the point at once—money."

"I guessed as much."

"Yes, there's no denying it; I'm regularly stumped. I suppose you were surprised now to hear I wasn't flush, after seeing me so well got-up? But it's a deal of it dummy. These pins now,—Lowther Arcade! No ticker at the end of this guard; nothing but a key-look!" And he twitched a key out of his waistcoat-pocket. "My boots too are infernally leaky; and my hat has become quite limp from being perpetually damped and ironed. Yes, I want money badly."

"Look here, Mr.——"

"Effingham."

"Mr. Effingham, you have taken, as you yourself admit, an immense deal of trouble to hunt me up, and having found me you ask me for money, on the ground of your being the brother of an infernal scoundrel whom I had once the ill-luck to be associated with—don't interrupt me, please. It wasn't Tony Butler's fault that I didn't die on a dunghill, or that I am not now—"

"In Norfolk Island," said Mr. Effingham, getting in his words this time.

Sir Charles glared fiercely at him for an instant, and then continued: "Now I expected I should have to encounter this sort of thing from the people who pillaged me when I was poor, and would make that an excuse for further extortion, and I determined not to accede to any application. But as you're the first who has applied, and as you've neither bullied nor whined, I'll tell you what I'll do. I'll give you, on condition I never see or hear of you again, this five-pound note."

Mr. Effingham laughed, a real hearty laugh, as he shook his head, and said: "Won't do: nothing like enough."

Sir Charles lost his temper, and said: "Stop this infernal tomfoolery, sir! Not enough! Why, d—n it, one would think you had a claim upon me!"

"And suppose I have, Sir Charles Mitford, what then?" said Mr. Effingham, leaning forward in his chair and confronting his companion.

"What then? Why—pooh, stuff! this is a poor attempt at extortion. You don't think to get any money out of me by threatening to tell of my connection with the Albatross crew? You don't think I should mind the people to whom you could tell it knowing it, do you?"

"I don't know; perhaps not; and yet I think I shall be able before I've done to prove to you I've a claim on you."

"What is it?"

"All tiled here, eh? Nobody within earshot? That sleek cove in black that wouldn't let me see you, not listening at the door, is he?"

"There is no one to hear," said Sir Charles, who was getting more and more uncomfortable at all this mystery.

"All right, then. Sorry to rake up disagreeables; but I must. You recollect making a slight mistake about your Christian name once, fancying it was Percy instead of Charles; writing it as Percy across a stamped bit of paper good for two hundred quid, and putting Redmoor as your address after it?"

"Well, what if I do?" His lips were so parched he could hardly frame the words.

"It would be awkward to have anything of that sort brought up just now, wouldn't it?"

Sir Charles hesitated for an instant, then gave a great sigh of relief as he said: "You infernal scoundrel! you think to frighten me with that, do you? To make that the ground for your extortion? Why, you miserable wretch, I myself burnt that—that—document in Moss's office!"

"How you do run on, Sir Charles! I just mentioned something about a little bill, and you're down upon me in a moment. I guessed that was destroyed; at all events I knew it was all safe; and Sir Percy's dead, so it don't much matter. But, Lord! with your memory you must surely recollect *another* little dockyment,—quite a little one, only five-and-twenty pound,-where you mistook both your names that time, and accepted it as Walter Burgess:—recollect?"

The pallor had spread over Mitford's face again, and his lips quivered as he said: "That was destroyed—destroyed by Tony Butler long since—before the other one was done."

"Yes, yes, I know this was the first,—a little one just to get your hand in. But it ain't destroyed. It's all right, bless you! I can see it now with a big black 'FORGED' stamped across it by the bank-people."

"Where is it?"

"Oh, it's in very safe keeping with a friend of mine who scarcely knows its value. Because, though he knows its a forgery, he don't know who done it; now, you see, through my brother Tony, I do know who done it; and I do know that Walter Burgess is alive, and is a large hop-factor down Maidstone way, and owing you a grudge for that thrashing you gave him in the billiard-rooms at Canterbury, which he's never forgotten, would come forward and prosecute at once."

"You—you might prove the forgery; but how could you connect me with it?"

"Not bad, that. But I'm ready for you. People at the bank will prove you had the money; and taken in connection with the other little business, which is well known, and which there are lots of people to prove, a jury would convict at once."

Sir Charles Mitford shuddered, and buried his face in his hands. Then, looking up, said: "How much do you want for that bill?"

"Well, you see, that's scarcely the question. It's in the hands of a man who don't know its value, and if he did he'd open his mouth pretty wide, and stick it on pretty stiff, I can tell you. So we can let him bide a bit. Meantime I know about it, and, as Tony told me, I intend to make it serve me. Now you want to get rid of me, and don't want to see me for some little time? I thought so. I'm not an extravagant cove; give me fifty pounds."

"Until that bill is destroyed, you will wring money from me when you choose."

"If you refused me money and I cut up rough, the bill should be produced, and you'd be in quod and Queer Street in a jiffy! Better do as I say—give me the fifty, and you shan't see me for a blue moon!"

Whether Sir Charles was stimulated by the period named or not, it is certain he sat down at his desk, and producing his cheque-book, began to write. Mr. Effingham looked over his shoulder.

"Make it payable to some number—295, or anything—not a name, please. And you needn't cross it. Lord! you didn't take much trouble to disguise your fist when you put Walter Bur—, beg pardon! quite forgot what I was saying. Thank you, Sir Charles. I'll keep my word all right, you shall see. I'm not an idle beggar; I'm always at something; so that I shan't depend entirely on this bit of gray paper; but it'll ease my springs and grease my wheels a bit. Good-day to you, Sir Charles. Never mind ringing for that solemn cove to let me out; I ain't proud. Good-day."

Mr. Effingham gave a very elaborate bow, and departed. As the door shut upon him, Sir Charles Mitford pulled his chair to the fire, and fell into a deep reverie, out of which he did not rouse himself until his wife's return.

CHAPTER VIII.

KISMET.

It was not because Laurence Alsager had been for a twelvemonth in the East that he believed in the Mohammedan doctrine of fatalism. That had been an unacknowledged part of his creed long before the disappointment which sent him flying from the ordinary routine of life had fallen upon him. Even under that disappointment he allowed the power of the wondrous "to be," and, bowing to its influence, accepted his exile with far greater equanimity than many others would have done under similar circumstances. He had suffered his plans—undecided when he left England—to be entirely guided by chance; had followed suggestions for his route made by hotel-landlords or conveyance-advertisements; had dallied over one part of his journey and hurried over another, simply in obedience to the promptings of the feeling of the moment; and had finally decided on returning to be present at the first night of Spofforth's play at the Parthenium in the haphazard spirit which had prompted all his movements.

His belief in Kismet had been enormously strengthened since his return. It was "arranged" that Lady Mitford should be present on the occasion in question; that he should be presented to her after trying to avoid her and her party; that Lord Dollamore should be at the Club, and should give utterance to those sentiments which had aroused so deep a disgust in Laurence's breast. As to the events of the next day,— the visit to Saunderson's, the drive to Acton, the trial of Sir Launcelot and its consequences,—therein was the most marvellous illustration of the doctrine of Kismet that ever he had yet seen.

He thought of all this as he woke the next morning; and clearly saw in an instant that it would be running directly contrary to his fate to go down to see his father just then. He felt impelled to remain in London, and in London he should stay. He felt— Ah, how beautiful she looked as he dragged her out from amidst the *débris* of the carriage and the plunging hoofs of the ponies, though her face was as pale as marble, and the light of her eyes was quenched beneath the drooping lids! It was Kismet that had kept that handsome oaf, her husband, at home, and prevented his interfering with the little romance. Not that Sir Charles Mitford was by any means an oaf; he was a man of less worldly experience, of less polish, of social standing, higher in rank, but decidedly lower in reputation, than Laurence; and so Laurence regarded him as an oaf, and, since the pony-carriage adventure, began to find a little hatred mingling with the contempt with which he had previously regarded the latest addition to the baronetage.

This last feeling may have been in accordance with the rules of Kismet, but it certainly was not in accordance with the practice of the world. There were many men in his old regiment, and generally throughout the brigade of Guards,—men who, as professedly *coureurs des dames*, held that, for the correct carrying out of a flirtation with a married woman, an intimacy of a certain kind with the lady's husband was almost indispensable. And, though not good at argument, had they been put to it, they could have indorsed their *dicta* with plenty of examples. They could have told of picnics improvised solely for the pleasure of madame's society, when monsieur was of the greatest assistance, the life and soul of the party, opening champagne, finding salt, cracking jokes; the only man who could induce the gathered leaves to burst into a fire for kettle-boiling purposes; the first to volunteer to sit in the rumble with the captain's valet on the journey homewards. They could have told of visits paid in opera-boxes at a time when it was certain that monsieur was just smacking his lips over something peculiar in claret at a dinner at the Junior, specially given by the captain's brother-officer, the major. They could have told of capital fishing and excellent shooting obtained by them for monsieur with a tendency in that direction; stream or lake, moor or stubble, always happening to be at a very remote distance from monsieur's family abode. There were even some of them who for the time being would thoroughly interest themselves in monsieur and his affairs, would bear with his children, would listen to his stories, would, on rare occasions, be seen about with him, and would, when very hard hit, invite him to the Windsor mess, or give him a seat in the Derby drag.

But that sort of thing did not do for Laurence Alsager. Such a line of conduct might have suited him once; but it would have been years ago, and with a very different style of wife and husband from Lady Mitford and Sir Charles. He could not think of her with any feeling that was not deeply tinged with respect, and that in itself was sufficient to remove this new passion from the category of his past loves. His new passion? Yes; he could not deny it to himself; he felt a singular interest in this woman; there was an attraction in her such as he had never experienced in any one else. He smiled as he recollected how in the bygone times he would have called her "cold" and "statuesque;" how he would have despised her slight figure, and thought her manners rustic, if not *gauche*. How he had sneered at love, as distinguished from intrigue, when he was a mere boy; and now, at thirty, after thirteen years of hard life of all kinds—traces of which might be seen in a few lines round the eyes and on the forehead—he was lapsing into the calf-love which boys at school feel for the master's daughter. He laughed; but he knew it was all true, nevertheless.

He must see her that day, of course; at least, he must call—mere politeness required so much after the events of the previous day. Meanwhile he would go down to the club, to read the papers and get some luncheon, and kill time.

There were several men in the morning-room at the club, some of whom he had seen on the first night of his arrival, others whom he met now for the first time since his return.

Lord Dollamore was there, his legs up on a sofa, reading a newspaper, with a very peculiar grin upon his face.

"Here he is!" he said, looking towards the door as Laurence entered the room; "here's the man himself! Why don't we have a band to play 'See the conquering'?"

"So we ought, by Jove!" said Cis Hetherington. "Hallo, Laurence, old boy! no sling or anything?"

"Looks well after it, don't he?" said another; while several old gentlemen looked up from their newspapers, partly in admiration, partly in awe.

"Fire away, gentlemen!" said Laurence. "Be as funny as you please; it's all lost upon me. What the deuce do you mean by 'sling,' Cis?"

"He's been so long away, that he's forgotten the English language," sneered Dollamore.

"O no, he hasn't, Lord Dollamore, as he'd quickly show you, were there the least occasion," said Laurence. "But," added he more quietly, "what is the joke? I give you my honour I don't know what you're talking about."

"A lovely lady and a gallant knight! Bring forth the steed! The accident; the leap; the rescue! Ha, ha! she's saved! Slow music and curtain! Stunnin' draymer it would make. I can introduce you to several enterprising managers if you'd like to tour in the provinces," said jolly Mr. Wisconsin, who spent nearly all his time and two-third's of his income amongst theatrical people.

"Why, how on earth did that story get here?" asked Laurence, on whom the truth was beginning slowly to dawn.

"Here! why, it's all over town—all over England by this time. It's in the papers."

"In the papers! Ah, you're selling me."

"Take it, and read for yourself," said Wisconsin. "Open the paper, and knock it back with your hand—that's the legitimate business."

"Doosid well Alsager pretends to be astonished, don't he, considering he put that in the paper himself?"

"No, he didn't do it himself; he got Cis Hetherington to do it."

"Cis couldn't have spelt it," said Lord Dollamore. "There are some devilish long words, over which Cis would have come a cropper."

While his friends were thus pleasantly discussing him, Laurence was reading a remarkably full-flavoured and eloquent description of a "Serious Accident and Gallant Conduct," as the paragraph was headed, in which Lady Mitford's name and his own figured amongst the longest adjectives and most difficult adverbs. How the wildly excited steeds dashed away at a terrific pace; how the grasp of the lovely charioteer gradually relaxed, and how her control over the fiery animals was finally lost; how the attendant groom did everything that strength and science in equine matters could suggest, until he was flung, stunned and breathless, into the mire; and how finally, the gallant son of Mars, mounted on a matchless barb, came bounding over the hedge, and extricated the prostrate and palpitating form of the lovely member of the aristocracy from utter demolition at the hoofs of the infuriated animals. All this was to be found in the newspaper paragraph which Laurence was reading. This paragraph originated in a short story told by the groom in the bar of a public-house close to the mews, whither he had gone to solace himself with beer after the indignities he had suffered at Mr. Spurrier's hands, and where he had the satisfaction of repeating it to a broken-down seedy man, who "stood" a pint, and who took short notes of the groom's conversation in a very greasy pocketbook.

Laurence was horribly disgusted, as could be seen by the expression of his face, and the nervous manner in which he kept twisting the ends of his moustache. The amusement of the other men was rather increased than diminished at his annoyance, and was at its height when Cis Hetherington asked:

"What the doose is a 'matchless barb,' Alsager? I've seen all sorts of hacks in my time, but never met with one of that kind."

"What do you mean by hacks?" said another. "A barb is a fellow that writes plays, ain't it? They call Shakespeare the immortal barb."

"Ah, but they call him a Swan, and all kinds of things. There's no making out what a thing is by what they call him."

Meanwhile Lord Dollamore had risen from the couch, and strolled over to the rug in front of the fire, where Laurence was standing.

"You've begun your duties quickly, my dear Alsager. There are few fellows who get the chance of falling into their position so rapidly."

"What position?"

"That of champion of beauty in distress."

"Position! I declare I don't follow you, my lord."

"My dear Alsager, surely the East has not had the effect of rendering obtuse one of the keenest of men. Don't you recollect our talk the other night?"

"Perfectly."

"When I then expressed my opinion that Lady Mitford would have to go through the usual amount of danger, of course I meant moral, not actual, peril. However, the actual seems to have come first."

"Ye-es. A smashed carriage and plunging horses may, I suppose, be looked upon as actual danger."

"Ah, she'll have worse things than those to contend against and encounter. You were lucky enough to save her from a fractured skull; I suppose we shall see you doing the 'sweet-little-cherub' business, and watching over her generally, henceforth."

"You seem to forget that Lady Mitford has a husband, Lord Dollamore."

"Not for an instant, my good fellow. But so has—well, Mrs. Hammond—and so have lots of women; but then the husbands are generally engaged in taking care of somebody else. Well, well, to think that *you* should become a sheep-dog,—you whose whole early life was spent in worrying the lambs!"

"Whose whole *early* life—that's it! *Quand le diable est vieux il se fait ermite!*"

"Ye-es; but if I were the husband of a very pretty young wife, I doubt whether I should particularly like you being her father confessor."

"You need not alarm yourself, my lord; I'm not going in for the position."

"*Qui a bu, boira*, my dear Alsager. I distrust sudden conversions, and have no great reliance on sheep-dogs whose fangs are scarcely cleared of wool."

Laurence might have replied somewhat sharply to this, had he heard it; but he was off on his way to the coffee-room to his luncheon, which had been announced by the waiter; that finished, he started off for Eaton Place.

He had sufficient matter for reflection on his walk. This preposterous story which had crept into the papers would of course form a splendid subject of gossip for all those who had nothing better to do than to talk about such things. There was already a certain amount of interest attaching to the Mitfords from the fact of Sir Charles having inherited the baronetcy in a singular and unlooked-for manner, and from his wife's having had the audacity—although sprung from an unknown family—to have a beautiful face and agreeable manners. For this presumption Alsager felt that a terrible retribution was in store for her, poor child, when the regular season came on, and the dowagers brought up their saleable daughters to the market. Then the notion that a common country parson's daughter had been beforehand with them, and had carried off an unexceptionable *parti* before he had been regularly advertised as ready for stalking, would drive these old ladies to a pitch of rankling and venomous despair which would find vent in such taunts, hints, insinuations, and open lies as are only learnt in the great finishing-school of London society. Lady Mitford's beauty, style, and position were in themselves quite sufficient to render her an object of dislike to nine-tenths of the other women in society, who would eagerly search for something against her, however slight it might be. Had not that unfortunate accident and its result given them this "something"? Laurence had been too long amongst the ranks of *nous autres* not to recognize the meaning of the grins and winks which went round the assembled circle of club-men when the newspaper paragraph was read, not fully to understand every sneering inflexion of Lord Dollamore's voice. Thus was the sin of his youth visited on him in later life, with a vengeance. Hundreds of other men might have done exactly as he had—an act simply of manly impulse—without anything having been said about it save praise; but with him, that infernal reputation for gallantry, of which he was once so proud, and which he now so intensely loathed, would set shoulders shrugging and eyebrows lifting at once. The old story! Laurence Alsager again! What else could be expected? For an instant, as all these thoughts came rushing through his mind, he stopped short, wondering whether it would not be better to retrace his steps to the hotel, and to fulfil his first-formed resolution of paying a hurried visit to his father, and then quitting England at once. Yes; it would be much better; it would save any chance of scandal or talk, and—And yet he did not like to miss the chance of being thanked by those sweet eyes and that soft voice. He had thought so much of how she would look, not as he had hitherto seen her in full evening-dress or in her bonnet, but in that simple morning-costume in which all charming women look most charming. Besides, it was his duty as a gentleman to call, after the events of the previous day, and see whether she was suffering from any result of her accident, or from any fright which might have arisen from it. Yes; he would first call and see her, and then go away;—at least, he was not quite certain whether he would go away or not. He was not sure that it would not be far more advisable that he should stay in England, and be on the spot to put a stop at once to any preposterous talk that might arise; and especially to watch over her in case of any attempts which might be made by men of the Dollamore class. Lord Dollamore was a most dangerous fellow, a man who would stick at nothing to gain his ends; and what those ends were, it was, to a man of Alsager's experience, by no means difficult to imagine. Besides, he was merely the type of a class; and if all he had stated about Sir Charles Mitford were really true, if the baronet were a man of dissolute tastes and habits, and utterly unable to withstand the temptation which his wealth and position would at once open up to him, it was absolutely necessary that some one should be there to prevent his wife's falling a prey to the numerous libertines who would immediately attempt to take advantage of her husband's *escapades*, and ingratiate themselves into her favour.

When the wish is father not merely to the thought, but to the subsequent argument, it is by no means difficult to beat down and utterly vanquish the subtlest and most logical self-reasoning. Three minutes' reflection and balancing served to show Laurence how wrong he had been in thinking of absenting himself at such a critical time; and though for a moment the "still small voice" ventured to insinuate a doubt of the soundness of his argument, yet he felt that leaving future events to take such course as they might ultimately fall into—it was at least his bounden duty to go then and inquire after Lady Mitford; and onwards he proceeded.

Lady Mitford was at home. In a charming drawing-room—everything in it bearing evidence of exquisite womanly taste,—he found her, dressed, as he expected, in the most lovely of morning-costumes—a high violet-silk dress with a simple linen collar and cuffs; her hair perfectly plain, showing the small classic head in all its beauty: she looked to him the loveliest creature he had ever seen. She rose at the announcement of his name, and came forward with a pleasant smile on her face and with outstretched hand Laurence noticed—not, perhaps, without a little disappointment—that there was not the smallest sign of a blush on her cheek, nor the slightest tremor in her voice.

"I'm so glad to see you, Colonel Alsager," she said frankly; "I'm sure I've thought a hundred times since we parted of my *gaucherie* in not thanking you sufficiently for the real service you did me yesterday."

"Pray don't say another word about it, Lady Mitford; it was a simple duty which merits no further mention."

"Indeed, I don't think so. It was a very gallant act in itself, and one which, so far as I'm concerned, renders me your debtor for life."

"The acknowledgment cancels the obligation. I only trust you are none the worse for the mishap."

"Thank you, not in the least.. I was a little shaken and unstrung by the fall, and rather stupid yesterday evening, I'm inclined to think; but the night's rest has set me perfectly right. You know I'm country-bred, and therefore what my husband would call in good condition; and I've had so many tumbles off ponies, and been upset so many times in our Devonshire lanes by papa,—who, I'm afraid, is not a very good whip, bless him!—that I'm not entirely unused to such accidents."

"That accounts for your pluck, then. I never saw any one go through what—now it's over—I may say was a very ugly runaway, with more perfect calmness."

"Ah, that's what I wanted to ask you. I lost my head just as we started down that descent, and knew nothing afterwards. I do so hope I didn't scream."

"You may make yourself thoroughly easy on that score. You were perfectly mute."

"I am delighted at that!" she laughed out with childish glee. "Charley asked me the very first thing whether I hadn't 'yelled out,' as he called it; and I told him I thought not. It was very weak of me to faint, and I fought against it as long as I could; but I felt it must come, and it did."

"You would have been more than woman if you could have deprived yourself of that treat," said Laurence "How is Sir Charles?"

"Well, not very well. I fancy that this accident has upset him very much, poor fellow. I think he blames himself for having allowed me to go without him; and yet he couldn't come, as he had some horrid man here on business. But he's been very dull and preoccupied ever since. He'll be annoyed at having missed you, as he went out specially to call and thank you for your great kindness. We did not know your address, and he went down to Mr. Bertram's office to get it from him."

"Oh, Bertram is a very old friend of mine. It was from him I first heard of you."

"Yes, he knew Charley at Oxford. He is a kind gentle creature, I should think; a man that it must be impossible for any one to dislike. And really his silence is sometimes anything but disagreeable—at a theatre, you know, and that sort of thing."

"Silence! I can assure you, Lady Mitford, that when you are the theme of his discourse, he is a perfect Demosthenes. 'The common mouth, so gross to express delight, in praise of her grew oratory,' as Tennyson says.. He is one of your stanchest admirers."

Lady Mitford looked uncomfortable and a little vexed, as she said, "Indeed!" then smiled again as she added, "You also have the effect of loosening the dumb man's tongue. In Mr. Bertram you have the loudest of trumpeters. In fact, ever since he heard from you of your intended return, we have grown almost tired of hearing of your good qualities."

"I hope you won't banish me, as the Athenians did Aristides for the same reason. Old George is one of the best fellows living. Do you know many people now in town, Lady Mitford?"

"No, indeed. Our Devonshire neighbours have not come up yet, and will not, I suppose, until Parliament meets. And then Sir Charles having been—been away for some time, and I not having lived in society, we scarcely know anybody yet; at least, I mean—I—some of Charley's old. friends have found us out. Mr. Bertram, Captain Bligh and Major Winton, and Lord Dollamore."

"Ah, Lord Dollamore! yes, to be sure. And what, if it's a fair question, do you think of Lord Dollamore?"

Georgie laughed. "It certainly is *not* a fair question, and if Charley were here, I should not be allowed to answer it; but I don't mind telling you, Colonel Alsager, that I have a great horror of Lord Dollamore."

Laurence smiled grimly, but with the greatest inward satisfaction, as he said, "Poor Dollamore! And will you tell me why you have a horror of him, Lady Mitford?"

"I can scarcely say. I'm sure I ought not to bare it, as he is always studiously polite to me; but there is something strange to me in his manner and in his conversation, something such as I have never met with before, and which, though I don't comprehend it, rouses my antipathy and makes me shudder. I never know what to say to him either, and he always seems to be watching every word that you speak. Now you're laughing at me, Colonel Alsager; and I can't explain what I mean."

Her cheeks flushed as she said this, and the heightened colour added to her beauty. Laurence found himself staring mutely at her, in sheer wonderment at her loveliness; then roused himself and said, "Indeed, I was not laughing, and I can fully comprehend you. Now tell me; the ponies are none the worse for their race?"

"Not much. One has a cut fetlock, and both have had a good deal of air rubbed off; but nothing to signify. I was round in the stables the first thing this morning, and came in great glee to tell Charley how little harm had been done to them. But he's dreadfully angry about it, and declares they shall both be sent away. And all because I was too weak to hold them."

"Well, I should like to be on your side; but I don't think your husband is very far wrong in the present instance. They are plainly unfit for any lady's driving, unless she is what no lady would like to be,—undeniably horsey, and masculine, so far at least as her wrists are concerned."

"Ah, and your horse; that splendid fellow that took the tremendous leap,—Mr. Saunderson told me this; I knew nothing of it at the time,—what of him?"

"Oh, he's wonderfully well. He landed splendidly; but just heeled over for a second and touched his knees,—the merest graze, and that all through my clumsiness; but I was too much excited at the time to attend to him. But it's a mere hair-scratch, and he'll be as right as ever in a week or two."

"Well, the whole thing seems to me like a dream; but a dream from which I should never have woke, had it not been for your promptitude and presence of mind. Those I have said I shall never forget; and—Now here comes Charley to indorse my gratitude."

As she spoke, a heavy tread was heard on the staircase; the door opened, and Sir Charles Mitford entered, full of life and radiant with happiness. Any preoccupation or anxiety, for which his wife had prepared her visitor, seemed entirely to have disappeared. He advanced with open hand, and in his cheeriest manner said, "My dear Alsager, delighted to see you! A thousand thanks, my dear fellow,—much more than I can express,—for your conduct yesterday! I've heard all about it, and know how much

I owe to you. Tremendous pluck! O yes, I know; you needn't pretend to be modest about it. I've been round to Saunderson's, and seen Spurrier; and he tells me that it was just one of the pluckiest things ever done. You staked the horse, or did something damaging to him, didn't you? so of course I told Spurrier to enter him in my account."

"You're very good; but you're a little late, Sir Charles. I bought him on the spot, and would not part with him for treble his price."

Laurence could not resist stealing a glance at Lady Mitford as he said this. Her eyes were downcast; but a bright red spot burned on her cheeks, and her brows were contracted.

"Well, you've the right of refusal, and you know a good fencer when you see one, Alsager, I know. I only wished to have the horse as a memento of the day."

Laurence muttered something inaudible.

"I went down to call upon you, to thank you for all your kindness to my wife," continued Sir Charles; "and then finding I didn't know your address, I looked up Bertram at the Foreign Office; and after being handed about from one room to another, I found him, and he took me to your hotel. Don't seem to have much to do, those fellows at the Foreign Office. Bertram had only just arrived; but he left immediately when I told him I wanted him to come with me."

"I'm very sorry I was not at home."

"Well, so was I partly, and partly not. Of course I should have wished to have given you my thanks for your kindness the very first thing; but then of course you understand that I meant all that. When a man rescues another man's wife from tremendous danger, of course he understands that her husband is tremendously thankful to him, unless it's in a book or play, or that kind of thing, where husbands wish their wives were dead. And then again, if you had been in, I should have missed being introduced to such a charming woman."

"To such a what, Charley?" asked Lady Mitford.

"Oh, don't you be frightened, dear; it's all square and above-board. She asked me if she might call upon you; and she'll be here to-morrow or the next day; so mind you're at home to receive her."

"Her? who?"

"O yes, I forgot. I'll tell you all about it. When we found Alsager was not at his hotel, Bertram evidently didn't want to go back to his office, so he proposed a stretch round the Park. I said I was quite agreeable, and off we started; right round the Oxford Street side, back by the powder-magazine, and so into the Drive. When we got there, there was not a single trap to be seen—not one, I give you my honour; but as we stumped along, and Bertram—most delightful companion!—never opened his mouth, I saw a pair of bright chesnuts in black harness come whirling a low pony-phaeton along; and as it passed, Bertram took off his hat to the lady driving. She pulled up, and we went to the trap, and Bertram introduced me. She was a very pretty little woman, and had a sable cloak;—you must have a sable cloak, Georgie; I'll find out where she got hers;—and there was another woman whom I could not see—kept her veil down, and looked like companion or something of that sort-sitting by her. She certainly drove splendidly. I couldn't help thinking if she'd had those grays of yours yesterday, Georgie, she'd have mastered them."

"I sincerely wish she had," said Lady Mitford with a little petulance; "I can't say I entirely relish the adventure, even though it called forth Colonel Alsager's assistance." ["That's a thorough woman's blow," thought Laurence, listening.] "But you haven't told us the name of this charming Amazon."

"I don't know anything about Amazon or not," said Sir Charles, who began to be a little bit nettled; "the lady's name is Hammond—Mrs. Hammond, wife of a man who was something in the government service. Ah, you know her, Alsager. Yes, by the way, I recollect her asking Bertram whether you had come back."

The mention of Mrs. Hammond's name seemed to throw rather a damp upon the conversation. Lady Mitford did not appear in the least to share her husband's rhapsodies,—as how should she, being ignorant of their object?—and Colonel Alsager's expression was moody, and his voice silent. But when he rose to take his leave the expressions of gratitude were renewed both by husband and wife, each in their peculiar manner—Sir Charles was boisterously hearty; Lady Mitford quietly impressive.

"We shall see a good deal of you now, I hope, Alsager; you won't stand on any ridiculous ceremony, or anything of that sort, but come in and out just as you like. There's no one who will be more welcome here, and no one who's earned the right so much, for the matter of that. It rests with you now entirely how far you pursue the acquaintance."

"Goodbye, Colonel Alsager," said Lady Mitford with a sweet smile; "and I'll promise, when you do come to see us, not to give you so much trouble as I did yesterday."

Laurence was equally averse to commonplaces and to committing himself, so he bowed and smiled, and went away.

"Kismet," he muttered to himself as he strode down the street,—"Kismet in full force. Laura Hammond back in England, and an acquaintance formed between her and Mitford already. Taken with her, he seemed too. She's just the woman that would fetch such a man as he. Well, let Kismet do its worst; I shall stand by and see the play."

CHAPTER IX.

MR. EFFINGHAM'S PROCEEDINGS.

When Mr. Effingham found himself with fifty pounds in his pocket outside the bank where he had changed Sir Charles Mitford's cheque, he could scarcely contain his exultation. His dealings with bankers had been few, and not always satisfactory. He had had cheques in his possession which he had been too bashful to present in his own proper person, but had employed a little boy to take to the counter while he waited round the corner of an adjacent street; he had had cheques which he had presented himself, but the proceeds of which, when asked "how he would have," he had always taken in gold, as a more convenient and untraceable medium. On the present occasion, however, he had walked boldly in; had rapped on the counter, to the horror and dismay of the old gentleman behind banking-firm, passing through the public office on his way to the private parlour, peered at Mr. Effingham. under his bushy-grey eyebrows curiously; but Mr. Effingham did not mind that. The porter sitting on a very hard stool just inside the swing doors rubbed his nose and winked significantly at the policeman in plain clothes stationed just outside the swing-doors, whose duty was to help rich old-lady customers in and out of their carriages. Both porter and policeman stared very hard at Mr. Effingham, and Mr. Effingham returned the stare with all the eye-power at his command What did he care? They might call him back and inspect the cheque if they liked, and then they would see what they would get for attempting to molest a gentleman.

In his character of gentleman, Mr. Effingham felt that his costume was scarcely so correct as it might have been; in fact, that in the mere quality of being weather-tight it was lamentably deficient. So his first proceeding was to visit an outfitter's, and then and there to procure what he termed "a rig-out" of the peculiar kind most in accordance with his resonant taste. The trousers were of such an enormous check pattern that, as the Jew tailor humorously remarked, "it would take two men to show it;" the hat shone like a bad looking-glass; the coat, though somewhat baggy in the back, was glossy, and had a cotton-velvet collar; and the Lowther-Arcade jewelry glistened in the midst of a bird's-eye scarf of portentous height and stiffness.

His outer man satisfied, Mr. Effingham thought it time to attend to his inner; and accordingly turned into a City chop-house of renown, where his elegant appearance made an immense impression on the young stockbroking gents and the junior clerks from the banks and Mincing-Lane houses, who commented, in no measured tones, and with a great deal of biting sarcasm, on the various portions of his costume. Either not hearing or not heeding this banter, Mr. Effingham ordered a point steak and potatoes and a pint of stout; all of which he devoured with an appearance of intense relish. An old gentleman sitting in the same box opposite to him had a steaming glass of fragrant punch, the aroma of which ascended gratefully into Mr. Effingham's nostrils and almost impelled him to order a similar jorum; but prudence stepped in, and he paid his bill and departed, Not that he did not intend to indulge in that after-dinner grog, which was customary with him whenever he had the money to pay for it himself, or the luck to get anybody to pay for it for him; but he wished to combine business with pleasure; and so started off for another tavern nearer the West End, where he knew the combination could be accomplished.

The chosen place of Mr. Effingham's resort, though properly designated the Brown Bear, was known to all its frequenters as "Johnson's," from its proprietor's name. It was a commonplace public-house enough, in a street leading out of the Strand, and sufficiently near the large theatres and newspaper offices for its parlour to be the resort of actors and press-men of an inferior grade. The more eminent in both professions "used" the Rougepot in Salad Yard, a famous old place that had been a house of call for actors, wits, and men-of-letters for generations, and where strangers seldom penetrated. The *habitués* of "Johnson's" were mostly young men just affiliated to their professions, and not particularly careful as to their associates; so that you frequently found in Johnson's parlour a sprinkling of questionable characters, men who hung on to the selvage of theatrical life, betting-book keepers, and card-sharpers. The regular frequenters did not actually favour these men, but they tacitly allowed their presence, and occasionally would join in and listen to their conversation, from which they gleaned new notions of life.

When Mr. Effingham pushed open the parlour-door and looked into the room on the afternoon in which he had conducted his banking operation with such signal success, the place was almost deserted. The large corner-boxes by the fire, where the professional gentlemen usually congregated, were empty; but at a table in the far end of the room were seated two men, at sight of whom Mr. Effingham's face brightened. They were flashily-dressed, raffish-looking men, smoking rank cigars, and busily engaged in comparing betting-books.

"Hollo!" said one of them, looking up at the noise made by the opening of the door; "I'm blessed if here ain't D'Ossay Butler! And the regular D'Ossay cut too—sprucer than ever; might pass for the Count himself, D'Ossay!"

"What's happened to the little cove now, I wonder?" said the other, a thin man with a shaved face and a tall hat, which he had great difficulty in keeping on his head; "what's happened to him now? Has he stood-in on a steeple-chase, or robbed a bank? Look at his togs! What a slap-up swell he is!"

Mr. Effingham received these compliments with great equanimity, sat down by his friends, and seeing their glasses empty, said: "Any lap? I'm game to stand anything you like to put a name to;" rang the bell for the waiter, and ordered three nines of brandy hot.

"What an out-and-out little cove it is!" repeated the first man with great admiration. "Well, tell us, D'Ossay, all about it. How did it come off? What was it?"

"Come off!" said Mr. Effingham; "what do you mean? Nothing's come off that I know of; at least nothing particular. You know that gentleman in the City that I told you of, Griffiths?" he asked, with a private wink at the man in the high hat.

"I know him fast enough," replied that worthy with a nod, partly confirmatory, partly to keep the tall hat on his head. "Did he pull through in that matter?"

"Pull through!" said Mr. Effingham; "he won a lot of money; and as I'd given him the office, and put him on a good thing, he said he'd behave handsome; and he didn't do amiss, considerin.'"

"What did he part with?" asked the first man.

"A tenner."

The first man's eyes glistened, and he instantly made up his mind to borrow half-a-sovereign if he could get it—five shillings if he could not—of Effingham before they parted.

"Ah, and so you went and rigged yourself out in these swell togs, D'Ossay, did you, at once? You always had the notions of a gentleman, and the sperrit of a gentleman, that's more. I wish you'd put me on to something of that kind; but, there, it wants the way to carry it out; and I haven't got that, I know well enough."

While this speech was in progress, Mr. Effingham had caught the eye of the tall man, and winking towards their friend, pointed over his shoulder at the door. The tall man repeated the nod that did the double duty, and after looking up at the clock, said, "You'd better be off Jim; you'll be just in time to catch that party down at Peter Crawley's, if you look sharp."

Jim, thus admonished, finished his grog and took his leave, asking Mr. Effingham if he could have "half a word" with him outside; which half-word resulted in the extraction of a half-sovereign, as Jim had predetermined.

"Now for it," said Griffiths, as soon as Effingham returned, "I'm death to hear all that's happened, only that fool wouldn't go. Wanted something, of course, outside, eh? Ah, thought so. What did you square him for?"

"Half-a-couter."

"You appear to be making the shiners spin, Master D'Ossay; that swell at the West End must have bled pretty handsome. Tell us all about it. What did he stand?"

"Well, I won't try and gammon you. He stood fifty."

"What, on the mere gab? without your showing him the stiff, and only telling him you knew about it? Fifty quid! that's a cow that'll give milk for many a long year, Master D'Ossay, if only properly handled. Come, hand us over what you promised for putting you on. By George!" he added, as Effingham drew a bundle of notes from his pocket, "how nice and crisp they sound!"

"There's your termer," said Effingham, selecting a note from the roll and handing it to his friend; "I'm always as good as my word. That squares us up so far."

"No fakement about it, is there?" said Mr. Griffiths, first holding the note up to the light, then spreading it flat on the table, and going carefully over it back and front.

"I've been dropped in the hole too often by flimsies not to be precious careful about 'em. No. Matthew Marshall—all them coily things in the water-mark and that; all right. I think you ought to make it a little more; I do, indeed."

"Make it a little more! I like that. Why, what the devil could you have done without me? It's true you first heard of the coppered stiff from Tony; but you didn't trouble a bit about it. Who set all the boys to hunt up this cove? who found him at last? and who walked in as bold as brass this morning, and checked him out of fifty quid without a stitch of evidence? Why, you daredn't have gone to his crib, to start with; and if you had, he'd never have seen you; the flunkey would have kicked you out for an area-sneak or a gonoph. Why, even I had some bother to get in; so what would have become of you?"

Mr. Effingham was only a little man, but he swelled so with self-importance as, in the eyes of his companion, to look very big indeed. He bounced and swaggered and spoke so loud as quite to quell the unfortunate Griffiths, who began, with due submission, to apologize for his own shortcomings and deprecate his friend's wrath.

"Well, I know all that fast enough, and I only just hinted; but you're down upon a cove so. However, it's a fine thing for us both, ain't it? He'll be as good as a bank to us for years to come, will this swell."

"I'm not so sure of that," said Mr. Effingham thoughtfully.

"How do you mean, not so sure of that?" asked Griffiths.

"Well, you see, he's a long way off being a fool; he's not half so soft as Tony led us to believe. He downed on me once or twice as quick as lightning; and I think it was only my way of putting it, and his being taken sudden on the hop, that made him shell out."

"You think that after he's thought the matter over he'll fancy he's been a flat?"

"Well, not exactly that. You see the higher a fellow climbs the worse it is when he falls. This Mitford wouldn't have cared a cuss for this thing in the old days; he'd have stood the racket of it easy. But it's different now; he's a big swell; its 'Sir Charles' and 'my Lady,' pony-phe-aton and 'orses and grooms, nice wife, and all that. He'd come an awful smasher if anything was to trip him up just now, and he knows it. That's our hold upon him."

"And that's what will make it easy for us to squeeze him."

"No, not entirely. That very fear of being blown upon, of having to bolt or stand a trial—my eye! how blue he turned when I mentioned Norfolk Island to him!—that very fear will make him most anxious to get rid of every chance of coming to grief, to prevent any one being able to lay hold of him."

"There's only one way for him to do that, and that's to burn the bill."

"Yes; but he must get it first, and that's what he'll want, you may take your oath. The next time I go to him, it'll be, 'Where is it? let me see it! name your outside price, and let me have it!' That's what he'll say."

"Likely enough; and what'll you say then?"

"Cussed if I know!" said Mr. Effingham ruefully. "If I say I haven't got it, he'll stop the supplies until I bring it; if I say I can't get it, not another mag from him."

"You must fall back on the bounce, like you did to-day, and tell him you know of there bein' such a thing, and that you won't keep your mouth shut unless you're paid for it."

"Oh, you're a leery cove, Griffiths, you are!" said Mr. Effingham with great disgust. "You never heard of attemptin' to extort money, did you? You don't think he'd ring the bell and send for a bobby, do you?"

"No, I don't. He wouldn't have the pluck."

"Oh, but I do though; and as you see it's me that the bobby would lay hold of, I'm rather pertickler about it. Besides, it's not such a pleasant thing finding yourself at Bow Street; for even if one could square this Mitford and get him not to prosecute, there'd be heaps of bobbies there to prove previous convictions. Clark of the G's getting up: 'Known as D'Ossay Butler, your worship. I had him for passing base coin in '43;' and all that kind of game. No, no, Griffiths! bounce won't do, my boy; won't do a bit."

"What will do, then? what shall we try? Shall we shy up the sponge and think ourselves lucky to have got this fifty, and never try him any more? That seems hard lines with such a chance."

"It would be; and we won't do it. No; there's only one thing to be done—we must go the whole hog; we must have the bill."

"Ah! and we must have lamb and green peas in Febooary; and a patent shofle cab to ride in, so as not to tire ourselves; and pockets full of 'alf-bulls to toss with! We *must*; but you see we 'aven't, D'Ossay, my boy! And as for getting' that bill, we're done at the very first step: we don't know who's got it."

"You fool! if we did know who'd got it we'd have it, fast enough. There ain't many of 'em that could keep it away from me!"

"You are a plucked 'un!" said Griffiths, regarding him with admiration; "I can't help sayin' so, though you do lose your temper and call your friends ugly names. No; I don't think there is many as could keep you off it if you knew where it was. But how we're ever to find that I can't tell."

"Let's go over the business all again," said Effingham. "It was Tony that always had a fancy for that bit of stiff. He stuck to it when it wasn't worth more than the stamp and the paper it was wrote on; but he always thought something would come of this Mitford, and then it would be a first-class screw to put on him, and make him do as Tony liked. But you see he died before anything turned up; and though he told you about the stiff, he didn't say where it was."

"He wouldn't. I asked him scores of times; but he always said 'Time enough for that,' he says, or 'That'll keep;' he says. He was a mistrustful cove was Tony,—always suspecting people."

"Ah, he'd seen a good deal of the world, Griffiths. What an infernal nuisance I hadn't got back from Yankeeland before he popped off! I'd have had it out of him. Who took his traps after his death?"

"Well, old Lyons had 'em, I think. There wasn't much; two or three boxes and a little dressin'-case,—for Tony, though not such a swell as you, D'Ossay, was always natty and spruce,—and a walkin'-stick or two. Old Lyons had lent Tony money, and stood in with him generally; and after he stepped it, old Lyons cleared off the things."

"Do you know where to find old Lyons?"

"Reethur! Why?"

"We'll go there next week when I come back to town. You may take your oath he's got the bill; and if he's heard nothing about Mitford's fortune, we may get it for next to nothing."

CHAPTER X.

SOUVENT FEMME VARIE.

No; Laurence Alsager was certainly not best pleased at all he heard about Mrs. Hammond. Mrs. Hammond, a pretty little woman, coming to call upon you—great Heaven! Is that the way that that oaf Mitford talked of her who two years ago was Laura Molyneux, the mere mention of whose name caused Alsager to thrill to his finger-tips; and whose low *trainante* voice, long steady passionate glances, and rippling shoulders could have led him to destruction? Drove her chestnuts well, eh? Yes, by Jove! there were few women could touch her either in riding or driving, and— Laurence laughed grimly to himself as he strode along. What was it Dollamore had said about Mitford's readiness to go to the bad, to shake a loose leg, to enjoy those advantages of health, wealth, and position which had before been denied to him? Why, here was the very woman to ensnare him, to act as his evil genius, the very counter-charm of Lady Mitford's quietude and girlish grace; a woman of the world, bright, sharp, active, and alert; with plenty of *savoir faire*, an enormous talent for flirtation, and not the smallest scrap of heart to throw into the balance against any of her whims. No, by George, not a scrap. Laurence bethought him of a certain December morning in Kensington Gardens, and the whole scene rose vividly before him. The trees all stripped and bare, and stridently clanging in the bitter wind; the thick dun clouds hanging over the horizon; the greatcoated park-keeper stamping vigorously over the gravel, and banging himself with his arms with vague notions of generating calorie; and he himself pacing up and down by Laura Molyneux's side. The arguments he had used, the very phrases which he had employed to induce her to reconsider the determination then announced to him, were ringing in his ears. He recollected how he had humbled himself, how he had implored her to reconsider her decision, how even he had begged for time, and how he had been met with one stern pitiless refusal; and how he had gone away to weep bitter tears of mortified pride, and rejected love, and savage disappointment; and how she had stepped into the neat little brougham waiting for her at the gate, and been whirled off to accept the hand and heart of Mr. Percy Hammond, a retired civil-servant from India, a widower with one daughter, who had shaken the pagoda-tree to some purpose and returned to England with a colossal fortune.

That was the then finale of the intimacy between Laura Molyneux and Laurence Alsager. In the course of the next week he started on his tour; in the course of the next month St. George's, Hanover Square, was the scene of her marriage,—a bishop welding the chains. And now two years had elapsed, and he was back in London, pretty much the same as if he had never left it; and she was asking whether he had returned, and he had begun to feel a great interest in Lady Mitford; and Sir Charles Mitford evidently thought Mrs. Hammond a most delightful person, and every thing was *à tort et à travers*, as it has been, is, and always shall be, in the great world of London.

Nil admirari is the motto on which your precocious youth piques himself; but which is adopted in all due seriousness and sobriety by the calm student of life. Who wonders at anything?—at the peevishness of your wife; at the ingratitude of the child for whom you have pinched and slaved; at the treachery of the one familiar friend; at the enormous legacy left you by the uncle whose last words to you were that you were a jackanapes, and, so far as he was concerned, should be a beggar? The man of the world is surprised at nothing; he is not *l'homme blasé* of the caricaturist; he is not an atom astonished at finding nothing in anything; on the contrary, he finds plenty of novelty in every variety of life; but nothing which may happen to him excites the smallest wonderment on his part. So that when Colonel Alsager walked into the Guards club to dinner, and received from the hall-porter a small note with an address in a handwriting perfectly familiar to him, he was not in the least surprised.

But he looked at the note, and twisted it between his fingers, and even put it into his waistcoat pocket, as he walked up to the table whereon stood the framed menu, and left it there while he walked round and spoke to two or three men who were already at dinner; and it was not until he was comfortably seated at his little table, and had eaten a few mouthfuls of soup, that he took it from his pocket, leisurely opened it, and bringing the candle within range, began to read it. Even then he paused for a moment, recollecting with what heart-throbs of anxiety and sensations of acute delight he used to read the previous epistles from the same source; then, as with an effort, he set himself to its perusal.

It was very short.

"I shall be at home to-morrow at three, and hope to see you. I hear all sorts of rumours, which you alone can solve. *Chi non sa niente non dubita di niente!* It will be for you to read the riddle. L."

He smiled outright as, after reading it and restoring it to his pocket, he said to himself, "The old story; she always made a mystery when there was no other excitement; but I'll go, for all that."

During his wildest times, Laurence had always been a punctual man; and even the irregular manner of his life during the two last years had not altered him in this respect. On the next afternoon, as the clock was striking three, he presented himself at Mrs. Hammond's door, and was immediately admitted and shown into her presence.

He was apparently a little too punctual; for a tall young woman, looking half lady, half nursery-governess, was standing by her and listening respectfully. Mrs. Hammond rose at the announcement of the Colonel's name, and coming forward, pressed his cold motionless hand with a tight grasp.

"Pray excuse me for one instant, Colonel Alsager," said she; "the doctors have said that we were all wrong in leaving Florence; that it's impossible Mr. Hammond can remain in London during this awful weather, and that he must go at once to Torquay. So I'm sending Miss Gillespie down there to get a house for us, and arrange matters before we go down.—Now, Ruth," turning to her, "I don't think there's any more to say. Not facing the sea, recollect, and a six-stall stable and double coach-house. You know all about the rest,—bed-rooms, and those sort of things,—and so goodbye."

Miss Gillespie touched lightly the outstretched tips of Mrs. Hammond's fingers, bowed gracefully to Laurence, and departed.

Mrs. Hammond watched the door close again, and obviously ill at ease, turned to Laurence, and said: "Miss Gillespie is the most invaluable person. She came at first as governess to Miss Hammond; but she has really made herself so useful to me, that I don't know what I should do without her. Housekeepers and all regular servants are so stupid; and I hate trouble so."

She stopped, and there was a dead silence. Mrs. Hammond coloured, and said: "Have you nothing to say, Colonel Alsager?"

"On the subject of Miss Gillespie, nothing. If you sent for me to expatiate to me on Miss Gillespie's virtues, I am sorry; for my time could have been better employed."

"Than in coming to see me? You did not think so once."

"Then we didn't talk about Miss Gillespie. Your note said that you had heard rumours, or riddles, which you wanted me to explain. What have you heard?"

"In a word, nothing. I wrote the first thing that came into my mind because I wanted to see you, Laurence Alsager. Because I have hungered to see you for two years; to hear your voice, to—You were at Vienna? at Ischl? and at Trieste?"

"I was at all three—some little time at each."

"You saw the *Times* occasionally on your travels?"

"While I remained in Europe, frequently. O yes, Laura, I received all your letters at the places you mention; and I saw the advertisement in the *Times*, under the signature and with the ciphers by which we used to correspond in the old days."

"And why did you take no notice?"

"Because my love for you was gone and dead; because I was tired of being dragged about and shown-off, and made to display the abject state of docility to which you had reduced me. I told you all this that January morning in Kensington Gardens; I said to you, 'Let us finish this scheming and hiding; let our engagement be announced, and let us be married in the spring.' And you apparently assented; and went home and wrote me that letter which I have now, and shall keep to my dying day, declaring that you had been compelled to accept an offer from Mr. Hammond."

"You knew, Laurence, that my mother insisted on it."

"I knew you said so, Mrs. Hammond.—When I was acquainted with Mrs. Molyneux she was not much accustomed to having any influence with her daughter. Then I went away; but at first not out of the reach of that London jargon which permeates wherever Englishmen congregate. I heard of your marriage, of your first season, of the Richmond *fête* given for you by the Russian Prince, Tchernigow. I heard of you that autumn as being the reigning belle of Baden, where Tchernigow must have been at the same time, as I recollect reading in *Galignani* of his breaking the bank.

Before I went to the East I heard of you in a score of other places; your name always connected with somebody else's name—always '*la belle Hammond, et puis*—' I never choose to be one in a regiment; besides—"

"Besides what?"

"Well, my time for that sort of thing was past and gone; I was too old for it; I had gone through the phase of existence which Tchernigow and the others were then enjoying. I had offered you a steadfast honest love, and you had rejected it. When I heard of the Tchernigow alliance, and the various other *passe-temps*, I must say I felt enormously grateful for the unpleasantness you had spared me."

"I cannot say your tour has improved you, Colonel Alsager," said Mrs. Hammond calmly, though with a red spot burning on either cheek. "In the old days you were considered the pink of chivalry, and would have had your tongue cut out before you would have hinted a sneer at a woman. You refuse to believe my story of compulsion in my marriage; but it is true—as true as is the fact that I rebelled then and there, and, having sold myself, determined to have as much enjoyment of life as was compatible with the sale."

"I never denied it, Mrs. Hammond; I simply told you what I had heard."

"Then tell me something more, Laurence Alsager," said Mrs. Hammond, flushing brilliantly, and looking him, for the first time during their interview, straight in the face; "is it to be war between us two, or what?"

She looked splendidly beautiful just at that moment. She was a bright-looking little woman, with deep-gray eyes and long dark lashes, shining chestnut hair, a *retroussé* nose, a wanton mouth, and a perfect, trim, tight, rounded small figure. As she threw out this verbal challenge, her eyes flashed, she sat erect, and every fibre within her seemed quivering with emotion.

Laurence marked her expression, and for an instant softened, as the recollection of the old days, when he had seen her thus wilfully petulant only to make more marked the subsidence into placidity and devotion, rose before him; but it faded rapidly away, had utterly vanished before, no less in reply to her peering gaze than to her words, he said, "No, not war; neighbours who have been so nearly allied should never quarrel. Let us take another strategic phrase, and say that we will preserve an armed neutrality."

"And that means—?"

"Well, in our case that means that neither shall interfere with the other's plans, of whatever kind, without due warning. That once given and disregarded, there will be war to the knife; for I think under present circumstances neither will be inclined to spare the other."

"Your anticipations are of a singularly sombre character, Colonel Alsager. I think that—ah!" she exclaimed, suddenly clapping her hands, "I see it all! my eyes are opened, and the whole map lies patent before me."

"What has caused this happy restoration of sight?"

"Remembering a story which was told me a day or two ago by a little bird. The story of a *preux chevalier* and a lady in distress; of a romantic adventure and a terrific leap; of plunging hoofs and fainting-fits, and all the necessary ingredients of such a scene. *Je vous en félicité, Monsieur le Colonel.*"

Laurence's brow grew very dark as he said, "You are too clever a woman to give a leg-up to a manifestly limping story, however much it might temporarily serve your purpose. Of that story as it stands, turned, twisted, perverted as it may be, nothing can be made. The scandal-mongers don't know what they have taken in hand. They might as well try to shake the Rock of Gibraltar as that lady's good name."

Mrs. Hammond laughed a short bitter laugh and said, "You have even lost that grand virtue which you possessed—the power of concealing your emotions. With the gravity, you have attained the simplicity of the Oriental; and you now—"

She was interrupted by the servant's throwing open the door and announcing, "Sir Charles Mitford."

That gentleman entered immediately on the announcement of his name, with a certain air of *empressement* which vanished so soon as he saw Colonel Alsager's broad back. Laura Hammond prided herself on never having been taken unawares. When speaking to Alsager her face had been curling with sneers, her voice harsh and strident; but before Sir Charles Mitford had crossed the threshold, she had wreathed her mouth in smiles, and as she shook hands with him, though aloud she only uttered the ordinary commonplaces, in a lower tone she said, "I thought you would come to-day."

Alsager heard her say it. That was a singular property of his—that gift of hearing anything that might be said, no matter in how large a party, or how earnestly he might be supposed to be talking. It had saved his life once; and he had assiduously cultivated it ever since. Mitford heard it too, but thickly. He had not had as much experience in the cadences of the *demi-voix* as Laurence.

"How are you, Alsager? We seem to be always tumbling over each other now, don't we? and the oftener the better, I say.—How d'ye do, Mrs. Hammond? I say, what's all this that you've been saying to my wife?"

Laurence started, and then reverted to the album which lay on his knees. Mrs. Hammond saw the start, and the means adopted for hiding it, and smiled quietly.

"I don't know what I said in particular to Lady Mitford; nothing to frighten her, I hope," said Mrs. Hammond; "I was congratulating myself that she and I had got on so very well together."

"O yes, so you did, of course," said Sir Charles,—"sisters, and all that kind of thing. But I mean what you said to her about leaving town."

"Oh, that's perfectly correct. Mr. Hammond has seen Sir Charles Dumfunk and Dr. Wadd, and they both concur in saying that he ought not to have left Florence until the spring; and that he must leave London forthwith."

"And they have recommended Torquay as the best place for him; at least so my wife tells me."

"Quite right; and in obedience to their commands I have sent Miss Gillespie off this very day to take a house, and make all necessary arrangements."

"Who's Miss Gillespie?"

"My-well, I don't know what. I believe *factotum* is the Latin word for it. She's Miss Hammond's governess (my stepdaughter, you know), and my general adviser and manager. I don't know what I should do without her, as I told Colonel Alsager, who, by the way, did not pay much attention."

Laurence grinned a polite grin, but said never a word.

"She was with me in the pony-carriage the first day Mr. Bertram introduced you to me, Sir Charles. Ah, but she had her veil down, I recollect; and she asked all about you afterwards."

"Very civil of her to take any interest in me," said Sir Charles. "I recollect a veiled person in the pony-carriage; but not a bit of interest did I take in her. All that concentrated elsewhere, and that sort of thing;" and he smiled at Mrs. Hammond in a manner that made Laurence's stern face grow sterner than ever.

"Well, but about Torquay," continued Sir Charles. "I thought at first it was a tremendous nuisance your having to go out of town; but now I've got an idea which does not seem so bad. Town's horribly slow, you know, utterly empty; one does not know what to do with oneself; and so I've been suggesting to Georgie why not go down to Redmoor—our country place in Devon, you know—close to Torquay,—and one could fill the house with pleasant people, and you could come over from Torquay, and it would be very jolly indeed."

He said it in an off-hand manner, but he nevertheless looked earnestly up into Mrs. Hammond's face, and Laurence Alsager's expression grew sterner than ever.

Mrs. Hammond returned Sir Charles's glance, and said, "That would be thoroughly delightful! I was looking forward with horror, I confess, to a sojourn at Torquay. Those dreadful people in respirators always creeping about, and the stupid dinner-parties, where the talk is always about the doctor, and the quarter in which the wind is. But with you and Lady Mitford in the neighbourhood it would be quite another thing."

"O yes, and we'd get some jolly people down there.—Alsager, you'd come?"

"I don't think I'd come, and I'm anything but a jolly person. I must go to my father's at once."

"Gad, Alsager, you seem to keep your father always ready to bring forward whenever you want to be misanthropical. You were to have gone to him a week ago."

"Circumstances alter cases," said Mrs. Hammond with a short laugh; "and Colonel Alsager finds London more tolerable than he expected. Is it not so, Colonel?"

"'Very tolerable, and not to be endured,' as Dogberry says, since I am about to leave it," said Laurence. ("She would like to draw me into a semi-confidence on that subject; but she sha'n't," thought he.)

"No; but really, Alsager, do try and come, there's a good fellow; you can hold over your father until you want an excuse for not going to some place where you'll be bored. Now we won't bore you; we'll take down a rattling good team Tom Charteris and his wife—she plays and sings, and all that kind of thing, capitally; and Mrs. Masters, who's quiet to ride or drive—I don't mean that exactly, but she's available in two ways,—as a widow she can chaperon, and she's quite young and pretty enough to flirt on her own hook; and the Tyrrells—nice girls those; and Bligh and Winton,— Oh, and Dollamore! I'll ask Dollamore; he'd be just the man for such a party."

"O yes, you must have Lord Dollamore," said Mrs. Hammond; "he has such a delightfully dry way of saying unpleasant things about everybody; and as he never shoots or hunts, he is a perfect treasure in a country house, and devotes himself to the ladies." She shot one hasty glance at Laurence as she said this, which he duly perceived.

"O yes," said Sir Charles, "Dollamore's sure to come. And you, Alsager,—come, you've changed your mind?"

"Upon my word, the temptation you offer me is so great, that I'm unable to resist it. Yes, I'll come."

"I thought you would," said Sir Charles carelessly.

"I knew you would," said Mrs. Hammond in an undertone; then aloud, "What, going, Colonel Alsager? Goodbye; I'm so pleased to have seen you; and looking so well too, after the climate, and all the things you've gone through."

Laurence shook hands with Mitford and departed.

Yes, there was not much doubt about it: Sir Charles was tolerably well "on" in that quarter. An old poacher makes the best gamekeeper, because he knows the tricks and dodges of his old profession; and there was not one single move of Sir Charles Mitford's during the entire conversation which Laurence Alsager did not recognize as having been used by himself in bygone days. He knew the value of every look, knew the meaning of each inflexion of the voice; and appreciated to its full the motive-power which had induced the baronet suddenly to long for the country house at Redmoor, and to become disgusted with the dreariness of London. Determined to sit him out too, wasn't he? Lord! how often he, Laurence, had determinedly sat out bores for the sake of getting ten words, one hand-clasp, from Laura after they were gone! Yes, Mitford was getting on, certainly; making the running more quickly even than Dollamore had prophesied. Dollamore! ah, that reminded him: Dollamore was to be asked down to Redmoor. That, and the manner in which Mrs. Hammond had spoken of him and his visit, had decided Laurence in accepting Mitford's invitation. There could not be anything between them which—no; Dollamore could never have made a confidante of Laura and imparted to her—O no! Laura had not too much conscience in any case where her own passion or even her own whim was concerned; but she would shrink from meddling in an affair of that kind. And as for Lord Dollamore, he was essentially a man of *petits soins*, the exercise of which always laid those who practised them open to misunderstanding. He had a habit of hinting and insinuating also, which was unpleasant, but not very noxious. As people said, his bark was probably worse than his bite, and—

And at all events Laurence was very glad that he had accepted the invitation, and that he would be there to watch in person over anything that might happen.

CHAPTER XI.

DOWN AT REDMOOR.

Just on the highest ridge of the great waste of Redmoor, which is interspersed with dangerous peat-bogs and morasses, and extends about ten miles every way, with scarcely a fence or a tree, stands Redmoor House, from time immemorial—which means from the reign of Edward III.—the home of the Mitford family. Stands high and dry, and looking warm and snug and comfortable, with its red-brick face and its quaint gables and queer little mullioned windows. It is a house the sight of which would put spirit into a man chilled and numbed with looking over the great morass, and would give some vestige of credibility to the fact, that the sluggiest little stream born in the middle of the moor, and winding round through the gardens of the house, from its desolate birthplace flows down—as can be traced from the windows—through a land of plenty, of park and meadow, of orchard and cornfield, by the old cathedral-city, to the southern shore.

A grand old house, with a big dining-hall like St. George's Chapel at Windsor on a small scale, without the stalls, but with the knightly banners, and the old oak, and the stained glass, and the solemn air of antiquity; with a picture-gallery full of ancestors, beginning with Sir Gerard, temp. Henry VIII., painted by Holbein, a jolly red-bearded swashbuckler, not unlike *his* royal master, and ending with the late lamented Sir Percy, painted by Lawrence, with a curly head of hair, a fur collar to his coat, a smile of surprising sweetness, and altogether not unlike his royal master. There were drawing-rooms in blue and amber; a charming bow-windowed room hung with tapestry, and commanding a splendid view over the cultivated landscape, which, in the housekeeper's tradition, had been a boudoir for Sir Percy's lady, who died within three years of her marriage; a grand old library, the bookcases in black oak, and nearly all the books in Russia leather, save those bought under the auspices of the late baronet,—Hansard's Debates, and a legal and magisterial set of volumes all bound in calf and red-lettered at the back. There is a grand terrace in front of the house, and all kinds of gardens stretch round it: Dutch gardens, formal, quaint, and solemn, with a touch of old-world stiffness like the Mynheers; Italian gardens, bright and sunny and gaudy, very glittering and effective, but not very satisfactory after all, like the Signori; English gardens, with ample space of glorious close-shaved lawn, and such wealth of roses as to keep the whole air heavy with their fragrance. Great prolific kitchen-gardens at the back, and stables and coach-houses which might be better; but the late baronet cared for nothing but his quarter-sessions and his yacht; and so long as he had a pair of horses to jolt with him to join the judge's procession at assize-times, troubled himself not one jot how the internal economy of the stables was ordered.

This is all to be altered now. It was not very bright in Sir Percy's time, and it has been deadly-lively indeed since his death; but the Sleeping Beauty herself was never more astonished by the arrival of the prince than was Mrs. Austin, the old housekeeper at Redmoor, by the advent of a tall hook-nosed gentleman, who announced himself as Captain Bligh, and who brought a letter from Sir Charles Mitford, duly signed and sealed with the family arms, which Mrs. Austin knew so well, ordering implicit obedience to whatever orders the bearer might choose to give. With him came a sleek-looking man with close-cut hair and a white cravat, whom Mrs. Austin at first took for a clergyman, until she discovered, he was the stud-groom. This person inspected the stables, and the remnant of the late Sir Percy's stud, and reported to Captain Bligh that the stables was pigsties, and as for the hanimals, he should think they must be the 'osses as Noah put into the hark.

A fresh *régime* and fresh work to be done by everybody under it. No more chance for Tummus coachman and Willum helper to just ride harses to ex'cise and dryaive 'em out in trap whenever wanted to go crass to races or market, or give missus and young 'uns a little change. No more chance for Dawniel Todd the Scotch gardener to make his market of all the fruits, flowers, and vegetables, selling them to Mrs. Dean or Miss Archdeacon, or to the officers up in barracks. Not much chance for the head-keeper and his two under-trappers, who really had all their work to do to keep the game down after Sir Percy's death, so strictly had that terror of poachers preserved; though they thought they saw their way to balancing any loss which they might sustain from being unable any longer to supply the poulterers of the county town, in a house full of ardent sportsmen, with innumerable heavy tips after battue-days, and an occasional dog to break or to sell. The old lodge-gates had begun to grow rusty from disuse; but they are constantly on the stretch now, for carts with ladders and scaffolding-poles, and men in light linen blouses daubed with paint, were streaming in and out from morning till night. There is a new roof being put on the stables, and the outhouses are being painted and whitewashed throughout; and the mastiff, who has been bred on the true English principle of "keeping himself to himself," has been driven quite mad at the influx of new faces, and has shown such a convincing set of teeth to the painter's men, that they have declined proceeding with their work until he has been removed. So Tummus coachman and Willum helper have removed his big kennel to the back of the stables; and here Turk lies, with nothing but his black nose visible in the clean straw, until he catches sight of a painter or a tiler pursuing his occupation high up in mid-air, and then with one baleful spring Turk bounds out of his kennel, and unmistakably expresses his fervent wish to have that skilled labourer's life's-blood.

Captain Bligh too sits heavy on the lodge-keeper's soul. For the captain, after a cursory inspection of the vehicles at Redmoor louse, has sent down to Exeter for a dog-cart, and has duly received thence the nearest approach which the Exeterian coachbuilder had on hand. It is not a bad tax-cart, of the kind known as "Whitechapel," has a very big pair of wheels, and behind a long chestnut mare—which the captain found in a loose box in the corner of the yard, and which it seemed Tummus the coachman used to reserve for his special driving-runs remarkably well and light. In this tax-cart Captain Bligh drives to and from the station, where he is occupied watching the disembarkation of furniture coming direct from Gillow's—ottomans for the smoking-rooms, and looking-glasses for my lady's boudoir; to and from the market-town, where the painters and other workpeople are to be hunted up; to and from the barracks, where he has found that hospitality and good-fellowship which are invariable characteristics of the service. From the barracks the Captain is not unfrequently very late in returning, yelling out, "Ga-a-ate!" in the early hours of the morning, and frightening the lodge-keeper from peaceful dreams; and as the painter's men arrive at six, and the railway-van did not leave till eleven, the lodge-keeper begins to feel, on the whole, that life is not all beer and skittles, and rather wishes that the late baronet had never been drownded.

Now things begin to look a little straighter, and rumours are rife that it won't be long before the new baronet brings his wife down, and, regularly takes possession. The old stables have been re-tiled and touched up, four new loose boxes, "wi' sla-ate mangers and brass foxes' heads a-holdin' the pillar-reins," have been erected, the coach-houses have been cleaned and enlarged. The stud-groom, under whose directions all these alterations have been made, has watched their completion, and has then started for London, returning with a whole string of splendid creatures, all in the most perfect-fitting hoods and cloths embroidered with Sir C. M.'s initials and bloody hand, railed down to the nearest station, and brought over thence in charge of three underlings, also sleek-headed, tight-trousered, and white-cravated. Not in income, but in status do Tummus coachman and Willum helper feel the change. They are to be retained on the establishment at the same rate of wages; but they are simply to make themselves generally useful in the stables, and to have no particular duties whatsoever.

Very busy indeed has been Captain Bligh; but his labours are drawing to an end now, and he begins to think that he has been very successful He has been good in generalization, he thinks; there's nothing that any one could find particular fault with, looking at the materials he had to work upon, and the time he had to do it in. But there are two things about which he knows in managing for other people you should be particular. Take care that both the men and the women have a stunning good room of their own. You know the library is generally considered the men's room; but Charley ain't much of a bookworm; the *Times* of a day, and *Bell* of a Sunday, and that kind of thing; and the library's an infernal big room, with all sorts of plaster-casts of philosophic classic parties grinning at you off the tops of the shelves. Charley won't like that; so Bligh has fitted him up this little crib, next to his dressing-room, cosey and comfortable, good-drawing stove, little let-down flap for his grog, whip-rack, pipe-rack, and all snug—don't you think so? Bollindar and Smyth, of the 26th Cameronians, to whom the question is put, think so—rather! and look all round the room and nod their heads sagaciously, and clap Bligh on the back and tell him what a knowing hand he is, and then go off to try the new billiard-table which Thurston has just sent from London. That Lady Mitford's special room should also be something to be proud of, is also a desideratum with the Captain; but there he mistrusts his own taste. The late Mrs. Bligh had been a barrack-master's daughter, and having lived in barracks both before and after her marriage, had been accustomed, as her husband recollected, to think highly of any place where the doors would shut and the windows would not rattle. But the old campaigner recollected that Mrs. Barrington the widow, daughter of the Dean and Deaness, and then living at home with her parents in the Close, had, during the two happy years of her marriage to George Barrington, private secretary to Lord Muffington when keeper of the Gold Fish to her Majesty, lived in very decent society in London; and it was after Mrs. Barrington's idea that the bow-windowed boudoir had its bow-window filled with plate-glass, and a light chintz paper and maple furniture. Sipping a glass of '20 port with her lunch-biscuit (the cellars at Redmoor were splendidly stocked, and wanted no renovation), Mrs. Dean declared that the room was perfect; and poor pale peaky little Mrs. Barrington, looking round at the elegance and comfort, was reminded of the days when she was something more than a dependent on her parents' bounty, and when she had a husband whose chiefest delight was the fulfilment of her every wish.

So the Captain wrote up to his principal, and reported all in readiness; and the day for Sir Charles and Lady Mitford to come down was agreed upon. There was some talk of having a public reception; but the Captain did not think Sir Charles would care particularly about that, and so the scheme was given up. However, when the carriage which fetched them from the station dashed through the lodge-gates, the tenantry, some mounted on their rough little Redmoor ponies, some on foot, but all in their best clothes, were drawn up on either side of the avenue, and greeted their new landlord with reiterated cheers. They are an impressible people, these Devonians; and they were much gratified by the frank, hearty, sporting appearance of Sir Charles, "so different from Sir Percy, as were all dried-up like;" they liked the jolly way in which he stood up and waved his hat to them; while as for Lady Mitford, the impression she created was something extraordinary. The men raved about her, and the women seemed to feel the greatest gratification in repeating that she was "a pure Devon lass, as any one could tell by her skin."

Sir Charles had wished to bring all their friends down to Redmoor at the same time as they themselves came; but Georgie, who, ever since the visit to the ancestral home had been determined upon, had found her mistress-of-the-house position weighing on her mind, begged that they might be there for at least a day or two by themselves, that she might settle with Mrs. Austin the disposal of the various rooms, and the general arrangement of the household. To this Sir Charles agreed, and they came alone.

The "day or two" spent by themselves were very happily passed by Georgie. The whole of the first day was consumed in going from room to room with Mrs. Austin, listening to the family history, and thoroughly examining all the pictures, tapestry, and curios. The old lady was enchanted with her new mistress, who took so much interest in everything, and who, above all, was such an excellent listener. Then Georgie, whose housekeeping tastes had not had much opportunity for display in the parsonage at Fishbourne, under Mrs. Austin's guidance went "through the things," absolutely revelling in snowy linen and spotless damask, in glorious old china and quaint antique glass, in great stores of jams and preserves, and all Mrs. Austin's household treasures.

She did not take so much interest in the display of plate, though it was really very handsome and very valuable; not the least effective among the trophies being several splendid regatta-prizes won by the late baronet's celebrated yacht. With the boudoir Georgie was delighted; and when she heard from Captain Bligh that, feeling his utter ignorance in the matter, he had consulted Mrs. Barrington, after whose taste the room had been prepared, Georgie declared that Mrs. Barrington must be a very nice woman to have such excellent taste, would probably prove a delightful neighbour, and certainly should be called upon as soon as possible.

You see, if Georgie "gushed" a little at this period of her life, it was not unnatural, and was certainly excusable. She had been brought up very quietly, and had had, as we have seen, her little trouble and had, borne it with great pluck and determination; and now, as she imagined, she was thoroughly happy. Husband's love, kind, friends, wealth and position, were all hers; and as she was young and impulsive, and thoroughly appreciative of all these blessings, she could not help showing her appreciation. In those days, even more than in the present, it was considered in the worst taste to be in the smallest degree natural; a dull uncaring acceptance of events as they occurred, without betraying the least astonishment or concern, was considered the acme of good breeding; so that unless Georgie altered a great deal before the London season, she would be voted very bad *ton* by Lady Clanronald and the Marchioness of Tappington, those sovereigns of society. But there is some little time yet before the commencement of the season, and Georgie may then have become as unappreciative and as undemonstrative as the other women in her position. Just now she is thoroughly happy with Mrs. Austin and the contents of the linen and china-rooms.

Whether, as the woman is the lesser man, the feminine mind is much more easily amused than the masculine, or whether there was much more absolute novelty to Lady Mitford in her position than to Sir Charles in his (he had seen something of the external life of fashionable people, and, like most military men, had acquired a veneer of swelldom while in the army), it is difficult to determine; but it is certain that the "day or two" to be spent before the arrival of their friends seemed like a day or twenty-two to Sir Charles Mitford. He had gone over every room of the house, thoroughly examined the new stables and loose boxes, had out all the horses and critically examined them, had tried two new pairs and spent an hour or two in breaking them, had pulled the old mastiff's ears until the dog growled, had then kicked him for growling, had put all his whips and all his pipes into their respective racks, had smoked more than was good for him, had whistled every tune he could remember, and was utterly and horribly bored.

He was like the little boy in the child's story-book: he wanted somebody to come and play with him. Captain Bligh had been obliged to leave for London directly his friends arrived, and was coming down again with the first batch of visitors. And Sir Charles hated being alone; he wanted somebody to smoke with him, and to play billiards with him. He used to put a cigar in his mouth and go and knock the balls about, trying various new hazards; but it did not amuse him. He could not ask the officers of the neighbouring garrison to come over, as his plea to his friends had been the necessity for preparation in the house. He grew very cross towards the close of the second day; and after dinner, as he was going to smoke a sulky pipe in his own room, Georgie came up to him, and put her arm through his, and looked at and spoke to him so affectionately, that his conscience gave him a little twinge as he thought how lately he had let his fancy run on eyes and hair of a different colour from his wife's.

"What is it, Charley? You're all wrong, I see; not ill, are you, darling?"

"No, Georgie, not ill; only confoundedly bored."

"Bored?"

"Yes, bored! Oh, I know it's all very well for you, who have your house to look after and Mrs. Austin to attend to, and all that kind of thing—that passes the time. But I've had nothing to do, and nobody to speak to, and I'm regularly sick of it. If this is the kind of thing one's to expect in country life, I shall go back to town to-morrow."

"Oh, you won't feel it when your friends come down, Charley; they'll be here the day after to-morrow. It's only because you're alone with me—and I'm not much of a companion for you, I know—that you're moped. Now let us see, what can you do to-morrow? Oh, I have it,—why not drive over and see your friends the Hammonds at Torquay?"

He had thought of that several times, but had not mentioned it because—well, he did not know why. But now his wife had started the subject; so of course it was all right. Still he hesitated.

"Well, I don't know—"

"Now I think it a capital idea. You can drive over there, and they'll most probably ask you to stop to dinner, and you'll have a fine moonlight drive back. And then the next day all the rest of the people will come down."

After this Sir Charles did not attempt, however faintly, to interpose an objection, and was in a very good temper for the remainder of the evening.

CHAPTER XII.

DRAWING COVER.

It was part of the crafty policy of the tall-hatted Mr. Griffiths to keep his employer Mr. Effingham in good humour, and to show that he was worth seeing occasionally; and it was with this end in view that Mr. Griffiths had spoken so confidently of Mr. Lyons's undoubted knowledge of the whereabouts of the forged bill and of his (Griffiths's) intention of seeking an immediate interview with Lyons. But, in sober truth, Mr. Griffiths merely had a faint notion that Lyons, from his previous connection with Tony Butler and his general acquaintance with the shady transactions of the deceased, might possibly give a guess as to the hands in which the bill then was, while he had not the remotest idea where to find the redoubtable Mr. Lyons himself, with a view to obtain from him the necessary information.

For Mr. Lyons, as is the case with many gentlemen of his persuasion, did not confine his energies to the exercise of one calling, but dabbled in a great many. To some men he was known as a jeweller and diamond-merchant; to others as an importer of French clocks, whistling bullfinches, and German mustard; to some he was known in connection with the discounting of stamped paper; to others as a picture-dealer, a cigar-merchant, a vendor of *objets d'art* of a very peculiar kind. He had no residence—that is to say, he had a great many, but none particularly tangible or satisfactory. He would write to you dating from a number in Clement's Inn; and when you called there, you would find the name of Mr. Glubb over the door, with a painted square of tin by the letter-slit announcing that Mr. Glubb had removed to Great Decorum Street, and that letters for him were to be left with the porter; and lower still you would find a dirty scrap of paper, with "M. Lyons" faintly traced upon it; and on the door being opened, you would find M. Lyons in a room with one chair, one table, a blotting-pad, pen and ink, and a cheque-book. He was in the habit of making appointments at coffee-houses and taverns; and when he sent the clocks or the bullfinches, the cigars or the *objets d'art*, to their purchasers, they arrived at night, being left at the door by mysterious boys, to whom they had been given, with the address and twopence, by a man whom they had never seen before, but who was just round the corner. There was, it was said, one permanent address which Mr. Lyons had kept up for a great number of years; but this was known only to those with whom in their relation with Mr. Lyons a melting-pot was associated, and these were very few in number.

Mr. Griffiths was getting desperate, for the last half-crown out of the ten pounds lay in his pocket, and his principal Mr. Effingham had already spoken to him rather sharply on the matter. He had been to all Mr. Lyons's known haunts; he had spoken to a dozen people who were known to be of his intimates; but he could obtain no tidings of him. Some thought he might be at Amsterdam, where the diamond-sale was going on; others had heard him mention his intention of visiting Frankfort about that period; some laughed, and wondered whether old Malachi had heard of the plate-robbery, "thalvers ath big round ath a cart-veel, and thpoonth, all new, not a bit rubbed!" which had lately taken place. But no one could give any precise information. And time was going on, and Mr. Effingham's patience and Mr. Griffiths's stock of ready-money were rapidly becoming exhausted.

One night, going into "Johnson's" as usual, Mr. Griffiths saw his principal seated at one of the tables, and not caring to confront him just then, was about quietly withdrawing as much of his tall hat as he had already protruded through the swing-door, when he was espied and called to by Mr. Effingham.

"Come in, there; don't think I didn't see you, because I did. What a slimy cove you are, Griffiths!—that's what I complain of; nothing fair and above-board in you."

"Who's to be fair and above-board," growled Mr. Griffiths, "if they're to be everlastingly growled at and badgered? What I come here for is to be quiet and 'ave a little peace, not to be worritted and downed upon. D'rectly I see you sittin' here, I knowed it'd be, 'Well, and wot's up?' and 'Ain't you got no news?' and 'Wot a feller you are, not to 'ave learned somethink!' so, as I didn't seem to care about that, I was goin' away agen."

"Poor feller," said Mr. Effingham with great contempt, "don't like being worried or having to work for your livin', don't you? I wonder you didn't get yourself a government berth, where pokin' the fire and whistlin' tunes is what they do when they're there, which is only the three winter months of the year. So you've brought no news?"

"Not a stiver, not a ha'porth, not a blessed word. There, you may as well take it all at once!" said Griffiths in desperation.

"And you've been everywhere likely?"

"Everywhere,—in every gaff and crib where there was the least chance of hearin' of the old boy; but not a word."

"Now you see what a thing luck is," said Mr. Effingham sententiously; "I believe that old City cove who said he couldn't afford to know an unlucky man was right after all; and I'm not at all sure I'm right, Master Griffiths, in not dropping your acquaintance, for certingly you're an unlucky buffer, if ever there was one."

"Well, p'raps I am, D'Ossay," said Griffiths, who began to see how the land lay; "perhaps I am in some things; but it ain't only luck,—I'm as lucky as most of 'em; but it's the talent as does it—the talent; and there's none of us has got that like you, D'Ossay, my boy."

"Well, luck or talent, or whatever it is," said Effingham, pulling the bell, "it helps me on.—Bring some brandy and hot water here.—I come in here to have a mouthful o' bread and cheese and a glass o' ale about two this afternoon, and Pollock was in here; Jack Pollock they call him,—the fellow that writes the plays, you know."

Mr. Griffiths, over his first gulp of brandy-and-water, nodded his head in acquiescence.

"Things is going on rather bad at the Garden," continued Mr. Effingham; "I don't know whether you've heard. Their pantomime's been a reg'lar failure this year, and Wuff's paper's beginning to fly again. I suppose old Lyons is in that swim, for Pollock says to me, 'Didn't I hear you askin' after Mr. Lyons?' he says. 'I did,' I says. 'I thought so,' he says; 'and I told him so when I saw him just now in Wuff's room at the Garden. And he says, "I've just come back from abroad, and I don't reckleckt Mr. Effingham's name," he says; "but if he's one of the right sort, he'll find me among the lemons on Sunday morning."' So I thanked Pollock, and winked my eye, and nodded my head, and made believe as though I knew all about it; but I don't."

"You don't?"

"Not a bit of it; I'm as far off as ever, save for knowing that the old man's in England."

"You ain't fly to what's meant by 'among the lemons,' eh?"

"Not a bit of it, I tell you. What are you grinning and chuckling away at there, Griffiths? That's one of your disgustin' ways,—crowin' over me because you know something which I don't."

"Don't be riled, D'Ossay; don't be riled, old feller. It's so seldom that I get a chance of findin' anything that you don't know, young though you are, that I make the most of it, I confess."

"Well, there, all right. Now do you know what he meant by 'among the lemons'?"

"Of course I do."

"And what does it mean?"

"'Among the lemons' is magsman's patter for 'Houndsditch.' There's a reg'lar gatherin' of sheenies there every Sunday mornin', where they have a kind of fair, and sellin' all sorts of things,—clothes, and books, and pictures, and so on."

"Well, but old Lyons is a cut above all that sort of thing."

"I should think he was."

"He wouldn't be found there."

"Well, not sellin' anything; but he might be on the lookout for some magsmen as work for him, and who may have had the office to be about there. But if he's not there, I'd know where to lay hands on him, I'd take my oath."

"Where's that?"

"At the Net of Lemons, a public where sheenies of all kinds—diamond-merchants, fences, all sorts—meet on the Sunday."

"Do you know the place?"

"Know it! I should think so, and Mr. Eliason as keeps it; as respectable an old gent as walks."

"They'd let you in?"

"Ah, and you too, if I squared it for you."

"Very well, then; we'll hunt up old Lyons on Sunday morning."

Mr. Effingham was so pleased with his chance of success, that Mr. Griffiths thought he might borrow half-a-sovereign; and what is more, he got it.

On the following Sunday morning Mr. Effingham found himself by appointment opposite Bishopgate Church as the clock struck ten, and Mr. Griffiths there waiting for him. As he approached, Mr. Effingham took stock of his friend's personal appearance, and mentally congratulated himself that it was at the East and not at the West end of London that they were to be seen in company together; for those mysterious means by which Mr. Griffiths went through "the fever called living" had not been very productive of late, and his wardrobe was decidedly seedy. The tall hat shone so as to give one the idea that its owner had forgotten to remove it when he applied the morning macassar to his hair, and the suit of once-black clothes looked as if they had been bees-waxed. Mr. Effingham must have allowed his thoughts to be mirrored in his expressive countenance, for Mr. Griffiths said as he joined him:

"Looking at my togs, D'Ossay? Well, they ain't as nobby as yours; but you see, I don't go in to be a 'eavy swell. They'll do well enough for the caper we're on to-day, though; better perhaps than your gridironed kickseys."

At another time Mr. Effingham might have shown annoyance at thus having his check trousers sneeringly spoken of; but something which Griffiths had said had rather dashed him, and it was with a little hesitation that he asked:

"They—they ain't a very rough lot that we're going amongst, are they?"

"Well, there's more rough nor smooth hair among 'em; but they won't do you no harm; I'll look after you, D'Ossay. Shovin you won't mind, nor elbers in every part of your body at once. Oh, and I say, don't leave any-think in your 'ind-pockets, and put your fogle in your 'at. Like this, look. I carry most things in my 'at."

And Mr. Griffiths whipped off the tall hat, and showed in it a handkerchief, a greasy parcel suspiciously like a ham sandwich, a pocket comb, and a paper book with the title "The Olio of Oddities, or the Warbling Wagoner's Wallet of Wit and Wisdom."

Mr. Effingham took his friend's advice, and transferred all his portable property from the tail-pockets of his coat to other less patent recesses, and the pair started on their excursion.

Crossing Bishopgate, and turning short round to the right up a street called Sandy's Row, past a huge black block of buildings belonging to the East India Company, and used as a store-house for costly silks, round which seethed and bubbled a dirty, pushing, striving, fighting, higgling, chaffering, vociferating, laughing mob, filling up the narrow street, the small strips of pavement on either side, and what ought to have been the carriage-way between them. It was Sunday, and may have been observed "as such" elsewhere, but certainly not in Sandy's Row or Cutler's Row. There were shops of all kinds, and all at work: tool-shops,—files, saws, adzes, knives, chisels, hammers, and tool-baskets displayed in the open windows, whence the sashes had been removed for the better furtherance of trade; hatters', hosiers', tailors', bootmakers' shops, the proprietors of which had left the calm asylum of their counters and stood at the doors, importuning the passers-by with familiar blandishments; for in the carriage-way through which Effingham and Griffiths slowly forced a passage, were peripatetic vendors of hats, hosiery, clothes, and boots,—hook-nosed oleaginous gentry with ten pairs of trousers over one arm, and five coats over the other, with enormous boots, a few hats, and a number of cloth caps. Mr. Effingham soon learned the value of his friend's advice, for there were thieves of all kinds in the motley crowd; big burly roughs, with sunken eyes and massive jaws, sulkily elbowing their way through the mass, and "gonophs" or pickpockets of fourteen or fifteen, with their collarless tightly-tied neckerchief, their greasy caps, and "aggerawater" curls. Delicate attention was paid to Mr. Effingham before he had been five minutes amongst them. The hind-pockets of his coat were turned inside out, and he was "sounded" all over by a pair of lightly-touching hands. Whether Mr. Griffiths was known, or whether his personal appearance was unattractive and promised no hope of adequate reward, is uncertain; but no attempt was made on him.

While Mr. Effingham was vaguely gaping about him, staring at everything and thoroughly impressed with the novelty of his situation, Griffiths had been taking stock of the crowd, and keeping a strict lookout for Mr. Lyons. Jews were there in shoals, and of all kinds: the grand old Jewish type, dignified and bearded, than which, when good, there is nothing better; handsome sensual-looking men, with bright eyes, and hook-noses, and scarlet lips; red frizzy-headed Jews, with red eyelids, and shambling gait, and nasal intonation; big flat-headed, stupid-looking men, with thick lips, and tongues too large for their mouths, and visibly protruding therefrom;—all kinds of Jews, but Mr. Lyons not among them.

So they pushed on, uncaring for the chaff of the mob, which was very facetious on the subject of Mr. Effingham's attire, saluting him as a "collared bloke," in delicate compliment to his wearing a clean shirt; asking whether he was a "Rooshan;" whether he were not "Prince Halbut's brother," and other delicate compliments,—pushed on until they arrived at the Clothes-Exchange, a roofed building filled round every side and in the centre with old-clothes stalls. Here, piled up in wondrous confusion, lay hats, coats, boots, hob-nailed shoes, satin ball-shoes, driving-coats, satin dresses, hoops, brocaded gowns, flannel jackets, fans, shirts, stockings with clocks, stockings with torn and darned feet, feathers, parasols, black-silk mantles, blue-kid boots, belcher neckerchiefs, and lace ruffles. More Jews here; salesmen shrieking out laudations of their wares, and frantically imploring passers-by to come in and be fitted: "Here'th a coat! plue Vitney; trai this plue Vitney, ma tear." "Here'th a vethkit for you, thir!" shouted one man to Effingham; "thuch a vethkit! a thplendid vethkit, covered all over with blue-and-thilver thpright." Mr. Effingham cast a longing eye at this gorgeous garment, but passed on.

No Lyons here, either among sharp-eyed vendors or leering buyers. Mr. Griffiths was getting nonplussed, and Mr. Effingham growing anxious. "We must find him, Griffiths," he said; "we must not throw away this chance that he's given us; he may be off to the Continent, Lord knows where, to-morrow. Why the devil don't you find him?"

Mr. Griffiths intimated that so far as eye-straining could be gone through, he had done his best; and suggested that if the man they sought were not there, all the energy in the world would not discover him. "But there's the Net of Lemons yet," he said; "that's, after all, the safest draw, and we're more likely to hit upon him there than anywhere else."

So they pushed their way through the steaming, seething, struggling crowd, and found themselves in a quiet dull little square. Across this, and merely glancing at several groups of men dotted here and there in its midst, loudly talking and gesticulating with energy which smacked more of the Hamburg Börsenhalle or the Frankfort Zeil than the stolid reticence of England, Mr. Griffiths led his companion until they stopped before the closed door of a public house, aloft from which swung the sign of "The Net of Lemons." At the door Mr. Griffiths gave three mystic raps, at the third of which the door opened for about a couple of inches, and a thick voice said, "Who is it?"

"All right, Mr. Eliason. Griffiths, whom you know. Take a squint, and judge for yourself."

Mr. Eliason probably followed this advice, and finding the inspection satisfactory, opened the door to its extent, and admitted the pair; but raising his bushy brows in doubt as to Mr. Effingham, Griffiths said, "A friend of mine—come on partickler business, and by appointment with Mr. Lyons. Is he here?"

The reference was apparently satisfactory, for Mr. Eliason, a fat good-looking big man in a soft wideawake hat, said, "You'll find him inside;" and shut the door behind them.

Mr. Effingham walking through, and following his conductor, found himself in a low-roofed, square-built, comfortable room, round three sides of which were ranged tables, and on these tables were placed large open trays of jewelry. There they lay in clusters, thick gold chains curled round and round like snares; long limp silver chains such as are worn by respectable mechanics over black-satin waistcoats on Sundays; great carbuncle pins glowing out of green-velvet cases; diamond rings and pins and brooches and necklaces. The best emeralds in quaint old-fashioned gold settings nestled by the side of lovely pale opals; big finger-rings made up after the antique with cut cornelian centrepieces; long old-fashioned earrings; little heaps of rubies, emeralds, and turquoises set aside in the corners of the trays; big gold and silver cups and goblets and trays and tazzas; here and there a clumsy old epergne; finger-rings by the bushel, pins by the gross; watches of all kinds, from delicate gold Genevas to the thick turnipy silver "ticker" of the schoolboy; and shoals of watchworks without cases. On this Tom Tidler's ground were crowds of customers, smoking strong cigars, walking about without let or hindrance, and examining—ay, and handling—the jewels without creating the least consternation in the breasts of their vendors.

There was a slight movement among the company at the entrance of the new-comers; but Griffiths seemed to be known to a few, with whom he exchanged salutations, and the appearance of Mr. Eliason with them settled any wandering doubts which might have arisen in the minds of the others. As for Mr. Effingham, he began to think he was in the cave into which Aladdin descended to get the lamp at the bidding of the magician; and he went moving round, gazing first on one side, then on the other, lost in wonder. But Mr. Griffiths, to whom the scene was tolerably familiar, went at once to business, scrutinizing with keen glance the buyers and sellers, poking his nose into the groups of domino-players in the corners, hunting about with admirable patience and forbearance, but for a long time with no result.

At last he stopped before a group of three. One of these was an old Jewish gentleman, with strongly-marked features, overhanging bushy eyebrows, hooked nose, and long white beard. He held in his hand a blue paper, such as generally contains seidlitz-powders, but its contents were diamonds. These were being carefully inspected by the other two men, each of whom had a bright steel pair of pincers, with which he selected a specimen from the glittering heap, breathed upon it, watched it carefully, and in most instances finally laid it on one side for purchase. When this transaction had been gone through and was at an end, the old gentleman folded up his paper with such diamonds as remained in it, placed it in his waistcoat-pocket, and was calmly walking away, when Griffiths touched him on the arm, saying interrogatively, "Mr. Lyons?"

The old man turned in an instant, and threw a sharp look of inquiry over his interlocutor, as he said: "Yes, ma tear sir, that's mai name; not ashamed to own it any veres. Vot might you vant with me?" As he spoke he had covered his waistcoat-pocket with his hand, and stood prim and spry.

"This gentleman—Mr. Effingham—has been looking for you some little time. You told a friend of his—Mr. Pollock—that you would be here to-day, and we've come on purpose to meet you."

"Effingham! Pollock!" said the old man, musing. "O yes, Pollock, who writes those funny burlesques for my friend Wuff; O yes—Effingham," he said. "How do you do, ma tear? Now vot is it? A leetle advance, or something you've got that you don't know how to get rid of, and think I might fancy it, eh?"

"Well, it ain't either, Mr. Lyons," said Effingham. "Its a little information you're in possession of that you might be inclined to give us, and—"

"You're not traps?" asked Mr. Lyons, turning pale.

"Not a bit of it, Mr. Lyons," said Griffiths, striking into the conversation. "Quite different from that. You and I have done business before. I was with—" and here he whispered into Lyons's ear.

"Ah, I reckleckt," said the old gentleman. "That vos a very good plant, and bothers them all in Scotland Yard to this day. Ha, ha! I reckleckt. Now vot did your friend say? Information? Veil, you know, I never *give* information."

"No, no, of course not," said Griffiths, winking at Effingham.

"O no, sir," said that worthy. "I'm prepared to pay, of course, anything reasonable for what I require."

"Vell, vell, ma tear, let's know vot it is."

"You were great pals with my brother, I believe?"

"No. Effingham? No;—never heard the name."

"No, no; not Effingham. That's merely—you understand?"

"O ah! O yes! I qvite understand; but vot is the name?"

"Butler! You knew Tony Butler well?"

"Knew him vell; I should rather think I did. A good fellow; a clever fellow; oh, a very clever fellow, ma tear."

"Yes; well, I'm his brother."

"Not like him," said Mr. Lyons. "More dressy, and not so business-like. A rare fellow for business, Tony."

"That may or may not be," said Effingham, slightly offended. "Now, when he died, you cleared off his traps."

"Only a few sticks; very poor sticks. Ah, ma tear, vot I lost by that transaction! Vy, there vosn't enough to clear me in a sixth part of vot I'd advanced to Tony."

"Well, I'm not here to enter into that—that was your lookout. But amongst what you took away there was a desk."

"Vos there? 'Pon my soul I can't reckleckt; not that I'm goin' to gainsay you. Vos there a desk, now?"

"And in it," continued Effingham, not seeming to heed him, "there was an overdue bill for twenty-five pounds accepted by Walter Burgess."

"Lord now! Vos there indeed?"

"Look here, Mr. Lyons. If you don't know anything, all right. We won't waste our time or our money, but we'll go to those who can help us."

"Vot a headstrong boy it is! Who said I couldn't help you? Go on now,—a bill accepted by Walter Burgess?"

"Exactly. Now that bill's no use to any one, and we want you to give it to us."

"Ha, ha! clever boys, clever boys! Vot large-hearted fellows too, to want to buy a bill that ain't of any use to any vun! O, vot generous boys!"

"It's no use, Griffiths," said Effingham angrily; "he either don't know or won't say anything about it."

"Steady," said Griffiths. "Come, Mr. Lyons, say you've got the stiff, and name your price."

"Accepted by Walter Burgess, eh?" said the old gentleman; "yes, I reckleckt that bill; O yes, I reckleckt him."

"Well now, bring your recklecktion into something practical, and I'll give you this for that bill," said Mr. Effingham, producing a five-pound note.

The old Jew's eyes glistened at the sight of the money; and then his face fell, and he looked horribly disappointed.

"You should have it for that," said he; "you should have it for that, and velcome; only there's vun little reason vy I can't make it over to you."

"What's that?" cried Effingham.

"Vell, it's a strong reason, as you'll allow ven I tell it to you. I can't let you have the bill, because—because I haven't got it myself."

Mr. Effingham swore a sharp oath, and even Mr. Griffiths looked disconcerted.

"Come along," said the former,—"we've wasted time enough with the pottering old fool, who's only selling us, and—"

"Vait a minute," said Mr. Lyons, laying his hand on the other's arm,—"vait a minute, ma tear. Though I haven't got the leetle bill myself, perhaps I know who has."

"That's likely enough," said Griffiths, "well, who has?"

"Ah, that's tellings, ma tear. I shall vant—just a leetle something to say."

"I'll give this," said Effingham, producing a sovereign.

"Vell, it ain't enough; but you're such headstrong fellows. There!" said Mr. Lyons, slipping it into his pocket; "now do either of you know a gal who was under Tony Butler's thumb at vun time, but who hated him mortal, and vos very sveet on vun of Tony's friends?"

"I do!" cried Griffiths; "Lizzie Ponsford."

"That's the same; a fine gal too, a reg'lar fine gal. Vell, I'd no sooner got Tony's traps over at my place than that gal comes to me, and she says, 'You've got a desk that b'longed to Tony Butler,' she says. And ven I says 'yes,' she offered me a pound for it. It vosn't vuth five shillings; so I knew there vos something in it she vanted, though I'd hunted it through and found nothin' but old diaries and memorandums and such-like. 'I von't sell it,' I says. 'May I look at it?' she says. 'You may,' I says; and vith that I fetched it down; and ven she see it, she touched a spring, and out flew a secret drawer vith this bill in it. 'Hands off,' I says, for she vos going to clutch it at vunce. 'Let me have it,' she says; 'I'll pay for it.' So I looked at it, and saw it had been overdue eighteen months, and reckleckted hearin' it was all wrong; so I says, 'Vot'll you give?' 'A sovereign,' she says. 'Make it two, and it's yours,' I says. So, after a little, she give me two skivs, and she took the bill and valked away vith it."

Mr. Effingham looked at Griffiths, and the latter returned the glance.

"It would be almost worth another crown to know if these are lies you are telling us, old gentleman," said the former; "but it sounds something like truth. Now one question more. Where is Lizzie Ponsford?"

"Ah, that beats me. A reg'lar clever gal; nice-looking and reg'lar clever. I'd have given something to find out myself; but it vos all of no use. She vent away from all the old haunts, and hasn't been heard of for a long time. I've all sorts of people about, and they'd tell me, bless you, if she'd ever show'd up. But she's gone, and no vun can find her."

"Very good," said Effingham; "now you take this commission from me. If you hear of her within the next month, and can let me know where she is, find out Griffiths at Johnson's, and it'll be a fiver in your pocket. You understand?"

Mr. Lyons made no verbal reply, but struck his forefinger against his nose and looked preternaturally sagacious.

"All right! now goodbye;" they shook hands and parted.

When they got into the street again Mr. Effingham said, "So Lizzie Ponsford has the bill. What the deuce made her want it? unless some day to revenge herself on Mitford. But she's not likely to have heard of his having turned up such trumps. Now, Mr. Griffiths, our pursuit begins again. Lizzie Ponsford has that bill. Your business and mine is to find out Lizzie Ponsford, and by some means or other—no matter what—get that bill from her."

CHAPTER XIII.

SIR CHARLES'S VISIT.

Sir Charles Mitford was up betimes the next morning, for he had a twenty-miles' drive before him. The weather was bright, clear, and frosty; Sir Charles's spirits were high; he was radiant and buoyant, and thoroughly in good temper with himself and everybody else. He was specially kind and affectionate to Georgie, and after breakfast insisted upon seeing her commence her day of work before he started on his day of pleasure; and he complimented Mrs. Austin on the progress her pupil had made under her directions, and on the care, cleanliness, and order observable throughout the house, and by his few words made a complete conquest of the old lady, who afterwards told Georgie that though Sir Percy had been an upright man and a good master, it was all in a strait-laced kind of way, and no one had ever heard him say a kind word to herself, let alone any of the servants. And then when the chestnuts had been brought round in the mail-phaeton, and were impatiently pawing at the gravel in front of the hall-door, and champing at their bits, and flecking with foam their plated harness and their sleek sides, Sir Charles gave his wife an affectionate kiss and drove away in great glee.

Mrs. Austin's instruction of her mistress was shortened by full five minutes that morning—five minutes during which Lady Mitford was occupied in leaning out of the window and watching her husband down the drive. How handsome he looked! in his big heavy brown driving-coat with its huge horn buttons, his well-fitting dogskin gloves, and his natty hat—wideawakes had not then been invented, but driving-men used to wear a hat low in the crown and broad in the brim, winch, though a trifle slangy, was in some cases very becoming. The sun shone on his bright complexion, his breezy golden whiskers, and his brilliant teeth, as he smiled his adieu; and as he brought the chestnuts up to their bearings after their first mad plunges, and standing up got them well in hand and settled them down to their work, Georgie was lost in admiration of his strong muscular figure, his pluck and grace. It was a subject on which she would have been naturally particularly reticent, even had there been any one to "gush" to; but I think the tears of pleasure welled into her eyes, and she had a very happy "cry" before she rejoined Mrs. Austin in the still-room.

And Sir Charles, what were his thoughts during his drive? Among all the wonderful revelations which the publication of the Divorce-Court trials has made public, the sad heart-rending misery, the brutal ruffianism, the heartless villany, the existence of which could scarcely have been dreamed of, there is one phase of life which, so far as I have seen—and I have looked for it attentively,—has never yet been chronicled. The man who leaves his wife and family to get on as they best can, while he revels in riot and debauchery; the man who is the blind slave of his own brute passions, and who goes headlong to destruction without any apparent thought save for his own gratification; the man who would seem in the iteration of his share of the marriage-service to have substituted "hate" for "love," and who either detests his wife with savage rancour, or loathes her with deep disgust, for better for worse, for richer for poorer, in sickness and in health, until the Judge-Ordinary does them part; the respectable man, so punctual in the discharge of his domestic duties, so unswerving in the matter of family-prayers, whose conjugal comfort is one day wrecked by the arrival of a clamorous and not too sober lady with heightened colour and blackened eyelids:—with all these types we are familiar enough through the newspaper columns; but there is another character, by no means so numerously represented, nor so likely to be brought publicly under notice, who yet exists, and with specimens of which some of us must be familiar. I mean the man who, with great affection for his wife and strong desire to do right, is yet so feeble in moral purpose, so impotent to struggle against inclination, such a facile prey to temptation, as to be perpetually doing wrong. He never grows hardened in his vice, he never withdraws his love from its proper object—for in that case it would quickly be supplanted by the opposite feeling; he never even grows indifferent: after every slip he inwardly upbraids himself bitterly and vows repentance; in his hour of remorse he institutes comparisons between his proper and improper attractions, in which the virtues of the former are always very bright and the vices of the latter always very black; and then on the very next occasion his virtuous resolutions melt away like snow, and he goes wrong again as pleasantly as possible.

Sir Charles Mitford was of this class. He would have been horrified if any one had suggested that he had any intention of wronging his wife; would have said that such an idea had never crossed his mind—and truthfully, as whenever it rose he immediately smothered it; would have declared, as he believed, that Georgie was the prettiest, the best, and the dearest girl in the world. But he was a man of strong passions, and most susceptible to flattery; and ever since Mrs. Hammond had seemed to select him for special notice, more especially since she had assumed the habit of occasionally looking pensively at him, with a kind of dreamy languor in her large eyes, he had thought more of her, in both senses of the phrase, than was right. He was thinking of her even then, as he sat square and erect in his phaeton, before he passed out of Georgie's gaze; thinking of her large eyes and their long glances, her full rounded figure, a peculiar hand-clasp which she gave, a thrill without a grip, a scarcely perceptible unforgettable pressure. Then his horsey instincts rose within him, and he began to take coachman's notice of the chestnuts; saw the merits and demerits of each, and almost unconsciously set about the work of educating the former, and checking the latter; and thus he employed himself until the white houses of Torquay came within sight, and glancing at his watch he found he should have done his twenty miles in an hour and forty minutes.

Mrs. Hammond had told him that he would be sure of finding their address at the Royal Hotel; so to the Royal Hotel he drove. The chestnuts went bounding through the town, attracting attention from all the valetudinarians then creeping about on their shopping or anteprandial walks. These poor fellows in respirators and high shawls, bending feebly on sticks or tottering on each other's arms, resented the sight of this great strong Phoebus dashing along with his spinning chariot-wheels. When he pulled up at the door of the Royal, a little crowd of invalids crept out of sunny nooks, and sheltered corners, where they had been resting, to look at him. The waiter, a fat greasy man, who used to let the winter-boarders tear many times at the bell before he dreamt of answering it, heard the tramp of the horses, and the violent pull given to the door-bell by Sir Charles's groom, and in a kind of hazy dream thought that it must be summer again, and that it must be some of the gents from the yachts, as was always so noisy and obstreperous. Before he could rouse himself sufficiently to get to the door, he had been anticipated by the landlord, wit° had scarcely made his bow, before Dr. Bronk, who had noticed the phaeton dashing round the corner, fancied it might be a son or a nephew on the lookout for quarters—and medical attendance—for some invalid relative, came into the portico, and bestowed the greatest care in rubbing his shoes on the hall-mat.

Mr. Hammond? No, the landlord had never heard the name. Constant change of faces renders landlords preternaturally stupid on this point, they can never fit names to faces or faces to names. Hammond? no, he thought not. John! did John know the name of Hammond? But before John could sufficiently focus his wits to know whether he did or not, Dr. Bronk had heard all, had stepped up to the side of the phaeton, had made a half-friendly, half-deferential bow, and was in full swing.

Mr. Hammond? a middle-aged gentleman,—well, who perhaps might be described as rather elderly, yes. Bald,—yes. With a young daughter and a very charming wife? Yes, O yes; certainly he knew them; he had the honour of being their medical attendant,—Dr. Bronk of the Paragon. Lately had come down to Torquay, recommended to him by his—he was proud to say—old friend and former fellow-pupil, Sir Charles Dumfunk, now President of the College of Physicians. Where were they? well, they had been really unfortunate. Torquay, my dear sir, every year rising in importance, every year more sought after,—for which perhaps some little credit was due to a little medical brochure of his, *Torquay and its Climate*,—Torquay was so full that when Mrs. Hammond sent down that admirable person, Miss Gillespie,—whom of course the gentleman knew,—there was only one house vacant. So the family had been forced to content themselves with a mansion—No. 2, Cleveland Gardens, very nice, sheltered, and yet with a charming sea-view. Where was it? Did the gentleman see the bow-windowed shop at the corner? Second turning to the right, just beyond that—"Se-cond turn-ing to the right!" This shouted after Sir Charles, who, with a feeling that the chestnuts were too rapidly cooling after their sharp drive, had started them off the minute he had obtained the information.

The second turning to the right was duly taken, and No. 2, Cleveland Gardens, was duly reached. It was the usual style of seaside-house, with stuccoed front and green veranda, and the never-failing creeper which the Devonians always grow to show the mildness of their climate. The groom's thundering knock produced a smart waiting-maid, who acknowledged that Mrs. Hammond lived there; and the sending in of Sir Charles Mitford's card produced a London flunkey, on whom the country air had had a demoralizing influence, so far as his outward appearance was concerned. But he acknowledged Sir Charles's arrival with a deferential bow, and begging him to walk in, assured him that his mistress would come down directly. So the groom was sent round, to put up his horses at the stables of the Royal, and Sir Charles followed the footman into the drawing-room.

It was not an apartment to be left alone in for long. No doubt the family of the owner, a younger brother of an Irish peer, found it pleasant and airy when they were down there in the summer, and the owner himself found the rent of it for the spring, autumn, and winter, a very hopeful source of income; but it bore "lodging-house" on every scrap of furniture throughout it. Sir Charles stared round at the bad engravings, at the bad old-fashioned artists on the walls; looked with concentrated interest on a plaster-model of the Leaning Tower of Pisa, and wondered whether the mortar shrinking had warped it; peeped into two or three books on the table; looked out of the window at the promenading invalids and the green twinkling sea; and was relieved beyond measure when he heard a woman's step on the staircase outside.

The door opened, and a woman entered—but not Mrs. Hammond. A tall woman, with sallow cheeks and great eyes, and a thickish nose and large full lips, with a low forehead, over which tumbled waves of crisp brown hair, with a marvellous lithe figure and a peculiar swinging walk. Shifty in her glance, stealthy in her walk, cat-like in her motions, her face deadly pale,—a volcano crumbled into ashes, with no trace of its former fire save in her eyes,—a woman at once uncomfortable, uncanny, noticeable, and fearsome,—Miss Gillespie.

The family of the younger brother of the Irish peer owning the house prided themselves immensely on certain pink-silk blinds to the windows, which happened at that moment to be down. There must have been some very peculiar effect in the tint thrown by those blinds to have caused Sir Charles Mitford to stare so hard at the new-comer, or to lose all trace of his ordinary colour as he gazed at her.

She spoke first. Her full lips parted over a brilliant set of teeth as with a slight inclination she said, "I have the pleasure of addressing Sir Charles Mitford? Mrs. Hammond begs me to say that she is at present in attendance upon Mr. Hammond, who is forbidden to-day to leave his room; but she hopes to be with you in a very few minutes."

A polite but sufficiently ordinary speech; certainly not in itself calculated to call forth Mitford's rejoinder—"In God's name, how did you come here?"

"You still keep up that horrid habit of swearing! *Autre temps, autres moeurs*, as I teach my young lady from the French proverb-book. What was it you asked?"

"How did you come here? what are you doing here?"

"I came here through the medium of the Ladies' Association for Instructors, to whom I paid a registration-fee of five shillings. What am I doing here? Educating youth, and making myself generally useful. I am Miss Gillespie, of whom I know you have heard."

"You have seen me before this, since—since the old days?"

"I don't know what is meant by 'old days.' I was born two years ago, just before Mrs. Hammond married, and was christened Ruth Gillespie. My mother was the Ladies' Association for Instructors, and she at once placed me where I am. Except this I have no past."

"And your future?"

"Can take care of itself: sufficient for the day, &c.; and the present days are very pleasant. There is no past for you either, is there? so far as I am concerned, I mean. I first saw Sir Charles Mitford when I was sitting in Mrs. Hammond's phaeton in the Park with my Shetland veil down, I recollect; and as I had heard the story of the romantic manner in which he had succeeded to the title and estates, I asked full particulars about him from—well—my mistress. I learned that he had married, and that his wife was reported to be very lovely—oh, very lovely indeed!" she almost purred as she said this, and undulated as though about to spring.

"Be good enough to leave my wife's name alone. You say there is no past for either of us. Let our present be as wide asunder as possible."

"That all rests with you."

"I wonder," said Sir Charles, almost below his breath, "what infernal chance has sent you here!"

"If 'infernal' were a word to be used by a lady—I doubt whether it should be used in a lady's presence; but that is a matter of taste—I should reiterate your sentiment; because, if you remark, you are the interloper and intruder. I am going on perfectly quietly, earning my living, giving every satisfaction to my employers,—living, in fact, like the virtuous peasant on the stage or in the penny romances,—when chance brings you into my line of life, and you at once grumble at me for being there."

"You can understand fast enough, I suppose," said Sir Charles, sulkily, "that my associations with my former life are not such as I take great pleasure in recalling."

"If a lady *might* say such a word, I should say, upon my soul I can't understand any such thing. Though I go quietly enough in harness, and take my share of the collar-work too, they little think how I long sometimes to kick over the traces, to substitute Alfred de Musset for Fénelon in my pupil's reading, or to let my fingers and voice stray off from *Adeste Fideles* into *Eh, ioup, ioup, ioup, tralala, lala*! How it would astonish them! wouldn't it?—the files, I mean; not Mrs. Hammond, who knows everything, and I've no doubt would follow on with *Mon père est à Paris* as naturally as possible."

Sir Charles was by no means soothed by this rattle, but frowningly asked, "How long do you mean to remain here?"

"How long? Well, my movements are of course controlled by Mrs. Hammond. It is betraying no confidence to say that I know she is expecting an invitation to Redmoor (you see I know the name of your place); and as this house is not particularly comfortable, and your hospitality is boundless, I conclude, when once we get there, we shall not leave much before we return to town for the season."

"We!" exclaimed Sir Charles; "why, do you mean to say that you are coming to stay at my house?"

"Of course I am. Mrs. Hammond told me that she gave you distinctly to understand that she must bring Miss Gillespie with her when she came to stop at Redmoor."

"True; but then—"

"Then you did not know Miss Gillespie. Well, you'll find she's not a bad fellow, after all."

"Look here," said Mitford with knitted brows and set teeth: "there's a point to which you may go, but which you sha'n't pass. If you dare to come into my house as my guest, look to yourself; for, by the Lord, it shall be the worse for you!"

"The privileges of the salt, monseigneur!" cried Miss Gillespie, with a crisp laugh; "the salt, 'that sacred pledge, which once partaken blunts the sabre's edge.' You would never abuse the glorious rites of hospitality?"

"You were always fond of d—d stage-jargon; but you ought to have known me long enough to know that it would have no effect on me. Take the warning I've given you in good part, and stay away."

"And take the warning I give you in good part and in good earnest, Charles Mitford," said Miss Gillespie, with a sudden change of voice and manner; "I've been tolerant to you hitherto for the sake of the old times which I love and you loathe; but don't you presume upon that. I could crush you like a snail: now this is no stage-jargon, but simple honest fact. You'll recollect that though perhaps a little given to rodomontade, in matters of business I was truthful. I can crush you like a snail; and if you cross me in my desires,—which are of the humblest; merely to be allowed to continue my present mode of life in peace,—so help me Heaven, I'll do it!"

All claws out here.

"You mean war, then?"

"Hush! not a word; here's Mrs. Hammond coming down. I do mean war, under circumstances; but you won't drive me to that. Yes, as you say, Sir Charles, it is the very place for an invalid."

As she spoke Mrs. Hammond entered the room, looking very fresh and pretty; her dark-blue merino dress with its close-fitting body displaying her round figure, and its sweeping skirts, and its tight sleeves, with natty linen cuffs. She advanced with outstretched hand and with a pleasant smile, showing all her fresh wholesome teeth.

"So you've come at last," she said; "it's no great compliment to say that we have anxiously expected you—for anything like the horror of this place you cannot imagine. Everybody you meet looks as if that day were their last, and that they had just crawled out to take farewell of the sun. And there's not a soul we know here, except the doctor who's attending Mr. Hammond, and he's an odious little chatterbox. And how is dear Lady Mitford? and how did you find the house? and did Captain

Bligh make the arrangements as nicely as we thought he would? Come, sit down and tell me all about it."

It was at this period, and before they seated themselves, that Miss Gillespie said she thought she would go and see what Alice was doing. And Mrs. Hammond asked her to tell Newman that Sir Charles Mitford would dine with them; and that as he had a long drive home, they had better say six-o'clock dinner. And charged with these messages, Miss Gillespie retired.

Then Mrs. Hammond sunk down into a pleasant ottoman fitted into a recess close by the glowing fire, and Sir Charles Mitford, looking round for a seat, obeyed the silent invitation conveyed to him in her eyes and in the movement of her dress, and seated himself by her side.

"Well, you must have a great deal to tell me," she commenced. "I saw in the Post that you had left town, and therefore imagined that Captain Bligh's arrangements were concluded. And how do you like Redmoor?"

"It's a glorious place, really a glorious place, though I've been rather bored there for the last two or three days—wanted people there, you know, and that sort of thing. But the place itself is first-rate. I've chosen your rooms. I did that the first day."

"Did you?" said she, her eyes sparkling with delight; "and where are they?"

"They are in the south wing, looking over the civilized side of the country, and are to my thinking the very best rooms in the house."

"And you chose them for us, and thought of us directly you arrived! How very, very kind of you! But suppose we should be unable to come?"

"What! unable to come! Mrs. Hammond, you're chaffing me, eh?"

"No, indeed. Mr. Hammond's health is in that wretched state, that I doubt whether Dr. Bronk would sanction his being moved, even to the soft air and all the luxuries of Redmoor."

"Oh, do him good, I'm sure; could do him no possible harm. He should have everything he wanted, you know; and the doctor could come spinning over there every day, for the matter of that. But at any rate *you* won't disappoint us?"

"I don't think my not coming would be keenly felt by many."

"It would by me," said Mitford in a low voice.

She looked him full in the face for an instant. "I believe it would," said she; "frankly I believe it would;" and she stretched out her hand almost involuntarily. Sir Charles took it, pressed it, and would have retained it, but she withdrew it gently. "No, that would never do. Mrs. Grundy would have a great deal to say on the subject; and besides, my place is at his side." If "his side" were her husband's, Mrs. Hammond was far more frequently out of place than in it. "My place is by his side," she repeated. "Ah, Sir Charles, you've no idea what a life I lead!"

He was looking at her hand as she spoke, was admiring its plumpness and whiteness, and was idly following with his eye the track of the violet veins. There is a something legible in the back of a hand, something which chiromancy wots not of, and Sir Charles Bell has left unexplained. Mitford was wondering whether he read this problem aright when the last words fell on his ear; and feeling it was necessary that he should reply, said, "It must be dull, eh?"

"Dull! you've no conception how dull. And I often think I was meant for something different,—something better than a sick-man's nurse, to bear his whims, and be patient under his irritability. I often think—But what nonsense I'm talking!—what are my thoughts to you?"

"A great deal more than you know of. Go on, please."

"I often think that if I had been married to a man who could understand me, who could appreciate me, I should have been a very happy and a good woman. Good and happy! God knows very different from what I am now."

With her right hand she touched her eyes with a delicate little handkerchief. In her left hand she had held a small feather fan, with which she had screened herself from the fire; but the fan had fallen to the floor and lay there unnoticed, while the hand hung listlessly by her side close by Sir Charles. Gradually their hands touched, and this time she made no effort to withdraw hers from his clasp.

There was silence for a few moments, broken by her saying, "There, there is an end of that! It is but seldom that I break down, and show myself in my true colours; but there is something in you which—inexplicably to myself—won my confidence, and now I've bored you with my troubles. There, let me go now, and I'll promise never to be so silly again." She struggled to free her hand, but he held it firmly.

"Leave it there," said he; "you have not misplaced your confidence, as you know very well. Oh, you needn't shake your head; you know that I would do anything to serve you."

He spoke in a low earnest voice; and as she looked up at him with one of her long deep dreamy looks, she saw a sudden thrill run through him, and felt his hand which held hers tremble.

"I *do* know it," she said; "and we will be the best, the very best of friends. Now let us talk of something else."

He was with her the whole of that day in a state of dreamful happiness, drinking in the music of her voice, watching her graceful motions, delighted with a certain bold recklessness, a contempt for the conventional rules of society, a horror of obedience to prescribed ordinances, which now and then her conversation betrayed. They saw nothing more of Miss Gillespie, save at dinner, when Mitford noticed that Mrs. Hammond made no alteration in her manner towards him, unless indeed it was a little more *prononcé* than when they had been alone. Miss Gillespie did not appear to remark it, but sat and purred from time to time in a very amiable and pleasant manner. She retired after dinner, and then Sir Charles's phaeton was brought round, and it was time to say adieu.

He said it in the little library, where the brother of the Irish peer kept his boots and his driving-whips, as he was lighting a cigar for which Mrs. Hammond held a cedar-match. As he bent over her, he felt her breath upon his face, and felt his whiskers touch her scented hair. He had not been inattentive to some Burgundy, which the invalid upstairs had specially commended to him in a message, and his blood coursed like fire through his veins. At that moment Miss Gillespie appeared at the open door with a glove which she had found in the hall, and with her dark-green eyes gleaming with rage. So Sir Charles only took Mrs. Hammond's hand, whispering "Friends?" receiving a long pressure and "Always!" for answer; and passing with a bow Miss Gillespie, whose eyes still gleamed ferociously sprang into his phaeton and drove off.

That last pressure of Mrs. Hammond's hand was on his hand, that last word of hers rung in his ear all the way home. All the way home his fevered fancy brought her image alluringly before him—more frequently, more alluringly than it had been in his morning's drive. But there was another figure which he had not thought of in the morning, and which now rose up;—the figure of a woman, green-eyed, pale-faced, cat-like in her motions. And when Sir Charles Mitford thought of her, he stamped his foot savagely and swore.

CHAPTER XIV.

IN THE TOILS.

Sir Charles Mitford had not been guilty of any exaggeration when he announced his intention of filling his house at Redmoor with a very pleasant set of people. If a man have a kindly genial temper, a sense of humour, a desire to be pleasant to his fellow-creatures, such qualities, however they may have hitherto been concealed, will make themselves felt during a sojourn at a friend's well-filled country-house. There the heavy man, who has sat by one at a dozen dinner-parties during the season and never opened his mouth except to fill it, is discovered to be full of antiquarian erudition about the old castles and abbeys in the neighbourhood; and imparts his information, pleasantly studded with quaint anecdote and pungent remark. There Lady Katherine gives up her perpetual simper, and rests her aching lips, and occasionally covers her gleaming teeth. There Mrs. Phillimore mixes for a while with people in her own rank of life, and temporarily denies herself the pleasure of hunting orphans into asylums, and dealing out tea and Bibles to superannuated crones. Grinsby would have gone through life despised as a cockney *littérateur*,—indeed, they intended to have immense fun out of him at the Duke's,—if he had not knocked over that brace of woodcock, right and left barrel; if, in fact, he had not made better shooting than any other man of the party; and Tom Copus would never have given that delicious imitation of little Mr. Loudswell, the blatant barrister, had it not been coaxed out of him during the private theatricals at Eversholt Park. What glorious flirtations, what happy marriages, what fun, enjoyable at the time, and lasting source of retrospective enjoyment for long after, have arisen from the gatherings in country-houses! In these days of imitation it is also gratifying to know that country-house society is essentially English. Monseigneur le Duc de Hausse et Baisse has a gathering at his *terre*, or the Graf von Hasenbraten fills his ancestral castle at Suchverloren with intending assistants at a *treibejagd*: but the French people are very unhappy; they long to be back in Paris, and they seek consolation in dressing and behaving exactly as if they had never quitted that city; while the manner of life among the Germans alters never;—to shoot a very little, to eat and drink a great deal, and the "sooner it's over the sooner to sleep,"—such are the simple conditions of Teutonic happiness.

The party at Redmoor was large and well constituted. Captain and Mrs. Charteris, whom everybody knew, were there. Tom Charteris had been in the Enniskillens; had run through all his money, and was in daily expectation of being sold up, when his uncle, the senior partner in a large distillery, died, leaving Tom such a share in the business as would bring him in an excellent income, on the sole condition that he should leave the army, and personally attend to the management of the distillery. It is probable that Tom would have been sufficiently idiotic to refuse compliance with these conditions; but, fortunately, he had taken to himself a wife, a young lady who was the daughter of the church-organist in a little town where the Enniskillens had been quartered, and who gave lessons in music and singing to the resident gentry. She was a pretty *piquante* little person; and Tom, lounging out of the barrack-window while he smoked his after-breakfast pipe, had seen her tripping to and fro, always neat, active, and sprightly, and always displaying a remarkably pretty foot and ankle. Admiration of pretty feet and ankles was among Tom's weaknesses, and he watched the little music-mistress with great interest, and began to look forward to her daily appearance with delight. Then he got an introduction to her,—without any definite end or aim, for good or for bad, but simply to amuse himself; then he became fascinated by her, and finally he married her. It was Mrs. Tom who insisted upon big jolly old Tom giving up the army and taking to the distillery and the money. She was a funny little woman, and would make her intimates shout with laughter at her imitation of Tom striding about the counting-house among the clerks (he never could get rid of his dragoon-swagger), and talking a haw-haw to the publicans who came to borrow money or beg for time. They had a pretty little house in Clarges Street, whence Tom would bowl away every morning at 9.30 to the distillery in Barbican, remaining there till half-past four, when Mrs. Tom would call for him in the brougham, and air him in the park till dinner-time. Everybody knew them, and hats were bobbing off over the iron-railings all down the Drive as they passed. Whenever a stoppage occurred Tom had to stand a running fire of chaff, being asked what it was a quartern, whether he'd like a drop of something short, with other jokes, in which the phrases "white tape" and "blue ruin" played conspicuous parts. The little house in Clarges Street was a great resort for a select few after the Opera, and many well-known men would drop in to have the claw of a lobster and a glass of champagne, or to smoke a final cigar whilst listening to Mrs. Tom's brilliant playing—till two A.M., when Tom turned his guests out, declaring he was a poor tradesman, and had to be up early to business. The house was a pleasant one, where there was a certain amount of *laissez-aller* freedom, but where Tom took care that his wife was thoroughly respected.

Then Mrs. Masters, always spoken of as "pretty Mrs. Masters," or "the pretty widow," was of the party,—a tall handsome woman with large eyes and masses of floating light brown hair, relict of old Dr. Masters, who had left her a capital income, which she seemed determined to keep to herself. Not more than eight-and-twenty, and eminently attractive, she was a source of wonder to her friends, who could not understand why she did not marry again. She had numbers of visitors, male and female; she went into society constantly, and did her due share of dancing and flirtation; but the latter was so mild in kind, and so general in its nature, that no man's name had ever been coupled with hers. Her most intimate enemies raised a report that she was at one time madly in love with Colonel Alsager; but if there was any truth in the rumour, she managed her madness so admirably as never to show a trace of it. She was invaluable in a country-house, for she was thoroughly good-tempered, entered heart and soul into everything that was proposed, and was a great bait for vain bachelors, whose vanity was specially piqued at her long resistance to the charms of their sex. With Mrs. Masters came her cousins, two young ladies named Tyrrell, whose father was a judge in India, who were of the ordinary stamp of pretty, pert, self-satisfied twenty-year-olds.

The other ladies in the house do not call for description. Chief amongst the men was Captain Bligh, who, as he walked about and inspected the alterations which had been made under his directions, wondered whether his old father would ever relent, and whether he should have a chance of putting the old hall down in Norfolk in order for himself; or whether he should go on betting and billiard-playing and steeplechase-riding until he "went a tremendous mucker," and either blew his brains out or levanted. And there was Major Winton, who, dressed in a pair of enormous thigh-boots, a dreadnaught, and a sou'-wester, and accompanied by a keeper, went away every morning at dawn to lie out in the marshes for snipe and wild-fowl, and who did not return till dinner-time; immediately after which meal he was accustomed to retire to his bed-room, where a case-bottle of brandy, a jar of Cavendish tobacco, a huge meerschaum-pipe, and the adventures of the Chevalier Faublas, were awaiting him; and with these he would occupy himself until he went to bed. Laurence Alsager was at Redmoor also, though his visit to his father was yet unpaid; and so was Lord Dollamore. The officers of the garrison had called, and the officers of the frigate cruising off Torquay, and the neighbouring gentry; and the whole party seemed to enjoy themselves except Sir Charles Mitford,—whose happiness was not to be long delayed, for the Hammonds were expected on a certain day, which now dawned upon the impatient master of Redmoor.

He had returned home after luncheon, leaving the shooting party under the charge of Captain Bligh, and had been in a state of undisguisable anxiety all the afternoon, unable to settle himself to anything; now playing a stroke or two at billiards, and looking on at Tom Charteris, who was practising certain hazards preparatory to a match with Bligh; now strolling through the drawing-room, where Alsager was talking to Lady Mitford and Mrs. Masters; now interrupting Lord Dollamore, who was stretched out in an easy-chair in the library reading Montaigne. Sir Charles's impatience and restlessness was not unobserved by any of these. Tom Charteris supposed he was already sick of the quiet of the country, and contemplated recommending him a turn in the distillery by way of a cure. Lady Mitford could not understand his restlessness, and feared Charley had been annoyed about something. Mrs. Masters ascribed it to want of *savoir faire* on the Baronet's part, Only Colonel Alsager and Lord Dollamore guessed its real cause. The former frowned portentously as he watched his host; and the latter vas considerably amused.

"This is positively a very delicious experience of life," thought Dollamore, as he laid aside his book; "I could not have had a more charming field for study. So many different characters too! There is that remarkably uncouth person our host, who is so horribly raw and undisciplined as to be unable to behave himself decently when expecting the last object of his calf-love, And there's that modern Bayard, Alsager, who has undoubtedly a *tendresse* for our hostess, and who as undeniably wore Laura Hammond's colours a little time ago, and bolted because of some inexplicable row with her. And there's Laura Hammond herself—delicious creature—with a newly-caught mouse in her mouth; and yet her eye constantly roving over the late captive playing round her, lest he should escape beyond possibility of recapture. There's that good-looking widow, too, who is as cold as ice, but who is supposed to have thawed a little once in Bayard's favour. And then there's Lady Mitford herself, who is worth all the rest of the women put together. What grace, what beauty, what thoroughly unsophisticated charms and real naturalness of manner! By Jove! compared to her, the widow is a giraffe, and the Hammond a dairy-maid. Talk of their birth and breeding! why this country-parson's daughter has the air and manner of a duchess. They will try and set upon her when she comes to town,—that old Clanronald, who looks like a cook, and the Tappington with her three daughters like grenadiers in petticoats; but if she has any pluck—and I think she has, under all that quietude—she'll ride them down right and left; and she'll have all the men on her side, though I don't know that that's any pull. Meantime this oaf is entertaining an angel unawares, and neglecting her,—is standing at the door of his tent ogling the daughters of the Cities of the Plain. So much the better for Bayard and—and for others. But the *imbroglio* is delightful, and I couldn't wish for better fun than to stand by and watch the play; cutting-in of course when I see a chance of holding winning cards."

And then Lord Dollamore rubbed his hands with great gusto, and applied himself with renewed delight to his volume of French philosophy.

At length the noise of wheels on the hard drive was heard, and Sir Charles rang the bell and summoned the servants, and, had the hall-door thrown open, and stood on the steps ready to receive his guests in person. Drawn by four horses at full gallop, Mr. Hammond's carriage came thundering along the drive, and ere it pulled up at the door Lady Mitford had joined her husband, prepared to echo his words of welcome. With her came Colonel Alsager,—carrying in his hand a light shawl, which he pressed upon her acceptance when he saw the door open, and felt the rush of the cold air, which sent the flames roaring up from the great open fireplace,—and also Lord Dollamore, who smiled placidly to himself as he saw this act of attention. "None but your regular Bayard would have done that," said he to himself; "wonderfully thoughtful fellows they are, by Jove!" He suffered under a slight lameness, and always carried a Malacca cane, with an ivory crutch-handle, declared by the men at the club to be his familiar, the recipient of his confidence, and the suggester of many of his iniquities. He carried it now, and rapped it against his teeth, and laid it to his ear, as though he were listening to its counsel.

"There they are," he continued, "in a close carriage of course, because of my husband's health; but I'm at the open window, and remarkably well I look. Blue always became me, and my eyes are bright, and I've got a high colour. How do you do? My hand out at the window, and a very palpable squeeze to the oaf, who is blushing, by Jove, like a great schoolboy,—a very palpable squeeze. Steps down now, and, leaning heavily on his arm, out we jump, and—O yes, dear Lady Mitford! Kiss, kiss—you she-Judas!—and—hallo! rather astonished at seeing Bayard, eh? How do you do, Colonel Alsager? I scarcely thought you would be here. No, of course not; one string too many for her bow. Now for me!—Needn't ask you how you are, Mrs.

Hammond; never saw you looking more charming.—And she smiles and passes on. Lord help us! is this Percy Hammond, this unfortunate object that they are helping out now? Why, he's only a year or two older than I; left Haileybury while I was at Eton; but what an awful wreck he is! What on earth made him marry a second time,—especially such a woman as this! Hallo! who have we here? Tall young woman; severely got up, but a neat figure, and a good stepper too. Very cold bow from Sir Charles; little hand-shake from my lady. Must be the governess. O yes, that's it; and there's the child. Now, then, all the characters are assembled; ring up the curtain—the play's begun."

Lord Dollamore was right; it had been a palpable hand-squeeze, palpable to him, palpable to Laurence Alsager, palpable to her from whom it should have been specially hidden—Lady Mitford. She saw it, but could scarcely believe she had seen aright; but then she noticed the manner in which Mrs. Hammond leaned on Sir Charles's arm, and a certain look which passed between them as she alighted. The next instant her guest had caught hold of both her hands, and was embracing her with effusion; but just before Georgie had had time to steal one glance at Laurence Alsager's face, and to read in the lowering brow and compressed lips that he too had noticed the *empressement* of the meeting. The whole thing was so thoroughly strange to her, so utterly unexpected, that she did not know how to act. Her first impulse was to drag herself out of Mrs. Hammond's embrace, to call her a false bad woman, and to go off in a flood of tears; but fortunately she did not attempt this experiment. She did the very best thing under the circumstances, and that was—nothing. She freed herself from her visitor's embracing arms when she had unresponsive received her kiss, and murmured a few commonplaces about her delight at seeing her; and then she went forward to say a passing word of kindness to Mr. Hammond as he was helped past her by his servants, to exchange salutations with Miss Gillespie, and to kiss the child's forehead. By this time she was perfectly ready to do the honours of her house, and to follow her husband, on whose arm Mrs. Hammond was already leaning, to the suite of rooms prepared for the guests. These were, as Sir Charles had said, the best in the house; and as they entered them, Georgie remembered how he had specially reserved them for the Hammonds, and she winced as her eye lighted on a splendid bouquet of hot-house flowers arranged in a vase on the writing-table. The fires burned brightly, and there was a sufficient air of comfort to justify Mrs. Hammond in clasping her hands and exclaiming, "How very, very charming! Everything in such exquisite taste; and oh, what lovely flowers, Lady Mitford! you know my passion for flowers, and have indeed taken pains to gratify it. Georgie bowed in an icy manner, and Sir Charles glowed from his head to his feet.

"It's too late to look out now, but I've no doubt that the prospect's delightful."

"Looks towards the south. Good for Hammond, and that kind of thing," said Sir Charles, explanatorily.

"We'll leave you now, Mrs. Hammond; the first dinner-bell has just rung," said Georgie, moving towards the door.

"Anything you want you've only to ring for, you know; so find out something to ask for by dinner-time. Do! you know you've only to ask and have in this house."

Georgie did not hear this last remark. She was hurrying as quickly as she could towards her own room; and on reaching it she flung herself on a sofa, and burst into tears.

It was the custom at Redmoor to assemble previous to the announcement of dinner in the library,—a large room, rather solemn with its dark oak bookcases, and when lighted only by two or three moderator-lamps, placed on small tables. Such was Sir Charles's whim; he had a notion that the removal from darkness to light awoke a corresponding cheerfulness; and though it had been often combated by Georgie, on this occasion she was grateful for any respite from the public gaze, and every opportunity of recovering her wonted calmness. Clang! goes the gong. "Dinner is served." Through the indistinct gloom Mrs. Hammond is seen sailing away on the arm of Sir Charles. Alsager has the widow for his companion, and feels a thrill run up his coat-sleeve, to which the arm within his coat-sleeve does not respond. There are officers from the garrison, who file off with the Tyrrell girls and with the young ladies, members of the neighbouring families; and the procession is closed by Lady Mitford, escorted by Lord Dollamore, who takes the opportunity of saying, "Charming woman Mrs. Hammond; so frank, ingenuous, and open! So devoted to her poor invalid husband—don't you think so?" And when Lady Mitford responds, "Yes, O yes, quite so," Lord Dollamore lifts the ivory crutch-handle of his Malacca cane to his mouth, and seems whispering to it untellable jokes.

The dinner was very good; but that was more due to Bligh than to any one else, even to Lady Mitford. The *chef* who had been let to the Mitfords with the house in Eaton Place had stuck to his bargain, and refused to go into the country. He had his club, his *menus plaisirs*, and he declined to leave them. So the jolly Captain looked about, took Mrs. Austin the housekeeper into confidence, and found out from her that there was a woman who had lived as kitchen-maid in the first families, and who had always thought of bettering herself, but never had the chance, and was then at Sir John Rumbold's, hard by. This person was fetched over, and directed to try her prentice-hand at cooking a steak and a potato for Captain Bligh, that achievement being, as he opined, the great touchstone of the culinary art; and having been thoroughly successful, she was borrowed for a few days and further tried, and finally engaged. The dinner was so good that every one enjoyed it, even poor Percy Hammond, who had roused himself sufficiently to come to table, and whose eyes brightened under the influence of a bottle of the celebrated old Madeira placed at his side. It was not the old Madeira which caused Mrs. Hammond's eyes to brighten, but they had never shone more brilliantly, and her spirits had never been higher. She talked incessantly, addressing her conversation chiefly to her host, on whose right hand she was seated.

"I suppose you have some charming old places about here, Sir Charles?—abbeys, and ruins, and castles," said she after a pause.

"I daresay there are, but as I have only just come here, you know, I can't say. Major Maxse, no doubt, can tell you; they've been quartered in the neighbourhood for the last twelve months, and know every inch of it.—Maxse, Mrs. Hammond asks whether there are any old ruins, castles, abbeys, that sort of thing, in the neighbourhood. I tell her she should inquire of you, a the likeliest person to know."

Major Maxse, the gentleman addressed, a good-looking middle-aged man, replied, "Well, I really think I might earn an honest livelihood by setting up as guide to this region. Though we've been here little more than a twelvemonth, I've been so horribly bored that I think I have explored every nook and corner of the country within a circle of fifty miles; and I am very happy to tell Mrs. Hammond that there are all sorts of ruins for her to choose from, with all sorts of architecture, and all sorts of legends attached. For example, there's Egremont Priory."

"That's Boscastle's place, isn't it?" said Lord Dollamore, from the other end of the table; "who made the legend about that? one of the family probably; for there never was a Boscastle yet who was known to speak truth, even by accident."

"First-rate place for wild-ducks," said Major Winton: "don't send any confounded picnic people there, Maxse; they'll scare the birds."

"Even at the risk of being considered confounded picnic people, if it's a pretty place, and has a good story attached to it, I propose that we make a party and go," said Georgie.

She was a little astonished at herself when she had said this, but she had said it purposely. She was wondering what it was that had attracted her husband in Mrs. Hammond which she herself did not possess; and she thought perhaps it was a certain dash and verve, to which she had never pretended, but which her rival undoubtedly displayed. Poor Georgie felt that perhaps she had been a little too tame and sedate; and this speech was her first attempt in the opposite direction.

"Charmingly said, Lady Mitford; the very thing," said Mrs. Hammond. "And I think we could go, even if there were no story at all—"

"There's round tower which is occupied by an old woman, who'll boil potatoes, and lay the cloth, and that kind of thing—all under shelter, you know," said Captain Bligh, who was of an eminently practical turn.

"O no; but we must have the legend," said Lord Dollamore. "Come, Major Maxse, you don't get off telling us the Boscastle legend."

"Oh, it's the old story with the usual ingredients—love and a ghost," said Major Maxse.

"Yes; but what love? whose ghost?" asked Mrs. Hammond. "You promised to tell me, Major Maxse, and we're all attention."

"It is simply this. After the Restoration Roger Boscastle, who had been serving with the Royalists from the beginning of the war, and who had had to fly the country after Naseby, came back to his estates and to his wife, who during her husband's absence had been living with her own family, strict Parliamentarians. Lady Boscastle was a very lovely woman; but a little strict and rigid, and scarcely suited to a rollicking swashbuckler like her husband. One day there arrived at Egremont Priory a troop of horse escorting a beautiful lady and her father, both foreigners, who had done the king much service in time of need, and who had known Roger Boscastle when abroad. Roger seemed very much surprised to see them, and so did Lady Mildred; the latter more especially when first the old nobleman threw his arms round Roger's neck and exclaimed, 'Mon fils!' and then the young lady did ditto and exclaimed, 'Mon amour!' but they were neither of them so astonished as were the old gentleman and the young lady when Roger led Lady Mildred forward and presented her as his wife. They were thoroughly taken aback, and the young lady muttered to Roger under her breath something which Lady Mildred could not catch, but which, by the expression of her eyes, must have been very unpleasant. However, they took up their abode in the castle, whither they had been commended by the king; and they were very polite, especially the lady, to Mildred, who hated her with such hatred as is only felt by a woman who suspects another of carrying on with her husband."

"Bravo, Maxse!" interrupted Lord Dollamore; "gad, that's really quite graphic,— that last sentence. You've mistaken your profession, Maxse; you ought to have been an author."

"I'm afraid the last sentence was cribbed from the *Guidebook* to the county. However, to cut my story short, one night Lady Mildred overheard a conversation between her husband and Pepita (that was the foreign lady's name), from which it was pretty clear that Roger had represented himself as a single man when abroad, and had actually married Pepita. Then Mildred had a stormy interview with Roger, and told him of her intention to leave him the next day and go to her brother. But the next morning she was found dead, stabbed to the heart with a dagger, round the handle of which was a scrap of paper, inscribed 'In a Spaniard's way;' and Pepita, her father, and Roger Boscastle were all gone. The latter came back when quite an old man, but was found dead in his bed the morning after his arrival; frightened, it is supposed, by the ghost of Lady Mildred, which in stormy weather duly walks the castle, wringing its hands and waving the bloody dagger in the air."

"No, I don't like the last bit," said Lord Dollamore; "too much like Richardson's show. All the rest very good and dramatic; don't you think so, Lady Milford?"

"Oh, very good indeed—thoroughly interesting; and, as usual, the only innocent person in the story was punished."

"That was because she was innocent," said Lord Dollamore; "there must have been eligible persons, even among her Roundhead friends; how very much better to have consoled herself with—"

"As usual, you miss the point of the story, Lord Dollamore," said Alsager, hotly interrupting; "surely it would have been better to have been the murdered than the murderess in such a case."

"It's very lucky there are not any such cases now-a-days," said Sir Charles. "No woman would put a knife into another now."

"Into any one who stood between me and my love I would, for one," said Mrs. Hammond under her breath; and she looked for a moment so fierce, that Mitford said, "Gad, I believe you!" in a similar tone.

When the ladies had left the room Laurence Alsager said to Lord Dollamore: "You had heard that story before?"

"What story, my dear Alsager?"

"The legend of Egremont Priory."

"Had I? Not unlikely. You know I'm a very eccentric reader, and delight in odd stories."

"It's a pity you did not save Maxse the trouble of telling it again."

"Do you think so? Well, do you know I can't agree with you? Its recital seemed to bring out the character of some of our friends in the highest degree; and if there is anything I delight in, it is the study of character."

CHAPTER XV.

EGREMONT PRIORY.

Lady Mitford's proposition of a visit to Egremont Priory, though originally made in a kind of bravado, was remembered by most of her guests—notably by Mrs. Hammond, who saw in it a better chance of flirtation than she had had since her arrival at Redmoor. Ever since Georgie had noticed the warm lingering hand-pressure exchanged between her husband and her visitor on that occasion, she had been thoroughly on the *qui vive*, and, like most young women ignorant of the world's ways, had imagined that the best way to nip a flirtation in the bud was by being perpetually observant of all that took place, and by letting the guilty persons know that their conduct was watched. It requires considerable experience before a woman discovers that—so long as the affair is confined within certain bounds—totally to ignore its existence is her very best policy; a policy which saves her from infinite domestic discomfort, and is besides the only possible method of galling her rival.

But Georgie was not only young, but country-bred,—which means a great deal, for London girls at seventeen know more of the world than country girls at five-and-twenty,—and had had scarcely any experience. So she went to work naturally, and betrayed her anger in the plainest manner,—in perpetual supervision, in lip-bitings and hand-clenchings, in occasional tears, which *would* come welling up into her eyes, however far back she might hold her head, and were perfectly visible, however hastily brushed away. To Mrs. Hammond, who was a practised duelist, all this behaviour was delightful; she took it as a tribute to her own powers of fascination, and was proportionately pleased. Flirtation, in its strongest sense, was absolutely necessary to her existence; but she never condescended to boys, and she regarded officers, when merely officers and nothing more, as very small game. She liked to entangle men of position and celebrity, no matter how grave or how old (she had perfectly charmed a bachelor bishop; and the enemies of one of our greatest physicians declared that his wife rendered his home unbearable on account of his attentions to Mrs. Hammond); and the latest literary, artistic, or theatrical lion was usually to be found hovering about her. But far beyond anything else she liked a flirtation with the husband of an acknowledged pretty woman; and the more beautiful the wife, the more bent was Laura Hammond on captivating the husband That gave her greater *éclat* than anything else, and she liked *éclat*. She liked being talked about,—up to a certain point; she liked women to express their wonder at what men could see in her to rave about; she liked to have repeated to her what men said at clubs: "'Str'ord'nary little woman the Hammond! There's Cosmo Gordon been everywhere with her, leaving that lovely wife of his all by herself, by Jove! What the doose can there be in her?" and other speeches of a like nature. She also liked to be on good terms with the wives of her admirers—a thing by no means so difficult as might be imagined by the inexperienced. There are women so spaniel-like in their nature that they will fawn on those who injure them; and some of these consorted with Mrs. Hammond with a vain idea of propitiating her by their forbearance, and thus inducing her to give up the chase. She had at first thought that Georgie Mitford might be of this order; but she was by no means disappointed to find her otherwise. She gloried in a contest out of which she could come victorious, and despised all easy triumphs; there was pleasure in captivating a man whose position or celebrity reflected lustre on his enslaver; but there was tenfold pleasure when he, in his blind infatuation, set the rules of society at defiance, and openly neglected the wife whose beauty had hitherto been his greatest pride.

So Mrs. Hammond reminded Sir Charles that dear Lady Mitford had expressed a wish that they should go over in a party to Egremont Priory, and suggested that he had better see about it at once. Of course Sir Charles saw about it immediately; told Bligh to have some luncheon sent over the next day, and to mind that they had a big fire in the keep, for it was anything but picnic weather; wrote a line to Major Maxse and other officers to join them; and proceeded to poll his visitors as to how they would go over to the spot. How would Mrs. Hammond go? How? Oh, wouldn't dear Lady Mitford ride over with her on horseback? they could get some gentlemen to escort them; and it would be delightful. Dear Lady Mitford was much obliged, but would rather not. Mrs. Hammond could ride over on horseback if she chose, and doubtless would find plenty of cavaliers; but Lady Mitford would drive in a pony-phaeton. Ah, of course! Mrs. Hammond had forgotten Lady Mitford's charming experience of pony-phaetons; and as she said this she looked round with a light and pleasant smile at Colonel Alsager, who was pulling his black beard, and glowering horribly close by. Sir Charles Mitford had no objection to Georgie's going in a phaeton—no objection to her driving, for the matter of that; but since that accident, it would be better, he thought, to have some one reliable in coachmanship sitting by her: Lord Dollamore, for instance? But Dollamore declared he was the worst whip in the world; his horrible rheumatism had crippled his hands; and why should not that tremendous fellow Alsager, who had already earned the medal of the Humane Society—why should not he go? Ay, Alsager was the very man, Sir Charles thought; and Laurence, though he saw every atom of the play on Dollamore's part, and felt himself completely jockeyed into the position, could discern no way out of it, and assented with apparent delight. He was not too pleased to see a certain look of terror which had pervaded Lady Mitford's face when Dollamore was proposed as charioteer fade away when the other arrangement was finally decided upon. Many men would have taken the change as a compliment; but Laurence had had experience, and thought otherwise. Lord Dollamore, Tom and Mrs. Charteris, one of the Tyrrell girls, and Captain Bligh, might post over in the break; in which also went the luncheon-hampers. Fred Aspen, Ellen Tyrrell, and Major Winton, would ride. So the stud-groom had his orders, and all was arranged. Sir Charles had not said how he intended to go to Egremont Priory, and yet no one was surprised, when the cavalcade was on the point of setting out, to see his big horse Tambour Major brought out by the stud-groom, who was closely followed by a helper leading Lady Jane—a very dark iron-gray mare—with a lady's saddle on her. No one doubted for an instant for whom the lady's horse was intended. A bright red spot burned on Lady Mitford's cheek; and as she settled herself in the phaeton by Laurence's side, she said in a loud and marked tone, "I hope, Colonel Alsager, I shall not have occasion to-day to increase the debt of gratitude I already owe to you."

Mrs. Masters raised her eyebrows as Lord Dollamore assisted her into the break, and afterwards had two minutes' confidential whispering with Miss Tyrrell; and Mrs. Charteris had scarcely time to frown down old Tom, who was always full of his gaucheries, before he had ejaculated, "Making the running early, eh? ah, haw, haw!"

Sir Charles Mitford saw nothing of this little performance; but Mrs. Hammond, whose eyes and ears were everywhere at once, lost not one single scrap of it. So, just before the word for starting was given, while Mrs. Masters was doing her whispering, and Lady Mitford was burning with anger, and Captain Bligh was peering into the various hampers to see that nothing had been forgotten; while Sir Charles himself, intoxicated with her wonderful piquancy (she never looked to such advantage as in her riding-habit), was coming across to mount her, she turned calmly round, and said in a voice which could be heard by all round, "No,—thanks, Sir Charles—I won't trespass on your attention. As host you have all sorts of things to look after and to do.—Major Winton, if that chestnut will stand for half a minute—here, boy, look to his head!— I'll get you to mount me, and if you'll permit me I'll join your party. I'm the best of chaperons, Major; and when it's required, my talent for admiring the landscape is enormous."

This last was uttered *sotto voce*, and with a quick side-glance towards Ellen Tyrrell. It was a clever move; and though by no means convincing, had some effect on all the party. Sir Charles bowed, sprang on Tambour Major, and rode away with disgust plainly visible in every feature; Lady Mitford looked disconcerted; so did Alsager, though he understood it all; Dollamore took his familiar stick in consultation, and whispered to it that she was a devilish clever little woman; Tom Charteris winked quietly at his wife; and Major Winton was delighted. He told some friends afterwards, in the freedom of barrack-room conversation, that he didn't go in for women's society and that sort of thing, you know, and he'd no idea he was so d—d nice.

So they went on. The party in the break was very humorous; they kept up a running fire of jokes against Bligh about something being forgotten, and compelled him (naturally a nervous man, and very proud of his arrangement of such matters) to dive frequently to the bottom of hampers and return with the supposed missing article in his hand, his face purple with stooping and triumph combined. Captain Bligh was not a humorist, but he retorted with several broad allusions to Tom Charteris's distillery; and, a flash of old sporting experience having suddenly revealed to him that there was an affinity of meaning between the words 'gin' and 'snare,' he dilated thereon after a fashion that Mr. George Cruikshank might have envied. They were very quiet in the pony-phaeton, for Georgie was annoyed at having so plainly shown her anger; and Laurence, finding that his few remarks about the weather and the scenery only gained monosyllabic answers, soon lapsed into silence. Sir Charles was seen going across country at a great pace, apparently comforting himself by taking it out of Tambour Major, and clearing everything in first-rate style. The mounted party seemed to enjoy themselves most of all; Major Winton was in the seventh heaven, for Mrs. Hammond did all the talking, requiring him only to throw in an occasional word, and she looked so fascinating that he devoted himself to her during the ride, entirely neglecting Ellen Tyrrell—to that young lady's great gratification, be it said, as she regarded the Major as a fogie, and was infinitely better pleased with the attentions of one of the officers who joined the cavalcade just as it emerged on the Redmoor.

The winter picnic passed off much more pleasantly than might have been augured from its commencement. During the drive Georgie had had time deliberately to examine herself, and to arrive at the conclusion that what she was doing was very foolish, and more than that, she was afraid, very wrong. It might be that her own jealousy had jaundiced her ideas; it might be that the pressure of the hand from which her misgiving first dated, was entirely imaginary. What right had she to suspect Charley of fickleness? Had he not proved his truth in the noblest way, by coming back to her in the time of his prosperity and raising her to her present position? Was it likely, then, that he would so suddenly change? Yes, she had been very wrong to permit the growth of such horrible suspicions, and she would make up for it to Charley by tenfold warmth and affection. Georgie's already-suffused face deepened in hue as she remembered what, in the bitterness of her spirit, she had said to Colonel Alsager on taking her seat in the phaeton. What could he have thought of her? Whatever he may have thought, nothing could be gathered from the calm grave expression of his face. Very likely he guessed what was passing through his companion's mind; for from the little he had seen of Georgie, he believed her to possess more commonsense than is given to the average woman, and he was certain she could show it in no better way than by totally ignoring this business, at all events in its present stage. Laurence saw plainly enough Mrs. Hammond's intentions. There was not a point in her system of strategy which he did not comprehend; and he also saw that Mitford was morally weak, and obviously flattered by her attentions. In the present stage of affairs, however, for Lady Mitford to show herself annoyed was the very worst policy she could adopt; and while she kept silence Laurence guessed she was arguing the question within herself, and earnestly hoped she would come to the right decision. He knew she had done so when, just as they were nearing their destination, she looked up with a bright smile and said, "I have been a very dull companion, I am afraid, Colonel Alsager! but the truth is I was full of thought."

"A bad thing to bring out to a picnic, Lady Mitford. I should advise you to discard it as speedily as possible."

"I fully intend to do so, and hope every one else will follow your advice. By the way, I may say, 'Physician, heal thyself;' for you've been most sedate ever since we started."

"I was wondering," laughed Laurence, "among other things, what the groom seated behind us could think of us. He's young, I see, and may possibly therefore imagine that silence is a sign of good breeding."

"In that case, in his opinion we must be perfect aristocrats, for we've not exchanged a word. Ah, here comes the cavalcade; how well Mrs. Hammond looks!— doesn't she? and how perfectly she sits her horse!"

"Yes, she rides admirably, and—ah, I thought so; she has just discovered we were looking at her, or she would not have done that."

"That" was to put her horse at a bit of bank and hedge bordering the grass-meadow, on which she and her party were cantering. She cleared it admirably, and drew rein close by the phaeton. As her horse jumped, Mrs. Hammond caught Laurence's eye, and her own lighted up with a saucy triumph; the exercise had done her good, and she was in great spirits.

"Well, dear Lady Mitford, I hope you've enjoyed your drive; no accident this time, I see. But Colonel Alsager is a good whip.—I've heard your praises sung often by men who really understand the subject, Colonel Alsager. They say you have the very hand for a restive animal—light, but firm."

"They get away from me sometimes, though, Mrs. Hammond," said Laurence, looking up.

"Ah, that happens with every one," she replied; "but you always conquer at last, don't you?"

"Always; and when I get them in hand again, I make them remember their freaks, and pay for them."

"You're quite right," said she carelessly. "Ah, here is Major Winton. I assure you, Lady Mitford, the Major is the most perfect escort; full of talk and fun, he never suffers you to be dull for an instant. And there's the break arrived, and that energetic Captain Bligh managing everything as usual. What very large hampers! And I declare there's Sir Charles arrived before any of us, and superintending the laying of the cloth in that romantic-looking old tower."

Lady Mitford caught sight of her husband at the same time, and hurried off to him. She was full of penitence, and wanted to set herself right with him at once.

"Ah, and there's Lady Mitford off at the mere sound of his name. Look at that, Colonel Alsager, and—will you have the kindness to help me to dismount, Colonel Alsager?—No, thank you, Major, I won't trouble you; the Colonel is already on the ground. There, Laurence Alsager," she whispered, as she sprang from the saddle, "that is what I pine for,—domestic love;" and she heaved a little sigh, and tapped the ground with the delicate little riding-boot, which the lifting of her habit had exposed.

For an instant Laurence was taken off his guard, and said bitterly, "When you might have had it, you spurned it;" then recovering himself, he added, "However, we have had that out once, and—"

"And here is Major Winton," said Mrs. Hammond in her airiest manner. "Luncheon already, eh? then you shall give me your arm, Major, for this turf-hill is awkward to climb, especially in a habit."

Meanwhile Georgie had hurried away to where her husband was standing watching the laying of the cloth in the one room of the keep, by the old *châtelâine* and her granddaughter. Georgie made her way up to him, and with the tears rising in her eyes, said, "Oh, Charley, I'm so glad I have found you; I wanted to speak to you."

"Did you, little woman?" said he, looking down at her in great astonishment; "what about? Nothing left behind, is there?"

"No; that is—at least—I don't know; it was not about that I wanted to speak."

"What was it, then? Nothing the matter with the ponies?—not another accident, eh?"

"No, O no; I only wanted to say that I hoped you would not be annoyed at—at anything I did when we started from home to-day—about the way in which the party was divided, I mean."

"Why, you silly little woman, of course not; you had nothing to do with it. If Winton chose to make himself ridiculous, it wasn't your fault. There, come, dry your eyes, Georgie, and let's go and look after the people."

So, then, he had not noticed her anger or her foolish speech at all. Georgie hardly knew whether to be pleased or vexed at the discovery.

The indefatigable Captain Bligh had now brought his arrangements to a head, and all was ready for luncheon. A large fire burned in the great open fireplace of the old room, lighting up the grim old walls, and flickering through the narrow slips and embrasures, whence in old days the archers had done good service. Lady Mitford headed the table, with Lord Dollamore and Major Maxse, who had ridden over with some of his brother officers, on either side. Mrs. Masters was delighted to find herself next to Colonel Alsager; Tom Charteris was placed opposite the largest piece of cold beef, and told to go on carving it until somebody stopped him; Mrs. Charteris was acting as a kind of female aide-de-camp to Captain Bligh; and if Mrs. Hammond found Major Winton, who was on one side of her, unusually talkative, she could make no such complaint of Sir Charles Mitford, who sat on the other side, and was unusually silent.

The meal went off with great success. Everybody was hungry, and nearly everybody was good-tempered; there was abundance of champagne, and the officers and the young ladies had a great deal of laughter; and then they set out to explore the ruins, and there was that charming story of the murdered lady, and the spot where she appeared was pointed out by the old housekeeper, who told the legend in a deliciously-funny manner; and Tom Charteris hid himself behind a buttress, and at its conclusion bounced out among them with a great roar, clanking a dog-chain which he had picked up. All the ladies screamed, and Ellen Tyrrell was so frightened that she nearly fainted, and had to be supported by Frank Somers, the officer who had ridden with her from Redmoor; and even when she recovered she was so weak as to be compelled to walk very slowly, so that she and her companion were some distance behind the rest of the party.

With this exception they all kept together; and Georgie had the satisfaction of engaging her husband's arm during the greater portion of their stay. When the time came for their return, the only change made was, that Mrs. Masters had manoeuvred so successfully as to induce Lady Mitford to change places with her,—Georgie returning in the break, and Laurence driving the widow in the phaeton. But this time the equestrians all started together. Sir Charles did not tear away on Tambour Major; for though still annoyed with Mrs. Hammond, he had by this time got his temper under control. It was a trying time for Tambour Major, who hated being held back, and pushed and jumped so as to be very disagreeable company at close quarters. He was very disagreeable indeed to Major Winton, who had eaten a large lunch and wanted to digest it quietly; and equally disagreeable to Frank Somers and Ellen Tyrrell, who were engaged in a conversation which compelled them to keep their horses at a walking-pace. The only person who was really pleased was Mrs. Hammond, who in Tambour Major's struggles and plunges saw her way to the end which she had all along intended to accomplish.

"That's more show than business, I'm thinking, Sir Charles," said she, pointing with her whip to the horse as he gave a tremendous plunge.

"How do you mean 'show,' Mrs. Hammond? I only know it's all I can do to hold him steady."

"Let him have his head, then; he looks as if he would rush his fences, and had not the least notion of steady jumping."

"You should have seen him this morning; he—"

"You took good care I should not, by running away from us."

"He'd do just the same going home. I can take you the way I came, over some of the prettiest jumps you have ever seen," said Mitford, getting nettled about his horse. "Come, who'll follow?"

"I, for one," said Mrs. Hammond; but no one else spoke.

"They only want a lead; come, let us show them the way;" and as he spoke, Sir Charles turned his horse out of the high-road up a short sloping embankment on to a broad stretch of moorland, and with Mrs. Hammond close by his side, was away at full gallop. The rest of the riding party looked after them, but did not attempt to follow. Major Winton, finding himself decidedly *de trop*, lit a cigar, and jogged lazily along by himself, while the others continued their conversation.

Away go the big black horse and the dark iron-gray, side by side, flying over the purple moorland, Lady Jane holding her own well with her companion, let him tear and struggle as he may to shake her off. Now far away to the right looms dark the first obstacle, which Sir Charles points out with his whip, and at sight of which Mrs. Hammond rings out a merry little laugh. As they approach, it develops itself as a double line of posts and rails, good stiff oak timber, which must either be cleared or declined, through which there is no scrambling. Tambour Major sees it already, and rushes at it with a great snort of triumph, clearing it at a bound. Nor is the gray to be balked; scarcely has he alighted, foam-flecked and trembling, in the field beyond, than Lady Jane is by his side.

"That's number one," said Sir Charles; "the next we shall find just at the end of—" but Mrs. Hammond laid her whip upon his arm. She had previously looked round and marked that they were far out of the range of observation by their late companions.

"Quite enough," she said; "I am satisfied with Tambour Major's performances, and own I did him grievous injustice. From the manner in which he went at that, I am certain he could do anything. Besides," she added, bending forward and patting Lady Jane's neck with her pretty dogskin gauntlet, "I wanted to speak to you."

"To me, Mrs. Hammond?"

"Yes, to you—to you, alone. You are angry with me?"

"I—angry? 'Pon my word I can assure you—I—"

"Ah, don't deny it." Her voice dropped into its most musical and softest key. "Do you think I am not quick to read any change in your manner?"

"No, but really—I haven't the least right to—"

"The least right! I thought you had promised to be my friend,—my firm, steadfast, constant friend. Ah, if you knew how I have longed for such a friend,—one in whom I could confide, and who would advise me!"

She dropped her head on her breast as she said this, and the red rays of the dying sun touched the tight braids of her chestnut hair with gold.

"Such a friend you will find in me," said Mitford; "I meant it when I said it—I mean it now."

"No," said Laura plaintively, "no; you have other ties and other claims upon you, and it must not be. The world cannot understand such confidence as I would give and receive; it is too pure and too earnest for worldly comprehension.—Already—but I won't speak of that."

"Finish your sentence, please."

"No, it was nothing, really nothing."

"Then tell me, or I shall fancy it was something. Tell me."

"How you compel me to obey you! I was going to say—it's excessively silly of me; very probably it was only my own foolish notion, but I'm so nervous and anxious about anything which concerns—my friends; I thought that Lady Mitford seemed a little annoyed at your obvious intention of riding with me this morning."

She stole a look at him under her hat to see how he received this shot.

"Who? Georgie! annoyed? Oh, you must have been mistaken. I should have noticed it in an instant if that had been the case."

"You think so! Well, then, very likely it was my mistake. And I was so frightened, so fearful of causing any misunderstanding between you, so terrified at the thought of getting you into trouble, that I at once called that odious Major Winton into my service, and have suffered him to bore me with his *niaiseries* throughout the day."

"Oh, *that* was the reason that you flirted with Winton, then! I thought—"

"Thought what? Ah, I've caught you! You were angry then?"

"Well, perhaps,—just a little."

"I should have been deeply hurt if you had not been; it would have showed that you had no real interest in me, and that would be dreadful. Just before I knew you, I held my life as utterly valueless, the daily repetition of a dull dreary task,—nothing to live for, nobody to care for. And this morning, when I thought you were really angry with me, that feeling came back so hopelessly—oh, so hopelessly! I think I should die if I had no one to take interest in me now."

She moved her hand towards the little pocket in her saddle-flap for her handkerchief, but he stopped it in its descent and held it in his own.

"While I live," said he, "you will never have cause to make that complaint."

And their eyes met,—hers soft and dreamy, his fierce and eager. A delicious interchange of glances to the persons concerned, but perhaps not so pleasant to a looker-on. Apparently very displeasing to the only one then present—a tall slim woman, picking her way in a very cattish manner across the adjoining meadow; who stopped on catching sight of the equestrians, frowned heavily as she watched them, and crouched under the shadow of the hedge until they had passed.

CHAPTER XVI.

CHECK.

The day after the winter picnic Sir Charles Mitford sat in that little snuggery next his dressing-room, which had been so deftly fitted up for him by Captain Bligh, in the enjoyment of a quiet after-breakfast pipe. Breakfast was on the table at Redmoor from nine to twelve. Each guest chose his own time for putting in an appearance; rang for his or her special teapot, special relay of devilled kidney, ham, kipper, eggs, or bloater; found his or her letters placed in close proximity to his or her plate; breakfasted, and then went away to do exactly as he or she liked until luncheon, which was the real gathering hour of the day. On the morning in question everybody had been late, except Major Winton, who, deeply disgusted with the proceedings of the previous day, had routed up one of the under-keepers at daybreak, and trudged away to his usual shooting-ground. Sir Charles had turned out at ten, but had found no one in the breakfast-room save Captain Bligh, deep in the perusal of the newly-arrived copy of *Bell's Life*. So Sir Charles read his letters, which were of a prosaic business-like character, and ate his breakfast, which he rather enjoyed, and then went up to his room, taking the *Times* with him. Not, however, for the purpose of reading it— Charley seldom resorted to that means of passing time; he never could understand what fellows saw to read in the papers; for beyond the police intelligence and the sporting-news and the advertisements of horses to be sold, all that enormous sheet of news, gathered with such care and expense, was utterly blank to him. To-day he did not even want to read his usual portion of the paper; he took it up with him half-unconsciously; he wanted to smoke and to think—to smoke a little and to think a great deal.

So he sat before the cheerful fire in the cosey little room, the firelight glancing on the red-flock paper, and illumining the "Racing Cracks" and the "Coaching Recollections;" pictures which the Messrs. Fores furnished for the delectation of the sporting men of those days, and which are never seen in these. They were better and healthier in tone than the studies of French females now so prevalent, and infinitely more manly and national. The smoke from his pipe curled round his head, and as he lay back in his chair and watched it floating in its blue vapour, his thoughts filled him with inexpressible pleasure. He was thinking over what had happened the day before, and to him the picnic was as nothing. He only remembered the ride home. Yes; his thoughts were very, very pleasant; his vanity had been flattered, his fur had been stroked the right way. This was his first experience of flirtation since his marriage; and he stood higher than usual in his own opinion when he found that he had attracted the notice of—to say the least of it—a very pretty woman. Very pretty; no doubt about that! By Jove! she looked perfection in that tight-fitting robe. What a splendid figure she had,—so round and plump, and yet so graceful; and her general turn-out was so good—such natty gloves and jolly little white collars and cuffs, and such a neat riding-whip! And that lovely chestnut hair, gathered into that gleaming coil of braids under her chimney-pot hat! How beautifully she rode too! went at those posts and rails as calmly as though she had been cantering in the Row. He watched her as the mare rose at them; and but for a little tightening of the mouth, not a feature of her face was discomposed, while most women would have turned blue through sheer fright, even if they would have had pluck to face such a jump at all, which he doubted.

It was uncommonly pleasant to think that such a woman was interested in him; would look forward to his presence, would regret his absence, and would associate him with her thoughts and actions. What an earnest, impulsive, sensitive creature she was! She had seen in an instant what had annoyed him yesterday! Not like Georgie—he felt a slight twinge of conscience as he thought of her—not like Georgie, who had supposed he was vexed at something she had said, poor child! No; that other woman was really wonderful—so appreciative and intelligent. How cleverly she had befooled that hard-headed old Winton for the sake of keeping things square! Winton was like a child in her hands; and though he could not bear ladies' society, and was supposed to be never happy except when shooting or smoking, had cantered by her side and tried to make civil little speeches, and bowed and smiled like a fellow just fresh from Eton. And how cleverly she had managed that business about their getting away when she wanted to speak to him! Poor little thing, how frightened she was too at the idea of his being angry, as though one could be angry with a creature like that! And how pretty she looked when her eyes filled with tears and her voice trembled! Gad! she must feel something stronger than interest in him for her to show all that. Yes, by Jove!—there was no use in denying it to himself any longer,—this little woman was thoroughly fascinated. He recalled the events of that homeward ride—the talk, the looks, the long, long hand-clasp, the passionate manner in which, just before they reached the house, she had implored him to remember that she counted on him, and on him alone, for advice and aid in the troubles of her life. By the way what were the troubles of her life? She had dwelt very much upon them generally, but had never thought it necessary to go into detail. She spoke frequently of being tied to an invalid husband, of having been intended originally for something better than a sick man's nurse; but that could not prey upon her mind very much, as she was scarcely ever with her husband, or if it did, it was not a case in which any advice or any aid of his would be of much use to her. No; the advice and aid, and the intimate friendship, were devices by which she was endeavouring to blind herself and him to the real state of the case, to the fact that she was deeply, madly in love with him, and that he—well, he—What was that? a rustle of a dress in the passage outside, a low tap at the door. Can it be she?

The door opened, and a woman entered—not Mrs. Hammond, but Miss Gillespie. Sir Charles Mitford's heart had beat high with expectation; its palpitation continued when he recognized his visitor, though from a different cause. He had risen, and remained standing before the fire; but Miss Gillespie made herself comfortable in a velvet *causeuse* on the other side of the snug fireplace, and pointing to his chair, said:

"You had better sit down again. I shall be some time here."

As though involuntarily, Mitford re-seated himself. He had scarcely done so when she said:

"You did not expect me? You don't seem glad to see me?"

"Are you surprised at that?" he sneered. "I should be glad never to set eyes on you again."

"Exactly; as we used to say in the old days, 'them's my sentiments.' I reciprocate your cordial feelings entirely. And I can't conceive what adverse fate drove you to come with a pack of swaggering, sporting, vulgar people, into a part of the country where I happened to be quietly and comfortably settled; for, as I pointed out to you at our last interview, I was the original settler, and it is you who have intruded yourself into my territory."

"You did not come here to repeat that, I suppose?"

"Of course not; and that's exactly a point I want to impress upon you—that I never repeat. I hint, I suggest, I command, or I warn—once; after that I act."

"You act now, you're always acting, you perpetually fancy yourself on the boards. But it does not amuse me, nor suit me either, and I won't have it. What did you come here for?"

"Not to amuse you, Sir Charles Mitford, you may be certain, nor to be amused myself; for a heavier specimen of our landed gentry than yourself is not, I should hope for the credit of the country, to be found. You were never much fun; and it was only your good looks, and a certain soft manner that you had, that made you get on at all in our *camaraderie*. No; I came here on business."

"On business! Ah, it's not very difficult to imagine what kind of business. You want money, of course, like the rest of them."

"I want money, and come to *you* for it! No, Charles Mitford; you ought to know me better than that. You ought to know that if I were starving, I would steal a loaf from a child, or rob a church, rather than take, much more ask for, a single penny from you. Like the rest of them, did you say? So they have found you out and begun to bleed you!—the pitiful curs!"

"Well, what do you want, then? My time's precious."

"It is indeed, my friend; if you did but know all, you'd find it very precious indeed. But never mind that; now for my business. I want you to do something."

"And that is—"

"To give up making love to Mrs. Hammond. Now, be quiet; don't put yourself in a rage, and don't try those uplifted eyebrows, and that general expression of injured astonishment, on me, because it won't do. I was not born last week, and my capacity for gauging such matters is by no means small. Besides, I happened yesterday to be taking my walks abroad in a meadow not far from the western lodge of Redmoor

Park, the seat of Sir Charles Mitford, Bart., and I happened to witness an interview of a very tender and touching kind, which took place between a lady and a gentleman both on horseback. I imagined something of the kind was going on. I saw something when you were leaving the house that night at Torquay which would have surprised any one who had not learned as much of Mrs. Hammond as I had during the time I had been with her. But since we have been here my suspicions have been confirmed, and yesterday's proceedings left no doubt upon my mind So I determined to speak to you at once, and to tell you that this must not and shall not be!"

Mitford's face grew very dark as he said:

"And suppose I were to ask you how the flirtation which you allege exists between me and—and the lady you have named,—which I utterly and entirely deny,—suppose I were to ask how this flirtation affects you, and, in short, what the devil business it is of yours?"

"How it affects me? Why—no, but that's too preposterous. Not even you, with all your vanity, could possibly imagine that I have in my own mind consented to forget the past, that I have buried the hatchet, that I have returned to my *premier amour*, and am consequently jealous of your attentions to Mrs. Hammond."

"I don't suppose that. But I can't see what other motive you can possibly have."

"You can't, and you never shall. I don't choose to tell you; perhaps I have taken compassion on your wife, who is very pretty—of her style—and seems very good and all that, and very fond of you, poor silly thing! and I don't choose her to be tormented by you. Perhaps I want that poor wretched invalid to die in peace, and not to have his life suddenly snuffed out by the scandal which is sure to arise if this goes on. Perhaps—but no matter! I don't intend to give my reasons, and I've told you what I want."

"And suppose I tell you—as I do tell you—I won't do what you want, and I defy you! What then?"

"Then I will compel you."

"Will you? Do you think I don't know the screw which you would put on me? You'd proclaim all about my former life, my connection with that rascally crew, of whom you were one—"

"Who brought me into it?"

"No matter;—of whom you were one! You'd rake up that story of the bill with my uncle's name to it. Well, suppose you did. What then? It would be news to nobody here—they all know of it."

"No, they don't all know of it. Lord Dollamore does, and so does that good-looking man with the beard, Colonel Alsager, and perhaps Captain Bligh. But I doubt if one of the others ever heard of it: these things blow over, and are so soon forgotten. And it would be very awkward to have the story revived here. Why, the county families who have called, and are inclined to be civil—I heard you boasting of it the other day—would drop you a like red-hot coal. The officers quartered in the barracks would cut you dead; the out-going regiment would tell the story to the in-coming regiment; you would never get a soul over here to dinner or to stop with you, and you would be bored to death. That's not a pleasant lookout, is it?"

He sat doggedly silent until she spoke again.

"But that is not nearly all. I have it in my power to injure your position as well as your reputation; to compel you to change that pretty velvet lounging-coat for a suit of hodden gray, that meerschaum-bowl for a lump of oakum, this very cheery room for—But there's no need to dilate on the difference: you'll do what I ask?"

"And suppose I were to deny all your story."

"Ah, now you're descending to mere childishness. How could you deny what all the men I have mentioned know thoroughly well? They are content to forget all about it now, and to receive you as a reclaimed man; but if they were asked as men of honour whether or not there had been such a scandal, of course they would tell the truth. Come, you'll do what I ask?"

She had won the day; there was no doubt about that. Any bystander, had one been there, could have told it in a moment; could have read it in his sullen dogged look of defeat, in her bright airy glance of triumph.

"You'll do what I ask?"

"You have me in your hands," he said in a low voice.

"I knew you would see it in the right light," she said, "You see, after all, it's very little to give up; the flirtation is only just commencing, so that even you, with your keen susceptibility, cannot be hard hit yet. And you have such a very nice wife, and it will be altogether so much better for you now you are *rangé*, as they say. You'll have to go to the village-church regularly when you're down here, and to become a magistrate, and to go through all sorts of other respectabilities with which this style of thing would not fit at all. Now, goodbye;" and she turned to go.

"Stay!" he called out; "when may I expect a repetition of this threat for some new demand?"

"That rests entirely with yourself. As I have said from the first, I did not seek you; you intruded yourself into my circle. I like my present mode of life—for the present—and don't want to change it. Keep clear of me, and we shall never clash. Again, goodbye."

She made a pretty little bow and, undulating all over, left the room as quietly as she had entered it.

When she had closed the door Mitford rose from his chair with a long sigh of relief, loosened his cravat, and shook his fist.

"Yours to-day, my lady—yours to-day; but my chance will come, and when it does, look out for yourself."

CHAPTER XVII.

COUNTERCHECK.

Mr. Effingham began to think that the position of affairs was growing serious. A month had elapsed since his interview with old Mr. Lyons at the Net of Lemons, and he had not gained one scrap of information as to the whereabouts of the holder of the forged bill, which was to be held *in terrorem* over Sir Charles Mitford for money-extracting purposes, and which was finally to be given up for an enormous round sum. Not a single scrap; and worse than all, he had so devoted himself to this one scent, that his other chances of money-getting were falling into disuse. Not that there was much to be done elsewhere; it was the off-racing season, so that his trade of tipster and tout, with occasional sallies into the arena of welching, could not have been turned to very profitable purpose. The Bank authorities had lately been terribly wideawake; several packets of slippery greasy half-crowns, and many rolls of soft sleezy bank-notes, lay hid in their manufacturer's and engraver's workshops, waiting a better time for their circulation. There had been some notable burglaries both in town and country. Gentlemen with blackened faces who wore smock-frocks over their ordinary clothes had done some very creditable work in out-of-the-way mansions and London houses whose owners were entertaining company in the country, and the melting-pots of old Mr. Lyons and others of his fraternity were rarely off the fire. But this branch of trade was entirely out of Mr. Effingham's line. "He's a good 'un at passing a half-bull or at spinning a flash fiver. There's a air about him that goes down uncommon. He's fust-rate for that, is D'Ossay Butler; but as rank a little cur as ever waddled. When he thinks traps is on, he's off; and as to my cracksman's business, or anything where pluck's wanted, Lor' bless you, you might as well have a girl in highstrikes as D'Ossay." That was what his companions said of him, and it was pretty nearly true. Where a little swaggering bantam-cock demeanour was of use, D'Ossay succeeded; but where anything like physical courage or physical force was required, he was no good at all.

When the lion is on short commons, the jackal is generally in a very bad way. If Mr. D'Ossay Butler was hard up, the condition of tall-hatted Mr. Griffiths was necessarily frightful. That worthy member of society was financially at the lowest ebb, and had resorted to a trade which he reserved for the depths of despair, a mild cardsharping—a "three, two, and vun" game, in which it was an impossibility for the bystander to point out the exact position of the king—at low public-houses. During all his wanderings, however, he kept his eyes open to the necessity of obeying his instructions from D'Ossay Butler, to the necessity of discovering the whereabouts of Lizzy Ponsford, the holder of the bill. There was no slum that he visited; no public-house, where he first propitiated the landlord by the purchase of half-a-pint of ale, and then proceeded to suggest to the notice of the two or three sawney-looking men at the bar a "curious little game he had there, at which 'atfuls of money had been von, and which was the favourite recreation of the horficers of the Queen's Life-Guards at the Windsor Barracks, where he'd 'ad the pleasure of introducin' it 'imself;" no pedestrian ground, no penny-gaff, where he did not get into conversation with somebody connected with the premises, and try to worm out that all-important secret. But all was of no avail. Many of the persons he spoke to knew or had heard of Tony Butler, and paid many handsome compliments to the deceased—"a vide-avake vun and no mistake," "a feller as vould take your coat off your back on to his own," &c.; but very few had known Lizzie Ponsford, and those had not seen or heard of her for a considerable time.

So Mr. Griffiths began to keep clear of Mr. Effingham. There was nothing to be got from his employer but abuse, and that was an article of which Mr. Griffiths perhaps had a surfeit, especially after he had picked up a few stray eighteenpences from the frequenters of the Pig and Whistle, at the noble game of the "three, two, and vun." But one night, finding himself in the neighbourhood of the Strand, and having had rather a successful evening,—he had won fifteen shillings from a sailor, at a public-house in Thames Street; a sailor who paid him rigidly, and then cursed him for an adjective swab and kicked him into the street,—Mr. Griffiths thought he would take a little refreshment at Johnson's. On presenting the crown of his hat within the swing-doors, that article was immediately recognized by Mr. Effingham, seated moodily in the nearest box, and its owner hailed in the nearest approach to a voice of thunder which that small gentleman could accomplish.

"Come in; I see you!" called out the little man. "I've been wondering what had become of you all this time. I thought you'd gone to stay with some swell in the country for the hunting-season. I was goin' to ask if they had got your address at the *Morning-Post* office, that I might write you a line and see if you could find it convenient to lend me a trifle."

"You must be in luck to have such spirits, D'Ossay,—you must," said Mr. Griffiths sententiously. "Out of collar and out at elbows—that's what I've been out of. Look at my coat," pointing to his arms; "shining like bees-wax. Look at my crabshells," pointing to his boots; "as leaky as an old punt, reg'larly wore down to the sewin', and all through elberin' and cadgin' my way into every crib where I thought there was a chance of my comin' at what we wanted to know."

"And what good have you done with all that tremenduous exertion?"

"No good,—not a scrap. I suppose you've been at the same game? How have you got on?"

"About the same as you have. Just as 'ealthy my lookout is."

"Well, I'll tell you what I intend to do. I've worked high and low, here and there, like a blessed black slave, to find out where this gal is, and I've had no luck no more than you have. And I intend to cut it. I'm sick of all this dodgin' and divin', and askin' everybody after somebody that nobody knows. I intend to cut it. That's what I intend!"

"And let it go altogether, after all the trouble we've had; after— Not such a flat, Griffiths; don't you fear. Look here, my boy," said Mr. Butler, putting his hand into his waistcoat-pocket, and producing therefrom two sovereigns; "do you see that couple of quid? That, with a shilling and a fourpenny bit, is all that remains to your friend D'Ossay of the current coin of this realm—the real business, I mean, and no fakement. But these two simple skivs shall be turned into fifty or a hundred before the end of the week. And to show you that I'm not boasting, I'll stand a drink. Here, waiter!—brandy hot, two!"

Mr. Griffiths gazed in double admiration at his friend's generosity and pluck; but low as he was, he really admired the latter, from which he might possibly derive ultimate benefit, more than the former, from which he was about to receive immediate advantage. After the first sip of his grog he said—

"And how's it coming off?"

"I don't mind telling you," said D'Ossay. "There's nothing to hide—why should there be? I'm going to try it on again with our friend the Bart."

"Without the bill?"

"Of course, without the bill, considering that neither you nor I have been able to get hold of it. But didn't I raise a fiftier out of him without the bill before, and why shouldn't I do that, or double that, now?"

"Ah, why indeed?" said Mr. Griffiths, who always coincided when he did not know what else to do, and there was nothing to lose by so doing.

"You see, I thought he might down upon me with the extortion dodge, and hand me over to a bobby. But there's no bobbies where he is now; he couldn't ring the bell and send out that sleek-looking vally, and have me in Vine Street in a brace of shakes. He's down in the country ever so far away. I called at Eaton Place to-day, and they gave me his address."

"And how do you mean to get at him? Not by writin'? Don't trust your fist on paper."

"Teach your grandmother, Griffiths! How do I mean to get at him? Why, by paying one of those yellow-boys to a booking-clerk at 6.30 to-morrow morning, and going down by the Great-Western parliamentary to Torquay, which is close by the swell's place."

"And then?"

"Then I shall put up at some quiet crib, and go over the next morning and take him on the bounce—just as I did before."

"And suppose he shows fight and won't part?"

"Then I must send up a line to you, and you must get up a friendly lead, or something of that kind, and work me back to town."

"And you'll chance all that?"

"I'd chance a mile more than that for such stakes, where there's no knockin' about or head-punchin' business, Griffiths. I've not got what they call animal courage, which means I don't like being hurt. Some people do, I suppose, and they have animal courage. Now, let's settle where I'm to write to you, and all the rest of the business."

Mr. Effingham spoke thus cheerily, and seemed thoroughly determined on his undertaking and confident of his success, as he sat, late at night, in a warm brilliantly-lit tavern-parlour, with the odours of tobacco and hot spirituous drinks fragrant to him floating pleasantly about. He took quite another view of the subject when he turned out between five and six the next morning into a bald blank street, swept by torrents of rain, in which no one was visible but the policeman and the few vagrants huddling round the early-breakfast stall at the corner. Mr. Effingham wrapped himself up as best he might in his fifteen-shilling pea-jacket, and under cover of a big gingham umbrella, borrowed from his landlady, made the best fight he could against the wind and the rain, which, however, had so far the best of it that he was tolerably damp by the time he reached the Paddington station.

He took his ticket, and seated himself on the shelf in one of those wooden boxes which benevolent railway directors set aside for the conveyance of parliamentarians. His companions were two navvies, who had not slept off the effects of last night's drunkenness, and whose language made Mr. Effingham—albeit not unused to listening to "tall talk"—shrink with disgust; an old woman with steaming black garments, and an umbrella which would not stand up in any corner and would not lie under the seat, and got itself called most opprobrious names for its persistence in leaning against the nearest navvy; and a young woman with a swollen face tied up in a check cotton handkerchief. Mr. Effingham made an effort to let the very small window on his side down, but the young woman with the toothache had it up in an instant; while the aperture on the other side was constantly stuffed with the body of one or other of the drunken navvies, who fought for the privilege of leaning half out of the carriage, and running the chance of being knocked to pieces against arches and tunnel-walls. So the navvies fought and swore, and the old woman sniffed and took little snatches of sleep, waking with a prolonged snort and start; and the young woman moaned and rubbed her face, until Mr. Effingham was nearly mad. Circumstances were almost too much for him; he grew first desponding, and then desperate. He wished he had never started on his journey; he would get out at the next station at which the train stopped (and as the parliamentary duly stopped at every station, he would not have had to wait long); he would go back to London. No, he would not do that; he had boasted about his intention to Griffiths, and would lose all authority over that satellite if he did not show at least the semblance of a fulfilment of his purpose. He would get out at the next station, and wait at a public-house in the village until the next day, and then go back and tell Griffiths he had seen Sir Charles Mitford, and had found it impossible to get any money out of him. And then, just as the whistle shrieked out and the engine reduced its particularly slow pace to a slower still, preparatory to pulling up, Mr. Effingham's hands strayed into his waistcoat-pocket, where he found only a half-sovereign and a few shillings remaining—the extent of his earthly possessions. That decided him; he would go on, come what might! Such a state of impecuniosity nerved him to anything; and—the absence of policemen in rural districts still pleasantly remembered—he determined upon pursuing his original idea and of continuing his journey.

The next day Sir Charles Mitford, who had been compelled to devote the morning to dry details of business connected with his estate—details to which he listened conscientiously, over which he shook his head visibly, and which he did not in the least understand—had got rid of the man of business from the library about noon, and was just thinking he would go and see what Mrs. Hammond was doing, when Banks entered, and closing the door after him in a secret and mysterious manner, announced "That party, sir."

"What 'party,' Banks?"

"The party that called in Heaton Place, Sir Charles, and ast to see you, and you wouldn't see at first, but did afterwards, Sir Charles."

"I don't know yet whom you mean, Banks."

"The naval party, Sir Charles; though lookin' more like after the coats and humbrellas in the 'all. The naval party as served with you on board some ship, Sir Charles."

"Oh," said Mitford hurriedly, "I recollect now; one of—one of my sailors from my old yacht—yes, yes, of course. You can show him into my own room, Banks. I'll go up there at once."

"'Sailor,'" said Mr. Banks to himself as he walked down the passage, "'from my hold yacht,' did he say? Why, if what they say at the Club is right, the honly naval concern which he knew of before comin' in for the title was the Fleet Pris'n! This is a queer start about this feller, this is. I wonder why he wants to see Mitford, and why Mitford can't refuse hisself to him?—This way, young man." And he beckoned haughtily to Mr. Effingham, and preceded him to his master's room. Sir Charles had already arrived there, and was seated in his large armchair when the visitor was shown in.

Ah, what a different visitor from the Mr. Effingham who called in Eaton Place! Then full of vulgar confidence and brazen audacity; now, flinching, slouching, cowardly. His dress bedraggled from the previous day's wretched journey, his manner downcast from the preconceived notion of failure in his mission, and the impossibility of enforcing his previous demands. A very wretched specimen of humanity was Mr. Effingham as he stood before Sir Charles Mitford, shifting his limp hat from hand to hand, and waiting to be asked to sit down.

When Banks had retired and closed the door, Sir Charles looked up quietly and steadily at his visitor, and said, "Well, Mr.—I forget your name—you've broken your promise, as I expected, and come to try and extort money from me again!"

"Extort, Sir Charles! that's not the word, sir; I—"

"That is the word, sir! Sheer barefaced robbery and extortion—that's what has brought you down here; deny it if you can! Have you come to ask me for money, or have you not?"

"Well, Sir Charles, I—that is—"

"No shuffling, sir! no prevarication! Have you or not?"

"Well, suppose I have?"

"Suppose you have! And suppose that I, as a justice of the peace and magistrate for the county, make out a warrant for your committal to prison as a rogue and vagabond? We're a long way from London, and justice's law is to be had down in these parts. Besides, how could you appeal? to whom could you refer? I've made a point of having a few inquiries made about you since you last did me the honour of a call, and I find that if not a regular gaol-bird, you could at all events be recognized by the police as a swindler and an utterer of base coin. What do you think of that Mr.— Butler?"

What did he think of it? The realization of his worst fears, the overthrow of his strongest hopes! He ought to have relied on the presentiment which had told him that the man would take this course, though not so promptly or so strongly. He thought he would try one more bit of bounce, and he shook himself together and put as much impudence as he could command into his look as he said,

"How do you know I've not got that forged bill in my pocket?"

"By your face, sir! I can see that as plainly as if it were written there in big black letters! Ah, I knew I was right! Now, what have you got to say to this, Mr. Butler?"

Mr. Effingham fairly collapsed. "Nothing, Sir Charles," he stammered. "I've nothing to say-only have mercy, Sir Charles! I have not brought the bill with me, but I know where it is, and could lay my hand on it at any time, Sir Charles. And as to what you said about committing me as a rogue and a vagabond, O Lord! don't do it, Sir Charles! pray don't! I'm a poor miserable devil without a rap; but if you'll only let me go, I'll find my way back to town, and never intrude on you again, Sir Charles; I—"

All this time Mr. Effingham had been backing, and with his hand behind him feeling for the handle of the door. Having secured it, he was about to vanish, when Sir Charles called out to him "Stop!" and he stopped at once.

"You say you're hard-up, Mr. Butler?"

"I'm positively stumped, Sir Charles."

"Then you'd be glad to earn a little money?"

"If I could do so—" Mr. Effingham was about to say "honestly," but he thought this would be a little too glaring, so he finished his sentence by substituting "without incurring any danger, I should be delighted."

"There would not be the slightest danger—"

"By danger I mean, punching of heads and that kind of thing."

"Precisely; there would be nothing of that. The only person with whom you would be brought into contact would be a woman."

Mr. Effingham's barometrical mercury rose as quickly as it fell. "A woman!" he said, as he settled his limp collar and gave a pull at his dirty wristbands,—"a woman, Sir Charles! Oh, then, I've no fear."

"Wait and hear what you're required to do, sir, before you give an opinion. The person to whom I allude is at the present moment in this house. She is therefore, although not invited by me, to a certain extent my guest, and it would be impossible for me to appear in the matter. You comprehend me?"

"Perfectly."

"Especially as she is to be got rid of at once and for ever. When I say 'got rid of,' I don't mean it in the slang phrase of the penny romances—I don't mean that the woman is to be killed; but simply that she is to be told that she must remain here no longer, and the danger of doing so must be strongly pointed out to her."

"Exactly, je twig! Now will you please to tell me the name of this good lady, and what reason I'm to give for insisting on her leaving such a very swell and pleasant crib as this appears to be?"

"She is called here Miss Gillespie," said Sir Charles; "but You will have heard of her under a very different name—Lizzie Ponsford."

"What!" exclaimed Mr. Effingham, leaping from his chair; "Lizzie Ponsford here! She whom I've been—"

"Well, sir?" asked Sir Charles in astonishment.

"Whom I've been hearing so much about!" said Mr. Effingham, recovering himself. "Lizzie Ponsford here!" he continued, going off again. "Well, that is a rum start!"

"Be good enough to attend to me, sir. She is here, and she is in my way. Her presence worries me, bringing back all sorts of hideous associations that I thought I had got rid of, and never want to have revived. You must see her, talk to her, and get her to go at once; once gone, I could so arrange matters as to leave little chance of her returning."

"I see!" said Mr. Effingham. "Now the question is, how to work her out of this. What would be the best way to frighten her and get her under your thumb?"

"What is your notion on that point?"

"I scarcely know yet! It will want a little thinking over, but I've no doubt I shall be able to hit upon something. Is she pretty comfortable where she is—likely not to give it up without a struggle?"

"You may take your oath she will not move unless compelled—it is for you to find the something that will compel her."

"Exactly. Well, I don't think that there will be much difficulty about that—at least," said he, correcting himself, for he feared that comparative facility might lessen the reward—"at least, not much difficulty for a man whose head's screwed on the right way. Now about the payment?"

Sir Charles opened a drawer in his desk, and from a little *rouleau* of gold counted out ten sovereigns. The chink of the money sounded deliciously in Mr. Effingham's hungry ears.

"I will give you these ten sovereigns now," said Sir Charles; "and if you succeed in carrying out all I have told you, I will give you fifty more."

"Will you? Well, I always say what I think, and I say that's liberal. Now look here! Very likely I shan't see you again; perhaps I shall have to step it with her, in order to be sure she's safe off, and not dodging, or likely to walk back again. So when you find she's really gone, just you send a cheque for the fifty, made payable to bearer, mind, and not crossed, to this address;" and bending down over the table he took a pen and scrap of paper and wrote: Mr. Effingham, Mr. Johnson's, The Brown Bear, Shakespeare Street, Strand, London. "Will you do that?"

"I will."

"Having said so as an honourable gent, I know you'll keep your word. Now how am I to see her?"

"She walks out every day at three o'clock with her pupil—"

"Her pupil! Lizzie Ponsford's pupil! My eye!"

"With her pupil," repeated Sir Charles sternly, "in the chestnut avenue leading from the lodge-gate. A tall woman with very large eyes, and crisp wavy °hair over her forehead; a peculiar-looking woman—you couldn't mistake her."

"All right! As I go out of the lodge-gate now, I'll just say a few words to the old lady that keeps it, that she may know me again—don't you see?—and not be surprised at my coming in and out. And now, as I shall probably have to hang about here for two or three days, where can I put up?"

"You mustn't remain here in the house—"

"Lor' bless you, that would never do! isn't there a public near?"

"There is the Mitford Arms, within a quarter of a mile of the lodge."

"I saw it; the carrier's-cart which brought me over from Torquay stopped there. That'll do. I'll be a littery gent gettin' up information about the old county families, or an artist sketchin'—that'll do. Now give me a week clear: if nothing's done by then, you'll have spent ten pound very badly, and I shall have lost my time. But if within that time—and it might be to-morrow or any day—you find she's clean gone, you've got the address, and you'll send the cheque to it?"

"You may rely on me."

"I do thoroughly. Now how am I to get out? It wouldn't do for you to be seen with me—my togs, though just the sort of thing for the littery gent, ain't very swell."

"You can go down this staircase," said Sir Charles, leading him to a landing; "it guides on to the garden, take the first to the right, and you'll come at last to the avenue."

Mr. Effingham put his finger to the limp brim of his hat and departed.

But when he arrived in the chestnut avenue, and had looked carefully round, and found that he was out of sight of any one in the house, and that there was no one near enough to observe his conduct, he rubbed his hands together, and almost cut a caper in the air with delight.

"To think of it!" he said. "There never, never was such luck! D'Ossay, my boy, you've got the trick of it somehow. What will Griffiths say now? To think that I've been hunting for this woman all this time, and that she's now placed in my hands—and by this very swell too! Two birds with one stone now. Oh, there's a much bigger game than the Bart.'s cheque for fifty! But it'll take a deal of thinking over and planning; and if there's any one to do that, it's you, D'Ossay, my boy, and no one else!"

CHAPTER XVIII.

IN THE DRAWING-ROOM.

What was Laurence Alsager doing at Redmoor? He was beginning to ask himself that question very frequently. And that question led to another—why had he come down there at all? He had "done" country-houses and their amusements and had tired of them years before; he had not the slightest liking for any of the guests; he had a vague dislike of the host. Why, then, had he come? He was a man who rarely tried to deceive himself; and when he put this question point-blank to himself the answer was, Why? Why, because you take a certain interest in Lady Mitford—no, I allow that perfectly; nothing dishonourable, nothing which at present could even be described as a love-passion; but a certain interest. You think from all you have seen that she is not merely very charming in her innocence and simplicity, but really good; and you expect from certain signs which you detect, and with the nature of which you are familiar, that she will have to pass through a very perilous ordeal. It is obvious to you that in society, as it is now constituted, a woman of Lady Mitford's personal attractions and position must incur a very great deal of temptation. This, of course, would be to a great extent avoided if she were secure in the affections and certain of the attentions of her husband; but in the present instance you are constrained to admit, contrary to the opinion which you once publicly expressed, that Sir Charles Mitford is a weak, silly, vain person, who has fallen a victim to the wiles of a thoroughly heartless coquette, and who appears to be going from bad to worse as rapidly as possible. So that your certain interest has brought you down here to watch over the lady. Quixotic and ultra-romantic, is it not? You do not mean it to be so, I know—I give you full credit for that; but still that is the designation it would probably receive from any of your friends. The truth is, that this—I was almost going to call it parental, but we will say fraternal—this fraternal regard for a very handsome woman is a novelty to you; and hence your enjoyment of it. I said expressly a very handsome woman, because I don't believe that the fraternal sentiment could possibly blossom for an ugly one. Beware of it, my friend, if you please! it's the trickiest, most treacherous elf, this fraternal friendship, that exists; it goes on for a certain period perfectly steadily and properly, and then one morning you find it has deserted you, and left in its place a hot flaming *riotous passion that scorches you into tinder, makes you miserable, takes away your appetite, and, in fact, possesses all the qualities which, at one time, you knew so well.*

Such was the result of Laurence Alsager's self-examination, and he fully admitted its truth. It was the interest which he took in Lady Mitford that had induced him to visit Redmoor; it was the same feeling which kept him lingering there. Then the interest must have increased; for the necessity for his self-imposed task of protection and supervision had certainly diminished. The actual fact which had decided his coming was the announcement that Lord Dollamore was to be among the guests. He had always had his own opinion of Lord Dollamore's morality; and the way in which that nobleman had spoken of Lady Mitford in the smoking-room of the Maecenas had jarred horribly on Alsager's nerves. There was something too in Laura Hammond's look and in the tone of her voice when she spoke of the probability of Dollamore's being left constantly with the ladies, at which Laurence had taken alarm. But Lord Dollamore seemed to be perfectly innocuous. Laurence had watched him narrowly from the first, and, as in the case of the drive to Egremont Priory, he seemed rather to avoid than to seek opportunities of being in Lady Mitford's company *en tête-à-tête*, and, judging from that and one or two other instances, was apparently desirous of keeping in the background, and of pushing Laurence forward. Could he—? No; he was a man utterly without principle where women are concerned; but he would never attempt such a game as that, more particularly if he, Laurence Alsager, were involved in it. Certainly Sir Charles was going to the bad more rapidly than Alsager had anticipated; but then it was to be said for him that he clearly had fallen into able hands. There had been few such adepts in the art of flirtation in Europe as Laura Molyneux; and she seemed to have become even more fertile in resources and skilful in their development since her marriage. Anything like the manner in which she had flirted with Mitford during the first few clays of her visit to Redmoor, Laurence, in all his experience, had never seen; and he thought at the time of the Egremont Priory expedition that things were coming rapidly to an end. Lady Mitford had evidently noticed something that day, some *tendresse* between her husband and Mrs. Hammond, which had annoyed her very much; so much that she had almost called her friends' attention to her disgust. But the sweetness of her disposition had come to the rescue. Laurence knew, as well as if he had been able to read her thoughts, all that had passed in her mind during that drive in the pony-phaeton; he saw how she had reasoned with herself, and how she had finally determined that she had been hasty, inconsiderate, and in the wrong. He had seen her, immediately on alighting, slip away to join her husband; and he could fully understand that she had made silent atonement for what she imagined to be an outburst of groundless jealousy.

An extraordinary change had come over Mitford within the last few days. Before the picnic, and at the picnic, he had been enthralled, *entêté*, eagerly waiting for Mrs. Hammond's every look, every word, and scarcely able to behave with decency to anybody else. Since then he had acted quite differently. Had his conscience smitten him for neglecting his wife? No; Laurence did not believe in sudden conscience-smites with such men as Sir Charles Mitford; and he had further noticed that though there was no open flirtation, there was plenty of eye-telegraphy of a very peculiar and significant kind. They had come to some understanding evidently, for Mrs. Hammond now seldom addressed her conversation to her host, but kept her hand in by practising on the susceptible heart of Major Winton, or by coquetting with some of the officers who were invariably to be found dining at Redmoor. She had tried to *réchauffer* a little of the old story with Laurence, but had encountered something so much more marked than mere disinclination, that she suspended operations at once.

However, be this as it might, the necessity for Alsager's stay at Redmoor, even judged by his own peculiar notions, was at an end. The Dollamore question never had been mooted; the Hammond difficulty seemed entirely in abeyance. What further need was there for him to keep watch and ward over the Redmoor household? He could be back in town as soon as they could, go where they might; *something* would occur during the season, he thought, and he might as well be there on guard; but that was a matter of only a few hours from wherever he might happen to be.

Whither should he go, then? Not back to London—that was impossible. The week or two he had passed there had thoroughly sickened him of London for some time to come. Paris? No, he thought not! The *bals d'opéra* would be on then,— Frisotte and Rigolette, Celestine and Mogador, Brididi and the Reine Pomaré—O yes, he knew it all; it was a very long time since those exercitations of the *cancan*, rebuked by the *sergents-de-ville* in a low grumble of *"Pas si fort! pas si fort! point du télégraphe!"* had afforded him the slightest pleasure. Leicestershire? No, though he had purchased Sir Launcelot, and from merely that short experience of him at Acton, felt sure that he would "show them the way"—no, not Leicestershire this year, he thought, nor anywhere else, unless he went down to Knockholt to see his father. Yes, by Jove! he ought to have done that long since, and now he would do it at once.

He settled this in his own mind as he was dressing for dinner about a week after the winter picnic. Settled it not without long deliberation and a little sleep, for he began to give the matter his careful consideration after returning from a long day's shooting; and it was not until he had steamed and lathered himself in a warm bath, had pulled the little sofa in front of the fire, and was contemplating his evening clothes neatly arranged on an adjacent chair, that he began to consider the question. His deliberation involved the putting up of his feet on the sofa, and that proceeding caused him at once to drop helplessly off to sleep, only to be roused by the loud clanging of the second dinner-bell.

An addition accrued to the dinner-party that day, in the persons of Sir Thomas Hayter, a country neighbour, his wife and daughter. Sir Thomas was a hearty old Tory country squire, who during his one season in London had been captivated by and had married her ladyship; at the time of her marriage a *passée* beauty, now a thin chip of an old woman, still affecting girlish airs. Miss Hayter was a fine, fresh, dashing, exuberant girl, inclined to flirting, and fulfilling her inclination thoroughly. They infused a little new life into the party; for though Sir Thomas did not talk a great deal, he listened to everything that was said, and threw in an occasional "Ha! dear me!" with great vigour and effect, while Lady Hayter chirped away to Sir Charles Mitford, asking him about all sorts of London people of whom he had never heard, and quite bewildering him with her volubility. She succeeded better with Mr. Hammond, whose health was fast improving in the soft Devon air, and who, in spite of the strongly-expressed opinion of his wife, had come down to dinner that day. He was seated next to Lady Hayter; and shortly after dinner commenced, he found out that he had known her before her marriage, when she was Miss Fitzgibbon; "used to have the pleasure of meeting you at the Silvesters' in South Audley Street;" and then they entered upon a very long conversation about the acquaintances of their youth, while all the time each was stealing covert glances at the other, and wondering how it was possible—she, that that cadaverous, parchment-faced, bent invalid could be the handsome boy who in those days had just come up from Haileybury, and was going to India with such good prospects; he, that the old woman with the palpably-dyed purple hair, the scraggy neck, and the resplendent teeth—the gold springs of which were so very visible— could have been Emily Fitzgibbon, about whose beauty every one was raving in '25. Miss Hayter too was very happy; she was immensely taken by Laurence Alsager, next to whom she was seated. She had heard of him often; and two years before, when she was in London, he had been pointed out to her at the Opera; and she, then a young lady of seventeen, had gone home and written about him in her diary, and drawn portraits of him in her blotting-book, and thought him the handsomest creature in the world. She told him this, not of course in so many words, but with that charming quiet way of paying a compliment which some well-bred women possess; and she had also heard of the catastrophe with the ponies at Acton, and of his gallant conduct.

"For it was very gallant, you know, Colonel Alsager; any one could see that, even through that ridiculous newspaper report; and it was a splendid jump too. I was talking about it the other day to my cousin Fred Rivers, who knows you, I think; and he said he'd seen the place, and Mr. ——, I forget his name; the head man up there— said it was as fine a thing as ever was done in Leicestershire; and Fred said he thought so too; 'bar none,' he said, in that sporting way, don't you know, which he has of talking."

"You make a great deal too much of it, Miss Hayter," said Laurence, smiling; "I've seen Fred Rivers take many such jumps himself, for a better horseman never crossed country."

"Ah, yes, during a run, I daresay; but this was in cold blood, wasn't it?—not that I wonder at your doing anything for Lady Mitford. Isn't she lovely? I declare I never saw such a perfect face in my life."

Alsager was about to answer, when Major Maxse spoke from the other side of the table, "Oh, by the way, Colonel Alsager, what Miss Hayter was saying reminds me that you ought not to have driven that day we went to Egremont; you should have gone on horseback. There's a very neat country if you do but know it."

"Did you *drive* over, Colonel Alsager?" asked Miss Hayter in astonishment.

"Yes; I drove Lady Mitford in her pony-phaeton." ("Oh!" in a subdued tone from Miss Hayter.) "Sir Charles was the only one who rode."

"And Mrs. Hammond,—I beg your pardon, and Mrs. Hammond!" said Major Winton, the first words he had spoken since he sat down to dinner. "I too was on horseback, but I can scarcely be said to have ridden. But, coming back, they went away splendidly. I never saw anything better than the manner in which the first fence was cleared by them both. I daresay it was as good all over the course; but they got away after the first, and we never saw any more of them."

And Major Winton sipped his first glass of post-prandial claret with great gusto. He had paid off Mrs. Hammond for using him on the picnic-day, and throwing him off when she no longer required him. It was to be presumed, however, that Mrs. Hammond had not heard this remark; at least she gave no signs of having done so, being occupied in conversation with Captain Bligh. Sir Charles Mitford grew very red; Miss Hayter looked round, enjoying the fun; and an awkward pause ensued, broken by old Sir Thomas Hayter.

"Didn't I hear you say you were over at Egremont the other day, Mitford?"

"Yes, Sir Thomas; we went over there, and had a kind of winter picnic."

"You didn't see anything of Torn Boscastle, I suppose?"

"No; we only went to the ruins, and lunched in the keep. Besides, I don't know him."

"Ah! you wouldn't have seen him if you had known him. He keeps quite to himself just now."

"What's the matter? is he ill?"

"No, not ill in body, you know. What's that we used to learn in the Latin grammar— *'magis quam corpore, aegrotat'*—his mind, you know."

"That's bad; what has brought that about?"

"Well, you see, he's got a son, a wild extravagant fellow, who has run through I can't tell how much money, which poor Tom could very ill afford, as we all know; and the last thing the vagabond did was to get hold of his father's cheque-book, and forge his name to a terrible amount."

Had Sir Thomas been a gentleman of quick perception—a charge which had never been brought against him—he would have been very much astonished at the effect of his anecdote. Sir Charles Mitford turned deadly white. Colonel Alsager frowned heavily, and glanced towards Lady Mitford, who, pale as her husband, looked as if she were about to faint; Lord Dollamore glanced sharply at Sir Thomas Hayter, to see whether he had spoken innocently or with malice prepense. Mrs. Hammond was the only one who seemed to keep her wits thoroughly about her. She glanced at Lady Mitford, and then pushing her chair back sharply, as though obeying a signal from her hostess, rose from the table, followed of course by all the other ladies.

After their departure, and so soon as the door closed behind them, Lord Dollamore addressed himself to Sir Thomas, asking him if he had heard the report that the Whig Ministry intended to impose a new duty on cider—a subject which he knew would engross the old gentleman's attention, to the exclusion of Tom Boscastle and every one else. And, as Lord Dollamore said afterwards, it was an illimitable subject, for he himself invented the report as a herring across the scent; but under old Hayter's fostering care it grew into a perfect Frankensteinian monster. While they were talking, Sir Charles Mitford filled a bumper of claret, and after swallowing half of it, looked round the table to see the extent of the calamity. Then, for the first time, he acknowledged to himself how right the girl Lizzie Ponsford had been in what she had said. Dollamore evidently knew the story, and Alsager—perhaps Hammond, who was leaning back in his chair, enjoying his Madeira; but he could tell in an instant, by the expression of their faces, that none of the others had heard it. Another link had been forged this evening in the chain of his attachment to that charming Mrs. Hammond! how nobly she had behaved! Poor Georgie had lost her bead of course, and had very nearly made a mess of it by fainting, or screaming, or something; but that other woman did just exactly the right thing at the right time. And all for him! He was more infatuated with her than ever. He wondered whether he should ever have the chance of telling her so. He wondered how Butler was progressing in his mission.

By the time the gentlemen arrived in the drawing-room, all trace of the little awkwardness at the dessert-table had passed away. Indeed, Miss Hayter was the only one of all the ladies who had noticed Georgic's uneasiness, and she had not attributed it to its right cause. Now Lady Mitford was looking as serenely lovely as ever, listening to Mrs. Charteris warbling away at the piano; and she looked at her husband with such loving solicitude as he entered the room, that he could not refrain from going up to her, smiling kindly, and pressing her hand, as he whispered, "All right! quite blown over."

Then Sir Charles went in search of Mrs. Hammond. She was sitting in a low chair near the fire, with a little table bearing a shaded lamp close by her hand, and was amusing herself by turning over an album of prints. She never gave herself the smallest trouble when left alone with women; she did not care what they thought of her, and, save under peculiar circumstances, she made no effort to please them. She wished to stand well with Lady Mitford, but she considered she had done enough to that end for one day by executing the masterly retreat from the dinner-table. So she sat there idly under the shade of the lamp, and Sir Charles Mitford thought he had never seen her to such advantage. Her rounded figure showed to perfection in her violet-velvet dress trimmed with soft white lace; her head reclined lazily on the back of her chair, and her eyes rested with calm indifference on the pages of the album— indifference which was succeeded by bright vivacity as she raised them and marked her host's approach.

He dropped quietly into a chair close by hers and said, "You have increased my debt of gratitude to you a thousand-fold."

"Have I?" she replied; "it has been very easily increased. So easily that I don't know how it has been done."

"Don't you? Then your natural talent is wonderful. I should think there were few better or more useful stratagems in warfare than the diversion of the enemy's attention from your weak point."

"Oh," she said, "that is not worth remembering; certainly not worth mentioning again. I am so glad," she added, dropping her voice, "to see you by my side again. I have gone through all kinds of self-examination, imagining that I had in some way offended you; going over in my own mind all that I had said or done since that delicious ride home from Egremont, and I could not tax myself with having wittingly given you any cause for offence. But you seemed to avoid me, to shrink from me, and I cannot tell you how I felt it."

Voice very low here, looks downcast, and general depression.

"Don't speak in that way," said Sir Charles in the same tone; "you don't understand my position. I could explain, and I will some time or other when I have the chance; not now, because—Yes, you are quite right, Mrs. Hammond, Sir Thomas is a thorough specimen of the good old English—"

"Very sorry to interrupt so pleasant a talk, specially when on so charming a subject as Sir Thomas Hayter," said Lord Dollamore, approaching; "but I come as a deputation from the general company to beg that Mrs. Hammond will sing to us."

"Mrs. Hammond would be charmed," said that lady; "but to-night she is out of voice, and really cannot."

"Do, Mrs. Hammond; as a matter of mere charity, do," said Lord Dollamore. "That delightful person Mrs. Charteris,—most delightful, and kind, and all that,—has been trilling away every evening until one is absolutely sick of her thin little voice. Do, for pity's sake, change the note, and let us have a little of your contralto. Do."

"You're very polite, Lord Dollamore; and 'as a matter of mere charity' I should be delighted to help you, but really I am out of voice and cannot. Stay; the old rule in convivial societies was, or I am mistaken, that one should sing or find a substitute. Now I think I can do the latter. Miss Hammond's companion, governess, what you will,—Miss Gillespie,—sings charmingly. If Lady Mitford will permit me, I will send for her."

Georgie, appealed to, was only too well pleased to secure such an aid to the evening's entertainment; so a message was sent to Miss Gillespie, and she was requested to "bring some songs;" Miss Hayter filling up the interval by playing, sufficiently brilliantly, a *pot-pourri* of dance-music.

Towards the end of this performance the door opened and Miss Gillespie entered. All eyes were instantly turned towards her, and—in the case of all the men at least— the casual glance grew into a lengthened gaze. She was a very striking-looking woman, with her sallow cheeks, her large eyes, her brown hair rolling in crisp waves on her forehead. She was dressed in a tight-fitting brown-silk dress with handsomely-worked collar and sleeves, and in her hand she carried a roll of music, of which Lord Dollamore stepped forward to relieve her; but she thanked him with a slight bow and sat down on the chair close to the door, still retaining her roll of music in her hand.

When Miss Hayter had ceased playing, Lady Mitford crossed the room and shook hands with Miss Gillespie, offered her refreshment, thanked her very sweetly for the promptitude with which she had acceded to their request, and told her that Mrs. Hammond had already raised their expectation very high. Then Sir Charles Mitford came up somewhat stiffly, and offered his arm to Miss Gillespie and led her to the piano; and there, just removing her gloves, and without the smallest hesitation or affectation, she sat down, and with scarcely any prelude plunged at once into that most delightful of melodies, "Che farò senza Eurydice," from Glück's *Ofeo*. Ah, what a voice! clear, bell-like, thrilling, touching not merely the tympanum of the ear, but acting on the nerves and on the spinal vertebrae. What melody in it! what wondrous power! and as she poured out the refrain, "Eurydice, Eurydice!" what deep passionate tenderness! The company sat spell-bound; Lord Dollamore, an accomplished musician himself, and one who had heard the best music everywhere, sat nursing his knee and drinking-in every note. Laurence Alsager, rapt in admiration, had even been guilty of the discourtesy of turning his back on Miss Hayter, whose chatter began to annoy him, and was beating time with his head and hand. Tom Charteris had crept behind his wife, who, far too good a little woman to feel professional jealousy, was completely delighted; and the big tears were rolling down Lady Mitford's face. She was still a child, you see, and had not gone through the Clanronald furnace, where all tears are dried up for ever.

When the song was ended, there came a volley of applause such as is seldom heard in drawing-rooms, and far different from the usual languid "Thank you," which crowns the failure of the amateur. Miss Gillespie looked round elated, as though the sound was pleasant and not unfamiliar to her, and was about to rise from her seat, when Laurence Alsager, who was nearest the piano, advanced, and begged she would remain—he was sure he spoke in the name of all present. So Miss Gillespie, after looking him hard in the face, made him a little bow, and remained at the piano, this time starting off into one of Louis Puget's charming French ballads, "Ta main," which she sung with as much fire and *chic* as if she had never quitted Paris.

At the conclusion of the second song, Lady Mitford came across to the piano to thank the singer, and she was followed by Mrs. Charteris and Mrs. Masters. Mrs. Charteris was in the highest delight—a feeling; not at all decreased when Miss Gillespie assured her that she had frequently listened to her, Mrs. Charteris's, singing, and had often envied that lady her correct musical education. Mrs. Masters said her little complimentary say about the song, but was principally taken up by Miss Gillespie's costume. She was one of those women who never see anything new worn by any other woman without taking private mental notes of its every detail; thus setting at defiance any attempted extension of the Patent laws in regard to female apparel. So, with her eyes devouring Miss Gillespie's dress, Mrs. Masters said to her "Yes, so charming that Glück! so full of depth and power!—(Wonderfully good silk; stands by itself like a board!)—And the little French *chansonnette*, so sparkling and melodious, and—(O yes, certainly French I should think! no English house could—) may I ask you where you got that collar and those cuffs, Miss—Miss Asplin? They are most peculiar!"

"My name is Gillespie, madam; and the collar and cuffs I worked myself." After which Mrs. Masters bowed, and went back to her seat.

During this examination Laurence Alsager, who had seated himself next to Miss Hayter, in the neighbourhood of the piano, was conscious that Miss Gillespie's looks constantly strayed towards him. It is very odd. There was nothing coquettish in the regard, he knew every one in that category of glances of old; but these were strangely earnest looks, always averted when she found they were remarked. While they were full upon him, Miss Hayter, in reply to something he had said about his delight in ferns, expressed a hope that they would see him at her father's place, the Arme Wood, where there was a splendid fernery. Laurence, in reply, thanked her, and said how happy he would have been to go, but that he feared it would be impossible, as he intended to leave Redmoor in a day or two. He must be a dutiful son, and visit his father, whom he had not seen since his return to England. As he said this Miss Gillespie's eyes were full on him.

They were very singular eyes, he thought, as he undressed himself lazily before the fire in his bed-room. Very singular eyes; so large, and dark, and speaking. What on earth made the woman look at him so perpetually! He was growing too old to inspire love at first sight, he felt, smiling grimly as he inspected himself in the looking-glass; besides, she was not the style of woman for any such folly. How magnificently she sung! what depth and pathos there was in her voice! "Eurydice, Eurydice!"—those notes were enough to go through any man's soul; those notes were enough to—hallo, what's this?

He had strolled across to the dressing-table, and taken up a small sealed Dote, addressed in a thin fine female hand to Colonel Alsager.

He broke the seal and read:

"I heard you talk of leaving Redmoor. If not impossible I pray you to stay. Your presence will be a check upon two people, who, liberated from that, will go headlong to ruin, *dragging down a third in their fall.* For the welfare of this third person both you and I are solicitous. But it seems probable that my sphere of usefulness is ended; so all devolves upon you. Remember this, and for her sake, stay on."

"Ah!" said Laurence Alsager when he had perused this mysterious note for the second time—"there's no doubt that my anonymous correspondent is the handsome woman with the eyes and voice. What she means I'll find out in the morning."

CHAPTER XIX.

DIAMOND CUT DIAMOND.

On the morning after the day when Miss Gillespie had made so successful a debut among the company assembled at Redmoor, Mr. Effingham, lounging quietly up the road from the Mitford Arms, rang at the lodge-gate, and after a few minutes' conversation with the old portress, passed up the avenue. His conversation was purely of a pleasant character; there was no inquiry as to who he was, or what he wanted,— all that had been settled long ago. He was a gentleman from London, who was writing a book 'bout all the old fam'ly houses, and was going to put our place into it. He knew Sir Charles, and had his leave to come and go when he liked. A civil-spoken gentleman he was, and talked most wonderful; never passed the lodge without stopping to say something. Perhaps of all Mr. Effingham's peculiarities, this impressed the old woman the most; for, like all country people of her class who live a solitary and quiet life, she was thoroughly reticent, and it is questionable whether, beyond the ordinary salutations to those with whom she was brought in contact, she uttered more than a dozen sentences in a week. But Mr. Effingham's light airy chatter was very welcome to the old lady, and, combined with the politeness which he always exhibited, had rendered him a great favourite.

A considerable alteration had been effected in Mr. Effingham's outward man since his first visit to Redmoor. As in the former instance, his first step on receiving the ten pounds from Sir Charles was to purchase a new suit of clothes. He bought them at the neighbouring town, and in pursuance of his intention to assume a literary or artistic character, he had endeavoured to render his apparel suitable, or, as he called it, "to make up for the part." So he now wore a large slouch felt wideawake hat, a dark velveteen jacket, long waistcoat, gray trousers, and ankle-jack boots. Had he carried out his own views of literary attire, he would have adopted a long dressing-gown and Turkish trousers, such as he had seen in the portraits of celebrated authors; but he felt that these would be out of place in the country, and might attract attention. He, however, armed himself with a large notebook and a pencil of portentous thickness, with which he was in the habit of jotting down visionary memoranda whenever he found himself observed. By the initiated and the upper classes this last-described act may have been recognized as an indisputable literary trait; but by the lower orders Mr. Effingham was regarded as a mystic potentate of the turf, whose visit to the Mitford arms had mysterious connection with the proximity of Sir Danesbury Boucher's stables, where Lime-juice, the third favourite for the Derby, was in training; while the entries of the memoranda were by the same people ascribed to the exercise of a process known to them as the booking of bets.

The March morning was so splendid in its freshness and bright glittering sunlight, that Mr. Effingham, although little given to admiring the beauties of nature, could not resist occasionally stopping and looking round him. The old elms forming the avenue were just putting forth their first buds; far away on either side stretched broad alternations of turf in level, hill, and glade, all glistening with the morning dew; while on the horizon fronting him, and behind the house, could be seen the outline of the great Redmoor. The jolly old house stood like some red-faced giant, its mullioned windows winking at the sunlight, the house itself just waking into life. From the stable-yard came a string of rugged and hooded horses for exercise. The gardeners were crossing from the conservatory bearing choice flowers for the decoration of the rooms. At the porch was standing the head-keeper, accompanied by two splendid dogs; a groom on horseback, with the swollen post-bag slung round him, passed Mr. Effingham in the avenue; everywhere around were signs of wealth and prosperity.

"Yes," said Mr. Effingham to himself, as he stopped and surveyed the scene, "this is better than my lodgings in Doory Lane, this is! No end better! And why should this fellow have it, and not me—that's what I want to know? I could do it up pretty brown, here, I'm thinkin'; not like him—not in the same way, that is, but quite as good. There mighn't be so many nobs, but there'd be plenty of good fellers; and as for the nobs, Lord bless you, when they found there was plenty of good grub and drink, and good fun to be had, they'd come fast enough. I should just like to try it, that's all; I'd show him. And why shouldn't I try it? Not in this way, perhaps—not to cut it quite so fat as this, but still reg'lar comfortable and nice. A nice little box at Finchley or Hampstead, with a bit o' lawn, and a pony-trap, and chickens, and a spare bed for a pal,—that's my notion of comfort! And why shouldn't I have it, if I play my cards properly? Damme, I will have it! I'm sick of cadgin' about from hand to mouth, never knowin' what's goin' to turn up next. This bit o' stiff ought to be worth anything to me—anything in reason, that is to say. So, when I've once got it from our friend here, and that won't be just yet,—I must get her away from here, and have her well under my thumb, before I try that on,—when I once get, that docyment, I'll take it straight to Sir Charles, and let him have it for a sum down—must be a big sum too—and then I'll cut the whole lot of 'em, and go and live somewhere in the country by myself! That's what I'll do!"

L'appétit vient en mangeant. When Mr. Effingham was utterly destitute he accommodated himself to his position, and lived on, from hand to mouth, in the best way he could. He retired to the back-ways and slums then, and seeing very few people much better off than he was himself, his envy and jealousy were not excited. Sir Charles's ten pounds had disturbed the little man's mental equilibrium; the readiness with which they melted in his grasp showed him how easily he could get rid of a hundred, of a thousand, of ten thousand. The sight of the comfort and luxury of Redmoor contrasted horribly with the wretchedness of his own lodging, and lashed him into a storm of rage.

"It's too bad!" said he, striking his stick against the tree by which he was standing,—"it's too bad that there should be all this lot of money in the world, and that I should have none of it, while this cove here—O yes, if you please, my horses goin' out with the grooms; my gardeners a bringin' pines and melons and all the rest of it; my keeper a-waitin' to know how many pheasants I'm going to kill to-day! Damme, it's sickening!" Mr. Effingham struck the tree again, pushed his hat over his eyes, and started off in his walk. When he had proceeded about half-way up the avenue, he climbed the iron fence, and started off to the right over the park, until he reached a little knoll, on the top of which were two magnificent cedars. On the other side of these cedars, and completely hidden by them from the house, was a carved rustic seat. On reaching the top of the knoll, Mr. Effingham looked round, and seeing nobody, sat down, put his feet up, and made himself most comfortable.

A lengthened contemplation of the cedars, however, instead, as might have been expected, of bringing calm to his perturbed soul, served only to remind him that they, in common with all the surroundings, were the property of somebody else, and that on that somebody else he had a tremendous hold, provided he went properly to work.

"And I'll do it!" said he, taking his feet off the bench, and pushing the felt wideawake hat into all kinds of shapes in his excitement,—"I'll do it too! Now, let me see! My friend will be here presently—let me just run through what's to be done. Quiet's the game with her, I think; no bullyrag and bluster—quiet and soft. No connection with any one here—never even heard the name—sent by the other parties—I'm so innocent. Yes, I think that will do; then, when we've once started together, I can make my own terms.—How late she is! She must be awfully down on her luck at being spotted down here, and she must suspect something by the quick way in which she agreed to meet me here when I spoke to her yesterday as she was walkin' with the young 'un,—made no bones about it at all. She won't fail me, I suppose."

Oh no, she would not fail him. There she was, crossing the park apparently from the back of the stables, and making straight for the cedars. Could it be she? A figure bent nearly double, dressed in an old-fashioned black-silk cloak and a poke-bonnet, and leaning on a thick umbrella. It was not until she was well under the shadow of the cedars, that she straightened herself, pushed back her bonnet, and stood revealed as Miss Gillespie.

"Good-morning," said she, so crisply and blithely that Mr. Effingham, who had expected she would adopt a very, different tone, was quite astonished; "I'm afraid I'm a little late, Mr. ——; you did not favour me with your name; but the fact is, as you probably know, I am not my own mistress, and my services were required just as I was about to start."

"All right, miss," said Mr. Effingham, taking off his hat, and making a bow as near as possible after the manner of walking-gentlemen on the stage—a proceeding with which the limpness of the wideawake's brim interfered considerably; "my name's Effingham."

"Indeed! what a pretty name! so romantic. You would not mind my sitting down, would you? No; that's all right. And now, Mr. Effingham, I suppose you want something of me, don't you, after that mysterious communication which you made to me yesterday when I was walking with my pupil? Poor child! she's been in a state of wonderment ever since; and I've had to invent such stories about you. And what is it you want, Mr. Effingham?"

Mr. Effingham scarcely liked the tone; he felt he was being "chaffed;" so he thought he would bring matters to a crisis by saying, "My name's not Effingham—at least, not more than yours is Gillespie."

"Oh, I perceive," said she with a little nod.

"My name's Butler as much as yours is Ponsford. Now d'ye see?"

"O yes; now I see perfectly. Butler, eh? Any relation of a man named Tony Butler who is now dead?"

"Yes—his brother. He may have spoken to you of a brother in America."

"In America! ay, ay. Well, Mr. Butler," she continued with a bright smile, "now I know that you're the brother of Tony Butler, there's scarcely any need of repeating my question whether you wanted anything; for—pardon me—you could hardly belong to that interesting family without wanting something. The question is, what do you want? Money? and if so, how much?"

"No; I don't want money—"

"That's very unlike Tony Butler. I shall begin to discredit your statements," said she, still with the pleasant smile.

"At least not yet, nor from you. But I do want something."

"Ye-es, and that is—"

"I want you to go away from here with me at once."

"To go away from here! O no. *Connu*, my dear Mr. Butler; I see the whole of the play. This is not your own business at all, dear sir. You dance, and kick your legs and swing your arms very well; but you are a puppet, and the gentleman who pulls the strings lives over yonder;" and she pointed with her umbrella to Redmoor House.

"I can't make out what you mean."

"O yes, you can. 'A master I have, and I am his man.' You are Sir Charles Mitford's man, Mr. Butler; and he has set you on to tell me that I must leave this place and rid him of my influence. Now, you may go back to Sir Charles Mitford, your master, and tell him that I set him utterly at defiance; that I won't move, and that he can't make me. Do you hear that, my dear Mr. Butler?"

She had risen from her seat, and stood erect before him, looking very grand and savage. Her companion knew that the success of his scheme depended wholly upon the manner in which he carried out the next move, and accordingly he threw all his power into the acting of it.

"You're one of those who answer their own questions, I see," said he with perfect calmness. "I've met lots o' that sort in my travels, and I never found 'em do so much good as those that waited. All you've been saying's Greek to me. Who's Sir Charles Mitford? I've heard of him, of course, as the swell that lives in that house. They've never done talking of him at the Mitford Arms and all about there. But what's he to do with you? I suppose it don't matter to him who his friends' governesses is. He's not sweet on you, is he? If so, he wouldn't want you to go away. And what's he to do with me? and how's he likely to hear of my having been in the place? I haven't left my card upon him, I promise you," said Mr. Effingham with a grim humour.

Miss Gillespie looked at him hard, very hard. But his perfect command of feature had often stood Mr. Effingham in good stead, and it did not desert him now. The saucy laughter on his lips corresponded with the easy bantering tone of his voice; he sat swinging his legs and sucking his stick, the incarnation of insolence. So far he was triumphant.

She waited a minute or two, biting her lips, and turning her plans in her mind. Then she said, "Granting what you say—and it was rather a preposterous proposition of mine, I admit—you are still a puppet in somebody's hands. You had no knowledge of my previous life, and yet you come to me and say I must come away at once with you. Why must I come away?"

"Because you're wanted."

"And by whom?"

"By the crew of the Albatross. Ah, I thought you wouldn't be quite so much amused and so full of your grins when I mentioned them."

"Oh," said she, recovering herself, "I can still grin when there's anything to amuse me. But we seem to have changed places; now you're talking riddles which I cannot understand."

"Can't you? then I must explain them for you. If what I'm told is right—but it's very little I know—you belonged to that crew yourself once. My brother Tony was one of them, I understand; and though he's dead now, there's several of 'em left. Old Lyons, for instance,—you recollect him? Crockett, Griffiths—"

"Suppose, to avoid giving you further trouble, I say I do recollect them, what then?"

"You're angry, although you smile; I can see that fast enough. But what's the good of being angry with me? You know when a feller gets into their hands what chance he has. You know that fast enough, or ought to. Well, I'm in their hands, and have to do what they order me."

"And they've ordered you to come down to me?"

"They found out where you were, and sent me after you."

"Ha! And what on earth can have induced them, after a certain lapse of time, to be so suddenly solicitous of my welfare?" said Miss Gillespie, laughingly. "There was never any great love between any of those you have named and myself. I have no money for them to rob me of, nor do I see that I can be of any great use to them."

"I don't know that," said Mr. Effingham, laying his forefinger knowingly alongside his nose. "You see, you're a pretty gal, and you've rather got over me—"

"Flattered, I am sure," said Miss Gillespie, showing all her teeth.

"No, it ain't that," said he, with a dim perception that his compliment was not too graciously received; "it ain't that; but I do like a pretty girl somehow. Well, you see, they don't let me much into their secrets—don't tell me the reason why I'm told to do so and so; they only tell me to go and do it. But I don't mind tellin' you—taking an interest in you, as I've just said—that, from what they've let drop accidentally, I think you can be of great use to them."

"Indeed! have you any notion how?"

"Well, now look here. I'm blowin' their gaff to you, and you know what I should get if they knew it; so swear you'll never let on. From what I can make out, there's certain games which you used to do for them that they've never been able to find anybody to come near you in. I mean the Mysterious Lady, the fortune-tellin', and the electro-biology business."

Some scenes recalled to her memory by these words seemed to amuse Miss Gillespie, and she laughed heartily.

"But that's 'general work,'" continued Mr. Effingham; "what they want you particularly for just now is this. Some swell, so far as I can make out, came to grief early in life, and made a mistake in putting somebody else's name to paper; what they call forgery, you know."

She nodded.

"Old Lyons has got hold of this paper, and he wants to put the screw on the swell and make him bleed. Now there's none of the lot has half your manner, nor, as they say, half your tact; and that's why, as I believe, is the reason they want you back in town amongst them."

"Ah! to—what did you say?—'to put the screw on a swell and make him bleed,' wasn't it? How very nice! Well, now you've obeyed your orders, and it's for me to speak. And suppose—just suppose for the fun of the thing—I were to hold by my original decision and declare I would not come, what would you do?"

"I should go back to town and tell 'em all that had passed."

"And they?—what would they do?"

"I can tell you that, because that was part of my instructions. Old Lyons put that very plain. 'If she rides rusty,' he says,—'and she's got a temper of her own, I can tell you,—just let her know from me that I'll ruin her. I'll never leave her; she knows me of old; it won't be merely,' he says, 'her being turned away in disgrace out of where she is now; but I'll never leave her. She may go where she likes, but I've found her out once, and I'll find her out again; I'll foller her up, and I'll be the ruin of her,' he says, 'so sure's her name's what it is.'"

He looked up to see the effect of his speech, but Miss Gillespie was looking full at him with an expression of great interest and a very pleasant smile, as if she were listening to the narration of a thrilling story with which she had no connection save that of listener.

"Did he indeed say all that?" said she, after a pause. "Oh, he's a most terrible old man, and whatever he determines on, he never fails of carrying out. However, I think I won't put him to much trouble this time."

"How do you mean?"

"Well, do you know I've a strong mind to save you any further worry, and to crown you with glory by allowing you to carry me back in triumph."

"You don't say so! but this is too sudden, you know. I don't put much trust in such sudden conversions."

"Mine is not the least sudden. I generally act on the impulse of the moment. That now urges me to go back to my old life. The shackles of this respectability are beginning to strain a little. I feel cramped by them occasionally, and I suppose I have originally something of the Bohemian in my nature, for you have fired me with au ardent longing for freedom and irresponsibility."

"That's right!" cried Mr. Effingham, delighted at the success of his scheme; "that's just as it should be. It's all very well for those swells to live on here, and go on their daily round. They've got the best of it, so far as they know; but they haven't seen as much as we have. They don't know the pleasure of—well, of pitting your wits against somebody else who think themselves deuced sharp, and beating them, do they?"

"No," said Miss Gillespie, with her crispest little laugh; "of course they don't."

"Well, now," said Mr. Effingham, "you know what old Lyons is, reg'lar man of business; want's everything done at once, right off the reel. When will you be ready to start?"

"What a practical man you are, Mr. Butler!" cried she, still laughing; "it will be quite delightful to get back again into the society of practical people after all this easy-going *laissez-aller* time. But you must not be too hard upon me at first. I've several things to do."

"You won't be saying 'goodbye' to anybody or anything of that sort?"

"O no, nothing of that sort, you may depend."

"That's right; you mean putting your things together, eh?"

"Yes; packing and getting ready to start."

"Well, twenty-four hours will be enough for that, I should think. Suppose we say to-morrow at noon?"

"Ye-es, give me a little longer: say two in the afternoon, then I shall be perfectly ready."

"And where shall we meet?"

"We must get across to the rail at once. Not to Torquay; there's a small station nearer here, where they won't think of looking for us. Not that I suppose they'd take any trouble of that kind when they find I'm once gone. However, it's best to be prepared. Can you drive?"

"I should think so!" said Mr. Effingham with a chuckle. "I've driven most things, from a shofle-cab in town to the mail-sleigh in Canada!"

"How very nice!" said she; "that will do beautifully, then. You must get a gig or a dog-cart, or something light, from some place in Torquay. I shall have very little luggage, and have it all ready at a little side-gate of the park, which you can see—over there," again bringing the umbrella into requisition. "That gate is invisible from the house; it's perfectly quiet and unfrequented, and I have a key of it. That once closed behind me I'm thoroughly safe."

"And there's no chance of our being met, and you being recognized?"

"Not the very smallest. The people staying in the house will all be at luncheon; the gardeners and stable-people, should we come across any, will all be in that state of comatose repletion which succeeds the after-dinner tobacco. Besides, very few of them know me by sight; and the road which I have pointed out skirts the Redmoor, and is very little frequented."

"That'll do! that will be first-rate! Now, let me see if all's understood. A dog-cart to be ready to-morrow at yon gate of the park, at two o'clock sharp. There you'll be and your luggage—eh? By the by, how's that to get there?"

"I told you it would be very little; and there's a boy devoted to my service, who will carry it."

"All right,—I only wanted to know. Two o'clock to-morrow, then." He put out his hand, and as she lightly touched it with the tips of her fingers, offered to seize hers and convey it to his lips; but she slid it through his clumsy fist, and had pulled the poke-bonnet over her face, resumed the bent walk and the clumsy umbrella, and was making her way back across the park almost before he had missed her.

"And if ever a man did a good day's work, I've done one this blessed morning," said Mr. Effingham, as he strolled quietly back through the avenue. "They may talk about great genius, if they please. Great genius means getting hold of a good idea at the right minute, and strikin' while the iron's hot. That's great genius! and they was two great ideas which I've worked just now! That pretendin' to know nothin' of the Bart., and gammonin' her that old Lyons sent me after her, was first-rate! I thought old Lyons's name would bring her round. They're all afraid of him, it seems. Now when we've got some distance on the road, I'll tell her the truth, or, at least, as much as I choose, and just sound her about the bill. D'Ossay, my boy, you've done a good day's work, and can afford to go into Torquay and dine like a swell to-night!"

CHAPTER XX.

CHECKMATE.

Mr. Effingham fulfilled his design of going into Torquay and dining well. In his singular costume he created quite a sensation among the invalids on the Parade, who would have severely resented the healthy and sporting tone of his ankle-jacks if it had not been mitigated by his slouch wideawake hat and black jacket. As it was, they merely regarded him as an eccentric person staying at one of the country-houses in the neighbourhood, and they pardoned his not being consumptive on the score of his being probably either rich or distinguished. So he "did" the town and all the lions to his great satisfaction, and, as affording them subject-matter for conversation over their valetudinarian dinners, to the satisfaction of those whom he encountered. He made an excellent dinner at the hotel, and then was driven out of his rural lodgings in a fly, having given orders for a dog-cart to be in readiness for him at the particular gate of Redmoor Park which he described at two o'clock the next day.

It was a brilliant starlight night, and Mr. Effingham had the head of the fly opened; he was well wrapped up, and the air being very mild, he wished to enjoy the beauties of nature and the flavour of his cigar simultaneously. As he lay back puffing the smoke out before him, his thoughts again reverted to his morning's work, and again he found every reason for self-gratulation. There would be the fifty pounds from Sir Charles—that was safe to start with; he should go up and give him notice in the morning, that that cheque might come up by the evening's post. That would help him to tide over any delay there might be in getting this woman to give up the bill. What a funny one she was! what a regular lively one! how she kept on laughing! and how sly she looked when she said that she was tired of that humdrum respectability, and would like to run away to the old adventurous life! Not one to be trifled with, though; none of your larks with her; regular stand-offish party. Well, never mind; that did not matter; what he was about now was business, and she seemed thoroughly up to that. He did not think he should have much trouble in making her see what advantage to them both could be got out of a proper use of the forged bill. One point, on which he at one time had had some doubt, the interview of that morning had satisfactorily set at rest. She had been spoony on Mitford—so Griffiths told him—and he feared that the old feeling might still remain, and she would refuse to take any steps about the bill lest she might injure her old flame. But, Lord! he could see plainly enough she did not care a snuff of a candle for Mitford now; rather more t'other might be judged from the flash in her eyes and the sneer on her lips when she spoke of him. That was all right, so—Ah! perhaps her shrewd notions of business might lead her to seeing the value of the bill and to driving a hard bargain for it. He must be prepared for that; but when he got her up to London she would be much more in his power. The bill must be had somehow, by fair means or foul; and if she resisted—well, there would not be very much trouble in stealing or forcing it from her.

As the reflections passed through his mind the carriage in which he sat reached the top of a height, whence was obtained a view of Redmoor House; its outline standing black and heavy against the sky, its lower windows blazing with light. The sight turned Mr. Effingham's thoughts into a slightly different current.

"O yes! go it; that's your sort," he said to himself with a certain amount of bitterness; "fine games goin' on there, I've no doubt; the best of drink, and coves with powdered heads to wait on you; game o' billiards afterwards, or some singin' and a dance with the women in the droring-room. That's the way to keep it up; go it while you're young. But, my friend the Bart., you'd sing another toon and laugh the wrong side o' your mouth, and cut a very different kind o' caper, if you knew what was so close to you. I've heard of a cove smokin' a pipe and not knowing that what he was sittin' on was a powder-barrel; and this seems to me very much the same sort o' thing. To think that close under his nose is the dockyment that would just crop his 'air, put him into a gray soot, Cole-Barth Fields, Milbank, and Portland, and that cussed stonequarryin' which, from all I've heard, is the heart-breakin'est work. To think that he's been payin' me to get the bill, and I've been employin' Griffiths and givin' skivs to old Lyons and settin' half Doory Lane at work to hunt up the gal, and that there she was under his roof, the whole time—it's tremenjous!"

And Mr. Effingham laughed aloud, and lit a fresh cigar, and pulled the rug tighter over his legs.

"She's a rum 'un, she is. I wonder which of them lights is in her room. There's one a long way off the rest, up high all by itself; that's it, I shouldn't wonder. She's not fit company for the swells downstairs, I suppose. Well, perhaps not, if they knew everythin'! But what a blessin' it is people don't know everythin'! Perhaps if they did, some of 'em wouldn't be quite so fond of sittin' down with the Bart. I wonder what she's doin' just now. Packin' her traps ready for our start, I shouldn't wonder. What a game it will be! Yes, D'Ossay, my boy, this is the best days work you ever did in your life; and your poor brother Tony little thought what a power of good he was doin' you when he first let you into the secret of Mr. Mitford and his little games."

And with these reflections, and constantly-renewed cigars, Mr. Effingham beguiled the tedium of his journey to the Mitford Arms.

He was up betimes the next morning, making his preparations for departure. His very small wardrobe—its very smallness regarded by the landlady of the inn as a proof of the eccentricity of literary genius—was packed in a brown-paper parcel. He discharged his modest bill, and began to fidget about until it was time to give his employer a final and fancy sketch of how he had accomplished his mission. Entirely fictional was this sketch intended to be, as widely diverging from fact as possible. Mr. Effingham knew well enough that so long as the removal of Miss Gillespie, or Lizzie Ponsford, had been effected, Sir Charles Mitford would care very little indeed about the means by which it had been accomplished. And as Mr. Effingham was playing a double game, it would be necessary for him to be particularly cautious in making any statement which might reveal the real state of the case to Sir Charles. These reflections, bringing clearly again before him the great fact of the entire business,— that he was being paid for communicating with a person, to communicate with whom he would have gladly paid a considerable sum of money had he possessed it,—put Mr. Effingham into the most satisfactory state of mind, and caused the time, which would otherwise have hung heavily on his hands, to pass pleasantly and quickly.

He knew that there was little use in attempting to see Sir Charles before eleven o'clock; so about that time he made his way up the avenue, on this occasion cutting short the old portress, who, contrary to the usual custom, was beginning to enter into some little story. It was Mr. Effingham's plan—and one which is pretty generally adopted in this world, especially by the lower order of Mr. Smiles's friends, the "self-made" men,—to kick down the ladder after he had landed from its top; and as Mr. Effingham thought he should be able to make no more use of this old woman, he did not choose to be bored by her conversation. So he cut her short with a nod, and walked up the avenue with a swaggering gait, which she had never known before, and which very much astonished her. He met no one on his way; and when he reached the house he went modestly round to a side-door leading to the billiard-room, through the window of which he observed no less a personage than Mr. Banks, Sir Charles's man, who was by himself, with his coat off and a cue in his hand trying a few hazards. Mr. Effingham gave a sharp tap at the glass, which made Mr. Banks start guiltily, drop his cue, and resume his garment; but when he looked up and saw who had caused him this fright, he waxed very wroth and said, "Hallo! is it you? what do you want now?"

His tone did not at all suit Mr. Effingham, who replied sharply, "Your master; go and tell him I'm here."

"He ain't up yet," said Mr. Banks.

"Did you hear what I said? Go and tell him I'm here."

"Did you hear what I said, that Sir Charles ain't stir-run'?"

"It'll be as much as your place is worth, my man, if you don't do what I tell you. Have I been here before, or 'ave I not? Have I been let in to him at once before, or 'ave I not? Does he see me d'rectly you tell him who's waitin', or does he not? Now— go."

This speech had such an effect upon Mr. Banks, who remembered that the little man only spoke the truth in his statement of the readiness with which Sir Charles always saw him, that he opened the door, showed Mr. Effingham into the billiard-room (which was decorated with empty tumblers, fragments of lemon-peel, tobacco-ash, and other remnants of the preceding night, and smelt powerfully of stale tobacco), suggested that he should "knock the balls about a bit," and went up to tell his master.

When he returned he said, "He's just finished dressin', and I'm to take you up in five minutes. You seem quite a favourite of his."

Mr. Effingham laughed. "Yes," he said; "he and I understand one another."

Mr. Banks looked at him for a moment, and then said, "Was you ever in the Pacific?"

"In the what?"

"The Pacific."

Mr. Effingham changed colour. He did not half like this. He thought it was the name of some prison, and that the valet had found him out. But he put a bold face on and said, "What's the Pacific?"

"Ocean," said Mr. Banks.

"No," said Mr. Effingham, "certainly not—nothing of the sort."

"Not when you and he," pointing to the ceiling, "was together?"

"Certainty not."

"Ah!" said Mr. Banks, "kept at home, I suppose; it ain't so dangerous or such hard work at home, is it?—Portsmouth and round there?"

"It's hard enough at Portsmouth, from what I've heard," said Mr. Effingham; "that diggin' away at Southsea's dreadful work."

"Diggin' aboard ship!" said Banks in astonishment.

"How do you mean 'aboard ship'?" said the other.

"Why, I'm talkin' of when you and him was on board the—what was it?—you know—Albatross."

"Oh!" said Mr. Effingham, greatly relieved, and bursting into a fit of laughter; "we went everywhere then. And that's where I learned something I don't mind teaching you."

"What's that?"

"Never to keep Sir Charles waiting. The five minutes is up."

Mr. Banks looked half-annoyed, but his companion had already risen, so he made the best of it, pretended to laugh, and showed Mr. Effingham into Sir Charles Mitford's private snuggery.

Sir Charles was drinking a cup of coffee. He looked eagerly at Mr. Effingham, and when Banks had closed the door, said:

"By the expression of your face I should say you bring good news. In two words—do you, or do you not?"

"In two words—I do."

Mitford set down his cup. Through his mind rushed one thought—the spy over his flirtation with Mrs. Hammond was removed! henceforward he could sit with her, talk to her, look at her, with the consciousness that his words would reach her ear alone, that his actions would not be overlooked. His face flushed with anticipated pleasure as he said:

"How was it managed? Did she make much resistance?"

"Well, it wasn't a very easy job, and that's the fact. I've seen many women as could be got over with much less trouble. You see the party seems to be in very comfortable quarters here,—all right to eat and drink, and not too much to do, and that sort of thing."

"Well, what then?"

"Why, when parties are in that way they naturally don't like movin'. Besides, there's another strong reason I've found out why that young woman don't want to go."

"And that is—"

"She's uncommon fond, of you. Ah, you may shake your head, but I'm sure of it."

"If she made you believe that, Mr. Effingham," said Sir Charles with a very grim smile, "I'm afraid she's got the better of you altogether."

"Has she, by Jove! No, no. The proof of the puddin's in the eatin', Sir Charles; and whether I've done the trick or not you'll find out before I've finished. Any how, I'm satisfied."

"Well, as you say that, and as the payment of the fifty pounds depends upon the 'trick being done,' as you call it, I suppose before you've finished your story I shall be satisfied too."

"What was I saying? Oh, about her being nuts on you still,—O yes,—and I had to talk to her about that, and tell her it wouldn't do now you was married, and, in fact, that that was one of the great reasons for her to go, as parties had observed her feelin's. That seemed to touch her,—for her pride's awful,—and she began to give way, and at last, after a long palaver, she said she'd go, though not before I—"

"Beg your pardon, Sir Charles," said Banks, opening the door; "Mrs. Hammond, Sir Charles, wishes to speak to you, Sir Charles: she's here at the door."

"Show her in, by all means," said Mitford, turning to Effingham and laying his finger on his lips; then to him, *sotto voce*, "Keep your mouth shut!"

"I'm very sorry to trouble you, Sir Charles," said Mrs. Hammond, entering hurriedly, with a slight bow to the stranger and a glance of astonishment at his appearance; "but I will detain you only an instant. Have you heard anything of Miss Gillespie?"

"Of Miss Gillespie? I, Mrs. Hammond? Not a word. What has happened?"

"Of course you haven't, but the most extraordinary thing! This morning Miss Gillespie did not come into Alice's room as usual; so the child dressed by herself, and went to Miss Gillespie's room. She tried the door, and found it fast; so, concluding that her governess was ill,—she's subject to headaches, I believe,—Alice went down to breakfast. Afterwards she tried Miss Gillespie's door again, but with no better success; and then she came to me. I sent for Gifford, Mr. Hammond's man, you know; and after calling out once or twice, he burst the door open; we all rushed in, and found the room empty."

"Empty!" cried Sir Charles.

"The devil!" burst out Mr. Effingham. "I beg your pardon! What an odd thing!"

"Empty," repeated Mrs. Hammond. "The bed hadn't been slept in; her boxes were open, and some of the things had been taken out; while on the dressing-table was this note addressed to me."

She handed a small slip of paper to Sir Charles, who opened it and read aloud:

"You will never see me again. Search for me will be useless.

"R. G."

"Yes," said Mrs. Hammond, "she's gone. 'Search for me will be useless.' So provoking too; just the sort of person one liked to have about one; and I had got quite accustomed to her and all that. 'Never see me again;' I declare it's horribly annoying. Now, Sir Charles, I want to ask your advice: what would you do? Would you have people sent after her in all directions, eh?"

"Well, 'pon my word, I don't see how you can do that," said Sir Charles. "She hasn't taken anything of yours, I suppose,—no, of course not,—so, you see, she has a right to go away when she likes. Needn't give a month's warning, eh?"

"Right to go away! Well, I don't know,—I suppose she has—and I suppose I haven't any right to stop her; but it is annoying; and yet it's highly ridiculous, isn't it?" "What on earth can have driven her away? Nobody rude to her, I should think; she wasn't that sort of person. Well, I won't bore you any more now about it, particularly as you're busy. We shall meet at luncheon, and then we can talk further over this unpleasant affair." And with a smile to Sir Charles, and another slight bow to Mr. Effingham, she left the room.

"Well, you certainly have done your work excellently, Mr. Effingham," said Sir Charles, as soon as the door had closed; "in the most masterly manner!"

"Yes, it ain't bad, I think," said Mr. Effingham, with a ghastly attempt at a grin; "I told you it was all square."

"Yes; but I had no notion it would come about so quickly."

"Why, I hadn't half time to tell you about it. However, there it is, done, cut, and dried,—all finished except the payment; and I'm ready for that whenever you like."

"Our agreement was, that the cheque was to be sent to London, to an address which you gave me—"

"Yes, but as I'm here, I may as well take it myself. You haven't got it in notes or gold, have you? It would be handier."

"No, not sufficient; but they would change my cheque at the bank in Torquay, I've no doubt."

"No, thank you, never mind, it ain't worth the trouble. I shall have to go to town, I suppose, and I shan't want it till I get there—that is, if you can lend me a couple of sovereigns just to help me on my way. Thank you; much obliged. Now, you've got my address, and you know where to find me when you want me; and you may depend on not seein' me for a very long time. Good morning to you."

He took the cheque and the sovereigns and put them in his waistcoat-pocket, made a clumsy bow, and was gone. Then Sir Charles Mitford rose from his chair and walked to the window, radiant with delight. It was all clear before him now; the incubus was removed, and he was free to carry out his projects.

Mr. Effingham strode down the avenue, switching his stick and muttering:

"Done! sold! swindled!" he exclaimed; "regularly roped,—that's what I am! It was lucky I kept my face before the Bart., or I should never have collared the cheque; but that's all right. So far he thinks it was my doin', and forked out accordin'. That's the only bright part of it. To think that a yellow-faced meek-lookin' thing like that should have taken me in to that toon! What can her game be? To get clear of the lot of us?—that's it! Pretendin' to be all square with me, and then cuttin' and runnin' and shakin' it all off! Oh, a deep 'un, a regular deep 'un! Now what's my game? After her as hard as I can. Where will she make for? London, I should think,—try hidin' somewhere. Ah! if she does that, I'll ferret her out. It'll be a quiet place that I don't hunt her up in, with the means I have for workin' a search. Here's two skivs to the good from the Bart. I'll meet the dog-cart and get down to Torquay, and go up at once by the express. Hallo! gate, there!"

"Why, you are in a hurry, sir!" said the old portress, coming out; "mist as pressed as the young woman as knocked me up at day-dawn this morning."

"Ah! what was that?" said Mr. Effingham stopping short.

"I would have told you this morning when you came in; but you were so short and snappish!" said the old lady. "She came down wi' a little passel in her hand, and knocked at my door and ast for the key. And I got up to let her out, and there were a fly outside—Mullins's fly, and young Mullins to drive; and she got in, and off they went."

"Ay, ay where does Mullins live?"

"Just close by Mitford Arms. His father were wi' my father—"

"Yes, yes; thank you! all right! goodbye!" and Mr. Effingham rushed off up the by-lane to where he knew the dog-cart was waiting.

CHAPTER XXI.

COLONEL ALSAGER'S COUNSEL.

When Laurence Alsager awoke the morning after Miss Gillespie's piano-performance, his thoughts immediately turned to the mysterious note which he had received on the previous evening, and he stretched out his hand and took it from the dressing-table, where he had placed it just before dropping off to sleep. He read it again and again, and each perusal strengthened his belief. It was written by Miss Gillespie—of that he had little doubt—and was intended to convey a warning of proximate danger to Lady Mitford, and counsel to him to avert this danger if possible, by remaining at Redmoor. It seemed further to imply that some protection which had hitherto been extended over her would necessarily be withdrawn, and that his presence was consequently more than ever needful. At this conclusion Laurence arrived; it was but a lame and impotent one, after all, and he determined to seek the solution at an interview with Miss Gillespie as soon as possible.

He was the earliest in the breakfast-room, and found a batch of letters lying in his accustomed place. They were of all kinds,—foreign letters from men whose acquaintance he had made abroad, and the gist of whose correspondence lay in an endeavour to tempt him to come out to them again; a business letter or two about the investment of some spare cash; a line from Blab Bertram, wondering when L. A. was coming to town, and "what was the use of leaving Egypt if you stuck down in Devon?" and a thick old-fashioned letter, on yellowish gilt-edged paper, sealed with a large seal, and directed in a bold yet tremulous hand—his father's. Alsager's conscience pricked him as he came upon this letter at the bottom of the little pile; he had been two months in England, after two years' absence, and had not yet found time to visit his father. They had been always very good friends; indeed when Laurence was at Eton, the tie between them was of the strongest, and they were more like brothers than father and son. With the young man's life at Oxford their relations were a little less intimate; Laurence was beginning to see life with his coevals, and found Sir Peregrine's society a check and hindrance on his enjoyment. The father perceived this, and weakly allowed himself to be annoyed at it. He was hurt and jealous at his son's preference of younger companions, at his own inability to amuse or interest his son's friends; and from that time forth there was a slight estrangement between them. Laurence had the enjoyment of his mother's fortune on coming of age, so that he was perfectly independent of his father; and his joining the Guards was entirely his own doing, and to a certain extent against his father's wish. Sir Peregrine was of that old-fashioned school which abhorred London and its ways, and thought a country gentleman ought to live entirely on his own estate, in superintending which, and in joining the sports of the field, he would find plenty of amusement and occupation. Their ideas and tastes being thus different, it was tacitly felt by both that they were best apart, and during the last few years they had not met a dozen times. Sir Peregrine's annual visit to London was generally made in the winter, when Laurence was staying with country friends; and Laurence found little attraction in the dozy, prosy county-magistrate society which the old gentleman gathered round him at Knockholt.

But his conscience pricked him when he saw the old gentleman's letter, which had been forwarded to him from his club—pricked him sharply after he had opened it and read as follows:

"Knockholt, Friday.

"My Dear Lance,—If you have not any very particular engagements, I think it would be as well if you were to come down here for a day or two. There are some things I want to talk over with you, and I think the sooner our business is done the better. I had a nasty fall a fortnight ago, when I was out with Lord Hawkshaw's pack; and though Galton says it's nothing, I was a good deal shaken at the time, and feel it has jarred me more than they think; for I have an odd kind of all-overish pain, which I can't explain to them, and can't account for to myself. Not that I am going to die, that I know of; but one does not fall lightly when one weighs fifteen stone, nor get over a cropper quickly when one is sixty-seven years old. So, my dear Lance, put up with the old house and the old man for a few days, and come. I have a surprise for you.—Your affectionate father, P. A.

"P.S.—Captain Freeman saw you looking out of the club-window when he was in London in January. He says you had a beard like a billy-goat. For God's sake, my dear Lance, go to a barber before I see you! I hate all such foreign affectations. P. A."

Laurence looked grave over the letter, but could not help smiling at the postscript, so characteristic of his father. He did not at all like the aspect of affairs at Knockholt; his father was evidently far more hurt than either the doctors imagined or he himself would allow. His ward, Miss Manningtree, and her governess, resided with the old gentleman; but Laurence knew too little of either to feel confidence in their capacity, their care, or their judgment in the matter of medical advice. They might think Galton all-sufficient and infallible; he didn't. He would go down at once, at least as soon as he had learned from Miss Gillespie what really was meant by her mysterious letter. He had been too long dallying at Capri; but now that duty called him away, he would obey cheerfully. By the time he had finished his letter and formed his resolution, Captain Bligh had entered the room, and had plunged deeply into his breakfast, which he took standing, now making a dive at the toast-rack, now impaling a bloater, now walking round and pouring out a cup of tea; for there were no ladies present, and the captain was in a hurry, having much business on hand.

"Morning, Alsager," said the Captain, when Laurence looked up. "Queer start this, isn't it?"

"What? I'm only just down; I've seen nobody and heard nothing."

"Oh, about that girl that sung last night,—Mrs. Hammond's governess. What's her name?"

"Miss Gillespie?"

"Ah, that's she! Wouldn't have thought it of her—would you?"

"What's she done?"

"Done! Bolted, that's all!—bolted slick away, no one knows where!"

"What on earth for?"

"No one knows that either. Rummest thing is, that she hasn't taken anything with her—anything of anybody else's, I mean. Now, if she'd walked off with some of that little Hammond woman's swell clothes, or jool'ry, one could understand it; but she's left a lot of her own behind."

"Did she give no hint of this? Has she left no explanation?"

"Well, I don't know about explanation. She's left a note for Mrs. Hammond, which I've got in my pocket. Mrs. Hammond gave it to Mitford, and he sent for me and handed it over, and asked me what I thought of it."

"It's not private, I suppose. May I look at it?"

"By all means—nothing private about it. Can't conceive why Mitford gave it to me. I can do nothing with it." So saying Captain Bligh took out the little scrap of paper from his waistcoat pocket, and handed it to Alsager.

There was no longer the least doubt about Laurence's mysterious correspondent. Both notes were in the same handwriting.

At luncheon that day Miss Gillespie's disappearance was the principal theme of conversation, and many and various were the comments it evoked. Lady Mitford seemed a little scandalized at the circumstance; but Mrs. Hammond, her first astonishment over, treated it very lightly. She had always thought Miss Gillespie a "curious person," she said; there was always something "odd" about her. Very likely, when they got back to town, they would find she would return to them. Perhaps, after all, the reason of her flight was that she was a little bored in the country. And then Mrs. Hammond forgot all about Miss Gillespie in her delight at having Sir Charles Mitford sitting next her again, at finding him paying her little attentions and compliments, talking to her in a dropped voice, and regarding her with deep tender glances, just as he had done in the first days of her visit to Redmoor. She delighted in all this, and her delight was increased when she marked the grave gloom on Laurence Alsager's face, as she shot a glance of saucy triumph across at him. Then he guessed the meaning of Miss Gillespie's note more thoroughly than he had yet done. She had had some hold either on Mrs. Hammond or on Sir Charles; that was gone, and he alone was left to do his best to keep them in check. And what could he do? Any overt act of his would be misconstrued by Mrs. Hammond, and turned to her own purposes, while over Mitford he had not the smallest power. What could he do? Had Lord Dollamore given any sign of intending to persecute Lady Mitford with his attentions, Laurence thought that his staying in the house might be of some use; but Dollamore had hitherto been perfectly respectful. So Alsager determined that he would remain a couple of days longer, and then start off for Knockholt.

After luncheon a proposal was made to go and see some new horses which Captain Bligh had inspected when last in Torquay, and which he thought might be obtained as bargains. So most of the party adjourned to the stable-yard, where these horses had been brought; and the visit ended in a pair of them being put to, and Sir Charles and Mrs. Hammond mounting the phaeton to which they were harnessed. The horses were young and fresh, and plunged a great deal at starting; but Sir Charles had them well in hand, and with his companion by his side and a groom in the back-seat, went flying down the avenue. It was full an hour before they returned, and Sir Charles's verdict on the pair was that they were too hot to hold. He had had all his work, he said, to keep them at all within bounds. Mrs. Hammond looked flushed and elated; but she went straight up to Lady Mitford, and told her how she had enjoyed the drive, and was full of praises of Sir Charles's powers of coachmanship.

That evening Sir Charles took Mrs. Hammond in to the dining-room, and addressed his conversation principally to her. He drank a great deal of wine both with and after dinner, and was in more boisterous spirits than any of his friends had yet seen him. When they went into the drawing-room he made straight for Mrs. Hammond's chair, and there he remained the whole evening, talking to her in a lowered tone, and regarding her with glances the fire of which had by no means been subdued by the quantity of claret he had drunk. Poor Georgie! The events of this day, culminating as they were, had totally upset her, and had reduced her very much to the same condition as when she begged Alsager to be her charioteer to Egremont Priory. There could be no mistake about it now. Surely it was a flagrant case; and the colour flushed in her cheeks as she saw Mrs. Masters's shoulder-shrugs and marked Lord Dollamore's ill-disguised cynical manner. Poor Georgie! She asked Mrs. Charteris to sing, and sat and listened to her as usual, and thanked her at the end of the performance; and she chatted with the Tyrrell girls, and she took the deepest interest in Mrs. Masters's embroidery,—and all the time her heart was sick within her, and she kept stealing glances at the couple seated in the embrasure of the window, with their heads so nearly touching. All present noticed her state of mind; but no one understood it or pitied it like Laurence Alsager, who began to confess to himself that what Dollamore had prophesied at the club was undoubtedly coming true, so far as Mitford was concerned; and did, not the wife's future, even in Lord Dollamore's prophecy, hinge upon the husband's conduct? It was a most horrible shame; but how on earth was he to protest against it? He had no position to enable him to do anything of the kind. There was only one thing that he could do, and that was to speak to Laura Hammond. He could do that; it might not be of much use, but he would do it.

So, accordingly, the next morning after breakfast Colonel Alsager sent to Mrs. Hammond a polite little note, in which he presented his compliments, and requested the pleasure of a few minutes' conversation; and to which a verbal answer was returned to the effect that Mrs. Hammond would be delighted to see Colonel Alsager, if he could come up at once. He followed the lady's-maid, and found Mrs. Hammond in the boudoir, dressed in her habit and hat. She received him with great cordiality.

"I am so sorry to have sent what may have seemed a peremptory message, Colonel Alsager," she said; "but the fact is, Sir Charles has been round here just now, and we have arranged a little riding-party,—he and I, and Emily Tyrrell, and Captain Bligh, and Mr. Somers, and one or two more; and I promised to be ready by eleven."

"Make no excuses, pray," said Laurence, in a hard dry tone. "I won't detain you, as your time's valuable, by any preamble. I will simply ask, are you determined to persist in your present course?"

"In what course, my dear Colonel Alsager?"

"In bringing destruction on a household, Laura Hammond! In blighting the happiness of a young wife, and spreading snares for a foolish husband! In rendering yourself conspicuous, and your host contemptible! Do I speak plainly enough?"

"Scarcely," said she with a little smile; "for though you insult me, and give way to your own rage, you do not condescend to—or you dare not—explain your motives. Don't think that I am weak enough to imagine that you are jealous of me, Laurence. I know you too well for that. I know that whatever command I may have had over you is past and gone. But perhaps the passion, the *caprice* that I had for you—call it what you will—continues. Suppose it does? Suppose the sight of you, the meeting with you after so long a separation, has renewed the dormant flame? You scorn me, and I see you prostrate at the feet of a sweetly pretty piece of propriety and innocence—don't interrupt me, please—who then becomes my rival? Revenge is sweet, especially to women, you know. This child of the fields makes herself my rival,—I make myself hers! I show to you and others, that if you care for me no longer, there are others who will. I show to her and others, that if she is preferred to me by one I—yes, I love,—I am preferred to her by one she loves. As yet I have never run second for anything for which I've entered, Colonel Alsager, and I don't intend to do so now."

"You are arguing on utterly false premises,—you are talking worse than nonsense. Between me and the lady to whom you allude there is nothing. You need not smile in that way. I swear it! She is as pure as—"

"Oh, pray spare me! Don't fall into raptures about her purity,—there's a good creature. Dear me, dear me! this must be a very bad case, when a man like Colonel Alsager takes a poetical view of his lady-love, and talks about her purity."

"I came to ask you to abandon this shameless flirtation, Laura Hammond, for the sake of our old friendship,—as an act of kindness to me. Your reply is mockery and ridicule. I may use other means to bring about what I want."

"Ah, you threaten! Then I shall certainly get Mr. Hammond to fight you! He was out once at Nusserabad, or Hylunjee, or some such place, I believe. And we can prop him up on his crutches, and get his man to hold him, and I've no doubt he'd be strong enough to fire a pistol.—No," she added, suddenly changing her tone, "don't threaten, and don't thwart me; else let our innocent young friend look to herself. I'll break her heart, and then I'll spoil her name,—that's all. And now, I really must run away. Sir Charles will have been waiting for me full ten minutes." She touched the brim of her hat, in salute, with the handle of her riding-whip, gathered up her habit with her other hand, and left the room.

"And that is the woman," said Laurence, looking after her, "for whom I nearly broke my heart; whose rejection of my suit caused me to leave England,—intending, hoping, never to return. Great Heavens! once in that state, what idiots we become! Think of this fool flinging away a pearl of price, reputation, decency,—and all for *that!* Think of that poor child his wife having pinned her faith and her affections on to such a shallow oaf! There can be no doubt about Miss Gillespie's meaning now; no doubt that, partly from innate devilry, partly from pique, Laura Hammond will pursue her scheme to the very end. And I am powerless to interfere."

He went down to the library with the intention of writing a letter to his father announcing his immediate arrival; but as he entered the room, he saw through the deep bay-window fronting him, which looked down upon the terrace, the cavalcade departing down the avenue. At some considerable distance behind the others rode Sir Charles Mitford and Mrs. Hammond; and he was bending towards her, and talking in an apparently impressive manner.

Laurence shrugged his shoulders and turned away in disgust; but he had not reached the writing-table before he heard a deep sigh, succeeded by a passionate sobbing, and turning quickly round, saw Lady Mitford leaning against the window and half-hidden by the heavy curtains,—her face buried in her hands, her whole frame convulsed with the violence of her grief. Laurence would have retreated from the room, but his footsteps had attracted her attention; and as she looked their eyes met. He at once approached her, saying, "You will believe me when I say that it was quite by chance I entered the room, Lady Mitford,—without the least idea that you were here; but I am glad now that I came, for you are, I fear, very unwell; and—"

"It is nothing," she said, with a strong but ineffectual effort to resume her usual calmness; "it is nothing, indeed, Colonel Alsager; a little silly woman's weakness—nothing more. I am over-tired, I think; we have been up later the last few nights, you know, and I am so totally unused to dissipation even of the mildest kind."

"You will be better when you return to London, perhaps," said Laurence; "I have a strong notion that the marsh on this great Redmoor is anything but a sanitary adjunct to the property. I should really advise your getting back to town as soon as possible, now Parliament has met; and soon everybody will be there."

In London, Laurence thought, Mrs. Hammond will at all events be out of the house, and in other gaiety there might be a chance of Mitford's getting rid of his infatuation.

"Oh, I'm frightened at the very thought of returning to town; and yet, down here, there are—I mean—it's—how very silly of me!—you must excuse me, Colonel Alsager, I am anything but strong;" and poor Georgie's tears began to flow again.

"So I see," said Laurence, in a very gentle tone. She had seated herself in one corner of a low brown morocco-leather couch that stood across the window. Hitherto he had been standing, but he now placed himself at the other end of the sofa.

"I think," said he, bending forward, and speaking in the same low earnest voice,—"I think, dear Lady Mitford, that you will be disposed to give me credit for taking a deep and friendly interest in you."

She looked at him through the tears that still stood in her splendid eyes—a frank, trusting, honest glance; and as he hesitated, she said, "I know it—I have proved it."

"Then, though your sex is taught to believe that mine is thoroughly selfish and heartless,—never moving without some end for its own benefit in view,—you still believe that what I am about to say to you is dictated simply by the hope to serve you, the desire to see you happy?"

She bowed her head, but did not speak this time. Her tears were gone, but there was a painful look of anxiety in her eyes, and the spasmodic motion of the muscles of the mouth betrayed her agitation.

"You are very young," he continued, "and wholly unacquainted with the world. I am certainly past the freshness of youth, and I should think there are not many of my age more thoroughly versed in the world's ways. And one of its ways, dear Lady Mitford, one of its never-failing and most repulsive ways, is to rob life of the glamour with which youth invests it; to lift up a corner of the silken curtain of the fairy temple and show the rough bare boards and wooden trestles behind it; to throw stumbling-blocks in the paths of happiness, and to drag down those now falling to a lower depth; to poison truth's well, to blacken innocence, and to sow distrust and misery broadcast,—these are among the world's ways. To be pure, noble, and beloved, is at once to provoke the world's hatred. Is it any wonder then that some of its emissaries are plotting against you?"

A faint blush overspread her cheeks as she said, "I have done nothing to provoke them."

"Pardon me," said Laurence, "you have offended in the three ways I have just pointed out: there are few who offer such a combination of offences. And the world will have revenge for all. To besmirch your purity, to lower the nobleness of your nature, are tasks which as yet it dare not attempt. But to prevent your being beloved,—by those whose love you have a right to claim,—is apparently, not really, far more easily done."

"It is, indeed," cried poor Georgie, mournfully; "it is, indeed."

"I said apparently, not really," continued Laurence. "To defeat such an attempt as this is the easiest thing in the world, if you only have the *savoir faire*, and will use the weapons in your armoury. Even in the most purely pastoral times, love in marriage was not all that was requisite for happiness. If Phyllis had done nothing but sit at Corydon's feet and worship him—if she had not been his companion and friend as well as his wife,—now talking to him about the crop in the forty-acre pasture, now telling him of the pigs eating the beech-nuts under that wide-spreading tree where that lazy Tityrus used to lie in the summer; moreover, if Corydon had not had his farm and flock to attend to,—he would at a very early period of their married life have left her solitary, while he sported with Amaryllis in the shade, or played with the tangle of Neaera's hair."

He stopped as he marked her half-puzzled, half-frightened look. "Dear, dear Lady Mitford," he continued, "let me drop parable and mystery, and speak plainly to you. I am going away to-morrow or the next day, and should probably have left with this unsaid; but the accidental sight of your sorrow has emboldened me to speak, and— and you know I would say nothing which you should not hear."

At the last words she seemed reassured, and with a little effort she said, "Speak on, pray, Colonel Alsager; I know I can trust you entirely."

"Thank you," he said, with a very sweet smile; "I am very proud of that belief. Now listen: you married when you were a child, and you have not yet put away childish things. Your notion of married life is a childish romance, and you are childishly beginning to be frightened because a cloud has come over it. In his wife a man wants a companion as well as a plaything, and some one who will amuse as well as worship him. Your husband is essentially a man of this kind; his resources within himself are of the very smallest kind; he cares very little for field-sports, and he conjugates the verb *s'ennuyer* throughout the entire day. Consequently, and not unnaturally, he becomes readily charmed when any one amuses him and takes him out of himself,—more especially if that some one be pretty and otherwise agreeable. Why should not you be that some one? Why should not you, dropping—pardon me for saying it—a little of the visible worship with which you now regard him,—why should not you be his constant companion, riding with him, making him drive you out, planning schemes for his amusement? If you once do this, and get him to look upon you as his companion as well as his wife, there will be no more cause for tears, Lady Mitford, depend upon it."

"Do you think so?—do you really think so? Oh, I would give anything for that!"

"And get him to London quickly, above all things. You are to have your opera-box, I heard you say; and there is the Park; and in this your first season you will never be allowed to be quiet for an instant."

"Yes; I think you're right. I will ask Charley to go back to town at once. There will be no difficulty, I think. The Charterises are gone; Mrs. Masters and the Tyrrells go to-morrow; and Captain Bligh is going to Scotland to look at some shooting-quarters for Charley in the autumn. There are only—only the Hammonds."

"I really do not think it necessary to take them into account in making your arrangements," said Laurence. "Besides, unless I'm very much mistaken, when Mrs. Hammond finds the house emptying, Mr. Hammond's bronchitis will either be so much better that there will be no harm in his going to town, or so much worse that there will be imperative necessity for his consulting a London physician."

"And now, Colonel Alsager, how can I sufficiently thank you for all this kind advice?" said Georgie hesitatingly.

"By acting up to it, dear Lady Mitford. I hope to hear the best account of your health and spirits."

"To hear! Will you not be in London?"

"Not just at present. I am at last really going to my father's, and shall remain there a few weeks. But I shall hear about you from Bertram, and when I return I shall come and see you."

"There will be no one more welcome," said she, frankly putting out her hand.

Just at that moment the door opened, and Mr. Banks advanced and handed a closed envelope to Alsager, saying, "From the railway, Colonel."

It was a telegraphic message; and as such things were rare in those days, Laurence's heart sunk within him before he broke the envelope. It was from Dr. Galton at Knockholt, and said,

"Lose no time in coming. Sir Peregrine has had a paralytic stroke."

Half an hour afterwards Laurence was in a phaeton spinning to the railway. His thoughts were full of self-reproach at his having hitherto neglected to go to his father; but ever across them came a vision of Georgie Mitford in the passion of her grief. "Ah, poor child," he said to himself, "how lovely she looked, and what a life she has in prospect! I am glad I have left her, for it was beginning to grow desperate—and yet how I long, oh how I long to be at her side again!"

CHAPTER XXII.

KNOCKHOLT PARK.

The old home which Laurence Alsager had so long slighted, and to which his heart suddenly turned with a strange wild longing, almost powerful enough, he thought, to annihilate the space between it and Redmoor, had seen many generations of Alsagers beneath its peaked and gabled roof. The house stood in a fine park, and occupied a commanding situation on the slope of a well-wooded hill. The features of the scenery were such as are familiar in the midland counties: rich and fertile beauty, with uplands ankle-deep in meadow-grass, tall patriarchal trees, which stood in solemn unending conclave, group by group or singly, with benignant outstretched arms, and wide-spread mantle of green and russet; bright shallow streams, flashing under the sunbeams, and rippling darkly in the shade. All the land about the picturesque and irregular old house was laid out, partly by nature and partly by art, on ornamental principles; and away to the right and left stretched a wide expanse of farm-lands, whose aspect suggested a practical knowledge of the science of husbandry, and a satisfactory return in profit. The house was surrounded by a broad stone-terrace, bounded by a low balustrade, and flanked at each of the corners by a large stone-vase containing flowers, which varied with the season, but were never missing from these stately *jardinières*. These vases were tended, in common with the formal flower-garden and the particular pet parterre which she called "her own," by Helen Manningtree, the orphan ward of Sir Peregrine Alsager, whom Laurence remembered as a quiet pretty little girl, who had been frank and free with him in her childhood, timid and reserved when he had last seen her, just before he had been driven abroad by the furies of disappointment and wounded pride, and whom he was now to meet again, a graceful, gracious, well-disciplined, and attractive woman.

Knockholt Park was one of those rare places which present a perfect combination of luxury and comfort to the beholder, and impress the latter element of their constitution upon the resident visitor. *Bien-être* seemed to reign there; and the very peacocks which strutted upon the terrace, and tapped at the dining-room window as soon as Sir Peregrine had taken his accustomed seat at the head of the long table, seemed less restless in their vanity and brighter in their plumage than their *confrères* of the neighbouring gentlemen's seats. The brute creation had fine times of it at Knockholt Park, except, of course, such of their number as came under the denomination of vermin; and those Sir Peregrine was too good a farmer, to say nothing of his being too enthusiastic a sportsman, to spare. Horses were in good quarters in the stables and the paddocks of Knockholt Park; and well-to-do dogs were to be found everywhere, the kennel and the dining-room included. Sir Peregrine had the liking for animals to be observed in all kindly natures which are solitary without being studious, and which affords to such natures a subtle pleasure, a sympathy which does not jar with their pride, a companionship which does not infringe upon their exclusiveness.

Sir Peregrine Alsager was essentially a solitary man, though he hunted pretty regularly and shot a little; though he fulfilled the duties of county hospitality with resignation, which county perceptions mistook for alacrity; and though he associated as much as most resident country gentlemen with the inmates of his house. These inmates were Helen Manningtree and her *ci-devant* governess, Mrs. Chisholm, a ladylike accomplished person, and a distant relative of Sir Peregrine, who had offered her a home with him when the charge of Helen had devolved upon him, almost simultaneously with the death of Mrs. Chisholm's husband,—an overworked young curate, who had fallen a victim to an epidemic disease, in consequence of the prevalence of which in the parish his rector had found it necessary to remove himself and his family to a more salubrious climate, but had not found it necessary to procure any assistance for the curate. They were pleasant inmates, but scarcely interesting,— would hardly have been so to a younger man; and there was a certain reserve in Sir Peregrine's manner, though it never lacked kindness, and was distinguished for its courtesy and consideration, which maintained their relative positions quite unchanged. A young girl would have been an unintelligible creature to Sir Peregrine, even if she had been his own daughter; and he contented himself with taking care that all Helen's personal and intellectual wants were amply supplied, and all her tastes consulted and gratified: he left the reading of the enigma to others, or was content that it should remain unread.

Life at Knockholt Park had rolled on very smoothly on the whole, until the accident which recalled his son to his neglected home had befallen Sir Peregrine; and if the master of the fine old house and the fine old estate had had a good deal of loneliness, some bitterness, not a little wistful haggard remembrance and yearning regret, a sense of discordance where he longed for harmony, with a disheartening conviction that he had not the faculties requisite for setting it right, and would never find them in this world, among his daily experiences, the decent and decorous mantle of pride had hidden these discrepancies in the general order of things from every perception but his own. If the hale old gentleman, on whom every eye looked with respect, and who had filled his place with honour all the days of his life, had unseen companions in those walks shared visibly by his dog alone; if the handsome stately library where he sat o' nights, and read all that a country gentleman is ever expected to read, was haunted now and then by a shadowy presence, by a beckoning hand; if the gentle whisper of a voice, whose music was heard in its full melody among the angels only, came oftener and more often, as "the tender grace of a day that was dead" receded more and more into the past, and stirred the slow pulses of the old man's heart,—he was all the happier, with such solemn happiness as remembrance and anticipation can confer, and no one was the wiser.

If "county society" in those parts had been brighter as a collective body, or if the individuals who composed it had had clearer notions of military life, and the obligations of a lieutenant-colonel, the long absence of Laurence Alsager from his father's house might have been made a subject of ill-natured and wondering comment; but the particular county to which Knockholt and its master belonged was rather remarkable for obtuseness, and there was a certain something about the old baronet which rendered it impossible to say unpleasant things in his presence, and difficult even to say them in his absence; and so Laurence Alsager escaped almost scot-free. Helen Manningtree felt some indignant wonder occasionally at the only son's prolonged absence from his father—indignant, be it observed, on Sir Peregrine's account, not on her own. Helen was very sensible, and as little vain as it was possible for a nice-looking and attractive girl to be, without attaining a painful height of perfection; and so she did not wonder that Laurence Alsager had not been induced by curiosity to see her—of whom Sir Peregrine had doubtless frequently spoken to him— to visit his old home. Her life had been too simple and well regulated to enable her to comprehend an estrangement between father and son arising from diversity of sentiment alone; but it had also been so devoid of strong affections, of vivid emotions, that she was not likely to regard Laurence Alsager's conduct from a particularly elevated point of view. It was wrong, she thought, and odd; but if Laurence had gone to Knockholt at stated periods, and had conformed outwardly to filial conventionalities, Helen would have been the last person in the world to perceive that anything was wanting to the strength and sweetness of the relationship between Sir Peregrine and his only son.

Mrs. Chisholm-a woman who had known love and bereavement, struggle and rest, but who was childless, and in whom, therefore, that subtlest instinct which gives comprehension to the dullest had never been awakened—felt about it all much as Helen did; but she expressed less, and the little she permitted herself to say was cold and vague, Coldness and vagueness characterized Mrs. Chisholm, because sorrow had early chilled her heart, and no one whom she loved had ever addressed himself to the awakening of her intellect. The curate had not had time, poor fellow; he had had too much to do in persuading people to go to church who would not be persuaded; and his Sophy had been so pretty in the brief old time, so cheerful, so notable, so lovable and beloved, that it had never occurred to him that her mind might have been a little larger and a little stronger with advantage. The time was brief, and the curate died in the simple old faith, leaving his pretty Sophy to outlive him, his love, and her prettiness, but never to outlive his memory, or to cease to glory in that unutterably-precious recollection, that her husband had never found fault with her in his life. On the whole, then, Laurence Alsager was gently judged and mildly handled by the worthy people who had the best right to criticise his conduct; and perhaps the knowledge that this was the case added keenness to the pang of self-reproach, which made his self-inflicted punishment, with which he read the brief but terrible news flashed to his conscious heart along the marvellous electric wire.

Evening had fallen over stream and meadow, over upland and forest, at Knockholt. It had come with the restless and depressing influence which contrasts so strangely with the calm and peace it brings to the fulness of life and health, into the lofty and spacious chamber where Sir Peregrine lay, prostrate under the victorious hand of paralysis. The mysterious influence of serious illness, the shadow of the wings of the Angel of Death, rested heavily upon the whole of that decorously-ordered house; and the watchers in the chamber of helplessness, it may be of pain,—who can tell? who can interpret the enforced stillness, the inexorable dumbness of that dread disease?—succumbed to its gloom. Mrs. Chisholm and Helen were there, not, indeed, close by the bed, not watching eagerly the motionless form, but gazing alternately at each other and at the doctor, who kept a vigilant watch over the patient. This watch had, if possible, increased in intensity since sunset, at which time Dr. Galton had perceived a change, visible at first to the eye of science alone. The dreadful immobility had certainly relaxed; the rigidity of the features, blended with an indescribable but wofully-perceptible distortion of the habitual expression, had softened; the plum-like blueness of the lips had faded to a hue less startlingly contrasted with that of the shrunken and ashy features.

"He will recover from this attack, I hope—I think," said the doctor in answer to a mute question which he read in Helen's eyes, as he stood upright after a long and close investigation of the patient. "Yes, he will outlive this. I wish Colonel Alsager were here."

"We may expect him very soon," Mrs. Chisholm said; "he would start immediately of course, and we know the telegraph-message would reach him in time for him to catch the up-train."

As she spoke, wheels were heard on the distant carriage-drive. Sir Peregrine's room was on the north side, that farthest from the approach; and immediately afterwards a servant gently opened the door—ah, with what needless caution!—and told Mrs. Chisholm that the Colonel had arrived, and desired to see her. There was more awkwardness than agitation in Mrs. Chisholm's manner as she hurriedly rose to comply with this request, but was interrupted by Dr. Galton, who said:

"No, no, my dear madam,—I had better see him myself; I can make him understand the necessary care and caution better than you can."

Mrs. Chisholm returned to her seat in silent acquiescence; and for the ensuing half-hour she and Helen sat sadly looking at the helpless form upon the bed, and occasionally whispering to one another their several impressions of how Laurence Alsager "would bear it."

What Laurence Alsager had to bear, and how he bore it, was not for any one to see. He held himself aloof even from the gentle scrutiny he had so little reason to dread. In half-an-hour Dr. Galton reentered Sir Peregrine's room, looking very grave, and requested Mrs. Chisholm and Helen to withdraw.

"I am going to let Colonel Alsager see his father," he said; "and I think there should be no one else by. We can never know exactly how much or how little the patient feels, or knows, or is affected in eases like these; but one at a time is an admirable rule."

"He will find us in the long drawing-room when he wishes to see us," said Mrs. Chisholm; and then she and Helen left the room, and went in silence along the wide corridor, and down the broad flat staircase of fine white stone, with its narrow strip of velvet-pile carpeting and its heavy, carved balustrade, terminated by a fierce figure in armour holding a glittering spear, with a mimic banderol blazoned with the device of the Alsagers. The wide stone hall, at the opposite extremity of which the door of the long drawing-room stood open, the heavy velvet *portière* withdrawn, was hung with trophies of the chase and of war. Tiger-skins, buffalo-horns, the *dépouilles* of the greater and the lesser animals which man so loves to destroy, adorned its walls, diversified by several handsome specimens of Indian arms, and a French helmet, pistol, and sabretache. Four splendid wood-carvings, representing such scenes as Snyders has painted, were conspicuous among the orthodox ornaments of the hall. They were great favourites with Sir Peregrine, who had bought them in one of the old Belgian cities on the one only occasion when he had visited foreign parts—an awful experience, to which he had been wont to allude with mingled pride and repugnance. Helen glanced at them sadly as she crossed the hall; then turned her head carelessly in the direction of the great door, which stood open, and before which a huge black Newfoundland lay at full length upon the marble steps. At the same moment the dog, whose name was Faust, rose, wagged his tail, twitched his ears, and cantered down the steps, and across the terrace in an oblique direction.

"Who is that, Helen?" asked Mrs. Chisholm, as she caught sight of Faust's swift-vanishing form. "Some one is coming whom the dog knows."

"It is only Mr. Farleigh," answered Helen; but her reply must have been made quite at random, for she had not advanced another step in the direction of the door, and could not possibly have seen, from her position in the hall, who was approaching the house at that moment.

Mrs. Chisholm had a natural and spontaneous inclination towards curates. She respected—indeed, she admired all the ranks of the hierarchy and all their members, and she never could be induced to regard them as in any way divided in spirit or opinions. They were all sacred creatures in her eyes, from the most sucking of curates to the most soapy of bishops; but the curates had the preëminence in the order of this remarkably unworldly woman's estimation. Her Augustine had been a curate; he might, indeed, have become a bishop in the fulness of time, and supposing the order of merit to have been attended to by the prime minister *in posse*; but fate had otherwise decreed, and his apotheosis had occurred at the curate-stage of his career. For this perfectly laudable and appreciable reason Mrs. Chisholm liked the Reverend Cuthbert Farleigh, and would have liked him had he been the silliest, most commonplace, most priggish young parson in existence—had he had weak eyes and a weak mind, Low-Church opinions, and a talent for playing the flute. But the Reverend Cuthbert had none of these things. On the contrary, he was a handsome manly young fellow, who looked as if he possessed an intellect and a conscience, and was in the habit of using both; who had a tall well-built figure, fine expressive dark eyes, and an independent, sensible, cheerful manner, which few people could have resisted. Helen Manningtree had never made any attempt at resisting it. She had known Cuthbert Farleigh for eighteen months, and she had been in love with him just twelve out of the number. She was not aware of the circumstance at first, for she had had no experience of similar feelings; she had had none of the preliminary feints and make-believes which often precede the great passion of such persons as are calculated to feel a great passion, and the tepid sincerity of such as are not. Helen had never experienced a sensation of preference for any one of the limited and not very varied number of young country gentlemen whom she had met since she "came out" (the term had a restricted significance in her case); and when she did experience and avow to herself such a sentiment in the instance of the Reverend Cuthbert Farleigh, she readily accounted for it to herself by impressing on her own memory that, however young he might look and be, he was her spiritual pastor and master—and, of course, that occult influence affected her very deeply—and by making up her mind that he preached beautifully. And Cuthbert? What was the young lady with the brown eyes, and the brown curls, and the fresh healthful complexion; the young lady who was not indeed strictly beautiful, nor, perhaps, exactly pretty, but who was so charming, so graceful, so thoroughly well-bred; such an innate lady in thought, word, and deed, in accent, in gesture, in manner;—what was she to him? He had asked himself that same question many a time; he asked it now, as he came up to the open door—rarely shut at Knockholt Park, save in the rigorous depths of winter—and he came to the conclusion, as he thought of the manifest luxury and elegance in whose enjoyment Helen had been reared, and of the probable fortune which she would possess, that he had better postpone answering it until he should have become a bishop.

Helen, who did not try to analyze her own perturbations, and was wholly unconscious of Cuthbert's, received him with her accustomed gentle sweetness, but with a sedate and mournful gravity adapted to the circumstances. When the ladies had brought their lengthy and minute narrative to a close—a narrative which embraced only the history of twenty-four hours, for Cuthbert was a regular and attentive visitor—he inquired about Colonel Alsager. Had he been informed? had he been sent for? had he come?

"Yes, to all your questions, Mr. Farleigh. Colonel Alsager is now in the house, in Sir Peregrine's room; but as yet we have not seen him."

The sensitive and expressive face of the curate was clouded by a look of pain and regret. He and Colonel Alsager had never met; but the young clergyman knew Sir Peregrine better, perhaps, than any other person knew him, and respected him deeply. He could not regard Laurence's conduct so lightly, he could not acquit him as easily, as others did. He blamed him heavily, as he sat and listened to the women's talk; and with the blame keen compassion mingled; for he knew, with the mysterious insight of a sympathetic nature, all that he must suffer in realizing that regret must be in vain, must be wasted now, must be *too late*.

The occasion was too solemn to admit of so trivial a feeling as curiosity; but had it not been so, that feminine sentiment would undoubtedly have predominated among the emotions with which Mrs. Chisholm and Helen Manningtree received Colonel Alsager, when, after a lengthened interval, he made his appearance in the long drawing-room. As it was, their mutual greetings were kindly but subdued. The presence of illness and danger in the house superseded all minor considerations, and Colonel Alsager might have been a guest as familiar as he was in reality strange, for all the emotion his presence excited. Mrs. Chisholm introduced Cuthbert Farleigh, and added to the usual formula a few words to the effect that he was a favoured guest with Sir Peregrine, which led Alsager to receive the introduction warmly, and to prosecute the acquaintance with zeal. The curate thawed under the influence of the Colonel's genial manner,—so warm and attractive, with all its solemn impress of regret, fear, and uncertainty. After a little while the women went away again to resume their dreary watch; and Dr. Galton came down to make his report, and to join Alsager at his late and much-needed dinner. A telegraphic message had been sent to London to seek further medical assistance; but the great man, who could do so little, could not reach Knockholt before the morning. In the mean time there was little change in the state of the patient; but Dr. Galton adhered to the hopeful opinion he had formed at sunset. Cuthbert Farleigh went away from the Park, and sat down to the preparation of his Sunday's sermon with a troubled mind. "What a capital good fellow Alsager is," he thought, "with all his faults! What a number of questions he asked about *her*! He takes a great interest in her. Well, *it* would be a very natural and a very nice thing." It is granted, is it not, on all hands, that the abandonment of proper names and the substitution of pronouns—which, whether personal or impersonal, are at all events demonstrative—is a very suspicious circumstance in certain cases?

Sir Peregrine Alsager did not die, as Laurence had thought, and dreaded that he was to die, with the silence between them unbroken, the estrangement unremoved. Nothing could undo the past, indeed; but the present was given to the father and son; and its preciousness was valued duly by them both. In a few days after Laurence's arrival the paralysis loosened its grasp of his father's faculties; and though he still lay in his bed shrunk, shrivelled, and helpless, he could see, and hear, and speak. Sometimes his words were a little confused, and a slight but distressing lapse of memory caused him to pause and try painfully first to recall the word he wanted, and next to accomplish its utterance; but gradually this difficulty wore away, and the old man spoke freely, though little. He was greatly changed by his illness—was most pathetically patient; and his face, a little distorted by the shock, and never more to wear the healthy hue of his vigorous age, assumed an expression of tranquil waiting. The supremacy of his will was gone with the practical abolition of his authority. He let it slip unnoticed. He cared little for anything now but the presence of his son and the progress of the mornings and the evenings which were making the week-days of his life, and wearing towards the dawn of the eternal Sabbath. He loved to have Helen with him, and would regard her with unwonted interest and tenderness,—keenest when she and Laurence met beside his couch, and talked together, as they came gradually to do, very often at first for his sake, and afterwards, as he hoped, as he never doubted, for their own. Yes, the keen anxiety, the foresight, the intensifying of former mental attributes which characterize some kinds of physical decay in persons of a certain intellectual and moral constitution and calibre, showed themselves strongly in Sir Peregrine Alsager, and centred themselves in his son. He had asked nothing, and had heard little of his wandering and purposeless life; but that little had made the old man—held back now, on the brink of the eternal verity, by no scruples of coldness, of pride, of pique, or of scrupulosity—very anxious that his son should marry, and settle down to live at Knockholt Park at least a fair proportion of the year. With that considerate, but perhaps, after all, beautiful, simplicity which restores to age the faith of youth, and builds her shrines for all the long-shattered idols, Sir Peregrine reasoned of his own life and his own experience, and applied his deductions to his son's far different case. He was, however, too wise to put his wishes into words, or even to make them evident without words, to their objects. But there were two persons in the small group who tenanted Knockholt Park who knew that the dearest wish of Sir Peregrine's heart, that desire which overpassed the present and projected itself into the inscrutable future, when its fruition might perchance never be known to him, was that Laurence Alsager, his son, should marry Helen Manningtree, his ward. The two who had penetrated the inmost feelings of the old man were Cuthbert Farleigh and Mrs. Chisholm.

How sped the days with Colonel Alsager in the old home? Heavily, to say the least of it. He had undergone strong excitement of various kinds; and now reaction had set in, with the unspeakable relief of his father's reprieve from immediate death. During his journey from Redmoor to Knockholt he had been an unresisting prey to bitter and confused regrets; so bitter, they seemed almost like remorse; so unavailing, they touched the confines of despair. The scenes in which he had lately played a part, the problems he had been endeavouring to solve, rushed from his view, and retired to the recesses of his memory,—to come out again, and occupy him more closely, more anxiously than ever, when the cruel grasp of suspense and terror was removed from his heart; when the monotony of the quiet house, and the life regulated by the exigencies of that of an invalid, had fairly settled down upon him; when all the past seemed distant, and all the future had more than the ordinary uncertainty of human existence. There was no estrangement between Laurence and his father now; but the son knew that there was no more similarity than before. Their relative positions had altered, and with the change old things had passed away. The pale and shrunken old man who lay patiently on his couch beside the large window of the library at Knockholt, at which the peacocks had now learned to tap and the dogs to sniff, was not the silent though urbane, the hale and *arriéré* country gentleman to whom his Guardsman's life had been an unattractive mystery, and all his ways distasteful. That Guardsman's life, those London ways, the shibboleth of his set, even the distinctive peculiarities of his own individuality, had all been laid aside, almost obliterated, by the dread reality which had drawn so near, and still, as they both knew, was unobtrusively ever nigh at hand. Father and son were much together at certain regulated times; and Laurence was unfailing in his scrupulous observance of all the wishes, his intuitive perception of all the fancies, of the invalid. Still there were many hours of solitude to be got through in every day; and Laurence Alsager held stricter and truer commune with his own heart, while they passed over the dial, than he had ever been used to hold. The quiet of the house; the seclusion of the park in which he walked and rode; the formal beauty of the garden, where he strolled with Helen Manningtree, and listened to her enthusiastic expectations of what its appearance would be when the time of flowers should have fully arrived; the regularity of the household; the few and trivial interruptions from without;—all these things had a strong influence on the sensitive temperament of Laurence Alsager, and gradually isolated him within himself. There was nothing to disturb the retrospective and introspective current of his thoughts; and in those quiet weeks of waiting he learned much of himself, of life, and of truth—knowledge which otherwise might never have come to him. It was not very long before his mind recurred painfully to Redmoor and its mistress, whom he had left in a position of difficulty and danger. He remembered the counsel he had given her, and he wondered whether it might avail. He pondered on all the eventualities which the *triste sagesse* of a man of the world taught him to anticipate, and longed for power to avert them or to alter their character. He learned some wholesome lessons in these vain aspirations, and looked deeper into the stream of life than he had ever looked before.

He looked at Lady Mitford's position from every point of view; he weighed and measured her trials, and then he began to speculate upon her temptations. All at once it struck him that he had ceased to fear Lord Dollamore; that that distinguished personage had somehow dropped out of his calculations; that he was occupying himself rather with her sentimental griefs than with the serious danger which he had believed, a little while ago, menaced her reputation and her position. He feared Laura Hammond, and he ardently desired to penetrate the full meaning of Miss Gillespie's warning. He perfectly understood the difficulty of conveying to a mind so innocent as that of Lady Mitford the full force and meaning of the counsel he had given her, the hopelessness of inducing her to arm herself with a woman's legitimate weapon—the strong desire to please,—and getting her to use it against her husband. She did not lack intelligence, but she did not possess tact; and her nature was too refined and straightforward to give her any chance in so unequal a contest as that into which her husband's worthlessness had forced her.

And now another truth came steadily up from the abyss into which Alsager was always gazing, and confronted him. That truth was the motive which animated his thoughts and inspired his perceptions; which gave him so clear an insight into Lady Mitford's position, and enabled him to read her heart with more distinctness than she herself could have interpreted it. One day Laurence Alsager knew, and acknowledged to himself, what this motive was, whence came this intuition. He loved Georgie Mitford. Yes; the idle speculation, the indignation of a true gentleman at beholding the innocent wronged and the trusting deceived; the loyal instinct of protection; the contemptuous anger which had led him to detest Laura Hammond and to desire her discomfiture; the tender and true sympathy of a world-worn man with a pure and simple woman, to whom the world and its ways are all unknown and unsuspected; the shrinking from beholding the suffering which experience must inflict,—all these had been evident—they had existed in utter integrity and vitality. Alsager had not deceived himself then, neither did he deceive himself now; and though they still existed, they had receded from their prominence,—they did but supplement another, a more powerful, a more vital reality. He loved her—he never doubted the fact, never questioned it more. He loved with a love as much superior to, as much stronger, holier, truer, and more vital than, any love which he had ever before felt or fancied— as his present self-commune was more candid, searching, and complete than any counsel ever previously held in the secret chambers of his brain and heart. He had settled this point with himself, and was moodily pondering on the possible consequences of the fact, and on the alteration in his own position towards Lady Mitford which it implied, when he received a letter from Georgie. It was not the first,—several notes had passed between them in the easy intimacy of their acquaintance; but it was the first since that acquaintance had strengthened into friendship. And now, for him, friendship too had passed away, and in its place stood love—dangerous, delicious, entrancing, bewildering love. So Georgie's letter had altogether a different value and significance for him now. This was the letter:

"Redmoor, — March 18—.

"Dear Colonel Alsager,—Sir Charles received your kind note, but has been too busy to write; so he has asked me to do so, and I comply with very great pleasure. I need hardly say how truly glad we were to hear of the improvement in Sir Peregrine's state, and how earnestly we hope he may completely rally. All things are going on here much as usual. Poor Mr. Hammond is very ill,—failing rapidly, I am sure; this week he is suffering fearfully from bronchitis. They talked of going away, but that is of course impossible. I am a good deal with him, and I think he likes me. Lord Dollamore has come back from town, and is staying here,—doing nothing but lounge about and watch everybody. Is there any chance that we shall have the pleasure of seeing you again if we are detained here much longer? I hoped Charley would have taken me to see my father, who has been ailing this cold spring weather; but I fear the long delay here will prevent that,—he will be impatient to get to town as soon as possible. Pray let us hear from you how Sir Peregrine is. Charley is out, but I know I may add his kindest regards to my own.—Yours, dear Colonel Alsager, always sincerely,

"Georgina Mitford.

"P.S. I have not forgotten your advice for a minute, nor ceased to act upon it, and to thank you for it from my heart. But—it is so difficult to write upon this subject— difficult to me to write on any, for, as you know, I am not clever, unfortunately for me. Could you not come?"

Laurence read and re-read this simple letter with unspeakable pain and keen irrepressible delight. She trusted him; she thought of him; she wished for his presence! Could he not come? she asked. No; he could not. But supposing he could—ought he? Well, he was a brave man and a true, and he faced that question also. How he answered it remains to be seen.

The days passed at Knockholt Park, and resembled each other very closely. Laurence saw a good deal of Cuthbert Farleigh, and liked him much. He wondered a little, after the manner of men, at the content yielded by a life so unlike his own, or any that his fancy had ever painted; but if he and the curate did not sympathize, they coalesced. Laurence wrote again to, and heard again from, Lady Mitford.

There was not much in her letter apart from her kind and sympathizing comments upon his; but he gathered a good deal from the tone which unconsciously pervaded it. He learned that she had not succeeded in breaking up the party at Redmoor; that Sir Charles had invited a fresh relay of county guests; that Mr. Hammond's health was very precarious; and that Georgie had not been gratified in her wish to see her father. The letter made him more uneasy, more sad, by its reticence than by its revelations. If he could but have returned to Redmoor!—but it was impossible. If he could have left his father, how was he to have accounted for an uninvited return to Sir Charles Mitford's house? He did not choose, for many reasons, to assume or cultivate such relations with the worthy Baronet as going there in an informal manner would imply.

So March and April slipped away, and Laurence Alsager was still at Knockholt, in close attendance upon his father. One day in the last week of April, Laurence was returning from a solitary ramble in the park, intending to read to his father for a while, if he should find that Sir Peregrine (sensibly feebler, and much inclined to slumber through the brightest hours of sunshine) could bear the exertion of listening. As he emerged from the shade of a thick plantation on the north side of the house and approached the terrace, he observed with alarm that several servants were assembled on the steps, and that two came running towards him, with evident signs of agitation and distress. He advanced quickly to meet them, and exclaimed, "Is anything wrong? Is my father worse?"

"I am sorry to tell you, Sir Laurence—" began the foremost of the two servants. And so Laurence Alsager learned that his father had gone to his rest, and that he had come to his kingdom.

CHAPTER XXIII.

LORD DOLLAMORE'S COUNSEL.

Lady Mitford remained in the library, where Colonel Alsager had bidden her farewell, for a long time after he had departed. She was sorely perplexed in spirit and depressed in mind. She was heartily grieved for Alsager, whom she had learned long ago to distinguish from the crowd of casual acquaintance by whom she had been surrounded as soon as her "brilliant marriage" had introduced her to the London world. Implicit confidence in him had come to reconcile her to the novel feeling of distrust towards others, which had gradually, under the deteriorating influence of her recent experiences, taken possession of her. He represented to her a great exception to a rule whose extent she had not yet thoroughly learned to estimate, and whose existence pained and disgusted her. His conversation with her just before his departure had ratified the tacit bond between them; and as Lady Mitford sat gazing idly from the wide window down the broad carriage-drive by which the riding-party had departed, she dwelt with grateful warmth upon every detail of Alsager's words, every variation of his manner and inflection of his voice.

"At least he is my friend," she thought; "and what a comfort it is to know that! what a support in the state of wretched uncertainty I seem doomed to!" Anon she ceased to think of Colonel Alsager at all, and her fancy strayed, as fancy always does, to scenes and subjects whence pain is to be extracted. If any stranger could have looked into that handsome and luxurious room just then, and seen its tenant, he would have recoiled from the contrast and contradictions of the picture. She sat, as Alsager had left her sitting, on a low brown-morocco couch, facing the deep bay-window; her hands lay idly in her lap, her small head was bent listlessly forward; but the gaze of the lustrous and thoughtful eves was fixed and troubled. The soft tempered light touched her hair, her quiet hands, the graceful outlines of her figure, and the rich folds of her dress with a tender brilliance, but no sunshine from within lighted up the pale brow or brightened the calm sorrowful lips. Time passed on, and still she sat absorbed in her thoughts, until at length the loud chiming of the clocks aroused her. She threw off her preoccupation by an effort, and saying half aloud, "At least they shall not return and find me moping here," she passed out of the library. She paused a moment in the hall, debating with herself whether she would betake herself at once to the piano in her dressing-room, or go and inquire for poor old Mr. Hammond, to whom she had not yet made her customary daily visit. Lady Mitford was in the mood just then to do a kindness; her heart was full of Alsager's kindness to herself, and she sent for Mr. Hammond's man, and bade him tell his master she requested admittance to his room if he felt able to see her.

"I suppose if he had not been," she added mentally, "his wife would have been afraid to have left him to-day."

Lady Mitford had made considerable progress in the science of life since the friend who had left her presence that morning had seen her for the first time at the Parthenium, but she had need to make a great deal more before she could be qualified to comprehend Laura Hammond.

Georgie found Mr. Hammond pretty well, and tolerably cheerful. The feeble old man liked his gentle and considerate hostess. He had liked her when he was in health; and he liked her still better now that the languor of illness rendered him liable to being fatigued by ordinarily dull or extraordinarily brilliant people. Georgie was neither;—she was only a gentle, refined, humble-minded, pure-hearted lady; and the old man, though of course he did not admire her at all in comparison with his own brilliant and bewitching Laura, and had considered her (under Laura's instructions) rather vapid and commonplace the preceding season, was in a position just then to appreciate these tamely admirable qualities to their fullest extent. She remained with Mr. Hammond until the sound of the horses' hoofs upon the avenue warned her that the cavalcade was returning. She then went hastily down the great staircase, and reached the hall just in time to see Mrs. Hammond lifted from her saddle by Sir Charles with demonstrative gallantry, and to observe that he looked into her face as he placed her upon the ground with an expression which rendered words wholly superfluous. The unborn strength which had been created by Alsager's counsel was too weak to bear this sharp trial. Georgie shrunk as if she had been stung, and, abandoning her brave purpose of giving her guests a cheerful greeting at the door, she took refuge in her own room.

On this day Sir Charles for the first time departed from the custom he had maintained since their marriage, of seeking Georgie on his return home after any absence. It was a significant omission; and as she took her place at the dinner-table, Lady Mitford felt that the few hours which had elapsed since Colonel Alsager had given her that counsel, which every hour became more difficult for her to follow, had made a disastrous difference in her position. She would make a great effort—she would do all that Laurence had advised, but how if Sir Charles estranged himself from her altogether?—and even to her inexperience there was something ominous in any marked departure from his accustomed habits,—what should she do then? He might either persist in a tacit estrangement, which would place her at a hopeless disadvantage, or he might quarrel with her, and end all by an open rupture. Georgie was beginning to understand the man she had married, without as yet ceasing to love him; and it is wonderful what rapid progress the dullest of women will make in such knowledge when they are once set on its right track.

Lord Dollamore took Lady Mitford to dinner, as usual, on that day, and Sir Charles gave his arm to Mrs. Hammond. He had entered the drawing-room only a moment before dinner was announced, and had not exchanged a word with his wife. Among the first topics of conversation was Colonel Alsager's departure, which Sir Charles treated with much indifference, and to whose cause Mrs. Hammond adverted with a pert flippancy, so much at variance with her customary adherence to the rules of good taste that the circumstance attracted Lord Dollamore's attention. He made no remark when she had concluded her lively sallies upon the inconvenience of fathers in general, the inconsiderateness of fathers who had paralytic strokes in particular, and the generic detestability of all old people; but he watched her closely, and when her exclusive attention was once more claimed by Sir Charles, whose undisguised devotion almost reached the point of insult to the remainder of the company, he smiled a satisfied smile, like that of a man who has been somewhat puzzled by an enigma, and who finds the key to it all of a sudden. A little was said about Miss Gillespie, but not much; she was speedily relegated to the category of "creatures" by Mrs. Hammond, and then she was forgotten. The general conversation was perhaps a little flat, as general conversation is apt to be under such inharmonious circumstances; and Lady Mitford's assumed spirits flagged suddenly and desperately. A feeling of weariness, of exhaustion, which quenched pride and put bitterness aside, came over her; a dreary loathing of the scene and its surroundings; a swift passing vision of the dear old home she had left so cheerfully—abandoned so heartlessly, she would now have said—of the dear old father of whom she had thought so little latterly, whose advice would be so precious to her now,—only that she would not tell him for the world; a horrid sense of powerlessness in the hands of a pitiless enemy—all these rushed over her in one cold wave of trouble. Another moment and she would have burst into hysterical tears, when a low firm whisper recalled her to herself.

"Command yourself," it said; "she is looking at you, though you cannot perceive it. Drink some wine, and smile."

It was Lord Dollamore who spoke, and Lady Mitford obeyed him. He did not give her time to feel surprise or anger at his interpretation of her feelings, or his interposition to save her from betraying them; but instantly, with the utmost ease and readiness, he applied himself to the task of enlivening the company, and that so effectually, that he soon gained even the attention of the preoccupied pair at the other end of the table, and turned a dinner-party which had threatened to become a lamentable failure into a success. It was a bold stroke; but he played it with coolness and judgment, and it told admirably. Lady Mitford lifted her candid eyes to his as she left the dining-room, and there was neither anger nor reproach in them; but there was gratitude, and the dawn of confidence.

"Just so," thought Lord Dollamore, as he drew his chair up to the table again; "she's the sort of woman who must trust somebody; and she has found out that her reclaimed Charley is not to be trusted. I'll see if I can't make her trust me."

It suited Laura Hammond's humour to exert her powers of pleasing on this evening, or perhaps even her audacious spirit quailed before the ordeal of the female after-dinner conclave, and she was forced to cover her fear by bravado. At any rate, she appeared in an entirely new character. The insolent indolence, the *ennui* which usually characterized her demeanour when there were no men present, were thrown aside, and she deliberately set herself to carry the women by storm. She talked, she laughed, she admired their dresses, and made suggestions respecting their *coiffures*. She offered one a copy of a song unpurchaseable for money and unprocurable for love; she promised another that her maid should perform certain miracles in millinery on her behalf; she sat down at the piano and played and sang brilliantly. Lady Mitford watched her in silent amazement, in growing consternation. The witchery of her beauty was irresistible; the power of an evil purpose lent her the subtlest seductive charm. The dark-grey eyes flashed fire, and glowed with triumph; the wanton mouth trembled with irrepressible fun.

It was an easy and a common thing for Laura Hammond to captivate men, and she really thought nothing about it, unless some deeper purpose, some remoter end, happened, as in the present instance, to be in view; but women, to tell the simple truth, always feared, generally envied, and frequently hated her; she enjoyed her triumph over the "feminine clique," as she disdainfully called them, at Redmoor thoroughly, and with keen cynical appreciation. She played her game steadily all that evening. When the gentlemen came into the drawing-room she almost ignored their presence; she was innocently, ingenuously polite, but she admitted no exclusive attentions; she never relapsed for a moment in her wheedling, but never overdone, civilities to the women. She brought forward the bashful young ladies; she actually played a perfect accompaniment, full of the most enchanting trills and shakes, to a feeble bleat which one of them believed to be a song; and when Sir Charles Mitford, whose ungoverned temper and natural ill-breeding invariably got the better of the conventional restraints which were even yet strange to him, endeavoured to interrupt her proceedings, she stopped him with a stealthy uplifted finger, and a warning glance directed towards his wife. Her victim was persuaded that he fully understood her; he rendered her admirable ruse in his feeble way, the warmest tribute of admiration; and he left the room with a vague consciousness that the indifference which had been for some time his only feeling towards his wife was rapidly turning into hatred.

Laura Hammond's own game was not the only one she played that night. Lord Dollamore had watched her quite as closely as Lady Mitford, and to more purpose. He saw that—where sheer recklessness or from some deeper motive,—which he thought he could dimly discern—she was hurrying matters to a crisis, and that he might take advantage of the position which she had created. They were dainty jewelled claws with which he proposed to snatch the fruit he coveted from the fire; but what of that; they were cruel also; and when they had done his work he cared little what became of them. Let them be scorched and burnt; let the sharp talons be torn out from their roots; what cared he? So he watched the feline skill, the deft, supple, graceful dexterity of the woman, with a new interest—personal this time; any he had previously felt had been mere connoisseurship, mere cynical curiosity, in a marked and somewhat rare specimen.

Every evidence of this observation, every sign Of this new interest, was carefully and successfully suppressed. When all other yes were turned on Mrs. Hammond, his never rested on her even by accident. She sang; and while the greater part of the company gathered round the piano, and those who could not obtain places near the singer kept profound silence, and listened with eager intensity, Dollamore ostentatiously suppressed a yawn, turned over the upholstery-books which ornamented the useless tables, scrutinized the chimney-decorations, and finally strolled into the adjoining room. Equally artistic was his demeanour towards Lady Mitford. He was delicately deferential and frankly cordial; but neither by word or look did he remind her of the service he had rendered her at dinner. Georgie might have been slow to comprehend genius and appreciate wit, but she recognized delicacy and good taste at a glance: and so it fell out that when she received Lord Dollamore's "goodnight," she thought, as she returned the valediction, "There is one man besides Colonel Alsager over whom she has no power. Lord Dollamore holds her in contempt."

The next morning at breakfast Lord Dollamore announced regretfully that he must leave Redmoor for a few days, but hoped to return by the end of the week. He addressed this announcement to Sir Charles Mitford, who was gazing intently on Mrs. Hammond as she broke the seals of several notes, and tossed them down one after another, half read, with a most reassuring air of indifference. Lady Mitford was not present; breakfast was a free and unceremonious meal at Redmoor, to which everybody came when everybody liked, and nobody was surprised if anybody stayed away. Sir Charles expressed polite regret.

"Dear me!" exclaimed Mrs. Hammond, "how very sorry Lady Mitford will be! Bereft of her two courtiers, she will be bereaved indeed. First Colonel Alsager, and now Lord Dollamore. She will be quite *au déspoir.*

"I wish I could hope to make so deep an impression by my absence, Mrs. Hammond," he answered in the careless tone in which one replies to a silly observation made by a petted child. "Mitford, can you come with me into the library a minute?" And he moved away, taking with him a parcel of letters.—"When you are spiteful, and show it, you grow vulgar, madam," he muttered under his breath—"after the manner of your kind—and a trifle coarse; but Mitford is not the man to see that, or to mind it if he did."

Half an hour later Lord Dollamore had left Redmoor; and as he leant back in the railway carriage which bore him towards town, he quietly reviewed all that had taken place during his visit, and arrived at a conclusion perfectly satisfactory to himself. Then he resolved to think no more of the matter till his return; and dismissed it with the reflection that "Mitford was a regular beast,—low, and all that;" but that she "was a devilish nice woman;—no fool, but not clever enough to bore one, and pretty enough for anything."

Matters continued pretty much in the same state at Redmoor during the week which followed Lord Dollamore's departure. Lady Mitford wrote to Colonel Alsager, and heard from him; but her letter—that which we have seen him receive at Knockholt—said as little as possible of the real state of affairs. The truth made a faint attempt to struggle out in the postscript; but pride, reserve, an instinct of propriety, the numberless obstacles to a woman in such a position as that of Lady Mitford telling it in its entirety to any man rendered the attempt abortive. Could he not come? she had asked him. Could he not come? she asked herself, in the weary days through which she was passing—days of which each one was wearier and more hopeless than its predecessor; for things were becoming desperate now. The other guests had taken their leave, but still the Hammonds remained at Redmoor. Not a woman of the party but had known Laura's hollowness and falsehood well—had known that the powers of fascination she had employed were mere tricks of cunning art; but they were all fascinated for all that. Laura had made the close of the time at Redmoor incomparably pleasant, whereas its opening had been undeniably dull; and there was another reason for their letting Mrs. Hammond down easily. They had remained as long as they could in the same house with her; and how were they to excuse or account for their having done so, if they disclosed their real opinion of her character and conduct? It was a keen privation, no doubt, not to be able to descant upon the "doings" at Redmoor, but they had to bear it; and the only alleviation within their reach was an occasional compassionate mention of Lady Mitford as "hardly up to the mark for her position and fortune, and sadly jealous, poor thing!"

It would have been impossible, in common decency, to have avoided all mention of the departure of the Hammonds; and accordingly Sir Charles Mitford told his wife, as curtly and sullenly as possible, that she might make her preparations for going to town, as he supposed they would be moving off in a few days. Georgie had suffered dreadfully, but the worst was over. The keen agony of outraged love had died out, and the sense of shame, humiliation, terrible apprehension, and uncertainty, was uppermost now. In her distress and perplexity she was quite alone; she had no female friend at all in any real sense of the word. It was not likely Sir Charles Mitford's wife should have any; and the only friend she could rely upon was away, and hopelessly detained. The only friend she could rely on—As she repeated the lamentation over and over again in the solitude of her room, and in the bitterness of her heart, did it ever occur to her that the only friend she could rely on might be a dangerous, though not a treacherous one;—that she was crying peace, peace, where there was no peace?

"When we know what the Hammonds are going to do, I shall write to Dollamore," said Sir Charles. He spoke to Georgie.

She felt an eager longing to see her old home, and to breathe a purer moral atmosphere than that of Redmoor. "I can only suffer and be perplexed here," she thought. "Let me get away, and I can think freely, and make up my mind to some line of action. Out of her sight, I should be easier, even in town; and how much easier at home!—once more in the old place, and among the old people, where I used to be before I knew there were such women as this one in the world." So she thought she would do a courageous thing, and ask Sir Charles to take her home for a little, as soon as the Hammonds should have left Redmoor.

She came to this resolution one morning before she went down to breakfast,—before she had to encounter Mrs. Hammond, who brought a fresh supply of ammunition to the attack on each such occasion; whose beauty was never brighter or more alluring than when she arrayed it in the elaborate simplicity of Parisian morning-dress; who was not sufficiently sensitive to be *journalière*, and who might always cherish a well-founded confidence in her own good looks, and the perfect efficiency of her weapons. Not that Georgie was fighting her any longer on the old *terrain*; she had retreated from that, and had no other object now than to shield herself from the perpetual sharp fire of Laura's polished impertinence, her epigrammatic sarcasms, her contemptuous pity. Lady Mitford, whose good sense was apt to do its proper office in spite of the tumult of feeling constantly striving to overpower it, wondered sometimes why Laura took so much trouble to wound her. "She has made sure of Sir Charles," the pure simple lady would say to herself, when some sharp arrow had been shot at her, and she felt the smart, not quite so keenly as the archer thought perhaps, but keenly still. "She does not need to turn me into ridicule before him, to expose my defects and *gaucheries*; she does not need to test his devotion to her by the strength and impenetrability of his indifference to me,—at least not now. She is clever enough to know that wit and humour, sarcasm and finesse, are all thrown away upon *him*, if she is showing them off for her own sake." Of a surety Lady Mitford was rapidly learning to estimate Sir Charles aright. "Her beauty and her unscrupulousness have fascinated him, and all the rest is more likely to bore him than otherwise. If she were in love with him she might not understand this; but she is not in love with him—not even after her fashion and his own; and I am sure she does understand it perfectly. What does she throw so much vigilance away for, then?—for she never loses a chance. Why does she waste so much energy on me? Of course, I know she hates me; and if she be as good a hater as such a woman should be, she would not be satisfied with the one grand injury she has done me; hatred might be pacified by so large a sop, but spite would crave for more. Yes, that must be the explanation—she is feeding spite."

If the old clergyman who had cried over Georgie Stanfield on her wedding-day, and uttered that futile blessing on the marriage which was so unblessed, could have heard her speak thus to her own heart, how utterly confounded and astonished that good but not "knowledgable" individual would have been! A few months in the great world to have turned Georgie into this woman, who seeks for motives, who reads character, who has all the dreary cunning in interpretation of the human heart which his life-long experience had failed to impart to him, though he had passed half a century in professional proclamation that "the heart of man is deceitful above all things, and desperately wicked." But it was not her short experience of the great world in any general sense which had so far forwarded her education in the science of life as to enable her thus to analyze conduct and motives,—she had had a surer, subtler teacher; she had loved, and been betrayed; she had hoped, and been deceived. She had dreamed a young girl's dream, and one by no means so exaggerated and exalted as most young girls indulge in; and the awakening had come, not only with such rudeness and bitterness as seldom accompany the inevitable disillusionment, but with such startling rapidity, that the lasting of her vision had borne no more proportion to the usual duration of "love's young dream," than the forty winks of an after-dinner nap bear to the dimensions of "a good night's rest." Experience had not tapped at the sleeper's door, and lingered softly near the couch, and insinuated a gently-remonstrative remark that really it was time to risk—tenderly letting in the garish light by tempered degrees the while—cheerfully impressing, without hurry or severity, the truth that a work-day world—busy, stirring, dutiful, and real—lay beyond the glorified realms of slumber, and awaited the passing of the foot going forth to the appointed task over the enchanted threshold. The summary process of awakening by which the sleeper has a basinful of cold water flung on his face, and is pulled out of bed by his feet, bears a stricter metaphorical analogy to that by which Lady Mitford had been roused from her delusion; and though she had reeled and staggered under it at first, the shock had effectually done its work. Georgie Mitford was a wiser woman than Georgie Stanfield could ever have been made by any more considerate process.

All Lady Mitford's newly-sprung wisdom, all the acuteness she had gained by being sharpened on the grindstone of suffering, did not enable her to reach a complete comprehension of Mrs. Hammond's motives. She had not the key to the enigma; she knew nothing of Laura's former relations with Colonel Alsager. If she had ever heard the story, or any garbled version of it, at all, it was before she had any distinct knowledge of, or interest in, either of the parties concerned,—when she was confused and harassed with the crowd of new names and unfamiliar faces,—and she had forgotten it. Even that advantage was her enemy's. Mrs. Hammond had been peculiarly bewitching to Sir Charles, and preternaturally impertinent to Lady Mitford, at the breakfast-table, on the morning when Colonel Alsager's first letter had arrived; indeed, she had a little overdone her part, which was not altogether unnatural. Fierce passions, a violent temper, and a cold heart, form a powerful but occasionally troublesome combination, and imperatively demand a cool brain and steady judgment to control and utilize them. Laura Hammond had as cool a brain and as steady a judgment as even a very bad woman could reasonably be expected to possess; but they were not invariably dominant. The cold heart did not always aid them successfully in subduing the violent temper; and when it failed to do so, the combination was apt to be mischievous. On the occasion in question, Mrs. Hammond had been, to begin with, out of sorts, as the best-regulated natures, and the most intent on their purposes in their worst sense, will occasionally be. Sir Charles bored her, and she was on the point of letting him perceive the fact, and thus giving her temper its head, when the cool brain interposed and curbed it in time. She exerted herself then to bewitch and enslave the Baronet, even beyond his usual condition of enchantment and subjugation. Her success was complete; but its enjoyment was mitigated by her perception that it had failed to affect Lady Mitford. The husband whom she had undoubtedly loved, and of whom she had been undeniably jealous, slighted her more openly than ever, and offered to her rival before her face undisguised and passionate homage; and yet Lady Mitford maintained perfect composure; and though she was occasionally *distraite*, the expression of her face indicated anything but painful thoughts as the cause of her abstraction. Her serene beauty was particularly impressive, and there was an indefinable added attraction in the calm unconscious grace of her manner. The quick instinct of hate warned her enemy that she was losing ground, and she listened eagerly, while she never interrupted her conversation with Sir Charles, for an indication of the cause. It came quickly. Alsager's letter was mentioned, and Lady

Mitford imparted its contents to Captain Bligh, who had dropped in late, and had not heard her communication to Sir Charles. She looked away from Mrs. Hammond while she spoke, and while she and Bligh discussed the letter, Sir Peregrine's state, Laurence's detention at Knockholt, and other topics connected with the subject. It was fortunate that she did not see Laura's face; the sight would have enlightened her probably, but at the cost of infinite perplexity and distress, deepening and darkening a coming sorrow, swooping now very near to her unconscious head. The look, which would have been a revelation, lasted only a moment. It did not deform the beauty of the face, which it lighted up with a lurid glare of baffled passion and raging jealousy; for that beauty owed nothing to expression—its charm, its power were entirely sensuous; but it changed it from the seductive loveliness of a wicked woman to the evil splendour of a remorseless devil. If Lady Mitford had seen it, the light which its lurid fury would have flashed upon her might have been vivid enough to show her that in the rage and torment whence it sprung, she was avenged; but Georgie was not the sort of woman to be comforted by that view of the subject.

Lady Mitford made her request of Sir Charles, and was refused more peremptorily than her letter to Laurence Alsager had implied. The increasing rudeness of Mitford to his wife was characteristic of the man. He had neither courage, tact, nor breeding; and when he went wrong, he did so doggedly, and without making any attempt to mitigate or disguise the ugliness of the aberration. His demeanour to his wife at this juncture exhibited a pleasing combination of viciousness and stupidity. He was maddened by the near inevitability of Laura's departure. The Hammonds must leave Redmoor, and there was no possibility of their going to town. Mr. Hammond's physician had prescribed Devonshire air, and in Devonshire he must be permitted to remain. Sir Charles heartily cursed the poor old gentleman for the ill-health by which he and Laura had so largely profited; but curses could do nothing,—the Hammonds must go. He must be separated from Laura for a time, unless indeed Hammond would be kind enough to die, or she would be devoted enough to elope with him. The latter alternative presented itself to Sir Charles only in the vaguest and remotest manner, and but for a moment. He had become very much of a brute, and he had always been somewhat of a fool; but he had not reached the point of folly at which he could have supposed that Laura Hammond would forfeit the wealth for which she had sold herself, and which in the course of nature must soon fall into her hands, for any inducement of sentiment or passion. He had been brooding over these grievances alone in the library, when Georgie, with whom he had not exchanged a dozen words for as many days, came in, and spoke to him, with a miserable affectation of unconsciousness, about a wish to visit her old home before their return to town for the season. He refused with curt incivility and obstinacy; and it is probable that the ensuing few minutes might have brought about a decided quarrel between the husband and wife, had not Captain Bligh entered the room abruptly, and called out, apparently without noticing Lady Mitford's presence:

"I say, Mitford, you're wanted. Hammond is ever so much worse. Gifford has been round to the stables to get a groom sent off for Dr. Wilkinson.—I beg your pardon, Lady Mitford,—I ought to have mentioned that Mrs. Hammond's maid is looking for *you.*"

Confusion reigned at Redmoor all that day, which seemed likely, during many hours, to have been the last of Mr. Hammond's life. Sir Charles felt that his morning meditation had had something prophetic in it; here was the other alternative almost within his grasp. At all events, whether he died a little sooner or lingered a little longer, Mr. Hammond must remain at Redmoor. The evil day was postponed. Lady Mitford simply devoted herself to the invalid, and behaved towards Mrs. Hammond with magnanimous kindness and consideration, which might have disarmed even Laura, had her inveterate coquetry and love of intrigue been the only animating motives of her conduct. She might have sacrificed the lesser passions to an impulse of the kind, but the greater—no. So she accepted all the delicate kindness which poor Georgie did her, she accepted the *rôle* of devoted and afflicted wife assigned to her before the household, and she hardened her heart against every appeal of her feebly-speaking conscience. With the following day the aspect of things changed a little. Mr. Hammond rallied; the doctors considered him likely to get over the attack; and Lord Dollamore arrived at Redmoor.

"I didn't hear anything from anybody, Mitford, and so I came on according to previous arrangement," said his lordship, as he greeted his host and looked about for Lady Mitford.

Lord Dollamore had strictly adhered to his programme. He never burdened his mind with the pursuit of two objects at the same time. He had completely disposed of the business which had called him away, and with which the present narrative has no concern; and he had come back to Redmoor as a kind of *divertissement* before the serious business of the season should commence. He entertained no doubt that he could resume his relation with Lady Mitford precisely at the point which it had attained when he left Redmoor. Georgie was not a fickle woman in anything; rather methodical, he had observed, in trifles. The impression he had made was likely to have been aided rather than lessened by the intermediate course of events at Redmoor. On the whole he felt tolerably confident; besides, he did not very much care. Lord Dollamore's was a happy temperament—a fortunate constitution, in fact—always supposing that life on this planet was *tout potage*, and nothing to follow. He could be pleasantly excited by the ardour of pursuit, and moderately elated by success; but failure had no terrors for him; he never fell into the weakness of caring sufficiently about anything to furnish fate with the gratification of disappointing him, in the heart-sickening or enraging sense of that elastic expression.

The Hammonds and Lord Dollamore were the only people now at Redmoor who could be strictly called guests. Captain Bligh was rather more at home than Sir Charles; and one or two stragglers, who had remained after the general break-up, addicted themselves to the versatile and good-humoured *vaurien*, and were generally to be found in his company. Accordingly, and as he anticipated, Lord Dollamore found Lady Mitford alone in, the drawing-room when he quitted the delectable society of the gentlemen. Mrs. Hammond had left the dinner-table, proclaiming her intention of at once resuming her place by her husband's side—a declaration by which she secured two purposes: one, the avoidance of a *tête-à-tête* with Lady Mitford; the other, the prevention of a visit by her hostess to the sickroom, on any supposition that Mr. Hammond might require extra attention. During dinner she had been quiet and subdued; her manner, in short, had been perfectly *comme-il-faut*, and she was dressed for her part to perfection. She had kept alive Lady Mitford's gentler feelings towards her; she had forged a fresh chain for Sir Charles, who, like "Joey B.," had great admiration for proceedings which he considered "devilish sly;" and she had afforded Dollamore much amusement of the kind which he peculiarly appreciated—quiet, ill-natured, and philosophical.

It does not much signify whether Laura went to her husband's sickroom at all, or how long she remained there; but there was some significance in the fact, which Lord Dollamore found eminently convenient and agreeable, that Sir Charles sent a footman to tell my lady that he had business to attend to in the library, and requested she would send his coffee thither; and there was a fortunate coincidence in the adjournment of Captain Bligh and his companions to the smoking-room, without any embarrassing drawing-room parade at all.

As Lord Dollamore entered the room, Lady Mitford was bidding goodnight to Mr. Hammond's little daughter, to whom she had been uniformly kind since the mysterious departure of Miss Gillespie. Lord Dollamore had, hardly ever seen the child, whom her stepmother wholly neglected, leaving her to the care of her maid, if the foreign damsel who officiated in that enviable capacity chose to take care of her,—and to chance, if she did not. Laura Hammond hardly knew that Lady Mitford had taken the child under her kindly protection, and had kept her with her during many of the hours of each day which she was not obliged to devote to her social duties; but the child's father knew the fact, and felt grateful to the one woman, after his senile fashion, without daring to express or even to feel any condemnation of the other. As the child left the room, Lord Dollamore looked after her for a moment before he closed the door; then he went up to Lady Mitford's sofa by the fireplace, and said quietly:

"Mrs. Hammond is as admirable as a stepmother as in all the other relations of life, I fancy."

Georgie made no reply, and he did not appear to expect any. Then came Sir Charles's message; and Dollamore watched Lady Mitford closely during its delivery, and until the servant had left the room, carrying a single cup of coffee on a salver.

"Does Mrs. Hammond disdain that celestial beverage?" he asked then, in a voice so full of meaning that Lady Mitford started and blushed crimson. This symptom of anger did not disconcert Lord Dollamore in the least. He had made up his mind to use the first opportunity which should present itself, and it had come. Of course she would start and blush, no matter how he phrased his meaning, but the start was rather graceful, and the blush was decidedly becoming.

"I don't know. I—what do you mean, Lord Dollamore? Mrs. Hammond has gone to her room; you heard what she said?"

"I did; and I don't believe a word of it. 'My poor dear Hammond' will have very little of her society this evening. Lady Mitford," he said, with a sudden change of tone, "how long do you intend to endure this kind of thing? Now I know what you are going to say; "—he put up his hand with a deferential but decided gesture, to prevent her speaking;—"I am quite aware that I have no business to talk to you about Mitford and Mrs. Hammond. I could repeat all that conventional catechism about the whole duty of men and women without a blunder; but it's all nonsense—all hypocrisy, which is worse. I am a man of the world, and you are a woman of the world, or nearly: you will very soon be completely so. Allow me to anticipate the period at which your education will be finished, and to speak to you with perfect frankness."

Georgie looked at him in complete bewilderment. What did this new tone which he had assumed mean?—To insult her? No; she had no reason to think, to fear anything of that kind. Had he not done her at least one substantial service—had he not saved her from ridicule, from affording her enemy a triumph? Had not his manner been always respectful, and, in his indolent way, kind? Even while he spoke of her as "nearly" a woman of the world, she knew that he was thinking of her newness, her ignorance of that very world, and of life. Perhaps she should only expose herself to ridicule on his part now, if she shrank from hearing him. It was certain that things had gone too far—the state of affairs had become too evident—for her to affect indignation or assume prudery, without making herself supremely ridiculous; besides, there was already a tacit confidence between them, which she could neither ignore nor recall. She wished vaguely that Colonel Alsager had been there; then, that some one might come into the room; but she felt, amid her perplexity and perturbation, a strong desire to hear what he had to say to her—to learn what was the view which a man so completely of society, and so capable of interpreting its judgment, took of her position and prospects. Nervously, yet not unreadily, she assented; and Lord Dollamore, standing on the hearth-rug and looking down at her bent head and drooping eyelids, spoke in a low tone:

"You are no match for Mrs. Hammond, Lady Mitford. You would not be, even if you did not labour under the insurmountable disadvantage of being Sir Charles's wife. That must be as evident to yourself—for you are wonderfully sensible and free from vanity—as it is to the lookers-on, who proverbially see most of the game. You have feeling and delicacy, and she is encumbered by no such obstacles to the attainment of any purpose she may set before her. But because you can't fight her on any ground, that's no reason why you should let her make you wretched, and, above all, ridiculous."

"She cannot. I—"

Georgie had looked up with an angry beautiful flush on her cheeks and a sparkle in her eyes, which Mrs. Hammond could not have managed by any contrivance to excel. But when she saw the look that was fixed on her, her eyes fell, and she covered her face with her hands. It was not a bold glance; it was quiet, powerful, and pitying—pitying from Dollamore's point of view, not of her grief, but of her "greenness."

"She *can*, and she *has*, Lady Mitford; but it will be your own fault, and a very silly fault too, if she has that power much longer. Look the truth in the face; don't be afraid of it. You have lost Mitford's affections, I suppose you will say; and there never was any one so miserable; and so forth. It's quite a mistake. Mitford never had any affections—he had, and has, passions; and they will be won and lost many and many a time, long after you will have ceased even to notice in what direction they may happen to be straying. Because your reign was short, you fancy Mrs. Hammond's will be eternal. Pooh! It will come to a timely end with the beginning of the opera-season; and nothing will remain to her of it but a rent in her reputation—which even that endurable material will hardly bear—and much mortification. Your reign is over, as you believe; and we will grant, for the sake of argument, that you are right. Well, what remains to you after this terrible imaginary bereavement of Mitford's affections? Why, Mitford's fortune, Mitford's rank, and a position which, if you were under his influence, might very possibly come to grief; but which you, free and blameless,—a very pleasant combination, let me tell you, and one that many a woman would gladly purchase at the price of a little sentimental blighting,—will elevate and dignify. If you will only realize your position, Lady Mitford, and act with good sense, you will have as brilliant a destiny before you as any woman not afflicted with a mission could possibly desire."

The dream she had dreamed—the home-life her fancy had pictured—came back in a moment to Georgie's mental vision; and she said, in a tone of keen distress:

"Don't say these things, Lord Dollamore. I know you don't mean them; but they sound cold and wicked. How could I care for any position? and what is wealth to me?"

"Pretty much what it is to every rational being, Lady Mitford—happiness; or if not quite the real sterling thing, the very best plated or paste imitation of it procurable in this state of existence. But you have not only wealth, rank, position, and a career of fashion and pleasure to look forward to; there are other things in your future. Think of your youth, estimate your beauty;—stay—no, you cannot do that; you never could conceive the effect it must produce on men who are gentlemen and have taste. If you ever learn to use its full power, you will be as dangerous as Helen or Cleopatra."

He had spoken in a calm business-like manner, which disguised the real freedom of his speech; but he lingered just a little over the last few words, and thou went on hurriedly:

"What charm do you think Mrs. Hammond, or all the women like her—who swarm like vipers in society—will have against you? I am not flattering you, Lady Mitford,—you know that; I am merely telling you the simple truth. Your experience has been narrow, and you think all, or most men, are like Mitford. Because she has beaten you in this inglorious strife, do you think she could rival you in a grander and higher warfare?"

"Inglorious!" she said, amazed. "Oh, Lord Dollamore, he is my husband!"

Dollamore smiled—not at all a pleasant smile; there was too much contemptuous toleration in it.

"Your husband! Yes, he is your husband; but is he therefore any the less a commonplace and vulgar-minded person? You are too clever, Lady Mitford" (he understood the art of praising a woman for those qualities which she does not possess), "to believe in or repeat the stupid methodistical cant which would limit a woman's perceptions, sympathies, and associations, to her husband only,—a worse than Eastern bondage; for it does not involve indulgence, and it sins against knowledge. You are not going to 'live forgotten and die forlorn,' because you have married a man who is certainly not much better than his neighbours, and who is really no worse. Of course he does not suit you, and he never would have suited you, if Mrs. Hammond had never existed. You would have found that out a little later, and rather less unpleasantly, perhaps; but why not make the best of the early date of the discovery, which, after all, has its advantages? Mitford does not 'understand' you-that's the phrase, I think. Well, it's no worse because he does 'understand' some one of a lower calibre which is wonderfully like his own. He won't annoy you in any way, I daresay; he is ill at ease in society at the best, and he will keep out of it,—out of good society, I mean—*your* set. He will find resources at his own level, I daresay. Then do not trouble yourself about him; by and by, I mean, when the Hammond will be nowhere. Of course that business vexes you now; people always are vexed in the country by things they would never care about in town. It's the trees and the moon and the boredom, I suppose. Make up your mind not to trouble yourself about him; study the advantages of your position well, and determine to take the fullest possible enjoyment of them all."

He paused and looked at her, with a covert anxiety in his gaze. She sat quite still, and she was very pale; but she did not say a word. Her thoughts were painful and confused. Only one thing was clear to her: this man's counsel was very different from that which Colonel Alsager had given her. Which of the two would be the easier to follow? Georgie had strayed—at least a little way—into a dangerous path, when she acknowledged the possibility that it might be a struggle to act upon Alsager's, and might be even possible to follow Lord Dollamore's counsel. The pale face was very still; but Dollamore thought he could read indecision in it. He drew a little nearer to her, and bent a little more towards her, as he said:

"Do you really believe-do you even make-believe-that love is never more to be yours? Put such a cruel delusion far from you. You find it hard to live without love now; you grieve because you cannot keep the old feeling alive in your own heart, as keenly as you grieve because it has died in your husband's. You will find it impossible in the time to come. Then, when the tribute of passionate devotion is offered to you, you will not always refuse to accept it. Then, if one who has seen you in these dark days, radiant in beauty and unequalled in goodness,—one whom you have taught to believe in the reality of—"

A servant entered the room, and handed Lady Mitford a small twisted note. It was from Sir Charles, and merely said, "Come to me at once—to the library."

CHAPTER XXIV.

MR. EFFINGHAM'S PROGRESS.

When Mr. Effingham returned to town after his signal discomfiture at Redmoor by Miss Gillespie, he had only two objects in view: one to prevent Griffiths finding out that he had gone so near to achieving success, but yet had failed; the other to find out whither the young woman, who had so cunningly betrayed him, had betaken herself. The first was not very difficult. The meeting with the object of his search down at a country-house far away in Devon was too improbable to present itself to a far more brilliantly gifted person than Mr. Griffiths; while the receipt of five sovereigns (Sir Charles's donation had this time been represented at twenty-five pounds only) gave that gentleman an increased opinion of his friend's powers of persuasion, and rendered him hopeful for the future.

The accomplishment of the second object was, however, a different matter. Mr. Effingham's innate cunning taught him that after all he had said to Miss Gillespie—or Lizzie Ponsford—about the source of his instructions, the company of her old acquaintances—Messrs. Lyons, Griffiths, Crockett, and Dunks—was about the last she would be likely to affect; and yet in their society only would he have opportunities of seeking her. Through the oft-threaded mazes of that tangled web, in and out, from haunt to haunt, Mr. Effingham once more wended his way,—asking every one, prying into every corner, listening to every conversation,—all to no purpose. He began to think that the object of his search must have departed from her original intention, and instead of coming up to London, have halted on the way; but then, what could she have done alone, unaided, without resources, in any provincial town? Mr. Effingham took to frequenting the Devonshire public-houses and coffee-shops,—queer London holes kept by Devonshire people, who yet preserved a little clannish spirit, who took in a Devon paper, and whose houses were houses-of-call for stray children of the far West, sojourning for business or pleasure in London. Many a long talk was there in Long Acre or Smithfield, surrounded by the foetid atmosphere and the dull rumblings of metropolitan life, of the Exe and the Dart, of the wooded coast of Dawlish and the lovely bay of Babbicombe, of purple moor and flashing cataract, of wrestling-matches and pony-fairs. The cads who dropped in for an accidental half-pint stared with wonder at the brown countrymen, on whom the sun-tan yet remained, who talked a language they had never heard, in an accent they could not understand; who had their own jokes and their own allusions, in which the jolly landlord and his wife bore their part, but which were utterly unintelligible to the cockney portion of the customers. In these houses, among the big burly shoulders of the assembled Devonians, Mr. Effingham's perky little head was now constantly seen. They did not know who he was; but as he was invariably polite and good-natured, took the somewhat ponderous provincial badinage with perfect suavity, and was always ready to drink or smoke with any of them, they tolerated his presence and answered his questions respecting the most recent arrivals from their native county civilly enough. But all was unavailing; to none of them was the personal appearance of Miss Gillespie known. The presence of any stranger in their neighbourhood would not have passed unnoticed; but of the few sojourners who were described to him, none corresponded in the least to that person whom he sought so anxiously.

Would she not attempt to persevere in the new line of life which she had filled at Redmoor and succeeded in so admirably? As governess and companion she had been seemingly happy and comfortable; as governess and companion she would probably again try her fortune. Forthwith Mr. Effingham had a wild desire to secure the services of a desirable young person to superintend the studies of his supposititious niece; and Mrs. Barbauldson, who kept a "governess agency," and Messrs. Chasuble and Rotchet, who combined the providing of governesses and tutors with "scholastic transfers," vulgarly known as "swopping schools," the engagement of curates, and the sale of clerical vestments and ecclesiastical brass-ware, were soon familiarized with Mr. Effingham's frequent presence. He dropped in constantly at their establishments, and took the liveliest interest in the registers, looking through not merely the actual list of candidates for employment, but searching the books for the past three months. He paid his half-crown fees with great liberality, or else the manner in which he used to bounce in and out the waiting-room and examine the features of the ladies there taking their turn to detail the list of their accomplishments to the clerk, was, to say the least of it, irregular, and contrary to the regulations of the establishment. But all to no purpose,—he could learn nothing of any one in the remotest degree resembling Miss Gillespie: his search among the governess-agencies had been as futile as his visits to the Devonshire public-houses, and all Mr. Effingham's time and trouble had been spent in vain.

What should he try next? He really did not know. He had, ever since his visit to Redmoor, been rather shy of Mr. Griffiths, fearing lest that worthy person might learn more than it was necessary, in Mr. Effingham's opinion, he should know. Griffiths was to him a very useful jackal, and it was not meet that the jackal's opinion of the lion's sagacity and strength should be in any way diminished. Chance had so far favoured him that Mr. Griffiths had recently been absent from town, having accepted a temporary engagement of an important character, as occasional croupier, occasional doorkeeper, to a travelling band of gamblers, who were importing the amusing games of French hazard and roulette into some of the most promising towns in the Midland Counties.

One night Mr. Effingham was sitting in a very moody state at "Johnson's," sipping his grog and wondering vaguely what would be the next best move to make in his pursuit of Miss Gillespie, when raising his eyes, they encountered Mr. Griffiths,— Mr. Griffiths, and not Mr. Griffiths. Gone was the tall shiny hat, its place occupied by a knowing billy-cock; gone were the rusty old clothes, while in their place were garments of provincial cut indeed, but obviously costly material; a slouch poncho greatcoat kept Mr. Griffiths's body warm, while Mr. Griffiths's boots, very much contrary to their usual custom, were sound and whole, and hid Mr. Griffiths's feet from the garish eye of day. Moreover, Mr. Griffiths's manner, usually a pleasing compound of the bearing of Ugolino and the demeanour of the Banished Lord, was, for him, remarkably sprightly. He threw open the swing-door, and brought in his body squarely, instead of butting vaguely in with the tall hat, as was his usual custom; he walked down the centre of the room, instead of shuffling round by the wall; and advancing to the box in which Mr. Effingham was seated in solitary misery, he clapped him on the back and said, "D'Ossay, my buck, how are you?"

The appearance, the manner, and the swaggering speech had a great effect on Mr. Effingham. He looked up, and after shaking hands with his friend, remarked, "You've been doin' it up brown, Griffiths,—you have. They must have suffered for this down about Hull and Grimsby, I should think?" And with a comprehensive sweep of his forefinger he took in Griffiths's outer man from his hat to his boots.

"Well, it warn't bad," said Mr. Griffiths, with a bland smile. "The yokels bled wonderful, and the traps kept off very well, considerin' I'm pretty full of ochre, I am; and so far as a skiv or two goes, I'm ready to stand friend to them as stood friend to me, D'Ossay, my boy. No? Not hard up? Have a drink then, and tell us what's been going on."

The drink was ordered, and Mr. Effingham began to dilate on the various phases of his pursuit of Lizzie Ponsford. As he proceeded, Mr. Griffiths went through a series of pantomimic gestures, which with him were significant of attempts to arouse a dormant memory. He rubbed his head, he scratched his ear, he looked up with a singularly vacant air at the pendent gas-light, he regarded his boots as though they were strange objects come for the first time within his ken. At length, when Mr. Effingham ceased, he spoke.

"It must have been her!" said he, ungrammatically but emphatically, at the same time bringing his fist down heavily on the table to express his assertion.

"What must have been her, Griffiths?" inquired Mr. Effingham, who was growing irritated by the extremely independent tone of his usually deferential subordinate,— "why don't you talk out, instead of snuffling to yourself and makin' those faces at me? What must have been her?"

Successful though he was for the time being, Mr. Griffiths had been too long subservient to the angry little man who addressed him to be able to shake off his bonds. He fell back into his old state of submission, grumbling as he said:

"You're a naggin' me as usual, D'Ossay, you are! Can't let a cove think for a minute and try and recollect what he'd 'eard,—you can't. What I was tryin' to bring back was this—there's a cove as I know, a theatrical gent, gets engagements for lakers and that, and provides managers of provincial gaffs with companies and so on. He was down at Hull, he was, and he come into our place one night with Mr. Munmorency of the T. R. there, as often give us a look up; and when business was over—we was rather slack that night—we went round to his 'otel to have a glass. And while we was drinkin' it and talkin' over old times, he says to me, 'Wasn't you in a swim with old

Lyons and Tony Butler once?' he says. 'Not once,' I says, 'but a good many times,' I says. 'I thought so,' he says; 'and wasn't there a handsome gal named Ponsford, did a lot of business for them?' he says. 'There was,' I says; 'fortune-tellin' and Mysterious-Lady business, and all that gaff,' I says. 'That's it,' he says; 'I couldn't think where I'd seen her before.' 'When did you see her last?' I says. 'About three weeks ago,' he says, 'she come to me on a matter of business, and claimed acquaintance with me; and though I knew the face and the name, I could not think where I had seen her before.'"

"Didn't you ask him anything more about her?" said Mr. Effingham.

"No, I didn't. 'Twas odd, wasn't it? but I didn't. You see I wasn't on your lay then, D'Ossay, my boy, and I was rather tired with hookin' in the 'arf-crowns and calclatin' the bettin' on the ins and outs, and I was enjoyin' my smoke and lookin' forward to my night's rest."

"What a sleepy-headed cove you are, Griffiths!" said Mr. Effingham with great contempt. "What do you tell me this for, if this is to be the end?"

"But this ain't to be the end, D'Ossay, dear! Mr. Trapman's come back by this time, I dessay, and we'll go and look him up to-morrow and see whether he can tell us anything of any real good about this gal. He's a first-rate hand is Trapman, as knowin' as a ferret; and it won't do to let him know what our game is, else he might go in and spoil it and work it for himself. So just you hold your tongue, if we see him, D'Ossay, and leave me to manage the palaver with him."

Mr. Effingham gave an ungracious assent to his companion's suggestion, and, practical always, asked him to name a time for this meeting on the next day. Mr. Griffiths suggested twelve o'clock as convenient for a glass of ale and a biscuit, and for finding Mr. Trapman at home. So the appointment was made for that hour; and after a little chat on subjects irrelevant to the theme of this story, the worthy pair parted.

The biscuit and the—several—glasses of ale had been discussed the next day, and Mr. Griffiths was maunderingly hinting his desire to remain at Johnson's for some time longer, when Mr. Effingham, burning with impatience, and with the semblance of authority in him, insisted upon his quondam parasite, but present equal, convoying him to the interview with Mr. Trapman. Mr. Trapman's Dramatic Agency Office, so notified in blue letters on a black board, was held at the Pizarro Coffee-house in Beak Street, Drury Lane. A dirty, bygone, greasy, used-up little place the Pizarro Coffee-house, with its fly-blown playbills banging over its wire-blind, its greasy coffee-stained lithograph of Signor Poleno, the celebrated clown, with his performing dogs; its moss-covered basket, which looked as if it had been made in a property-room, containing two obviously fictitious eggs. The supporters of the Pizarro were Mr. Trapman's clients, and Mr. Trapman's clients became perforce supporters of the Pizarro. When an actor was, as he described it, "out of collar," he haunted Beak Street, took "one of coffee and a rasher" at the Pizarro, and entered his name on Mr. Trapman's books. The mere fact of undergoing that process seemed to revivify him at once. He was on Trapman's books, and would probably be summoned at an hour's notice to give 'em his Hamlet at South Shields: a capital fellow, Trapman!—safe to get something through him; and then the candidate for provincial histrionic honour would poodle his hair under his hat and take a glance at himself in the strip of looking-glass that adorned the window of the Roscius' Head, and would wonder when that heiress who should see him from the stage-box O.P., and faint on her mother's neck, exclaiming, "Fitzroy Bellville for my husband, or immediate suicide for me!" would arrive.

There was a strange *clientèle* always gathered round Mr. Trapman's door so long as the great agent was visible, viz. from ten till five; old men in seedy camlet cloaks with red noses and bleared eyes—"heavy fathers" these—and cruel misers and villanous stewards and hard-swearing admirals and libertine peers; dark sunken-eyed gray men, with cheeks so blue from constant shaving that they look as if they had been stained by woad; virtuous and vicious lovers; heroes of romance and single walking-gentlemen; comic men with funny faces and funny figures, ready to play the whole night through from six till twelve, in four pieces, and to interpolate a "variety of singing and dancing" between each; portly matrons—Emilias and Belvideras now-who have passed their entire life upon the stage, and who at five years of age first made their appearance as flying fairies; sharp wizen-faced little old ladies, who can still "make-up young at night," and who are on the lookout for the smart *soubrette* and singing-chambermaid's line; and heavy tragedians—these most difficult of all to provide for-with books full of testimonials extracted from the potential criticisms of provincial journals. The ladies looked in, made their inquiries as to "any news," and went away to their homes again; but the gentlemen remained about all day long, lounging in Beak Street, leaning against posts, amicably fencing together with their ashen sticks, gazing at the playbills of the metropolitan theatres, and wondering when their names will appear there.

Through a little knot of these upholders of the mirror, Mr. Effingham and Mr. Griffiths made their way up the dark dirty staircase past the crowded landing, until they came into the sanctuary of the office. Here was a dirty-faced boy acting as clerk, who exhibited a strong desire to enter their names and requirements in a large leather-covered book before him; but Griffiths caught sight of Mr. Trapman engaged in deep and apparently interesting conversation with a short dark man in a braided overcoat, and a telegraphic wink of recognition passed between them. As it was the boy's duty to notice everything, he saw the wink, and left them without further molestation, until Mr. Trapman had got rid of his interlocutor, and had come over to talk to them.

"Well, and how are you?" said he, slapping Mr. Griffiths on the back.—"Servant, sir," to Mr. Effingham.—"And how *are* you?" Slaps repeated.

"Fust rate," said Mr. Griffiths, poking him in the ribs. "This is Mr. Effingham, friend of mine, and a re-markably downy card!"

Wouldn't be a friend of yours if he wasn't, said Mr. Trapman, with another bow to D'Ossay. "Well, and what's up? Given up the gaff, I suppose. Seven to nine! all equal!—no more of that just now, eh?"

"No; not in town. Sir Charles Rowan and Colonel Mayne at Scotland Yard, they know too much,—they do. No; I ain't here on business."

"No?" said Mr. Trapman playfully. "I thought you might be goin in for the heavy father, Griffiths, or the comic countryman, since your tour in the provinces."

Mr. Griffiths grinned, and declared that Mr. Trapman was "a chaffin' him." "My friend, Mr. D'Ossay—Effingham is more in that line," he said; "a neat figure, and a smart way he's got."

"Charles Surface, Mercushow, Roderigo,—touch-and-go comedy,—that's his line," said Mr. Trapman, glancing at Mr. Effingham. "One fi'-pun-note of the Bank of England, and he opens at Sunderland next week."

Mr. Effingham had been staring in mute wonder at this professional conversation; but he understood the last sentence, and thought enough time had been spent in discussing what they didn't want to know. So he put on his impetuous air and said to Griffiths, "Go in at him now!"

Thus urged, and taking his cue at once, Mr. Griffiths said, "No, no; you've mistaken our line. What we want of you is a little information. Oh, we're prepared to pay the fee!" he added, seeing Mr. Trapman's face grow grave under a rapid impression of wasted time; "only—no fakement; let's have it gospel, or not at all."

"Fire away!" said Mr. Trapman. "I'm here to be pumped—for a sovereign!"

The coin was produced, and handed over.

"Now," said Mr. Trapman, having tested it with his teeth, and then being satisfied, stretched out his arm in imitation of a pump-handle, "go to work!"

"You recollect," said Griffiths, "telling me, when we met down at Hull, that one of our old lot had been to see you lately—a girl called Lizzie Ponsford."

"I do perfectly."

"It's about her we want to know—that's all."

"It ain't much to tell, but it was curious,—that it was. It's six weeks ago now, as I was a-sittin' in this old shop, finishin' some letters for the post, when I looked up and saw a female in the doorway with a veil on. I was goin' on with my letters, takin' no notice, for there's *always* somebody here, in and out all day they are, when the female lifted up her finger first warning-like, like the ghosts on the stage, and then pointin' to Tom, the boy there, motioned that he should go out of the room. I was a little surprised; for though I had enough of that sort of thing many years ago, I've got out of it now. I thought it was a case of smite; I did indeed. However, I sealed up the letters, and told Tom to take 'em to the post; and then the female came in, shuttin' the door behind her. When she lifted her veil, I thought I knew the face, but couldn't tell where; however she soon reminded me of that first-rate gaff, in—where was it?—out Oxford Street way, where she did the Mysterious Lady, and Seenor Cocqualiqui the conjurin', and Ted Spicer sung comic songs. I remembered her at once then, and asked her what she wanted. 'An engagement,' she says. 'All right,' I says; 'what for?' 'Singin'-chambermaid, walkin'-lady, utility, anything,' she says. 'Walkin'-lady, to grow into leadin' high comedy, 's your line, my dear,' I says: 'you're too tall for chambermaids, and too good for utility. Now, let's look up a place for you.' I was goin' to my books, but she stopped me. 'I don't want a place,' she says; 'I ain't goin' to stop in England; all I want from you,' she says, 'is two or three letters of introduction to managers in New York. You've seen me before the public; and though you've never seen me act, you could tell I wasn't likely to be nervous or stammer, or forget my words.' 'No fear of that,' I says. 'Very well then,' she says, 'as I don't want to hang about when I get there, but want them to give me an appearance at once, just you write me the letters, and'—puttin' two sovereigns on the table—'make 'em as strong as you can for the money.' Oh, a clever girl she is! I sat down to write the letters, and in the middle of the first I looked up, and I says, 'The bearer, Miss ——, what name shall I say?' 'Leave it blank, Mr. Trapman, please,' says she, burstin' out laughin'; 'I haven't decided what my name's to be,' she says; 'and when I have, I think I can fill it in so that no one will know it ain't your writin'.' So I gave her the letters and she went away; and that's my story."

Mr. Griffiths looked downhearted, and was apparently afraid that his patron would imagine he had not had his money's worth; but Mr. Effingham, on the contrary, seemed in much better spirits, and thanked Mr. Trapman, and proposed an adjournment to the Rougepot close by in Salad Yard, where they had their amicable glasses of ale, and discussed the state of the theatrical profession generally.

When they had bidden adieu to Mr. Trapman and were walking away together, Mr. Griffiths reverted to the subject of Miss Ponsford.

"There's an end of that little game, I s'pose," said he; "that document's lost to us for ever."

"Wait!" said Mr. Effingham, with a grin; "I ain't so sure of that. She's gone to New York, you see; now I know every hole and corner in New York, and I'm known everywhere there, as well as any Yankee among them. I could hunt her up there fifty times easier than I could in London."

"I daresay," said Mr. Griffiths; "but you see there's one thing a trifle against that; you ain't in New York."

"But I could go there, I s'pose, stoopid!"

"Yes; but how, stoopid? You can't pad the hoof over the sea; and them steamers lay it on pretty thick, even in the steerage."

"I'm goin' to America within the next week, Griffiths, and I intend a friend of mine to pay for my passage."

"What! the Bart. again?"

"Exactly. The Bart. again!"

"And what game are you goin' to try on with him now?"

"Ah, Griffiths, that's my business, my boy. All you've got to do is to say goodbye to your D'Ossay to-night, for he's got to journey down to that thunderin' old Devonshire again to-morrow; and before a week's out he intends to be on the briny sea."

For the second time Mr. Effingham travelled down to Redmoor, and obtained an interview with Sir Charles Mitford. He found that gentleman very stern and haughty on this occasion; so Mr. Effingham comported himself with great humility.

"Now, sir," said Sir Charles, "you've broken your word for the second time. What do you want now?"

"I'm very sorry, Sir Charles—no intention of givin' offence, Sir Charles; but—"

"You've not got that—that horrible bill?"

"N-no, Sir Charles, I haven't; but—"

"Then what brings you here, sir? more extortion?—a further attempt to obtain money under false pretences?"

"No, no; don't say that, Sir Charles. I'll tell you right off. I may as well make a clean breast of it. I can't find that document anywhere. I don't know where it is; and I'm sick of cadgin' about and spongin' on you. You know when I first saw you up in town I told you I'd come from America. I was a fool to leave it. I did very well there; and I want to go back."

"Well, sir?"

"Well, just as a last chance, do that for me. I've been true to you; all that business of the young woman I managed first-rate—"

"I paid you for it."

"So you did; but try me once again."

"Tell me exactly what you want now."

"Pay my passage out. Don't even give me the money; send some cove to pay it, and bring the ticket to me; and he can come and see me off, if he likes, and give me a trifle to start with on the other side of the water; and you'll never hear of me again."

Sir Charles reflected a few moments; then said, "Will you go at once?"

"At once-this week; sooner the better."

"Have you made any inquiries about ships?"

"There's one sails from Liverpool on Friday."

"On Friday-and to-day is Saturday; just a week. I shan't trust you in the matter, Mr. Butler," said Sir Charles, taking up a letter lying on the table. "I shall adopt that precaution which you yourself suggested. A friend of mine, coming through from Scotland, will be in Liverpool on Wednesday night. Yes," he added, referring to the letter, "Wednesday night. I'll ask him to stop there a day, to take your ticket and to see you sail; and with the ticket he shall give you twenty pounds."

Mr. Effingham was delighted; he had succeeded better even than he had hoped, and he commenced pouring out his thanks. But Sir Charles cut him very short, saying:

"You will ask for Captain Bligh at the Adelphi Hotel; and recollect, Mr. Butler, this is the last transaction between us;" and he left the room.

"For the present, dear sir," said Mr. Effingham, taking up his hat; "the last transaction for the present; but if our little New York expedition turns up trumps, you and I will meet again on a different footing."

On the Friday morning Mr. Effingham sailed from Liverpool for New York in the fast screw-steamer Pocahontas, his ticket having been taken and the twenty pounds paid to him on board by Captain Bligh, who stood by leaning against a capstan while the vessel cleared out of dock.

CHAPTER XXV.

A CRISIS AT REDMOOR.

When Mrs. Hammond left the dinner-table on the evening destined to add a new sorrow to Georgie Mitford's sorely-troubled lot, she really had gone, as she had announced her intention of going, to her husband's room. The old man was lying in his bed, propped up with pillows, his face turned to the large window, through which the rays of the moon were shining, and mingling in a cold and ghastly manner with the light in the room. The invalid had a fancy for seeing the dark clumps of trees on the rising grounds, and the cold moon shining over their heads. Gifford, his confidential servant, sat at the bed's head, and had been reading to his master. Mrs. Hammond asked him several questions in a tone of interest which sounded almost genuine as to how Mr. Hammond had been; and then saying she meant to remain with the invalid for a while, she dismissed him, and took her seat by the window, in a position enabling her to see quite distinctly a portion of the broad carriage-drive to the right of the entrance, across which the rays of the moon flung their uninterrupted radiance. Laura did not exert herself much for the amusement of the invalid. The few questions he asked her she answered listlessly, then sunk into silence. After a short time her stepdaughter came softly into the room to bid her father goodnight.

"You are rather late, Alice; where have you been?" said Laura, without turning her head towards the child, still looking fixedly at the patch of ground in the moonlight.

"With Lady Mitford, mamma," answered Alice.

"Have the gentlemen left the dining-room?"

"Lord Dollamore came into the drawing-room, and I saw Sir Charles crossing the hall into the library; but I don't know about the others," answered Alice.

Mrs. Hammond said no more; and Alice, having received an affectionate embrace from her father, and the coldest conceivable touch of Mrs. Hammond's lips on the edge of her cheek, went off to bed. The silence continued in the sick man's room, and Laura's gaze never turned from the window. At length a figure passed across the moonlit space, and was instantly lost in the darkness beyond. Then Mrs. Hammond drew down the blind, and changed her seat to a chair close by the bedside. She took up the book which Gifford had laid down, and asked her husband if he would like her to read on.

"If you please, my dear," said Mr. Hammond, "if it won't tire you; and you won't mind my falling asleep, which I may do, for I feel very drowsy."

Laura was quite sure it would not tire her to read, and she would be delighted if her reading should have so soothing an effect.

"If I do fall asleep, you must not stay with me, Laura; you must go downstairs again. Promise me you will; and you need not call Gifford,—I don't require any one; I am much better to-night."

Very well; Laura would promise not to stay in his room if he should fall asleep; and as she really did think him very much better, she would not summon Gifford.

Mrs. Hammond possessed several useful and attractive accomplishments; among others, that of reading aloud to perfection. She did not exhibit her skill particularly on this occasion—her voice was languid and monotonous; and the author would have had ample reason to complain had he heard his sentences rendered so expressionless. She read on and on, in a sullen monotone; and after a quarter of an hour had elapsed, she had the pleasure of seeing that her kind intention was fulfilled. Her voice had been very soothing, and her husband had fallen into a profound sleep. Then she passed through an open door into her dressing-room, and reappeared, wrapped in a dark warm cloak, the hood thrown over her head. If any one had taken the place she had so lately occupied at the window, that person would have seen, after the lapse of a few moments, a second figure flit across the moonlit space, and disappear into the darkness beyond.

About half an hour later Banks tapped at the door of the smoking-room, and was gruffly bidden to "come in" by Captain Bligh.

"If you please, Captain," said Banks, upon whom the atmosphere of that particular apartment always produced a distressingly-choky and eye-smarting effect,— "if you please, Captain, I can't find Sir Charles. He ain't in the library, nor yet in the droring-room, and he's wanted very particular."

"Perhaps he has gone up to see Mr. Hammond," suggested Bligh.

"No, Captain, he ain't; I've bin and ast Gifford, and he says as his missis has been along o' the old gentleman since dinner-time, and she's there now, and nobody ain't with them."

"That's odd," said Captain Bligh; "but who wants him? Perhaps I might do."

"I beg your pardon, Captain," said the peremptory Banks, "but nobody won't do but Sir Charles hisself. It's a party as has been sent up from Fishbourne, where my lady comes from, and his orders is to see Sir Charles alone, and not to let out his message to nobody else."

The good-natured Captain looked extremely grave. Only one occurrence could have rendered so much precaution necessary, and he conjectured at once that that occurrence had taken place.

"I fear Mr. Stanfield is dead," he said to his companions. "I must go and find Mitford. Just excuse me for a while, and make yourselves comfortable here, will you?—Come with me, Banks, and take care your mistress gets no hint of this person's being here."

"There ain't no fear of that, Captain," replied the man; "my lady's in the droring-room, along o' Lord Dollamore; and I knew that Sir Charles worn't there, so I didn't go to look for him."

The Captain found the messenger in the library, where Banks had sent him to await Sir Charles's appearance. He was a respectable elderly man, and he answered Captain Bligh's inquiry at once. He had been sent by poor Georgie's old friend, the curate, to convey to Sir Charles Mitford the melancholy intelligence of Mr. Stanfield's death, which had taken place early that morning; and particulars of which event were contained in a letter which he was charged to deliver to the Baronet. He had received special injunctions to communicate the event to Sir Charles alone, and leave it to be "broken" to Lady Mitford by her husband. The simple curate had little thought how difficult Sir Charles would find it to assume even a temporary sympathy with the feelings of his wife.

Captain Bligh ordered refreshments to be served to the bringer of evil tidings; requested him not to communicate with any of the other servants; and strictly enjoining Banks to secrecy, went out of the front door and into the shrubbery on the left of the house. Mitford was not unaccustomed to take fits of sullen moodiness at times, and the Captain thought that he might perhaps find him walking about and smoking, in all the enjoyment of his ill-humour.

The intelligent Banks had asked Gifford if he thought it likely that Sir Charles was in his master's room, in the presence of several of the ladies and gentlemen of the household, assembled in a comfortable and spacious apartment which the insolence of a dominant class caused to be known as the servants'-hall. Among the number of those who heard the question and its answer was Mademoiselle Marcelline, Mrs. Hammond's "own maid." She was a trim-looking French girl, who had not anything remarkable in her appearance except its neatness, or in her manner except its quietness. She was seated at a large table, on which a number of workboxes were placed, for the women-servants at Redmoor greatly affected needlework, and had a good deal of time to devote to it; and she was embroidering a collar with neatness, dexterity, and rapidity, eminently French. Mademoiselle Marcelline made no observation, and did not raise her eyes, or discontinue her work for a moment, during the discussion as to where Sir Charles could be, which had ensued upon Banks's inquiry. She had spoken only once indeed since his entrance. When Gifford had said Sir Charles Mitford could not be in Mr. Hammond's room, because her mistress had been, and was there still, he had asked, "Isn't she there still, mam'selle?" Mam'selle had answered, "Yes, Monsieur Giffore, madame is there still."

Mademoiselle Marcelline was so very quiet a little person, and differed so much from French ladies'-maids in general, by the unobtrusiveness of her manners and her extreme taciturnity—to be sure she spoke very little English, but that circumstance is rarely found to limit the loquacity of her class—that her exit from the servants'-hall was scarcely noticed, when she presently looked at her little Geneva watch, made up her embroidery into a tidy parcel, and went away with her usual noiseless step.

Mademoiselle Marcelline mounted the stairs with great deliberation, and smiling a little, until she reached the corridor into which the suite of apartments occupied by the Hammonds opened. The rooms were five in number, and each communicated with the other. They were two bed-rooms, two dressing-rooms, and a bath-room. The latter occupied the central space, and had no external door. Mademoiselle Marcelline entered the last room of the suite, corresponding with that in which Mr. Hammond lay,—this was Laura's bed-room,—and gently locked the door. She passed through the adjoining apartment—her mistress's dressing-room—and paused before a large wardrobe, without shelves, in which hung a number of dresses and cloaks. She opened the doors, but held them one in each hand, looked in for a moment, and then shut them, and smiled still more decidedly. Then she softly locked the door of this room which opened into the corridor, and passing through the bath-room secured that of Mr. Hammond's dressing-room also; after which, with more precaution against noise than ever, she glided into the old man's room. He was sleeping soundly still, and his face looked wasted and ashen in the abstraction of slumber. Mademoiselle Marcelline glanced at him, shrugged her shoulders, sat down on a couch at the foot of the bed, where she was effectually screened from view by the heavy carved bedpost and the voluminous folds of the purple curtain, and waited.

Meantime, Captain Bligh had not succeeded in finding Sir Charles, though he had sought for him in the shrubbery and in the stable-yard. He could not make out whither he had gone, and returned to the house to take counsel with Banks. That functionary suggested that Sir Charles might have gone up to the keeper's house; and though the Captain could not imagine why Sir Charles should have gone thither at such an inconvenient time, as he had no other to offer, he accepted this suggestion, and said he would go thither and look for him.

"Shall I go with you, Captain?" asked Banks, who felt curious to discover what "Mitford was up to."

Since Mr. Effingham's visit, and the polite fiction of the yacht—endeared to Mr. Banks by his own joke about the Fleet Prison, which he considered so good that society was injured by its suppression within his own bosom—the incredulous flunkey had experienced an increased share of the curiosity with which their masters' affairs invariably inspire servants. He was much pleased then that Captain Bligh answered,

"Yes, yes, you can come with me."

The keeper's cottage was not very far from the great house, from which, however, it was entirely hidden by a thick fir-plantation which covered a long and wide space of undulating land, and through which several narrow paths led to the open ground beyond. The Captain and his attendant struck into one of those paths, which led directly in the direction of the keeper's house.

"We can't miss Sir Charles, I think, if he really has gone up to Hutton's," said the Captain.

"No, sir, I think not, unless he has taken a very roundabout way," answered Banks.

They walked quickly on for some distance, the Captain's impatience momentarily increasing, and also his doubts that Mitford had gone in this direction at all. At length they reached a point at which the path, cutting the plantation from east to west, was intersected by one running from north to south. Here they paused, and the Captain said testily,

"By Jove, Banks, I hardly know what to do. The messenger from Fishbourne's shut up in the library all this time, and all the servants in a fuss, and Sir Charles not forthcoming! I wish I had broken the news of her father's death to Lady Mitford before I came out; it would have been by far the best plan. She's sure to hear it by accident now."

The Captain spoke to himself rather than to the servant, and in a particularly emphatic voice—a testimony to his vexation. Then he strode onwards with increased speed, little knowing that he had spoken within the startled hearing of the man whom he was seeking, and who was so near him, as he stood where the paths met, that he could have touched him by stretching out his arm,—touched him and his cowering frightened companion.

They kept a breathless silence until the Captain and Banks were quite out of hearing. Then Sir Charles said: "What is to be done? Did you hear what Bligh said, Laura? Some one has been sent from Fishbourne to tell me that Mr. Stanfield is dead, and they are searching for me everywhere. What a cursed accident! There is not a chance of concealing your absence. My darling, my life, what is to be done?"

She was very pale and trembling, and the words came hard and hoarse, as she replied,

"I know not. If we must brave it out we must; but there is a chance yet. Do you stay here, and meet Bligh as he comes back; you can be strolling along the cross path. Have you a cigar? No; you are in dinner-dress, of course. Stay; you have an overcoat on; search the pockets. Yes, yes; what luck! Here's a cigar-case, and your light-box hangs to your chain,—I'll never call it vulgar again,—light a cigar at once, and contrive to show the light when you hear them. I will go to the house. You left the side window open, did you not?"

"Yes, yes." His agitation was increasing; hers was subsiding.

"If I can get into the house unseen, all is right. I can pass through my own rooms into Hammond's. Send there for me if all is safe; the servants think I am there."

She turned away to leave him; but he caught her in his arms, and said in a tone of agony,

"Laura! Laura! if I have exposed you to danger—if—"

"Hush!" she said, disengaging herself; "you have not exposed me to danger any more than I have exposed myself; but don't talk of this as a hopeless scrape until we know that there is no way out of it." She was out of sight in an instant.

Mademoiselle Marcelline sat at the foot of Mr. Hammond's bed without the least impatience. She did not fidget, she did not look at the clock, she did not doze. The time passed apparently to her perfect satisfaction. The invalid slept on very peacefully, and the whole scene wore an eminently comfortable aspect. At length her acute ears discerned a light footfall at the end of the corridor, and then she heard the handle of Mrs. Hammond's dressing-room door gently turned—in vain. Then the footstep came on, and another door-handle was turned, equally in vain.

Mademoiselle Marcelline smiled. "It would have been so convenient for madame to have hung her cloak up and smoothed her hair before monsieur should see her, after madame's promenade in the clear of the moon," thought Mademoiselle Marcelline. "What a pity that those tiresome doors should unhappily be locked! What a sorrowful accident!"

The door opened, and Laura looked cautiously into the room. All was as she had left it; the sleeping face of her husband was turned towards her. The pathetic unconsciousness of sleep was upon it; she did not heed the pathos, but the unconsciousness was convenient. The minutest change that would have intimated that any one had entered the room would not have escaped her notice, but there was no such thing. She came in, and softly closed the heavy perfectly-hung door; she made a few steps forward, uttered a deep sigh of relief, and said in an involuntary whisper, "What a risk, and what an escape!"

Her heavy cloak hung upon her; she pushed back the hood, and her chestnut hair, in wild disorder, shone with red gleams in the firelight. She lifted her white hands and snatched impatiently at the tasseled cord which held the garment at the throat; and Mademoiselle Marcelline emerged from the shadow of the bed-curtains, and with perfect propriety and an air of entire respect requested that madame would permit her to remove the cloak which was so heavy, and also madame's boots, which must be damp, for the promenade of evening had inconveniences.

Laura started violently, and then stood looking at the demure figure before her with a kind of incredulous terror. Mademoiselle Marcelline composedly untied the refractory cords and removed the mantle, which she immediately replaced in the wardrobe. Would Madame have the goodness to consider what she had said about the boots, and to go into her dressing-room? Madame followed her like one in a dream. She placed a chair before the dressing-table, and Laura mechanically sat down; she took off her boots and substituted slippers; she restored the symmetry of the crushed dress; she threw a dressing-gown over the beautiful shoulders, folded it respectfully over the bosom heaving with terror and anger, and began to brush her mistress's hair with a wholly unperturbed demeanour. Laura looked at the demure composed face which appeared over her shoulder in the glass, and at length she said:

"How came you in that room?"

"Ah, madame, what a happy chance! One came to the salon of the servants, and demanded of Monsieur Giffore if Sir Charles might be in the chamber of monsieur. Then Monsieur Giffore say that no; that madame was there, and is there. And Monsieur Giffore asked me if he have reason; and I say, 'Certainly, madame is still in the chamber of monsieur.'"

"Well," said Laura, for Mademoiselle Marcelline had paused, "what has that to do with your being in that room?"

"It has much, if madame will take the trouble to listen. I know that servants are curious,—ah, how curious servants are, my God!—and I thought one of them might have curiosity enough to see for herself madame, so affectionate, passing the long, long evening with poor monsieur, who is not gay,—no, he is not gay, they say that in the salon of the servants. So, as it is not agreeable to be listened and spied, and as servants are so curious, I locked the doors of the rooms consecrated to the privacy of madame, and rejoiced to know that madame might read excellent books of exalted piety to monsieur, or refresh her spirits, so tired by her solicitude, with a promenade in the clear of the moon—madame is so poetic!—as she chose, without being teased by observation. I respect also that good Monsieur Giffore, and I would not have him disprove. 'Madame is still there, mam'sell?' he asks; and I say, 'Yes; madame is still there.'"

All the time she was speaking, Mademoiselle Marcelline quietly pursued her task. The long silken tresses lay now in a well-brushed shining heap over her left arm, and she looked at them with complacent admiration.

"Heaven! but madame has beautiful hair!" she went on, while Laura, pale and motionless, at taking into her heart the full meaning of this terrible complication of her position. "It is, however, fortunate that she does not adopt the English style, for promenades at the clear of the moon are enemy to curls—to those long curls which the young ladies, lastly gone away, and who were so fond of madame, wore. They avoided the damp of the forest in the evening, the young ladies; they were careful of their curls. But madame has not need to be careful of anything—nothing and nobody can hurt madame, who is so beloved by monsieur. Ah, what a destiny! and monsieur so rich!"

She had by this time braided the shining hair, and was dexterously folding the plaits round and round the small head, after a fashion which Laura had lately adopted. Still her mistress sat silent, with moody downcast eyes. As she interrupted her speech for a moment to take a fresh handful of hair-pins from the dressing-table, Banks knocked at the door of the adjoining room. Mademoiselle Marcelline did not raise her voice to bid him enter; always considerate, she remembered that an indiscreet sound might trouble the repose of the invalid, so she stepped gently to the door and opened it.

"Is Mrs. Hammond here, mam'sell?" asked Banks.

"Oh, but yes, Monsieur Banks, madame is always here."

"Not exactly," thought Banks, puzzled by her idiom; but he merely said, "Bad news has reached the family. My lady's father is dead, which he was a good old gentleman indeed; and she ain't seen him neither, not for some time; and my lady she's been a faintin' away in the libery like anythin'; and Sir Charles, he's been a holdin' of her hup, leastways him and Lord Dollamore, and there's the deuce to pay down there."

Mademoiselle listened with polite attention to Mr. Banks's statement of the condition of affairs; but she was not warmly interested.

"Monsieur Banks will pardon me," she said; "but at present I coif madame; I think he demanded madame?"

"Yes, I did, marm'sell," said Banks, abashed and convicted by this quiet little person of undue loquacity; "only I thought you'd like to hear. Mostly servants does; but," here Mr. Banks floundered again, "you ain't much like the rest of us, miss— mam'sell, I mean."

Mademoiselle Marcelline acknowledged the compliment with a very frigid smile, and again inquired what she might have the pleasure of telling madame, on the part of Monsieur Banks.

"Sir Charles begs Mrs. Hammond will come down to the libery if quite convenient to her, as he wishes to speak to her about some necessary arrangements."

Mr. Banks delivered his message with elaboration, and waited the reply with dignity. Mademoiselle Marcelline repeated the communication to her mistress, word for word, and did not suffer the slightest trace of expression to appear in her face.

"Yes, I will go down immediately," said Laura, much relieved at the prospect of escaping from the presence of her maid, and having time to consider her position.

Mr. Banks went away to deliver Mrs. Hammond's message, and mademoiselle, in perfect silence, removed the dressing-gown from her mistress's shoulders; and Laura, her dress in complete order, and her nerves to all appearance as well arranged, rose from her chair.

"Give me a lace shawl," she said, in her customary imperious manner; "if Lady Mitford has lost her father, she will not be gratified by my making my appearance in full-dress, and I have no time to change it."

"Madame is so considerate," remarked Mademoiselle Marcelline, as she folded a web of fine black lace round Mrs. Hammond's form; "and Lady Mitford owes her so much. Poor lady, she is sensitive; she has not the courage of madame. Madame must form her."

"Go for Gifford to sit with Mr. Hammond," said Laura. "You can wait for me in my room as usual;" and she walked out of the dressing-room, having previously ordered her maid to unlock the door, without any outward sign of disturbance. Slowly she went down the great staircase, and as she went she asked herself, "Shall I tell Charles? Could any worse complication arise out of my concealing this dreadful thing from him?" At length she made up her mind, just as she reached the door of the library. "No," she said, "I will not tell him. He has no nerve, and would blunder, and the less one tells any man the better."

Poor Georgie, now indeed lonely and desolate, had been taken to her room, and induced to lie down on her bed, by the housekeeper and her maid, who proposed to watch by their unhappy mistress all night. She and Sir Charles were to proceed to Fishbourne on the following day. She had earnestly entreated her husband to take her with him, and he had consented. She was quite worn-out and stupefied with grief, and had hardly noticed Mrs. Hammond's presence in the library at all. It was agreed that Lord. Dollamore should leave Redmoor on the following day, a little later than Sir Charles and Lady Mitford, and that the Hammonds should go to Torquay as soon as the physicians would permit their patient to make so great an effort.

"It is impossible to say how soon I shall get back, or how long I may be detained," said Sir Charles; "and it's a confounded nuisance having to go."

Lord Dollamore looked at him with tranquil curiosity, and tapped first his teeth and then his ear with his inseparable cane.

"I hope they will make you comfortable here. Bligh will see to everything, I know. Perhaps they won't let Hammond move at all—very likely, for there's an east wind—and you'll be here when we return."

Very gravely Mrs. Hammond answered him: "That will be impossible, Sir Charles. Lady Mitford could not possibly be expected to have any one in her house under such circumstances. Mr. Hammond *must* be brought to Torquay."

Sir Charles was puzzled; he could not quite understand her tone; he did not think it was assumed entirely, owing to the presence of Lord Dollamore, for that had seldom produced any effect on Laura. No, she was completely in earnest. She gave her hand to each gentleman in turn, but the clasp she bestowed on each was equally warm; and when Sir Charles, as she passed out of the door, shot one passionate glance at her, unseen by Dollamore, she completely ignored it, and walked gracefully away.

"By Jove!" said Lord Dollamore, when he had gotten rid of Mitford and was safe in his own room, "it was a lucky thing Buttons made his appearance just when he did. I should have hopelessly committed myself in another minute; and then, on the top of that fine piece of sentiment, we should have had the scene of this evening's news. No matter how she had taken it, I should have been in an awful scrape. If she had taken it well, I should have had to do a frightful amount of sympathy and condolence—the regular 'water-cart business' in fact; and if she had taken it ill, egad, she's just the woman to blurt it all out in a fit of conscience, and to believe that her father's death is a judgment upon her for not showing me up to Mitford! As it is, the matter remains in a highly-satisfactory condition; I am not committed to anything: I might have been pleading my own cause, or a friend's, or some wholly imaginary personage's; and I can either resume the argument precisely where I dropped it, if I think proper, or I can cut the whole affair. Bless you, my Buttons!"

As Georgie was driving over to the railway-station on the following day,—her maid and she occupying the inside of the carriage, and Sir Charles, availing himself of his well-known objection to allow any one but himself to drive when he was present, to avoid a *tête-à-tête* with his wife, on the box,—she raised her heavy veil for a while, and drawing a letter from her pocket, read and re-read it through her blinding tears. It was from Colonel Alsager. At length Georgie put it away, and lay back in the carriage, with closed eyes, thinking of the writer.

"He has suffered a great deal also," she thought; "and he has more to suffer. How sorely he must repent his neglect of his father! as sorely as I repent my neglect of mine." Here the tears, which had already burned her eyelids into a state of excruciating soreness, burst forth again. "What must he have felt when he read his father's letter!—the letter written to be read after the writer's death,—the letter he will show to me, he says, though to no one else in the world, except, I suppose, the young lady whom Sir Peregrine entreated him in it to marry. I wonder if he will,—I wonder if she is nice, and good, and likely to make him happy! It is strange that a similar calamity should have befallen him and me. He can feel for my grief now—I have always felt for his!"

CHAPTER XXVI.

MR. WUFF'S "NEW STAR."

"Miss Constance Greenwood, the new actress!" "Go and see Constance Greenwood on the 18th!" "Constance Greenwood as Lady Malkinshaw!" Such were the placards in enormous letters which glared upon Laurence Alsager from every dead wall and hoarding on his passage from the railway-station to his old rooms in Jermyn Street. Laurence could not forbear smiling as he glanced at them—could not forbear a laugh as, at the Club over his dinner, he read the advertisements of the forthcoming appearance of Miss Greenwood at the Theatre Royal, Hatton Garden, for which national establishment she had been secured by the *impresario*, Mr. Wuff, at an expense hitherto unparalleled—at least so said the advertisements.

Yes; Mr. Wuff had done it at last! He had cut himself adrift from the moorings of mediocrity, as his nautical dramatist expressed it, and it was now sink or swim with him. He was "going in a perisher," he said himself; and having set his fortune on a die, he was just waiting to see whether it turned up six or ace.

When Mr. Wuff came into a sum of money on the death of a distant relative, and, forsaking the necessary but hardly popular calling of a sheriff's-officer, took the Theatre Royal, Hatton Garden, and opened it with a revival of the legitimate drama in general and of Shakespearian plays in particular, he made a very great hit. It was so long since any one had attempted to represent Shakespeare, that an entirely new generation had sprung up, which, egged on by its elders, went religiously to the first performance of all the celebrated plays, and tried very hard indeed to think they both understood and liked them. The newspaper press too was very noble on the subject. Mr. Wuff, so said the critics, was the great dramatic resuscitator of the age.

What! People had said that the taste for the legitimate was exploded! The answer to that was in the crowds that thronged to T. R., Hatton Garden. And then the critics went on to say that the scenery by Mr. Slapp, with wonderful moonlight effects such as had never previously been seen, was thoroughly appreciated; and that the mechanical arrangement for the appearance of Banquo's ghost amongst the unconscious Thanes was a marvel of theatrical deception. Was it Shakespeare or Slapp who drew? Buncle, a heavy, ignorant, ill-educated man, who had played fourth-rate parts with the *Dii majores* in those "palmy days" of which we read, and who now, *faute de mieux*, found himself pitch-forked into the leading characters, thought it was Shakespeare—and Buncle! The knowing ones thought it was the novelty of the reproduction and the excellence of Slapp's scenery which caused the success; and the knowing ones were right. Shakespeare, as interpreted by Buncle, Mrs. Buncle, and Stampede—whom Buncle always took about with him to play his seconds—drew for a certain length of time. Then the audience thinned gradually, and Wuff found it necessary to supplement *King Lear* with the *Harem Beauties*—a ballet supported by the best band of *coryphées* in Europe; and that was a really good stroke of policy. While Buncle was lying down and dying as Lear, the club-men came trooping into the house; and Buncle's apostrophes to his dead daughter Cordelia were nearly inaudible in the creaking of boots and the settling into seats. The pit cried "Hush!" and "Shame!" but the swells did not care about the pit, and the curtain fell on Buncle thirsting for aristocratic blood. The ballet at first attracted largely. As the time for its commencement approached, the military clubs were drained of their members, who went away in a procession of hansoms from Pall Mall to Hatton Garden; and you could have counted more peers within Wuff's walls at one time than were to be found, save on special occasions, at St. Stephen's.

But the ballet, after a time, ceased to draw; and Mr. Wuff could not supplement it by another, for the *coryphées* had all returned to their allegiance to the manager of the Opera-house, whose season had just commenced. Mr. Wuff was in despair; he dared not shut the house, for he had to make up his rent, which was required with inexorable punctuality by the committee of gentlemen who owned the theatre. He must try something; but what was it to be? Wuff and his treasurer, Mr. Bond,—always known as Tommy Bond, an apple-faced, white-headed old gentleman, who had dropped into the theatrical world no one ever knew whence, and who had held a place of trust with all the great managers of the T. R., Hatton Garden, for thirty years,—were closeted together.

"What's it to be, Tommy?" repeated Mr. Wuff for the twentieth time. "They've had it all round, hot and strong; and what's the caper for 'em now, I don't know."

"What do you think of reviving *Julius Caesar?* The classic costume has not been seen on these boards for years."

"What! Billy's *Julius Caesar?* No, thank you! I've had enough of Bill to last me some time—and that brute Buncle drawing fifteen pounds a week, and bellowing his lungs out to thirty people in the pit! No, no! Is there a good lion-and-camel lot about?"

Mr. Bond shuddered; he was frequently prompted to shudder in his conversation with Mr. Wuff. He was a great believer in the elevating tendencies of the drama; and when he thought of lions and camels on the same boards which he had seen trodden at different times by those great actors and rivals, Grumble and Green, he could not refrain from shuddering. But his business instincts made him turn to a file of the *Era* on the table, and he said, after consulting it:

"There's Roker's troupe at North Shields."

"How long since they've been in town?"

"Oh, two years; and then they were only at the Wells—you can scarcely call that town; and it didn't interfere a bit with our people, you know."

"Roker's are performing lions, ain't they?"

"Yes; they'll let him do anything to them, when they're in a proper state."

"All right! Write to him about terms at once; and send to Darn and tell him we want a piece to bring out this lot at once. Must be Eastern, because of the camel—long procession, slaves, caskets, and all that kind of thing, and a fight with the lion for Roker. That's all Roker's to do, mind; he can't act a bit."

Mr. Roker was driving such an excellent trade with the pitmen of the North, that he refused to come to London except on terms which Mr. Wuff would not give; and so that enterprising manager was again in a strait. Mr. Trapman had been called into council, had ransacked his books and his brain in search for novelty, but all to no purpose; and things were looking very serious for Mr. Wuff, when one morning Trapman rushed from his office and arrived breathless in the manager's sanctum.

"What is it?" asked Wuff, who was sitting vacantly looking at Bond, poring over files of old playbills.

"We've got it at last, I think!" said Trapman, pointing to an open letter in his hand "You've heard of Constance Greenwood?"

"Yes, yes!" struck in Mr. Bond eagerly. "Milman was here last week, just arrived from New York,—and he says that for the leading-lady business—modern time, I mean—he'd never seen anything like her."

"Yankee, ain't she?" asked Wuff coldly.

"Not a bit of it," replied Trapman. "She's English bred and born; only been out there three months; never played anywhere before, and made a most tre-mendous hit. I saw the New York papers about her first night. They'd got up a report that she was the daughter of an English nobleman, and had run away because her father was cruel to her; and this crammed the house. The girl's acting did the rest. Every one says she's very clever, and she was making no end of dollars a-night."

"Well?" said Wuff, who was working up into excitement.

"Oh, I thought you did not care about it," said Trapman. "I've a letter from her here in my hand, saying she's taken a sudden desire to England, and wants me to get her an engagement in a first-class theatre. I've got newspapers by the same mail, describing her farewell benefit, and speculating, in the way those chaps do over there, about what can have made her want to go to England so suddenly. But there's no doubt she's a clipper, and I came at once to offer her to you."

"I'll have her!" shouted Wuff, jumping up. "First-class theatre she wants, eh? This is the shop. Let's have a look at her letter?"

"Can't do that,—it's a private letter," said Trapman; "but I'll tell you her terms: ten pound a-night settled, and a share after a hundred."

"That'll do. Now, Tommy Bond, just sit down and write a stunnin' advertisement, and put that story about her being a nobleman's daughter into shape,—only make her run away because she was in love, and wanted to earn money for the support of her lover, who was blind.—Eh, Trapman, that ought to wake 'em up?—And send the story to little Shiffon, who does that column of lies, and ask him to stick it in next week.—What's her line, Trapman?"

"Genteel comedy and interesting business of the highest class,—lady of the present day, you know."

"All right; then I shan't want Buncle."

"Not a bit; get rid of him at once. But I'll tell you what; Pontifex has quarrelled with the Parthenium people—he was with me yesterday—and I'd pick him up to support her."

Mr. Wuff agreed to this, and told Mr. Trapman to take the necessary steps; and that gentleman then took his departure.

"Wasn't going to let Wuff look at her letter," said he, as he walked away; "wouldn't do at all. What a doosed clever gal! What does she say?" and he pulled the letter from his pocket: "'Not a word to any one until after my appearance. After that I shan't care.' All right, my dear; you may depend upon me."

Mr. Wuff went to work with a will, and spared no expense in his bills and advertisements. The nobleman's daughter's story was duly filtered through the newspapers, and popular curiosity was excited. Miss Constance Greenwood arrived from America by the next mail, bringing with her an American play, founded on a French subject, full of interest, and what we should in the present day call sensation, but wretchedly written. This play was given to the accomplished Spofforth; and under his manipulation it became a very capital acting drama, with a splendid character for Miss Greenwood, and very good chances for Pontifex. Wuff, Bond, Spofforth, and Oldboy, the critic of the *Statesman*, had a little dinner at Wuff's house before the evening dress-rehearsal, which Miss Greenwood had requested before the production of the piece; and they were all delighted with what they saw. Oldboy was especially pleased. "I thought," said he, "that ladylike women left the stage with Miss Fortescue; but this girl restores my hopes." And Wuff winked at Spofforth, and they both knew that meant a column and a half the morning after the performance.

Sir Laurence Alsager drove straight from the railway-station to the Maecenas Club, where his servant was waiting for him with his dressing-things. As he pushed through the streets, the placards on the walls announcing the theatrical novelty for the evening recalled to his mind the night of his return from the East. Then he drove to the Club, then he had returned to be present at the first representation of a theatrical novelty; but ah, how different was his state of mind then from what it was now! Then the iron had passed over the slight scratch which he at that time imagined was a wound, and had completely cicatrized it; now a real wound was gaping and bare. Kismet! kismet! the old story. That night he saw Georgie Mitford for the first time; and ever since then what had he not suffered on her account! Ah, what had she herself not suffered, poor child! His absence from London and his manner of life down at Knockholt had precluded him from hearing any recent news of her; and he wondered whether the lapse of time had had any effect on Sir Charles Mitford's mad infatuation, or whether it still continued. More than anything else, Laurence wanted to know whether Lady Mitford's domestic misery was known to the world at large, or confined to the few acquaintances who had such splendid opportunities of inspecting in the quiet of Redmoor. He knew that her first appearance in society had excited a great deal of notice, a great deal of admiration, and, consequently, a great deal of envy; and he was too much a man of the world not to feel certain that anything to her disadvantage would be sought out with the greatest perseverance, and spread abroad with the greatest alacrity. And it was to her disadvantage in the eyes of society, that her home was unhappy; there were people in numbers who would declare that the result was her fault; that she was prim, puritanical, bad-tempered; that her jealousy was perfectly ridiculous; that her missy ways and affectation rendered it impossible for any man to live with her. There were numbers of people who would take an opposite view of the question, and who would pity her—not indeed with that pity which is akin to love, but from a feeling springing from a very different source,—a pity which consists in loudly denouncing the cause for compassion, and wondering how the person to be compassionated can endure what has to be gone through. There would be people who could not understand how anything otherwise could have been expected: a young person from the *bourgeoisie* introduced into the *nous-autres* class must expect that the silly fancy which had captivated her husband would not last, and must be prepared to take the consequences of her vaulting ambition. The Clanronald and Tappington set would infallibly regard it from this last-mentioned point of view, accordingly.

How Laurence Alsager's blood boiled within him as all these thoughts passed through his mind! During the quietude of his life at Knockholt, he had had sufficient opportunities so thoroughly to catechise himself, so perfectly to dissect the feelings of his breast, as to leave no doubt in his own mind that he loved Lady Mitford deeply and passionately. The notion of the guardian angel, the protecting genius, which he had so encouraged at first, had now entirely faded out, and he had not scrupled to show to himself the actual state of his feelings towards her. Not that they would ever be known; he had made up his mind to keep them rigidly locked in his own bosom. But still it was worse than horrible to think that the woman in whose service he would willingly have perilled his life, was in all probability dragging on a miserable existence, exposed to the perverse misunderstandings or degrading pity of the world! On these latter points he should soon be assured. They discussed everybody at the Maecenas; and if there had been anything sufficiently noticeable in the Mitford *ménage* to call for comment, it was sure to receive the freest and most outspoken discussion in the tabak-parliament of the Club.

Meanwhile, the mere notion of being back in London conduced in no small degree to raise Laurence's spirits. His time at Knockholt had been, he felt, far from unprofitably spent; he had had opportunities not merely of examining his own heart, but of making himself acquainted with the hopes and fears, the wishes and prospects, of some of those with whose lives he was to a certain extent concerned. He had had opportunities of carrying out certain pet projects of the good old man, whose last days he had been permitted to console; and he had been enabled to take up that position in his county which was required of him, not merely by the hollow ordinances of "gentility," but by the great binding rivets of society. He hoped in all honesty and humility to be able "to do his duty in that state of life unto which God had called him;" but he felt all the delight of a schoolboy out of bounds in laying-by the county magnate, the landed proprietor, the many-acred wealthy baronet, for a time, and making a very small unit in the grand population of London. The crowded streets, the gas-lamps, the dull rumble of the passing vehicles,—all were delightful to him; and as he drew up at the club-door he felt happier than he had done for many a long day.

He dressed himself and went down into the coffee-room, which he found thronged. Mr. Wuff's advertisements and bills had been so far fruitful, that two-thirds of the diners at the Maecenas seemed from their talk to be going to the Hatton-Garden Theatre. Laurence was welcomed with great cordiality by all who knew him, and had numerous offers of "joining tables;" but he expected George Bertram, and when he found that that pillar of the state did not arrive, he preferred dining by himself. The solitary life he had been leading, the event which had led to that life, the reflections which had engrossed him since he had led it,—all concurred to prevent him from suddenly plunging into the light gossip of a club-room. After dinner, finding that the piece in which Miss Constance Greenwood was to appear did not commence until half-past eight, he went into the smoking-room, where most of the diners had assembled, and in addition to them, Lord Dollamore. He looked up and saw Alsager's entrance; then stretched out his hand, and pointed to a vacant seat on the couch beside him.

"My dear Alsager, delighted to see you,—honestly and truly delighted! How are you? What a hermit you have become! though of course I understand,—family-business and all that; and what has brought you up at last—not this new play?"

"Well, I can scarcely say that; but I wanted a something to come up for—a something, I mean, beyond law-business—and perhaps this wondrous advertisement of Wuff's turned the scale."

"They tell me the gal's deuced good. Spofforth, who saw her last night, was here this morning, and says she's really wonderful. This is the second time you've done this sort of thing,—coming back on the first night of a great theatrical event. It's not half a bad idea, because you see a lot of people you know, and get rid of 'how-d'ye-do's' in one large parcel."

"There are some who were present on the last occasion whom I shall not see to-night, I suppose," said Laurence. "I was thinking," he added, as he saw Dollamore whispering to his stick, "of George Bertram."

"No!" said Dollamore, "the Blab has been missing for the last fortnight. It's rumoured that he has gone as a mute into the service of the Pasha of Egypt. I thought you were alluding to our friends in Devonshire: a nice business that."

"Indeed! I, as you know, have been absent from town for months, and have heard nothing."

"Well, you won't listen to me, I suppose, because you'll imagine I am prejudiced, recollecting all I said to you on the subject in this very room after Spofforth's play. But you won't deny that, so far as you had opportunities of judging while we were down at Redmoor, I was right?"

"Right so far as your estimation of the man went, certainly—"

"Oh, as for the lady, there is no one can entertain a higher opinion of Lady Mitford than myself. The degradation that that brute is bringing upon her—"

"Degradation! Do you mean to say that Mitford's infidelities are known—about—generally?"

"My dear Alsager, you think I colour and exaggerate. Let us pump that well of candour, Cis Hetherington. If there is an honest opinion about, it will be procurable from that son of Anak.—Well, Cis, going to the play?"

"Course I am," responded that scion of the aristocracy, lazily lifting his head from the ottoman; "everybody's going, seems to me. What's the woman like? Yankee, ain't she? Don't like Yankees,—all speak through their noses, and say 'I guess;' at, least, all that I've ever seen do, and that's only on the stage."

"She's not Yankee; she's an Englishwoman, they tell me; though of course that story of the nobleman's daughter is all bosh. However, Wuff has worked the oracle splendidly. Everybody's going. Here's Alsager come up to town on purpose."

"Is that Alsager sitting next to you?" asked Cis Hetherington, raising himself on his elbow and looking full at Laurence. "I thought it looked like him, and I wondered he didn't speak to me. But I suppose he's grown proud since he's become a Bart."

"You old idiot! I shook hands with you in the hall as I came in," said Laurence, laughing. "What's the news, Cis? how are all your people?"

"First-rate, old boy! Westonhanger's gone abroad—to America, I mean; Sioux Indians, and that sort of thing. Wanted you awfully to go with him, but thought you were doing monseigneur on your *terre*. Asked about you no end, give you my word! And the Duke's really tremendous! 'pon my soul, some fellow ought to put him in a book! Ever since the row about the repeal of the Corn Laws has been coming to a head, he's been like a lunatic. He thinks it's all up with everything, and is sure we shall have a revolution, and that he'll have his head cut off by the mob and stuck on a pike, and all that kind of thing."

"And Algy Forrester?" asked Dollamore.

"Algy Forrester was here to-day," said Hetherington; "came to me about a devilish unpleasant thing. That fellow Mitford, whom you both know" ("Now, then, listen!" said Dollamore),—"that fellow Mitford has asked him—Algy, I mean—to put him up here. And Algy came to ask if I'd second him, and I told him I'd see Mitford d—d first. And so I would. I ain't a strait-laced party, and don't go in for being particularly virtuous myself; but I'm a bachelor, and am on my own hook. But the way that fellow Mitford treats that nice wife of his is neither more nor less than blackguardly, I think; and so I wouldn't mind telling him, if I'd the chance."

"Hallo, Cis!" said Markham Bowers, who was sitting near; "shut your stupid old mouth. You'll get into a mess if you give tongue like that,—get cut off in the flower of your youth; and then what weeping and wailing there'll be among the ten tribes, and among those unfortunate Christians who have been speculating on your autograph. Not that you're wrong in what you say about Mitford; for if ever a cad walked this earth, that's the man."

"Ah! and isn't she a nice woman?" said Hetherington. "When she first showed in town last season, she took everybody's fancy; even Runnymede admired her, and the Duchess asked to be introduced, and they were quite thick. Wonderful! wasn't it? And to think of that snob Mitford treating her as he does, completely neglecting her, while he's—Well, I don't know; I suppose it's all right; but there ain't many things that would please me better than dropping on to that party—heavy."

"You're always dropping on to parties, Cis," said Bowers; "but you had better keep quiet in this case, please. You would have to make your own chance of getting into a row, for of course the lady's name must not appear—"

"Oh, don't you be afraid of me, Marky; I'm all right!" said Cis, rising and stretching himself. "You won't mind my stamping on Mitford's feet,—accidentally, of course,—if we find him in the stalls." And the two Guardsmen started away together.

"Well," said Lord Dollamore, leaning forward towards his companion, "was I right or wrong?"

"Right! terribly right!" said Alsager, with a set rigid face.

"You would not have accepted my testimony, thinking perhaps that I had motives for exaggeration, or was prompted by an *arrière pensée*, in which, on my word of honour, you're wrong. But those fellows are merely types of society; and their opinion, somewhat differently expressed, is society's opinion."

"Has not Mitford's madness cooled down at all?"

"It is worse, far and away,—worse than ever—"

"And that woman?"

"Ah," said Lord Dollamore, "she's been very quiet lately, owing to her husband's death. Poor old boy! poor old Percy Hammond! But she's up in town, I understand, now; and I don't think—" and here Dollamore's crutch-handled stick was evidently whispering confidences into his master's ear,—"I don't think Master Mitford will find it all straight sailing in that quarter just now."

"How do you mean? What would induce her to change to him?"

"Well, you see, she's a widow now, with a comparatively small income; for I suspect poor old Percy knew more than he ever let on, and instructed Trivett to prepare his will accordingly. So that, besides wanting a husband, she'll want him rich; for she's one of the best hands at getting through money in England. With a husband in posse, Mitford's attentions would not do at all."

"Ah, I see; but is not her character too well known?"

"Not a bit of it; her powers of attraction are enormous still. Why, if I'm rightly informed, a Russian whom you know, I think,—Tchernigow by name,-is making the running there already."

"I know him; he was madly in love with her, I heard, the season before last; followed her to Baden and about."

"That's the man! Well, he's *revenu*—not to his *premier*, which was probably some Cossack peasant-girl—but to one of his *amours*, and is desperate."

"He's enormously wealthy. If she accepted him, there might yet be a chance of happiness for Georgie,—Lady Mitford, I mean."

"Don't you believe that for an instant, Alsager!" said Dollamore, looking keenly at him; "you're not posted up in that family history. Matters have gone too far now; there is only one way in which Sir Charles Mitford could really be of service to his wife, and that is by dying. But I'm afraid she would not think so, poor girl!" Then seeing his companion looking very grave, he said, "Come, it's no use brooding over these matters; let us go to the theatre."

The theatre was crammed, as Mr. Wuff had anticipated. The audience was composed of pretty much the same class of people as those present on the first night of Mr. Spofforth's play at the Parthenium; with the exception of those who were most strongly remembered by Alsager. He had known that the Mitfords and Mrs. Hammond could not be there, and there was little to interest him among the audience. The curtain rose on the piece of the evening, and everybody's attention concentrated on the stage. Shortly afterwards came the appearance of the new actress, who was hailed with shouts of encouragement and applause by Mr. Wuff's supporters in boxes, pit, and gallery. She seemed not in the least overcome by her reception, but bowed gracefully, and entered immediately on the business of the piece. The character she played was that of a highbred wealthy girl, beloved by a young yeoman-farmer of the neighbourhood, who proposes to her, but she mocks at his gaucheries, and rejects him with scorn. He accepts his defeat, and goes away to travel on the Continent with his brother. It is not until he is gone that she finds how deeply she had really loved him; but he is gone never to return, and so she accepts the attention of, and is engaged to, a silly peer. Then comes the Nemesis. The girl's father is ruined, the peer jilts her, and she is left in wretchedness, when the yeoman-farmer comes back a polished gentleman. There is an admirable scene of intensity between them, and, of course, all ends happily. The character of the heroine seemed excellently suited for Miss Greenwood, who, gradually winning the confidence of the audience, worked them to a pitch of enthusiasm in the last scene, and brought down the curtain with a universal verdict of her combining thorough knowledge of the usages of society and ladylike manners with great dramatic power.

Of course she was recalled before the curtain; and then as she swept across the stage, clasping her bouquet to her bosom, and occasionally bowing low, her eyes lit full on those of Laurence Alsager. And then for the first time Laurence Alsager, who had been puzzling his brain about her ever since she appeared on the scene, recollected who she was, and said half aloud, "The woman who wrote me the note!— Miss Gillespie, without a doubt!"

CHAPTER XXVII.

LOVE AND DUTY.

Lady Mitford was alone on the afternoon of the following day, when Sir Laurence Alsager was announced. She was often alone now; for the world falls readily and easily away, not only from the forsaken, but from the preoccupied—from those to whom its gaieties are childish follies and its interests weariness. She had fallen out of the ranks, as much through inclination as in compliance with the etiquette of mourning; and it came to pass often that the afternoon hours found her, as on this occasion, sitting alone in her splendid, vapid, faultless, soulless home. The softened light which reached her stately figure and irradiated her thoughtful lace showed the grace and loveliness which distinguished her untouched, undimmed. Under the discipline of sorrow, under the teaching of disappointment, her face had gained in expression and dignity,—every line and curve had strength added to its former sweetness; the pure steadfast eyes shone with deeper, more translucent lustre, and the rich lips met each other with firmer purpose and more precision. The perfecting, the refinement of her beauty, were sensibly felt by Alsager as he advanced towards the end of the room where she was seated in the recess between a large window and a glittering fireplace. She sat in a deep low chair of purple velvet; and as she leaned slightly forward and looked at him coming rapidly towards her, his eye noted every detail of the picture. He saw the glossy hair in its smooth classic bandeaux, the steadfast eyes, the gracious, somewhat grave, smile, the graceful figure in its soft robe of thick mourning silk, and its rich jet trimmings; he saw the small white hands, gentle but not weak,—one extended towards him in welcome, the other loosely holding an open book. In a minute he was by her side and speaking to her; but that minute had a deathless memory,—that picture he was to see again and again, in many a place, at many a time and it was never to be less beautiful, less divine for him. He loved her—ay, he loved her—this injured woman, this neglected, outraged wife, this woman who was a victim, crushed under the wheels of the triumphal car which had maimed him once on a time, though only slightly, and by a hurt soon healed by the balsam of contempt. Was she crushed, though? There was sorrow in that grand face—indeed, to that look of sorrow it owed its grandeur,—but there was no pining; there was sad experience, but no weak vain retrospection. All the pain of her lot was written upon her face; but none could read there a trace of what would have been its mortification, its bitter humiliation to commoner and coarser minds. It mattered nothing to her that her husband's infatuation and their mutual estrangement were topics for comment to be treated in the style current in society, and she herself an object of that kind of compassion which is so hard to brook: these were small things, too small for her range of vision; she did not see them—did not feel them. She saw the facts, she felt their weight and significance; but for the rest! If Lady Mitford had progressed rapidly in knowledge of the great world since she had been of it, she had also graduated in other sciences which placed her above and beyond it.

"I am fortunate in finding you at home, Lady Mitford," said Alsager.

She answered by a smile They had got beyond the talking of commonplaces to each other, these two, in general; but there was a sense of oppression over them both to-day, and each was conscious that it weighed upon the other. The remembrance of the talk to which he had listened at the Club, of the light discussion of Sir Charles's conduct, of the flippant censure of the woman who had won him from his wife, was very strong upon Alsager; while she,—of what was she thinking? Who could undertake to tell that? who could categorize the medley which must occupy the mind of a woman so situated? Was she suffering the sharp pangs of outraged love? or was she enduring the hardly less keen torture of discovering that that which she had believed to be love, had cherished in her breast as the true deity, had given, in that belief, to her husband, was not love, but only a skilful (and innocent) counterfeit, only a mock jewel which she had offered in good faith for the flawless pearl of price? Who can tell? She could hardly have answered such a question truly, if she had put it to herself at the close of the interview which began after so commonplace a fashion.

"I have not seen you since your father's death," said Lady Mitford, gently; and in a tone which lent the simple words all the effect of a formal condolence. "You have not been long in town, I'm sure?"

"No, indeed," he said; "I have but just returned. There is so much to be done on these occasions; there are so many forms to be gone through; there is so much immediate business to be transacted, in the interests of the living, that—that,"—he hesitated; for he had neared that precipice so dreaded by all now-a-days, the exhibition of natural emotion.

"That one has to wait for leisure to mourn for the dead," said Lady Mitford. "Ah, yes, I understand that. But you remain in town now, do you not?"

There was a tone of anxiety in the question which struck on Alsager's ear with a sound of music. She had missed him, then,—she would miss him if he went away again! He loved her well, ay, and worthily, contradictory though that may seem; but his heart was stirred with a joy which he dared not analyze, but could not deny, at the thought. He answered hurriedly, "Yes, I remain here now." And then he changed his tone, and said eagerly,

"Tell me something of yourself. How has it been with you since we met last?"

"Of myself!" she replied sadly; and her colour flushed and faded as she spoke, and her restless fingers trifled with the ornaments of her dress. "Myself is an unprofitable subject, and one I am weary of. I have nothing new to tell,—nothing you would care to hear."

He dissented by an eager gesture; but she appeared not to perceive it, and went on, with attempted gaiety:

"We have missed you dreadfully, of course. I need not tell you what a void your absence must necessarily make. We all know you are beyond spoiling."

She looked at him, and something in his face warned her not to pursue this tone. She felt vaguely that the position was unreal, and must be changed. He knew, as she supposed, what she was thinking of; she knew, as he fancied, what he was thinking of; and though, as it happened, each was wrong, it was manifestly absurd to carry on false pretences any longer. Woman-like, she was the first to brave the difficulty of the situation.

"You have come to me," she said steadily, and looking at him with the clear upheld gaze peculiar to her, "because you have heard something which concerns me nearly, and because, man of the world,—of this heartless world around us,—as you are, and accustomed to such things, still you feel for me; because you would have prevented this thing if you could; because you tried to prevent it, and failed; because you knew—yes, Sir Laurence Alsager, because you knew the extent and the power of the danger that menaced me, and my helplessness: say, am I right?—for these reasons you are here to-day."

The composure of her voice was gone, but not its sweetness; her colour had faded to a marble paleness; and her hands were firmly clasped together. Alsager had risen as she spoke, and was standing now, leaning against the low velvet-covered mantelpiece. He answered hurriedly, and with scant composure:

"Yes, Lady Mitford, for these reasons, and for others."

"For what others?"

This almost in a whisper.

"Never mind them now," he said impetuously; and then the superficial restraint which he had imposed upon himself gave way, broke down before that strongest and most terrible of temptations, the sight of the sorrow and the silent confidence of the woman one loves, granted at the moment when a hope, a guilty hope, that that love may not be vain, begins to stir, like life, at one's heart. She shrank a little back in the chair, but she looked at him as earnestly as before.

"It's all true, then," he said,—and there was a tone of deep and bitter hatred in his voice,—"all true. The prophecy I heard among those fellows the first time I ever heard your name—the coarse language, the cynical foresight,—all true. That heartless demon has caught his shallow nature in her shallow lure, and worked the woe of an angel!"

His voice rang with a passionate tremor, his eyes deepened and darkened with the passionate fervour which glowed in them. His impetuous feeling mastered her. She had no power to arrest him by a conventional phrase, though he had overstepped more than conventionality by invading the sacred secrecy of her domestic grief.

"Yes, Lady Mitford," he went on; "I have returned to find that all I feared,—more than I feared,—has befallen you. It was an unequal contest; you had only innocence and purity, an old-fashioned belief in the stability of human relations and the sanctity of plighted faith; and what weapons were these in such a fight? No wonder you are vanquished. No wonder she is triumphant—shameless as she is heartless. I wound you," he said, for she cowered and trembled at his words; "but I cannot keep silence. I have seen shameful things,—I am no stranger to the dark passages of life; but this is worse than all. Good God! to think that a man like Mitford should have had such a chance and have thrown it away! To think that—"

"Hush, Sir Laurence!" she said, and stretched her hand appealingly towards him; "I must not hear you. I cannot, I will not affect to misunderstand you; but there must be no more of this. I am an unhappy woman—a most wretched wife; all the world— all the little world we think so great, and suffer to torment us so cruelly—knows that. Pretence between us would be idle; but confidence is impossible. I cannot discuss Sir Charles Mitford's conduct with any one, least of all with you." She seemed to have spoken the last words unawares, or at least involuntarily, for a painful blush, rose on her face and throat.

"And why," he eagerly asked,—"why least of all with me? I have been honoured by your friendship,—I have not forfeited it, have I? I know that conventionality, which is a systematic liar and a transparent hypocrite, would condemn in theory a woman to keep her garments folded decorously over such mortal heart-wounds; I know that poets snivel rhymes which tell us how grand and great, how high and mighty, it is 'to suffer and be strong.' I know how easy some people find it to see others suffer, and be perfectly strong in the process; but such rubbish is not for you nor for me. I cannot return to London and hear all that I have heard; I cannot come here and look upon you—" his voice faltered, but he forced it into the same hurried composure with which he had been speaking. "I cannot see you as I see you now, and talk to you as an ordinary morning visitor might talk, or even as we have talked together, when these things were coming indeed, but had not yet come."

She was leaning forward now, her face turned towards him, but hidden in her hands. He gazed at her with a kindling glance, and strode fiercely backward and forward across the wide space which lay before the window.

"I am not a good man," he went on, "according to your standard of goodness, Lady Mitford; but I am not a bad man according to my own. I have had rough tussles with life, and some heavy falls; but I swear there is a dastardly, cold, heartless ingratitude in this business which I cannot bear; and in the sight of you there is something terrible to me. Men know this man's history; we know from what degradation you raised him; we are not so blind and coarse that we cannot guess with what fidelity and patience you loved him when it was at its deepest. And now, to see him return to it; to see him, without any excuse of poverty or struggle, in the enjoyment of all that fate and fortune have blindly given him; to see him play the part of a liar and a villain to you—to you—to see you left unprotected, openly neglected and betrayed, to run the gauntlet of society such as ours! I cannot see all this, Lady Mitford, and pretend that I do not see it; and what is more, you do not wish that I could. You are too true, too womanly to form such a wish; and you are too honest to express it, in obedience to any laws of cant."

He went near to her; he bent down, he lowered his voice, he gently drew away the hands that hid her face from him; they dropped into her lap, nerveless and idle; the first tears he had ever seen in her eyes dimmed them now.

"You mean kindly, as you have always meant to me, Sir Laurence," she said; "but we cannot discuss this matter,—indeed we cannot. I am weaker than I ought to be,—I should not listen to this; but oh, God help me, I have no friends; I am all alone, all alone!"

If she had been beautiful in the pride and dignity of her sorrowful composure, if his strong heart had quailed and his firm nerve had shrunk at the sight of her pale and placid grief, how far more beautiful was she now, when the restraint had fallen from her, when the eyes looked at him from the shadow of wet lashes, and the perfect lips trembled with irrepressible emotion.

"No!" he said vehemently; and as he spoke he stood close before her, and stretched his hands towards her, but without taking hers; the gesture was one of mingled denial and appeal, and had no touch of boldness in it; "no, you are not alone; yes, you have friends,—at least you have one friend. Listen to me,—do not fear to hear me; let us at least venture to tell and listen to the truth. This man, to whom you were given as a guardian angel, is quite unworthy of you. You know it; your keen intellect accepts a fact and all its consequences, however terrible to your woman's heart, and does not palter with the truth. Are you to be always miserable because you have been once mistaken? If you had known, if you had been able to comprehend the real nature of this man, would you, could you ever have loved him?"

She put up her hand with a faint gesture of protest; but he impetuously waved it away, and went on, once more striding up and down.

"No, no; I must speak! There can be more reticence now. You would not, you could not have loved him, this heartless, ungrateful profligate, as tasteless and low as he is faithless and vicious,—this scoundrel, who, holding good in his grasp, has deliberately chosen evil. Ay, I will say it, Lady Mitford! You *could* not have loved him, and you know it well; you have admitted it to yourself before now, when you little dreamed that anyone—that I—would ever dare to put your thought in form and shape before you. What did you love? A girl's fancy,—a shadow, a dream! It was no reality, it had no foundation, and it has vanished. Your imagination drew a picture of an injured victim of circumstances,—a weak being, to be pitied and admired, to be restored and loved! The truth was a selfish scoundrel, who has returned in wealth with fresh zest to the miserable pleasures for which he lived in poverty; a mean-hearted wretch, who could care for your beauty while it was new to him indeed, but to whose perception you, your heart and soul, your intellect and motives, were mysteries as high and as far off as heaven. Are you breaking your heart, Lady Mitford, under the kindly scrutiny of the world, because the thistle has not borne figs and the thorn has not given you purple grapes? Are you sitting down in solitary grief because the animal has done according to its kind, because effect has resulted from cause, because the wisdom of the world, wise in the ways of such men, has verified itself? Do you love this man now? Are you suffering the pangs of jealousy, of despair? No, you do not love him; you are suffering no such pangs. You are truth itself,—the truest and the bravest, as you are the most beautiful of women; and you cannot, you dare not tell me that you love this man still, knowing him as you know him now." He stopped close beside her, and looked at her with an eager, almost a fierce glance.

"Why do you ask me?" she gasped out faintly. There was a sudden avoidance of him in her expression, a shadow of fear. "Why do you speak to me thus? Oh, Sir Laurence, this—this is the worst of all." She was not conscious of the effect of the tone in which these words were spoken, of the pathos, the helplessness, the pleading tenderness it implied. But he heard them, and they were enough. They were faint as the murmur of a brook in summer, but mighty as an Alpine storm; and the barriers of conventional restriction, the scruples of conscience, the timidity of a real love, were swept away like straws before their power.

"Why?" he repeated, "because I love you!"

She uttered a faint exclamation; she half rose from her chair, but he caught her hands and stopped her.

"Hush!" he said; "I implore you not to speak till you have heard me! Do not wrong me by supposing that I have come here to urge on your unwilling ear a tale of passion, to take advantage of your husband's crime, your husband's cowardice, to extenuate crime and cowardice in myself. Before God, I have no such meaning! But I love you—I love you as I never even fancied I loved any woman before; though I am no stranger to the reality or the mockery of passion, though I have received deep and smarting wounds in my time. I wish to make myself no better in your eyes than I am. And I love you—love you so much better than myself; that I would fain see you happy with this man, even with *him*, if it could be. But it cannot, and you know it. You know in your true heart, that if he came back to his allegiance to you now—poor bond of custom as it is—you could not love him, any more than you could return to the toys of your childhood. I read you aright; I know you with the intuitive knowledge which love, and love only, lends to a man, when he would learn the mystery of a woman's nature. You are too noble, too true, to be bound by the petty rules, to be governed by the small scruples, which dominate nine-tenths of the women who win the suffrages of society. You have the courage of your truthfulness."

He stood before her, looking steadfastly down upon her, his arms tightly folded across his chest, his breath coming quickly in hurried gasps. She had shrunken into the recesses of her velvet chair, and she looked up at him with parted lips and wild eyes, her hands holding the cushions tightly, the fingers hidden in the purple fringes. Was it that she could not speak, or that she would not? However that may have been, she did not, and he went on.

"Yes, yes, I love you. I think you knew it before?" She made no reply. "I think I have loved you from the first,—from the moment when, callous and *blasé* as I had come to believe myself—as, God knows, I had good right to be, if human nature may ever claim such a right—I could not bear to see the way your fate was drifting, or to hear the chances for and against you calculated, as men calculate such odds. I think I loved you from the moment I perceived how completely you had mistaken your own heart, and how beautifully, how innocently loyal you were to the error. While your delusion lasted, Lady Mitford, you were safe with me and from me, for in that delusion there was security. While you loved Mitford, and believed that he returned your love, you would never have perceived that any other man loved you. But you are a woman who cannot be partially deceived or undeceived; therefore I tell you now, when your delusion is wholly at an end, when it can come no more to blind your eyes, and rend your heart with the removal of the bandage, that I love you,—devotedly, changelessly, eternally. You must take this fact into account when you meditate upon your future; you must number this among the component parts of your life. Hush! not yet. I am not speaking thus through reckless audacity, availing itself of your position; you know I am not, and you must hear me to the end."

She had made a movement as if about to speak, but he had again checked her; and they maintained their relative positions, he looking down at her, she looking up at him.

"We are facing facts, Lady Mitford. I love you, not as the man who left you, in your first year of marriage, for the worthless woman who forsook me for a richer lover, and would have wronged the fool who bought her without a scruple, could she have got me into her power again—not as he loved you, even when he came nearest to the truth of love. That woman, your enemy, your *rival*,"—he spoke the word with a stringent scorn which would have been the keenest punishment in human power to have inflicted on the woman it designated,—"she knows I love you, and she has struck at me through you; struck at me, poor fool—for she is fool as well as fiend—a blow which has recoiled upon herself. She has taught me how much, how well, how devotedly I love you, and learned the lesson herself thereby, for the intuition of hate is no less keen than that of love. But why do I speak of her? Only to make you understand that I am a portion of your fate,—only to lay the whole truth before you; only to make it clear to you that mine is no chance contact, no mere intrusion. I am not a presumptuous fool, who has dared to use a generously-granted friendship as a cover for an illicit passion. Have patience with me a little longer. Let me tell you all the truth. You cannot dismiss me from your presence as you might another who had dared to love you, and dared to tell you so; you cannot do this."

"Why?" she asked faintly, but with an angry sparkle in her eyes. For the second time she said that one word.

"Because I have injured you, Lady Mitford,—injured you unconsciously, unintentionally; and that is a plea which cannot fail, addressed to such as you. Had I never crossed your path, the woman for whom your husband has wronged you would never have crossed it either. I am the object, you are the victim, of the hatred of a she-devil. You don't suppose she cares for Mitford, do you?"

"Not if she ever loved you," was the reply.

Alsager passed it over, but a sudden light flashed into his face.

"Of course she does not. She has played her ruthless game skilfully according to her lights, and your happiness has been staked and lost. Indirectly, I am the cause of this. Was the feeling which came over me the first time I saw you a presentiment, I wonder? Well, no matter; you see now that I am a portion of your fate. You see now that a hidden tie binds us together, and the folly, the delusion of my youth, and the mistaken love of your girlhood, have borne mysterious common fruit."

She sat like one enthralled, entranced, and listened to him; she bent her head for a moment as he took an instant's breath, but she did not attempt to speak. His manner changed, grew softer, and his voice fell to almost a whisper:

"May not this mysterious tie of misfortune mean more to us?" he said. "May not the consolation come, as the curse has come, and all the designs of our enemies be disconcerted? I do not say my love is worthy of your acceptance,—I am too much travel-stained in my wanderings in the world's ways to make any such pretension; but it is yours, such as it is—faulty, imperfect, but loyal and eternal. I love you, Lady Mitford, and I ask nothing of you but permission to love you freely and fully; I ask your leave to give you all the devotion of my heart, all the loyalty of my life. I know how the world would hold such a demand; but I care nothing for the world, and I fancy you know it too well to care much for it now. You cherished a delusion long and sacredly; it was at least a noble one, but it is gone, and the world can neither satisfy you for its loss nor substitute another. Dearest—" he paused; she shivered, but she said not a word,—"dearest, what remains? Inexpressible tenderness was in his voice, in his bending figure, in his moistened eyes. There was a moment's silence, and then she spoke, replying to his last words:

"Duty, Sir Laurence,—duty, the only thing which is not a delusion; that remains."

He drew back a little, looking at her. She raised herself in her chair, and pointed to a seat at a little distance from her own. She was deadly pale, but she did not tremble, and her voice was firm and low as she said:

"Sit down, and listen to me."

He obeyed, silent and wondering. Perhaps he had not told himself exactly what he had expected,—perhaps no one ever does, when the emotions of the heart are called into evidence; but he knew that it was not this. Had he more to learn of this woman whom he had so closely studied; had her nature heights which he had not seen, and depths which he had not comprehended? Breathless he waited for her words. In an agony of suspense he looked at her averted face, which appeared to address itself to something in the distance,—which had settled into a wondrous composure at the command of the strong will. He had not estimated that strength of will aright; he had made the common mistake of overlooking a quality because he had not seen it in active employment. There was neither confusion nor weakness in the manner of the woman to whom he had just spoken such words as no woman could hear unmoved; and there mingled strangely with his love something of wonder and of awe.

After a little interval, which seemed endless to him, she turned her face towards him again, laid her hand heavily upon her breast, and spoke:

"You have been cruel to me, Sir Laurence, in all that you have said; but men, I believe, are always cruel to women if they love them, or have loved them. I acquit you of intentional cruelty, and I accept all you say of the necessity for the truth being spoken between us in the new phase of our relation which you have brought about to-day."

The intensity of her face deepened, and the pressure of her hand grew heavier. He muttered a few words of protest, but she went on as if she had not heard him.

"You have spoken words to me, Sir Laurence, which I should not have heard; but they have been spoken, and the wrong cannot be undone. It may be atoned for, and it must. Neither these words nor any other must be spoken between us henceforth—"

He started up.

"You cannot mean this," he said; "it is impossible; I do not believe it.—I will not bear it."

"Be still and hear me," she replied; "I kept silence at your desire,—you will not, I am sure, do less at mine. I too must speak to you, uninterrupted, in the spirit of that truth of which you have spoken so eloquently and with such sophistry—yes, with such sophistry."

Once more she paused and sighed.

"Speak to me, then," he said; and there was true, real anguish in his tone. "Say what you will, but do not be too hard on me. I am only a mortal man; if I have offended you, it is because you are an angel."

"You have not offended me," she said very slowly: "perhaps I ought to be offended, but I am not. I think you judge me aright when you say that truth holds the foremost place in and for me: therefore I tell you truth. You have grieved me; you have added a heavy burden to a load which is not very easy to bear, though the world, which you exhort me to despise and to deny, cannot lay a feather's weight upon it. Your friendship was very dear to me,—very precious; I did not know how dear, I think, until to-day."

How eagerly he listened to the thrilling voice! how ardently he gazed into the dreamy beautiful eyes! how breathlessly he kept the silence so hard to maintain!

"If I could use any further disguise with myself, Sir Laurence, if self-deception could have any further power over me, I might terminate this interview here, and tell you, and tell myself, that it should be forgotten. But I have done with self-deception."

"For God's sake, don't speak in that bitter tone!" Alsager said entreatingly; "spare me, if you will not spare yourself."

"No," she replied; "I will spare neither you nor myself. Why should I? The world has spared neither of us—will spare neither of us; only it will tell lies, and I will tell truths,—that's all."

Her colour was heightened, and her eyes were flashing now; but the pressure of her hand upon her bosom was steady.

"You have read my story aright: I know not by what art or science—but you have read it. If, as you say, you have an involuntary share, an unconscious responsibility in my heavy trial, it is a misfortune, which I put away from my thoughts; I hold you in no way accountable. My sorrow is my own; my delusion is over; my duty remains."

"Do you speak of duty to Sir Charles Mitford?" asked Alsager with a sneer.

"Yes," she said gently; "I do. Your tone is unworthy of you, Sir Laurence; but I pass it by; for it is the tone of a man of the world, to whom inclination is a law. Can my husband's faithlessness absolve me from fidelity? Is his sin any excuse for my defection from my duty? You say truly, I cannot love him now as I loved him when I did not know him as he is; but I can do my duty to him still—a hard duty, but imperative. The time will come when this woman will weary of him, of her vain and futile vengeance; and then—"

"Well, Lady Mitford, and then—?" asked Alsager in a cold hard voice.

She looked at him with eyes in which a holy calm had succeeded to her transient passion, and replied:

"Then he will return to me, and I must be ready to meet him without a shade upon my conscience, without a blush upon my cheek."

He started up angrily, and exclaimed:

"You pass all comprehension! What! You are no longer in error about this man; the glamour has passed. You know him for the cold cynical profligate he is; and you talk of welcoming him like a repentant prodigal; only yourself it is you are prepared to kill—your own pride, your own delicacy, your own heart! Good God! what are good women made of, that they set such monstrous codes up for themselves, and adhere to them so mercilessly!"

"He is my husband," she faltered out; and for a moment her courage seemed to fail. The next she rose, and standing by the mantelpiece, where he had stood before, she went on, with hurry and agitation in her voice: "Don't mistake me. Love is dead and gone for me. But this world is not the be-all and the end-all; there is an inheritance beyond it, reserved for those who have 'overcome.' Duty is hard, but it is never intolerable to a steadfast will, and a mind, fixed on the truth. Time is long, and the round of wrong is tedious; but the day wears through best to those who subdue impatience, and wrong loses half its bitterness when self is conquered. I have learned my lesson, Sir Laurence, and chosen my part."

"And what is to be mine?" he said with angry impatience,—"what is to be mine? You moralize charmingly, Lady Mitford; and your system is perfect, with one little exception—and what is that? A mere nothing, a trifle—only a man's heart, only a love that is true! You are all alike, I believe, bad or good, in this,—you will pine after, you will endure anything for, a man who is false to you, and you will tread upon the heart of one who is true. What do you care? We do not square with the moral code of the good among you, nor with the caprice and devilment of the bad; and so away with us! I am 'cruel' to you, forsooth, because I tell you that you no longer love a worthless profligate, who sports with your peace and your honour at the bidding of a wanton! I am 'cruel' because I tell you that I, who have innocently wronged you, love you with every pulse of my heart and every impulse of my will! Is there any cruelty on your side, do you think, when you talk, not puling sentiment—I could more easily pardon that; it would be mere conventional silliness—but these chilly, chilling moralities, which are fine in copy-books, but which men and women abandon with their writing-lessons?"

"Do they?" she said with imperturbable gentleness; "I think not. You are angry and unjust, Sir Laurence,—angry with *me*, unjust to *me*!"

The keen pathos of her tone, its innocent pleading, utterly overcame him.

"Yes," he cried; "I *am* unjust, and you are an angel of goodness; but—I love you,—ah, how I love you!—and you reject me, utterly, utterly. You reject me, and for him! You give *her* a double triumph; you lay my life waste once more."

He stopped in his hurried walk close to her. She laid her hand upon his arm, and they looked at one another in silence for a little. She broke it first.

"And if I did not reject you, as you say—if I accepted this love, this compensating truth and loyalty, which you offer me, what should I be, Laurence Alsager, but her compeer? Have you thought of that? Have you remembered that there is a law in marriage apart from and above all feeling? Have you considered what she who breaks that law is, in the sight of God, in the unquenchable light of her own conscience, though her conduct were as pure from stain as the ermine of a royal robe? I am speaking, not chilly, chilling moralities, but immortal, immutable truth. In the time to come you will remember it, and believe it; and then there will be no bitterness in your heart when you recollect how I bade you farewell!"

The lustrous eyes looked into his with a gaze as pure as an infant's, as earnest as a sibyl's, and the gentle hand lay motionless upon his arm.

"How you bade me farewell!" he repeated in a hoarse voice. "What do you mean? Are you sending me from you?"

"Yes," she answered; "I am sending you from me. We have met once too often, and we must meet no more. You say you love me;" she shrunk and shivered again,—"and—and I believe you. Therefore you will obey me."

"No," he said resolutely; "I will not obey you! I will see you,—I must. What is there in my love to frighten or to harm you? I ask for nothing which even your scrupulous conscience might hesitate to give; I seek no change in the relation that has subsisted between us for some time now."

"Dreams, dreams," she said, sadly; "unworthy of your sense,—unworthy of your knowledge of the world. Nothing can ever replace us on our old footing. The words you have spoken to me can never be unsaid. They are words I never ought to have heard—and—" In a moment her firmness deserted her, her voice failed; she sank into a chair, and burst into passionate tears.

"You would not have them unsaid!" he cried; "tell me that you would not! Tell me that the coldness and the calm which those streaming tears deny are not true, are not real! Tell me that I am something in your life,—that I might have been more! Dearest, I reverence as much as I love you; but give me that one gleam of comfort. It cannot make your heavenly rectitude and purity poorer, while to me it will be boundless riches. Tell me that you could love me if you would; tell me that the sacred barrier of your conscience is the only one between us! I swear I will submit to that! I will not try to shake or to remove it. Nay, more, I will leave you,—if indeed you persist in commanding my absence,—if only you will tell me that under other circumstances you would have loved me. Tell me this! I ask a great, a priceless boon; but I do ask it. Dearest, will you not answer me?" Her agitation, her tears, had reassured him, had broken the spell which her calmness had imposed. The hope that had come to him once or twice during their interview came again now, and stayed.

There was no sound for a while but that of her low rapid sobs. The clocks upon the mantelpieces in the suite of rooms ticked loudly, and their irritating metallic voices mingled strangely with the rushing pulses of Alsager's frame, as he leant over her,— one arm round the back of her chair, the other hand upon its velvet arm. His face was bent above her drooping head; his thick moustache almost touched the waved ridges of her scented hair. He implored her to speak to him; he poured out protestation and entreaty with all the ardour of his strong and fiery nature, with all the eloquence which slumbered in him, unsuspected even by himself. Little by little she ceased to weep, and at length she allowed him to see her face. Again he renewed his entreaties, and she answered him.

"You try me too far, and I am weak. Yes, I would love you, if I might!"

"Then you *do* love me!" he exclaimed. "You and I are no dreaming boy and girl, no Knight and Dame of old romance, but man and woman; and we know that these shades of difference are merest imagination. We love each other, and we know it. We love each other, and the acknowledgment makes the truth no truer. I am ungenerous, you would say; I am breaking the promise I have just made. Yes, I am; but I love you—and you love me!" He had dropped on one knee beside her chair now, and as he spoke he caught her hand in his. Without any sign of anger or prudery, she withdrew her hand quietly, but resolutely, and signed to him to rise and be seated. He obeyed her; but exultation shone out from every line and feature of his face.

"You *are* ungenerous," she said,—"very ungenerous, and very cruel; but I will not the less be true in these the last words I shall say to you. If I have dreamed of a life other than mine, of love well bestowed and faithfully returned, it was only in the most passing, transient visions. My lot is cast; my mind is made up; my heart is fixed. I linger here for a few moments longer because they are the last I shall ever pass alone with you. Do not interrupt me, or I terminate this interview on the instant. This subject must never be renewed,—indeed it never can be; for you know my resolution, and I know you will respect it. The past remains with us; but the future has no common history for you and me. When I have ceased speaking, and that door has closed behind you, you must remember me, if you do not see me, and regard me if you do, as a woman wholly devoted to her wifely duty, of whom to think otherwise is to do a deadly wrong."

He stood before her as pale as she had been; something wrathful and something reverential contended in his expression. She waved her hand with a slight gesture, and went on "Now I have done with myself; there is no more question of me. But of you, Sir Laurence, there is much and serious question. Your life is aimless and unreal. Give it an object and an aim; invest it with truth, occupy it with duty. I am speaking with you face to face for the last time, and I go back to the old relation which you have destroyed for a few minutes. In that relation I speak to you of your father's death-bed request. Fulfil it; and by doing so, end this vain and sinful strife,—quell this demon which deludes you."

"You mean that I should marry my father's ex-ward, I presume?" said Alsager, coldly.

"I do."

"Thank you, Lady Mitford. Your proposition is full of wisdom, however it may lack feeling. But there are sundry objections to my carrying it into effect. The lady does not love me, nor do I love the lady."

"You hardly know her," Lady Mitford said with a timid smile; "you have not given yourself any opportunity of testing your power of obedience to your father's dying wish. You cannot judge of how she would be disposed towards you." Once more she smiled timidly and sadly. "You would have little cause to fear ill-success, I should think."

"Except that in this case, Lady Mitford, the lady's affections are preëngaged, and she is doubtless a miracle of constancy."

"You speak bitterly, Sir Laurence, but your bitterness will pass, and your better nature will assert itself."

"Is this all you intend to say to me, Lady Mitford?"

"This is all. My words will supplement themselves in silence and reflection, and you will acknowledge that I have spoken the truth—that I am as true as you believe me."

"And are we to part thus?" he asked in a slightly softened tone.

A quick spasm crossed her face, but she answered him at once, and looked at him as she spoke, "Yes!"

He bowed profoundly. She held out her hand, On the third finger was a heavy-looking seal-ring, which she constantly were. As he coldly took the hand in his, his eyes fell upon this ring. She marked the look, and when he released her hand, she drew off the ring and offered it to him.

"You are angry with me now," she said; "but your anger will pass away. When no shade of it remains, wear this for my sake, and make its motto, which is mine, yours."

He took the ring, and without looking at it, dropped it into his waistcoat-pocket. Then he stood quite still as she passed him with her usual graceful step, and watched the sweep of her soft black robe as she walked down the long room, and disappeared through a door which opened into her boudoir.

Late that night Alsager, angry still, dark and wrathful, tossed the ring with a contemptuous frown into a jewel-case; but he first took an impression of it in wax, and read, the motto thus: "Fortiter—Fideliter—Feliciter."

CHAPTER XXVIII.

SIR LAURENCE'S LETTER.

Helen Manningtree and Mrs. Chisholm pursued their customary mode of life at Knockholt Park after, as before, the departure of Sir Laurence. Helen missed the grave and courteous gentleman whom she had learned to like so much, and her at first distant association with whom had grown into intimacy and confidence. Sir Laurence was a most agreeable companion; well-informed; and entirely without any sort of pretension. He had seen a great deal of the world—in the geographical sense of the term, as well as in every other; and his anecdotes of travel and descriptions of foreign lands had unflagging interest for Helen, whose experience had indeed been narrow, but whose reading had been various and extensive. In the thoughtful mood into which Alsager had fallen—in the serious frame of mind which had become almost habitual with him now—he would probably have been voted a bore by "society," supposing that he had placed himself within reach of its suffrages; but Helen knew nothing of the tastes and fashions of the great world, and to her Laurence was all that was most companionable and pleasant. He was not indeed so gifted, so cultivated a creature as Cuthbert Farleigh; but then,—who was? who could be expected to be? And Helen, whose circle of acquaintance included a dozen unmarried men at the most, believed with perfect good faith that she had exercised the soundest judgment and discretion in her selection of the Reverend Cuthbert, from "all the world," as the individual to whom alone she could render unqualified respect and intrust the happiness of her future life. That resolution, before mentioned, by which the curate had bound himself, to himself, to wait until he should be a bishop, or for the occurrence of any other equally improbable event, was rather in the way of Helen's happiness, either present or future; but she was not much disquieted by the delay. Cuthbert had seen no symptoms of an alarming nature to indicate any "intentions" on Colonel Alsager's part prior to Sir Peregrine's death, and he was ignorant of the existence of the old Baronet's letter, in which he had urged a marriage with Helen upon Sir Laurence. He had begun to think, within a very few days of Colonel Alsager's arrival at Knockholt, that he had been foolishly apprehensive in the first instance. Was it at all likely that, at Colonel Alsager's age, and in his position, with his opportunities of seeing, and recommending himself to, the fairest and most fascinating women in the world, he should be entirely heart-free and ready to fix his affections upon his father's ward? Of course Cuthbert was quite aware that Laurence Alsager could never by any possibility have met any one half so worthy of admiration and of love as Helen Manningtree; but he was a young man of candid mind, and ready to acknowledge that a man might be preoccupied to the extent of being unable to recognize the unapproachable excellence of Helen without being guilty of absolute stupidity or unpardonable bad taste. So, on the whole, these young people were tolerably comfortable in their minds, and felt an equable though unexpressed confidence in their mutual affection and in the future. The circumstance of Sir Peregrine Alsager's will making no mention of Helen—in fact, having been made before she became his ward, and during Lady Alsager's lifetime—had taken them both by surprise, and affected them differently. Helen had always known that her own very moderate income—which Sir Peregrine had always supplemented by a liberal allowance—was all that she actually possessed, or had any positive right to expect. But she had never entertained any doubt that her guardian intended to leave her a handsome provision, and she experienced a considerable shock when she learned that he had not done so. She could not understand it, and she was still more puzzled and surprised when Sir Laurence told her that he found himself a very much richer man than he had ever expected to be. Helen had too much good sense, and even in her secluded, life had learned to estimate facts and to eschew sentimental fallacies; so she did not affect to be indifferent on the subject, or to think that it was quite as well to be poor as to be rich, to be dependent as to be independent; but she did think and feel with very consoling sincerity that Cuthbert would have no more scruples about asking her to share his lot when her own had ceased to be of a nature to contrast with it. So she accepted her altered position cheerfully, and asked Sir Laurence what he would advise her to do, with a true-hearted freedom from anger or jealousy which elevated her to a great height in the mind of the new Baronet. Sir Laurence made her an evasive answer, and begged her to defer any decision on the subject until his return to Knockholt. He was going away, first to town, and then abroad, he told her, most probably; and she and Mrs. Chisholm must remain and take charge there for him. He would keep up the establishment just as it had been, with the exception of the stable department. Helen acquiesced with great readiness. She was too completely a lady to feel any awkwardness in such an arrangement, and she knew well that Laurence's interests would be best served by her accepting his offer.

"I will stay here then," she said, "and go on just as usual. I don't know whether you are aware that I was Sir Peregrine's almoner. Am I to be yours? The farm-bailiffs, the keepers, and all the rest of your people, are my excellent good friends. I shall get on capitally with them, and go my old rounds in the village, and so forth. But I want to know what I am to do about the charities, the schools, and the promiscuous applications to the 'great house.'"

"I would give you unlimited credit with Todd, Helen, for all your requirements in that way, but that I fear you would be too conscientious to make sufficient use of it. But stay; the best plan will be to arrange it with Farleigh. Yes; I'll speak to him, and tell Todd he is to give him anything he asks for. I daresay he won't mind a little additional trouble in the cause of his poor people; and you can do the visiting and all that as usual, and report to him."

Sir Laurence looked at Helen as he made this remarkably convenient proposition for rendering the intercourse between the Park and the Rectory (for Cuthbert lived at the rector's house; that is to say, in a corner of it) more frequent than it was at present. Helen grew extremely red, and then turned the conversation.

"So, I suppose," said she to Mrs. Chisholm, after Sir Laurence had taken his leave, and the two women were talking over his visit and all the late events,—"so I suppose we shall live here until Sir Laurence is married; and then, when he brings a handsome, dashing, fashionable Lady Alsager down here, you and I, dear old woman, will go and live in the village; perhaps that pretty little house with the roses and the little white fountain, just big enough for the two ducks that are always swimming in it, may be vacant then; and I daresay Laurence would give it to us rent-free, and we should be very snug there; but we would not have ducks, except for dinner; and Lady Alsager would have us up to tea, I daresay, when there were no fine people at the Park. What do you say to all this, Mrs. Chisholm? doesn't it sound pleasant? What a cosy little place it is! don't you think so?"

"My dear Helen, how you do run on?" said the calmer Mrs. Chisholm; "you are quite in spirits to-day."

She was; for in her sketch of the rural abode with the roses there had been an unmentioned element. Helen thought the house would be quite the thing for a curate. Helen was always thinking about a curate; and in that respect there was considerable sympathy between her and her companion, for Mrs. Chisholm was almost always thinking of a curate too. Helen's curate was living; Mrs. Chisholm's was dead. The girl's heart was in a dream of the future; the woman's, in the memory of the sacred past.

Cuthbert Farleigh had received the intelligence of Sir Peregrine Alsager's unaccountable conduct towards Helen Manningtree with mingled feelings. He was by no means a commonplace young man, though not the light of learning and the mirror of chivalry which Helen believed him. Her over-estimate of him did him no harm, for he entertained a tolerably correct opinion of himself; and if the future were destined to unite them, it would probably not militate against her own happiness either. The mistake she made was in degree, not in kind,—a distinction which makes all possible difference. A sensible and dutiful woman may find out that her husband is not possessed of the qualities with which she has believed her lover to be endowed, to the extent with which she accredited him, and her love and esteem may not suffer by the discovery. She would probably recognize that if she had over-rated him (and what a dreadful woman she would be if she had not!) on some points, she had also failed to discover his merits on others, until the intimacy of domestic life had restored the balance of judgment. The mistake, which lays a woman's life waste in its rectification, is that which endows a man with qualities which he does not possess at all,—the mistake which leads to the conviction that the man she has married is not the man she loved, and burdens her with an actual duty and a lost ideal. If Helen Manningtree were ever to marry Cuthbert Farleigh, she would incur no such danger; she would have to pay no such price for the indulgence of undisciplined imagination. He was a good and a clever man, and was as highly and wholly disinterested as it is possible for a human being to be, to whom the consideration of meat, drink, clothing, and house-rent is one of rational importance.

He regarded his position with respect to Helen as very much improved by the fact that Sir Peregrine Alsager had not left her the fortune, which the gossips of the neighbourhood had taken for granted, and even announced "on authority." On the other hand, he grieved that she should be deprived of the luxurious home and the opulent manner of life to which she had been so long habituated; and as he was not at all a conceited man,—albeit flattered and exalted by all the ladies in the parish, which is ordinarily the bane of curates,—it did occur to him that perhaps Helen might have been better and happier if Sir Peregrine had left her the fortune, and he had adhered to his resolution of leaving her to its enjoyment, unwooed by him. Such a supposition was not likely to last long; its cold chill would pass off in the sunshine of free and acknowledged love. Free and acknowledged love? Yes, the curate was going to tell Helen, as soon as he should have learned the particulars of her position, that she had not erred in believing that he loved her, aid to ask her to take all the risks and all the cares of a life which could never have any brilliancy or any luxury to offer her, for the sole consideration of sharing them with him. He had not the smallest doubt of his success. Helen's nature was too true, and too well known to him, to render a misgiving possible; still the near approach of the assurance of his hope made him grave and solemn. The orphan-girl loved and trusted him; without him she was alone—alone in a world which is not very easily gotten through with the best of help and companionship. The sense of a great responsibility rested upon him, and his heart was lifted up in no merely conventional or professional prayer. So Cuthbert made up his mind, and felt very quiet and solemn about it. That mood would pass away; it would be succeeded by the dazzling delight, the splendid triumph, the fertile fancy, and superhuman hope and exultation of love, as it ought to be; but it is a good omen for any woman whose lover addresses himself to his wooing in such a temper.

Thus it fell out that Helen and Cuthbert, standing together by a window which opened on the broad stone terrace, and watching poor Sir Peregrine's peacocks, as they marched up and down outside, talked of a future which was to be common to them both, and was to date from the expiration of the year of mourning for Sir Peregrine Alsager. Helen had told Cuthbert how she had sketched such a charming picture for Mrs. Chisholm, of the house with the roses; and they had talked a good deal of the nonsense incidental to their position, and which is so much pleasanter than sense,—about whether she had thought of him; and if she had, why she had?—for there is a subtle resemblance to Jack Bunsby's monologue in the dialogues of lovers;—and then the conversation drifted away to Sir Laurence Alsager.

"We must tell him, my own Helen," said the curate; "he has been very kind to you, and I daresay will be very much disgusted at your making so poor a marriage."

The girl looked reproachfully at him, but smiled in a moment, and said, "Go on, Cuthbert; you are not worth contradicting, you know."

"No, but—" said Cuthbert, remonstrating, "you must let me set the world's view before you. No doubt Sir Laurence will think you very foolish; but he will always be our friend,—I feel sure of that,—though I know he is so different, and lives in so different a world, under so different a system. Sometimes, Helen, I have had an idea that he found out my secret; though I never could see an inch farther into his life and his heart than it was his good pleasure I should look. Yes, my darling, he must know all about us, and soon; for you must remember that it may make a difference in all his plans and arrangements, if he finds you are not to remain here after next spring."

"I hardly think it will do that," said Helen; "I fancy he will establish Mrs. Chisholm here *en permanence*; that is to say, until he marries."

"Is he likely to marry? Have you heard anything of that sort?"

"O no! he has never talked of any girls to me. He has never said anything the least like intending to marry. The only woman he ever speaks of—and he does talk of her, and sometimes hears from her—is Lady Mitford; you remember, you told me about her marriage,—the daughter of Mr. Stanfield, your old tutor, you know."

"Of course, I remember. How strangely things come about! it really seems as if there were only two sets of people in the world; for one never meets any one with whom one has not some link of communication! And Georgie Stanfield is Laurence Alsager's female crony and correspondent! How and where is she?"

"In town, I believe; but I don't know much about her. He used to speak of her vaguely, in talking to me of the great world and its hollowness, as of one whom he greatly liked and esteemed, and who was unfortunately circumstanced. He said he would have asked Lady Mitford down here in the autumn, if he could have asked her without her husband; but that, of course, was impossible, and he could not invite Sir Charles Mitford. I believe they are very unhappy. Think of that, Cuthbert,—a husband and wife unhappy! a splendid home, with rank and wealth, and misery!" The girl lifted solemn eyes full of wonder and compassion to her lover's face. "Sir Laurence wished that I could know her, for her sake, he kindly said."

"I wish you could, Helen; you would comfort her and do her good: and yet I would not have you saddened, my child, and made wise in the possibilities of life, as you must be if you had the confidence of an unhappy wife. You are better without it, darling—far better without it."

Then the curate remembered the alarm he had felt when Colonel Alsager made his appearance at Knockholt Park; and he confessed it to Helen, who laughed at him, and pretended to scold him, but who was not a little pleased all the time.

"You stupid Cuthbert!" said the young lady, to whom the curate had ceased to be an object of awe since their engagement; "it never came into Laurence's head to wish to marry me; and I am certain it never crossed any human being's imagination but your own that such a thing could ever happen."

The Reverend Cuthbert was reluctantly obliged to break off the conversation at this point, and go about his parish business. So he took leave of Helen, enjoining her to write to Sir Laurence that very day, and to make him acquainted with their engagement,—as Mrs. Chisholm, who had just entered the room, and to whom he referred the matter, gave it as her decided opinion that the communication should be made by Helen.

The post was not a subject of such overwhelming importance at Knockholt Park, its punctuality was not so earnestly discussed, nor was there as much excitement on its arrival, as at the generality of country-houses. Mrs. Chisholm had very few correspondents; Helen had only two, exclusive of Sir Laurence; and no letters were "due" at this particular time: hence it happened that the ladies often left the breakfast-table before the arrival of the letter-bag, and that its contents awaited their attention undisturbed through more hours of the day than most people would believe possible. Mrs. Chisholm never read the newspapers until the evening, and Helen never read them at all, being content with Cuthbert's version of public affairs. On this particular morning, however, Helen thought proper to remain in the breakfast-room until the post should arrive. The truth was she shrank from the task of writing to Sir Laurence, and she knew she ought to set about it at once; so she lingered and fidgeted about the breakfast-room long after Mrs. Chisholm had betaken herself to her daily confabulation with the housekeeper. Thus she was alone when the letter-bag was brought in, and she turned over its contents, expecting to find them of the usual uninteresting nature. There were several letters for Sir Laurence "to be forwarded," a number of circulars, a few letters for some of the servants, the customary newspapers, and lastly—a missive for Helen herself. It was a large letter in a blue envelope, and directed in a lawyer-like hand Helen opened it, feeling a little frightened, and found that the cover enclosed a packet addressed to her, in the hand of Sir Laurence Alsager, and marked "Private."

"What on earth can Laurence be writing to me about that requires such precaution?" thought Helen anxiously; and then she rang the bell, handed over the other letters to the footman for proper distribution, and retired to her own room, where she read the following:

"Dover.

"My Dear Helen,—I am devoting the last evening which I shall pass in England for an indefinite period, to writing to you a letter, which I shall take the precaution of sending so that its existence may be known to none but you, at the present time. A certain portion of its contents must necessarily be communicated to others; but you will use your discretion, upon which in this, and all other things, I rely with absolute confidence.

"You must not let this preamble alarm you; there is nothing to occasion you any trouble or sorrow in what I am about to say to you. It will be a long story, and, I daresay, a clumsily—told one, for I am eminently unready with my pen; but it will interest you, Helen, for my sake and for your own. When I tell you that this story is not a new one,-that it does not include anything that has occurred after I left Knockholt, though I am indirectly impelled to write it to you by circumstances which have happened since then,—you will wonder why I did not tell it to you in person, during the period when our companionship was so close and easy,—so delightful to me, and I am quite sure I may add, so pleasant to you. I could not tell you then, because I was not sufficiently sure of myself. I had an experiment to try—an experience to undergo—before I could be certain, even in the limited sense of human security, of my own future; and until these were over and done with, all was vague for me. They are over and done with now: and I am going to tell you all about yourself, and a good deal about myself.

"You know that among the sorrows of my life there is one which must be life-long. It is the remembrance of my conduct to my father, and of the long tacit estrangement which preceded our last meeting, and which, but for a providential interposition, might never have been even so far atoned for and mitigated as it was before his death. It would be difficult to account for this estrangement; it is impossible to excuse it; there never was any reproach on either side,—indeed there could not have been on mine, for the fault was all my own,—and there never was any explanation. My father doubtless believed, as he was justified in believing, that any wish of his would have little weight with me;—he seldom expressed one; and I am convinced that one thing on which he had set his heart very strongly, one paramount desire, he cautiously abstained from expressing, that he might, by keeping me ignorant of it during his lifetime, give it the additional chance of realization which it might derive from the sanctity of a posthumous appeal to the feelings of an undutiful and careless son, when those feelings should be intensified by unavailing regret. I did learn, dear Helen, after the barrier of eternal silence had been placed between my father and me, that he had cherished one paramount desire, and that he had resorted to such an expedient in order to induce me to respect and to fulfil it.

"My amazement and discomfiture when I found that my father's will was of so far distant a date that it made no mention of you were great. I could not understand why he had not supplemented the will which existed by another, in which you would be amply provided for, and his wishes concerning your future fully explained. My long and wilful absence from my father had prevented my having any real acquaintance with you. To me you were merely a name, seldom heard, hardly remembered. Had I not gone to Knockholt when I did, you would have remained so; and there was no one else who could be supposed to take an obligatory interest in you. How came it, I thought, that my father had taken no precaution against such a contingency—which, in fact, had so nearly been a reality? You will say he trusted to the honour and the gentlemanly feeling of his son; and so I read the riddle also; but reflection showed me that I was wrong. A more strictly just man never lived than my father; and he must have been strictly unjust had he allowed the future fortunes of a young girl whom he had reared and educated—who had been to him as a daughter for years—to depend upon the caprice or the generosity of a man to whom she was an utter stranger, and between whom and herself the tie of blood was of the slightest description. Nor was delicacy less characteristic of my father than justice. (Ah, Helen, how keenly I can see all these things now that he is gone!) He would have shrunk as sensitively as you would from anything that would have obliged you and me to meet for the first time in the characters of pensioned and pensioner. I knew all this; and I was utterly confounded at the absence of any later will. I had the most complete and diligent search made; but in vain. There was no will, Helen, but there was a letter. In the drawer of the desk which my father always used, there was a letter. How do you think it was addressed? Not to 'my son'—not to 'Colonel Alsager;' but to 'Sir Laurence Alsager, Bart.'! It was a painful letter—painful and precious; painful because a tone of sadness, of disappointment, of content in feeling that the writer had nearly reached his term of life, pervaded it; precious because it was full of pardon and peace, of the fulness of love for his only son. I cannot let you see the letter,—it is too sacred for any eyes but those for which it was intended; but I can tell you some of its contents, and I can make you understand its tone. As a mother speaks to her son going forth into the arena of life, the night before their parting, in the dark, on her knees, by his bedside, with her head upon his pillow; as she speaks of the time to come, when she will watch and wait for him, of the time that is past, whose memories are so precious, which she bids him remember and be brave and true; as she makes light of all his faults and shortcomings,—so did my dear old father—my father who had grown gray and old; alone, when I might have been with him, and was not—write to me. God bless him, and God forgive me! He never reproached me, living; what punishment he has inflicted upon me, dead! The letter was long; and it varied, I think, through every key in which human tenderness can be sung. But enough of this.

"A portion of the contents concerned you nearly, my dear Helen. I can repeat them to you briefly. I knew, and you know, that your father and my father—very distant relatives—had been playmates in boyhood, and attached friends in manhood. We knew that your father died on his voyage home from India, and just after he had consigned you and your black nurse to the care of the captain of the ship, to be sent, on landing, to Knockholt Park. I believe you have your father's letter to my father, in which he solemnly, but fearlessly, entreats his protection for the orphan child, whose credentials it is to form. He had left your mother and her baby in an alien grave at Barrackpore, and I suppose he had not the strength to live for you only, 'little Nelly,' as they called you then. At all events, he died; and I knew in a vague kind of way about that, and my father's care of you, and how you grew up with him, and made his home cheerful and happy, which his only son left carelessly, and forsook for long. The letter recapitulated all this, and told me besides, that your mother had been my father's first love. Perhaps she was also his only love—God knows. He was a good husband to my mother during their brief married life, I am sure; for I remember her well; and she was always smiling and happy. But the girl he loved had preferred Robert Manningtree with nothing but his commission, to Peregrine Alsager with a large estate and a baronetcy for his fortunate future. My father, *preux chevalier* that he was, did not forget to tell me that she never repented or had reason to regret that preference. Thus, Helen, you were a legacy to him, bequeathed not alone by friendship, but by love. As such he accepted you; as such he prized you, calm and undemonstrative as he was; as such it was the cherished purpose of his life to intrust you to me—not that I was to be your guardian in his place, but that I was to be your husband. He thought well of me, in spite of all, you see; he did not despair of his ungracious son, or he never would have dreamed of conferring so great a privilege on me, of suffering you to incur so great a risk. He had had this darling project so strongly in his mind, and yet had been so convinced that any betrayal of it to me would only prevent my seeking you, that my persistent neglect of the old home had a double bitterness for him; and at length, two years ago, hearing a rumour that I was about to marry one of the beauties of the season, he relinquished it, and determined to make a will, bequeathing to you the larger portion of his unentailed property. The rumour was true as to my intentions, but false as to my success. The lady in question jilted me for a richer marriage, thank God! I don't say this from pique, but from conviction; for I have seen her and her husband, and I have seen her since her husband's death. She did not hold her perjured state long; nor did she win the prize for which she jilted me. I am a much richer man than her husband ever was, and he has left her comparatively poor. In a storm of rage and disgust I left England, without going to Knockholt—without having seen you since your childhood—without bidding my father farewell. This grieved him much: but I was free; I was not married. I was labouring under angry and bitter feelings towards all womankind. I should come home again, my father thought, still unmarried, and his hope would be fulfilled. He did not make the will. I remained away much longer than he supposed I should have done, and not nearly so long as in my anger and mortification I had determined to remain. You know the rest, dear Helen—you know that I lingered and dallied with time and duty, and did not go to Knockholt until it was all but too late. A little while before he met with the accident, my father had written a letter somewhat similar in purport; but he had not seen me then, and I suppose it was not warmly affectionate enough for the old man's liking, and he wrote that which I now mention at many, and, I fear, painful, intervals of his brief convalescence. It was finished just a week before he died.

"You will have read all this with emotion, Helen; and I daresay at this point your feelings will be very painful. Mine are little less so, and the task of fully explaining them to you is delicate and difficult. The truthfulness, the candour of your nature will come to my assistance when you read, as their remembrance aids me while I write. My first impulse on reading my father's letter was to exult in the thought that there was anything possible to me by which his wishes could be respected. My second—and it came speedily—was to feel that the marriage he desired between us never could take place. Are you reassured, Helen? Have you been frightened at the image your fancy has created, of a debt of gratitude to be discharged to Sir Peregrine at the cost of your own happiness, or disavowed at the cost of seeming cold, ungrateful, and undutiful? Have you had a vision of me in the character of an importunate suitor, half imploring a concession, half pressing a right, and wholly distasteful to you? If you have, dismiss it, for it is only a vision, and never will be realized to distress you. Why do I say this? Because I know that not only do you not love me, but that you do love Cuthbert Farleigh. Forgive the plainness and directness with which I allude to a fact yet perhaps unavowed to him, but perfectly well known by and acknowledged to yourself. No betrothal could make you more truly his than you have been by the tacit promise of your own heart—I know not for how long, but before I came to Knockholt Park, I am sure. If I had not seen the man, I should equally have discerned the fact, for I am observant; and though I have, I hope, outlived the first exuberance of masculine conceit, I did not err in imputing the tranquil, ladylike indifference with which you received me to a preoccupied mind, rather than to an absence of interest or curiosity about the almost unknown son of your guardian. Life at Knockholt Park has little variety or excitement to offer; and the advent of a Guardsman, a demi-semi-cousin, and an heir-apparent, would have made a little more impression, would it not, had not the Church secured its proper precedence of the Army? I perceived the state of things with satisfaction; for I liked you very much from the first, and I thought Cuthbert a very good fellow; just the man to hold your respect all his life long and to make you happy. In my reflections on your share, then, in the impossibility of the fulfilment of my father's request, I experienced little pain. My own was not so easily disposed of after his death as during his life. I was destined to frustrate his wishes. Had you and I met, as we ought to have done, long before; had I had the good fortune to have seen you and learned to contrast you with the meretricious and heartless of your sex, who had frittered away my heart and soured my temper, perhaps, Helen, I might have won you, and the old man might have been made happy.

"We met under circumstances which made any such destiny for us impossible, for reasons which equally affected both. My preoccupation was of a different sort from yours; it had neither present happiness nor future hope in it,—it had much of the elements of doubt and fear; but it was powerful, far more powerful than I then thought, and powerful it will always be. All this is enigmatical to you, dear Helen, and it must remain so. I would not have said anything about it, but that I owed it to you, to the friendship which I trust will never know a chill, to prevent your supposing that your share in the frustration of my father's wishes is disproportionate to mine. I would not have you think—as without this explanation you might justly think—that I magnanimously renounce my claims, my pretensions to your love in favour of the actual possessor. No, Helen; for us both our meeting was too late. We were not to love each other; I was not to be suffered to win the heart of a true and priceless woman, such as you are, when I had not a heart to give her in exchange. But though we were not to love each other, we were destined to be friends—friends in the fullest and firmest sense; and believe me, friendship between a man and woman, with its keen sympathy, its unrestrained, confidence, and its perfect toleration, is a tie as valuable as it is rare.

"Now I have told you almost all I have to tell about my father's letter. I suppose we shall both feel, and continue always to feel, that there was something hard, something almost cruel in the fate which marked him out for disappointment, and you and me for its ministers. But this must be; and we must leave it so, and turn to the present and vital interests of our lives. We shall think of him and mourn for him none the less that we will speak of this no more.

"Strong as was my father's desire for our marriage, dear Helen, and his persuasion that it would come to pass, in his abstraction and his want of observation he failed to take Farleigh into account; or perhaps, like all old people, he did not realize the fact that the child, the girl, had grown into a woman. He did not quite forget to provide for the contingency of its non-fulfilment. 'If, for any reason, it may not be. Lance,' he wrote—'if Florence Hillyard's child is not to be the mistress of the home which might have been her mother's, see that she has a dowry befitting my daughter and your sister.' No sentence in his letter touched me more with its simple trust than did that.

"I have seen very clearly into the state of your feelings, as I am sure you allow, and I don't think I have blundered about that of Farleigh's. He has not told you in formal words the fact patent to every one's observation, that he entirely reciprocates your devotion (don't be vexed, Helen; one may pet a curate, you know), because he's poor, and you were likely to be rich. He believes, as every one believes, that you are as poor as himself; a belief, by the way, which does not say much for the general estimate of my character—but that does not matter; and in that faith he will not hesitate any longer. Will you be discreet, and say nothing at all of my intention of carrying out this privately-expressed wish of my father? Will you prove your possession of the qualities I give you credit for, by leaving Cuthbert in the belief that he will have in you a portionless bride, save for your dowry of beauty and worth? I really almost think you will, Helen; especially as, though you do not need any further confirmation of Farleigh's nobility of mind than the silence he has hitherto kept, and the alacrity with which he will now doubtless break it, it will be well for Mrs. Chisholm and for myself, your only friends, to know how amply he fulfils our expectations. I almost think you will; but I intend to make assurance doubly sure by not giving you the slightest satisfaction on the subject of my intentions. When your marriage is near, you shall learn how I mean to fulfil my father's last injunction, but not till then; and if you tell Farleigh anything about it until I give you leave, I vow I won't give you a shilling.

"You see I have written myself into good spirits, dear Helen; the thought of you cheers me almost as your kindly presence would do. What more have I to say? Not much more of myself, or of yourself, save that the dearest and warmest wish I entertain is for your welfare.

"I shall send from my first halting-place on the Continent full instructions to Todd, in case my absence should be much prolonged. I cannot speak with any certainty of its duration; it does not depend on my own inclination.

"And now, in conclusion, I am going to ask you to do something for me, which I shall take as the truest proof that the friendship I prize and rely upon is really mine. I am sure you have not forgotten the friend I mentioned to you—Lady Mitford. I have seen her in town, and found her in much grief and perplexity. The cause of her sorrow is not one on which I can venture to enter to you; but it is deep-seated, incurable. I am much distressed for her, and can in no way defend or comfort her. She was an only child, motherless, and brought up in seclusion by her father,—an exemplary country clergyman, but a man whose knowledge of the world was quite theoretical and elementary, and who could not have trained her so that she would know how to encounter such trials as hers; he probably did not know that such could exist. As I told you at Knockholt, she has no female friend; unfortunately she has female enemies— one in particular. My great wish is to procure her the one, and defend her from the other. I may fail in the latter object; but you, Helen, can aid me, if you will, to fulfil the former. I have spoken to her about you, and have assured her that she might trust in your kindliness, though your inexperience is far greater than her own. I cannot bring you together now—there is no time or opportunity; but I want you to promise me that, if at any time during my absence from England Lady Mitford asks you to come to her, you will go promptly, and will be to her all that is in you to be to one unjustly oppressed, cruelly betrayed, and sorely afflicted. Will you do this for me, Helen? and will you give me an assurance that I may rely upon you to do it (this is the only portion of my letter which you need reply to, if you have any feeling that you would rather not) before next Wednesday, and addressed to me at the Hotel Meurice, Paris?—Always affectionately yours,

"LAURENCE ALSAGER."

CHAPTER XXIX.

A "TERCEL GENTLE."

Sir Laurence Alsager's angry mood was of short duration. The day after that interview in which he had spoke words that he had never intended to speak, and heard words which he had never thought to hear, he felt that a great change had fallen upon him. This woman who had rejected his love, not because she did not reciprocate it, but because it was unlawful; this woman who had had the strongest and subtlest temptation which can assail the human heart set before her—the temptation at once of consolation and of retaliation, of revenge upon the husband who had deceived and the enemy who had injured her, and who had met it with utterly disarming rectitude; this woman to whom duty was dearer than love,—she had changed the face of the world and the meaning of life for him. He had many times believed a lie, and not seldom had he worshipped a sham; but he has detected the one and exposed the other, and gone on his way not much the worse for the delusion, and a good deal wiser for the experience. Life had, however, never brought him anything like this before, and he knew it never would again. He should never love, he could never love, any other woman than this peerless one who could never be his, from whom her own mandate—he knew its power and unchangeableness—had severed him, whom he must leave in the grasp of sorrow and perplexity. He mused long and painfully over the interview of the preceding day, and he asked himself how it was that, dear as she had been to him, early as he had ceased to struggle against her influence, he had never understood the strength, the dignity, the perfect rectitude of her character before. It never occurred to Sir Laurence that he had not looked for these qualities; that he had never studied her disposition but in the most superficial way; that his love for her was founded upon no fine theory whatsoever; that it had sprung up partly in admiration of her exceeding beauty, partly in chivalrous compassion for her disastrous situation, and found its remaining constituent in a hearty contempt and abhorrence of Sir Charles Mitford. In short, Sir Laurence did not understand that he had done just as other people do,—fallen in love with a woman first, and found out what sort of woman she really was afterwards.

Sir Laurence's reverie had lasted a long time before the consideration of his own immediate movements occupied any place in it. When it did so, he formed his resolution with his accustomed promptitude. He had told them at Knockholt that he might perhaps go abroad; and now abroad he would go. He must leave London; he could not bear to witness the progress of this drama, in which he had so vital an interest, only as an ordinary spectator. He was parted from her; she was right—there could be no pretext of friendship in their case. Even if he could have obscured her clear perception and misguided her judgment; even if he could have persuaded her to receive him once more on the footing of a friend, he would have disdained to avail himself of such a subterfuge. The surest test a man can apply to the worth and sincerity of his love is to ask himself whether he would deceive its object in order to win her; if he can honestly say no, he is a true lover and a gentleman. Sir Laurence asked himself such a question, and was answered, no. He could not stand the Club-talk; he could not meet those men to whom she furnished matter for conversation,—not insolent indeed, so far as she was concerned, but intolerable in its easy, *insouciant*, flippant slang and indolent speculation in the ears of the man who loved her. He could not stop it; if he remained in town he must endure it, or forsake the society of all his customary associates, which was not to be thought of. Such a course of proceeding as that, in addition to depriving him of resources and leaving him nothing to do, would give rise to no end of talk and all kinds of surmises. If he started off suddenly, nobody knowing why, and went nobody knew where, it would be all right,—it would be only "Alsager's queer way;" but if he stayed in town and saw no one, or changed his set, then, indeed, that would be quite another matter. One's own set has toleration for one's queer ways, to which they are accustomed, but they decidedly object to any but habitual "queerness;" they will not bear with new developments, with running off the rails.

Yes, he would go; and the sooner the better. There was nothing to detain him now. He would have liked to see Miss Gillespie perhaps: but, after all, what good could it do? Her connection with the Hammonds, and through them with the Mitfords, had long been at an end; her mysterious note had warned him that her power was over; so that what could she do? and what had he to say to her? Persons of her sort were never safe to talk to, and were so full of caprice that she might either resent his visit or ignore the subject of Lady Mitford altogether; if she had ever had any interest in her, and it had been genuine, it was not likely she retained it now. No; he would not linger for the purpose of seeing her,—he would go at once. Whither? To Paris first, of course; and then he would consider. Was he always to be a wanderer? he thought; was he never to realize any of the good resolves, to put in practice any of the views, he had been indulging in lately? Was Knockholt to remain masterless, because he could not settle down to the interests and the occupations which sufficed for other and better men?—men who had not been exempted from the common lot either;—men, to many of whom their heart's desire had not been granted. Could he not now do as his father had done? No, not yet; the restlessness of mental trouble was upon him; the pain of unaccustomed moral processes; the shivering chill of the dawn of a new kind of light and a new system of thought. No doubt this would not be always so; after a time he could find rest and tranquillity in the duties and enjoyments of a country baronet's existence. Was this what she meant? Was this strength to do, and fidelity in adhering to duty, the noble law by which she ruled her life? Were they to bring him to the happiness which seemed so distant, so impossible? Were not the words upon the ring her message, her counsel, her command? Ah, well, if so, he might—he would try to follow them some day; but for the present he must get away. Like every wounded animal, he must seek refuge in flight, he must get him to the covert.

Sir Laurence Alsager did not remember, amid all his musings, that he was alone in the enjoyment of this resource; that *she* remained where her feet trod on thorns, and heart fed on bitterness—remained in the straight path of her duty, strong and faithful.

Yes, he would go at once,—that evening. He gave his servant the necessary orders, and then applied himself to writing letters on matters of business. While thus engaged a note was brought to him, and he was informed that the bearer awaited the answer. The note was enclosed in an oblong envelope, bordered with black about an inch deep, so that room was barely left for the address. He knew the handwriting well; he had been accustomed to see it in combination with every kind of coquetry in stationery; and he smiled grimly as he noted the mingled hypocrisy and coquetry of this very pretty and impressive affliction in black and white.

"What the devil is she at now?" thought Sir Laurence, as he broke the accurately-impressed seal. He had not had any communication with Mrs. Hammond since he left Redmoor in the spring; he had heard not quite all perhaps, but enough about her to make him shrink from any further acquaintance with her, as much from disgust of herself as from indignation on Lady Mitford's account; and he gave her too much credit for a sufficiently accurate knowledge of the machinery of London society, and the unfailing circulation of scandal, to entertain any doubt that she was well aware that he must inevitably hear, and had by this time heard, the stories that were rife about her. He was not in the least aware to how great an extent she had been actuated by torturing jealousy of him, though, as he had told Lady Mitford, he knew one of her motives was revenge; but he was prepared to give Laura Hammond credit for any amount of spite of which human nature is capable; still, what purpose could she have to serve by opening any communication with him? He read the note as he asked himself the question. It was dated from the house in Portman Square, and contained only a few lines. Mrs. Hammond had heard of Sir Laurence Alsager's arrival in town, and was particularly desirous of seeing him. She begged he would send her a line to say whether he could conveniently call upon her the same evening; she said evening, as no doubt his mornings were fully occupied with the business entailed by his acquisition of rank and fortune, on which she begged to offer her congratulations; and she equally, of course, did not go out anywhere, or receive (ordinary) visitors. She hoped Sir Laurence Alsager would comply with her request, as she wished to speak to him concerning a person in whom he was interested, and whom his acquiescence would materially benefit (underlined); and she remained his most faithfully.

"A snare and a bait," said Laurence, as he stood with the note in his hand, uncertain what reply he should make. His first impulse was to write that he was leaving London that afternoon; but he hesitated to do that, as it occurred to him she would be surprised at the abruptness of such a step, and setting her serpentine sagacity to work, might arrive at guessing something at least proximate to the truth. Curiosity; a strong conviction that Laura would not venture to tamper with his patience too far, and would not have dared to take this step without some motive; a vivid recollection of the interview which had taken place between them before the memorable visit to

Redmoor, of his threat, and Laura's evident appreciation of its sincerity; finally, an irresistible longing to hear what Laura might have to say about Lady Mitford, and a vague dread that a refusal might in some indescribable way injure her,—decided him.

He wrote a short formal note, to the effect that Sir Laurence Alsager would have the honour of calling upon Mrs. Hammond at eight o'clock that evening, despatched it, and then returned to his letters.

Sir Laurence did not dine at the Club that day; he was in no mood to meet the men whom he must have met, and who would have made him pay the price of his popularity by inopportunely insisting on his society. He dined at a private hotel, and eight o'clock found him at the door of Mrs. Hammond's house.

He was shown into an inner drawing-room, which was brilliantly lighted, and where he was left alone for a few minutes. Then Mrs. Hammond appeared, and came towards him holding out her hand.

"I cannot congratulate you on your appearance, Sir Laurence," she said, as she seated herself in a low deep chair and looked up at him. The look was a peculiar one; intent observation and some anxiety were blended in its expression. He had taken a seat at her invitation, and was quite grave and self-possessed, while he preserved with exactness the manner of a man who was there in obedience to a summons, not of his own wish or act, and who was waiting to learn the motive which had dictated it.

Laura Hammond looked handsomer than he had ever seen her, as she sat in the lighted room in her deep mourning dress, whose sombre hue and rich material toned down the sensuous style of her beauty, and lent it that last best touch of refinement in which alone it had been wanting. Sir Laurence Alsager observed this increased beauty, but merely with an artistic sense of its attraction. To him Laura Hammond could never be aught but despicable and repulsive; and he was just then in the mood in which a man believes that only one woman in the world is really beautiful. She had conformed to custom in her dress so far as the weeds went, but she did not wear a widow's cap. Nothing would have induced her to disfigure herself by such a detestable invention; and though she knew she should be talked about, she considered that a minor evil. Her fine silky chestnut-hair, preserved from contact with the hideous cap, was banded smoothly on her forehead, and gathered into an unadorned knot at the back of her head, showing the profile and the delicate little ears to perfection. More beautiful than ever she undoubtedly was; but yet, as Laurence looked at her with close attention, he noticed that she had grown suddenly older in appearance. Even supposing all her former light and dashing manner to be resumed, the sombre dress to be laid aside, and the brilliant toilette in which Laura had been unrivalled among English women to have taken its place, a change had come over her. A line above the brow,—a horizontal line, not the sharp perpendicular mark that intellectual toil sets; a tighter closing of the lips, too seldom closed before; a little, a very little, less elasticity in the muscles which produced and banished the ever-flitting smile,—these were faint, but certain, indications.

"I have not been ill, Mrs. Hammond," replied Sir Laurence gravely; "but I have had a good deal of trouble lately, and that does not improve one's looks. But," he went on, "you wished to see me; may I inquire why? I am leaving town shortly; and—"

He paused; his natural courtesy arrested him. He could not tell Mrs. Hammond so plainly that he was anxious to get away from her as soon as possible. She saw it though, and she reddened with sudden anger, which in an instant she brought under control.

"You are amazingly business-like, Sir Laurence! The influence of your late onerous experiences in the character of *Gentilhomme Campaynard*, no doubt. By the way, how do you like it all?"

"All? I hardly catch your meaning. Since my father's death I have been, as you suppose, very much occupied, and I cannot say I like the details of a transfer of property and responsibility much."

"Ah, but the property itself, I meant,—the title and the fortune, the 'county-magnate' business, and the ward;—above all, the ward."

She spoke in a playful tone; but she watched him closely, and Sir Laurence saw it.

"She had heard something about Helen, and she is on a false scent," he thought. "Perhaps it is just as well to let her deceive herself."

So he replied, still gravely, still unwarmed by her manner, which was half caressing and half contemptuous:

"They are all good things in their way, Mrs. Hammond; and if their way be not yet mine, mine will be theirs some day, I hope."

"Ah, then, it's true!" she exclaimed. "You are really going to marry and settle; you are going to assume the semi-sporting, semi-bucolic, but entirely domestic character, which is so very charming, and which will suit you so perfectly; and henceforth the all-conquering Colonel will be sought for in vain under so admirable a travesty!"

Still he was grave and immovable. Her *persiflage* had no more power to charm, her ridicule to annoy, than her beauty had power to please him. It was all silly chatter; and he wondered at himself as he remembered the time when he preferred the nonsense, occasionally adulterated by slang and invariably spiced with spite, which she had talked then and always, to any words of wit or wisdom. She still watched him, under cover of her light manner, narrowly.

"You know as well as I do what is the ordinary amount of truth in public rumour, Mrs. Hammond. But you must excuse me for again reminding you that I am here at your request, and that you summoned me hither with some purpose. It was not to talk of my affairs and prospects, I presume."

He spoke the last words in a harsh and angry voice involuntarily. Anger against her, and something very like hatred of her, were strong within him, and grew stronger rapidly. He looked at her careless face; he marked her sensuous *soignée* beauty; and he remembered the fair woman whom he had seen struck down by her merciless hand in the dawn of her innocent happiness, in the pride of her hope and love. He would make her say her say, and leave her, or he would leave her with it unsaid; he was sorry he had come. What could this woman do but harm to any one; to him, and to *her* most of all?

"No, Colonel Alsager,—I beg your pardon, Sir Laurence,—I cannot always remember how times are changed, you see,—it was *not*. It was for a purpose which you may think a little less welcome, and perhaps even more trifling; it was to talk to you—of myself."

"Of yourself, Mrs. Hammond! What can you have to say of yourself that I ought to hear, or you to speak?"

"Much," she said vehemently; and in a moment her manner changed. He had a perfectly distinct recollection of her on the last two occasions when he and she had spoken together, especially on the last, when she openly defied him; when she had declared that she still loved him; when she had furnished him with the clue to her conduct which he had unravelled for Lady Mitford's enlightenment; when she had said, "I will break her heart, and then I will spoil her name."

Had she done so? had this woman fulfilled her threat? Very nearly; she had almost broken Georgie's heart, and she would certainly ruin her reputation if he— Laurence Alsager—did not resolutely withdraw, and deprive her of any pretext for slander. And so it had come to this: the woman he had undertaken to defend, for whose sake he had foregone so much pleasure and neglected so much duty, could be saved only by his absence! He knew that Laura was "talked of," and therefore persons unskilled in the science of society might suppose that she could not do much harm by talking of another woman; but Alsager was an adept, and he knew that a stone will bruise and maim, and even kill, if well-aimed and sufficiently heavy, though the hand that throws it be ever so much stained with sin. He feared—he feared exceedingly for the woman he loved, and whom this she-devil hated. He noted the change in Laura's manner before she spoke, and he feared still more.

"I have much to say, and I *will* say it," she went on vehemently; "and you shall listen to me! What! am I to have won at last, and at the end of such deception and slavery, the reward I have done all and suffered all for, and then am I to keep a decorous silence, and see it all made waste and worthless? Don't look at me in that grave, polite, criticising way, Laurence, or you will drive me mad!"

Something of menace and something of appeal in her manner, a startling energy in her gesture, and the hoarse intensity of her voice, threw Alsager off his guard; this was so totally new to him. He had seen her in many moods, but never in one like this. Tenderness, coquetry, a mock gust of passion, all the tricks of fence of the most finished flirt he had seen her play, and he had found them out—perhaps she had never really deceived even when she had most completely fascinated him; but he had never seen her thus, he thought, and he was right. She was in earnest; he was about to understand her fully now. She had risen impetuously from her seat, and approached him, and he had risen also; so they stood confronting each other. There was nothing artificial in the expressive grace of her attitude; her figure was perfect, and she was graceful always—never more so than now, when she was carried away into a forgetfulness of her own beauty, which, if it had been habitual, would have made Laura Hammond irresistible. Her eyes flashed, and her smooth brow reddened; but her beauty gained by every subtle change of expression, as she poured out a torrent of impetuous words.

"Did you think I had forgotten our last meeting and our last parting? Did you think I had forgotten the words you spoke then, and those with which I answered them? Did you think the past was all blotted out, and those three horrid years were gone like an ugly dream; those years during which you banished yourself for love of me,—yes, Sir Laurence Alsager, for me,—you cannot deny it, you can't take *that* from me, you can't transfer that jewel to *her* crown of triumph,—ay, start and stare; I know it all, you see,—and then came back to torture me by indifference, by neglect, by preference of another—and *what* another! my God! that made it a thousand times worse—before my face! What do you take me for that you think I would endure this, and when the time came for speech keep silence!"

She was trembling violently now; but as he looked at her, with all the amazement he felt in his face, she put a strong control on herself and stood quite firmly.

"For God's sake, what do you mean?" stammered Sir Laurence. "What are you talking about? What is it that you must say? What is it that I have done?"

"You ask me what I mean; you—you—did I not tell you then—when you pleaded to me for the woman who had rivalled me with you—that I loved you? Did I not tell you then, I say, and did you not know it?"

"You did tell me that you loved me then, Mrs. Hammond, and I did not believe you. You had told me the same thing before, you know, many a time, and you married Mr. Hammond. You married him because he was very rich,—perhaps you might have hesitated had he not also been old and silly; but he was, and your calculations have succeeded;—you are rich and free. Once before, when we talked upon this subject, I said we would not go into it any more. To you it cannot be *profitable*" (he laid an emphasis upon the word), "and to me it is very painful. 'That time is dead and buried,' and so let it be. I cannot conceive why you have revived its memory; but, whatever your purpose, it can have no success dependent on me. I have no bitter memory of it now; indeed, for some time I have had no memory of it at all. I know it is hard for a woman to believe that a wound inflicted by her can ever heal, and I daresay men show the scars sometimes, and flatter the harmless vanity of their *ci-devant* conquerors. But I am not a man of that stamp, Mrs. Hammond; I have good healing flesh, I suppose, as the surgeons and the nurses say; at all events, I have no scars to show."

He made a step in advance, as if to take his hat from a small table; and she saw that he intended to leave her.

"No," she exclaimed; "you shall not go! I am utterly resolved to speak with you; and you must hear me. I will be as cold and as calm as you are; but you must hear me, if not for my sake or your own, for Lady Mitford's!"

She motioned him to his seat, and smiled—a little momentary smile and full of bitterness. He sat down again, and she stood by the mantelpiece, on which she laid her hand, and for a moment rested her head upon the palm. Something forlorn in the attitude caught Alsager's attention; then he knew that she was acting, and acting well. Fury, perhaps ferocity, might be natural to Laura Hammond under certain circumstances; but forlornness never. When she next spoke it was in a softer tone, and she kept her face towards him in profile. It was her best look, as he remembered, and as she remembered also; for though she was not acting now in all she said—though she was more real throughout the whole of their interview than she had ever been before, nothing, except indeed it might have been severe bodily pain, could have reduced Laura to perfect reality.

"I believe," she said, "the best way I can make you understand why I sent for you, and what I want to say to you, is to tell you the truth about those three years."

"As you please," he answered; "I cannot conceive how their history can concern me, except that portion of it which I have witnessed; and that has concerned, and does concern me. But I am here at your request, and I will go only at your dismissal."

"When I married, and you went away," she began, "I was not very unhappy at first; there was novelty and success, and there was luxury, which I love," she said with emphatic candour. "Mr. Hammond was not a disagreeable man, and I never suffered him to get into the habit of controlling me. He was inclined to try a little, but I soon convinced him it was useless, and, especially at his age, would make him uncomfortable. So he left off." Her voice hardened now into the clear metallic tone which Laurence remembered so well.

"By degrees, however," she continued, "everything grew irksome; and a horrid weariness and sense of degradation stole over me; not because I loved wealth and luxury any less, but because of the price I had to pay for it. And you had made it dearer to buy, for you had gone away."

"Yes," he said, "I had gone away; and you would have liked to have me stay, and be experimented on, and victimized for your delight,—I can understand that; but I should have fancied, Mrs. Hammond, you knew me too well to suppose you could have played such a game as that with me."

"I would not have played any game with you," she said—not angrily, rather sadly. "How unjust you are! how unjust men always are! they—"

He interrupted her. "Pray do not indulge me—with that senseless complaint which women who, like you, are the bane and the torment of men who loved them with an honest, and the utter ruin of men who loved them with a dishonest love, make of their victims. I have long ceased to be yours, Mrs. Hammond; but I am not unjust. I say again, you would have made me ridiculous as readily as you had made me wretched. I don't deny it, you see. I am much astonished, and rather ashamed, when forced to remember it; but I am not weak enough to deny a weakness. To be so would argue that it is not entirely corrected."

He was provoking her to anger, but not altogether unintentionally; his best means of coming at her real purpose would be by throwing her off her guard.

"I say again," she repeated, "you are unjust; I would *not* have played any such game. I would have become used to my position in time; I would have seen you in the world; I would have seen you gradually forgetting me. It would not have been our angry parting, and a dead dull blank,—time to feel to the utmost all the horrors of a marriage without love. No woman, I believe, would sell herself, at least in marriage, which must last, if she could estimate them aright. And then such a meeting as ours! Do you remember it, Laurence?" She stole a very affectionate look at him here.

"Yes, I remember it," he said shortly.

"A horrid interview we had then, full of sneers and bitterness on your side, and not in the least real on mine."

"Is this a pleasanter one, Mrs. Hammond?" said Sir Laurence, who perceived that her levity was coming up again, and desired to suppress it. "I cannot perceive the utility of this retrospect."

"I daresay not," she answered coolly; "but I do." The pretty air of command was entirely lost on Alsager. She saw that it was, and ground her teeth,—a pleasant symptom of passion which she never could suppress. "By the time we met again," she continued, "I was sick and weary—not only of the price I had to pay for the wealth I had bought, but of the wealth itself. Of course I never changed my opinion of the value of money. I don't mean that; but I did not get as much out of the wealth I had purchased as I might have done. I was very much admired, and quite the fashion, but somehow I tired of it all; and then—then, Laurence, I found out why. I found out that I really had more heart than I believed, and that it was in your keeping."

"Pshaw!" he said, angrily and impatiently; "pray don't talk like this. You are drawing on your imagination very largely, and also on my vanity. The latter is quite useless, I assure you."

"Think what you like, say what you will,—I loved you. I knew it by the listlessness that was always upon me; I knew it better by the disappearance of that listlessness when they said you were coming home; and I knew it best of all when—when do you think, Sir Laurence Alsager?"

"I really could not presume to guess when you made such a discovery, Mrs. Hammond."

"Indeed! I will tell you, then. I learned it best of all when the first pang of jealousy I had ever felt in my life seized me. I had often heard your name coupled with that of some woman of fashion. I had heard a multitude of speculations about your affairs of the heart; but I never feared them—I never believed in them; I never knew that I had so vital an interest in them until your own look, your own manner, your own indecision of purpose about the visit to Redmoor, betrayed you to me, and told me who was my rival."

"Your rival!" said Sir Laurence in astonishment. "Surely you did not suppose I had returned to England to be caught again in your toils?"

"I don't know what I thought; I don't care. I only know that when you and I parted, you loved me, and were angry with me,—it was passionate love and passionate anger,—and that when you and I met, not only had you ceased to be angry, but you were rapidly succumbing to the influence of another woman—a woman utterly different from me! Not more beautiful,—I deny *that*; she has not the art of being beautiful; she has only the material. A woman whom I hate; whom I should have hated and would have injured, I believe, if you had never seen her. Yes; and you actually dared to menace me on her account; you presumed to pit yourself against me as her champion. You forgot that such championship hardly serves its object, in the eyes of the world."

Sir Laurence uttered an exclamation of disgust; and was about to rise, when she stepped forward close to him, and laid her hands lightly upon his breast for an instant.

"No, no, Laurence," she said; "bear with me. I did not mean it; not quite that. Can you not understand me? Ah, my God! how pitiless men are! While they want to win us, where is the end of that toleration? We may sin as we please, provided we do not sin against them and their self-love. But when that is over, they cannot judge us harshly enough; they have even less pardon and pity for the sins into which they have driven us than for any others."

"You are talking utter nonsense, Mrs. Hammond," said Sir Laurence; "and nonsense it is painful for me to hear. Your temptations are of your own making, and your sins are of your own counselling, not mine. I would have made you my wife, but you preferred—and I thank you for the choice—another destiny. Am I to blame? You have chosen to cherish a distempered fancy which has no foundation in truth, and am I the ruthless being who has robbed you of it? You have chosen to solace the tedium of your uncongenial marriage by a proceeding as vile and unprincipled as any woman ever ventured on, to her eternal shame. Harsh words, Mrs. Hammond, but true; and now you endeavour to lend an air of melodrama to a transaction which was in reality as commonplace as it was coarse. You find it hard to put your relation with Sir Charles Mitford on a sentimental footing,—he is hardly a subject for sentiment, I think; and you have invented this tragical theory of an indirect revenge upon me. Tush! I gave you credit for more tact."

This was well and boldly said; for Sir Laurence had but one object in view,—to do the best he could for Lady Mitford in this encounter with her foe. He knew as he spoke, as he looked into the unmasked face before him—pale and deformed with jarring passions—that the motive was real, though secondary; it had indeed only come to supplement the first, which had led Laura to employ her fascinations upon Sir Charles; but it had always been stronger, and had latterly completely swallowed up the other.

"Shall I never make you understand me?" she said passionately; "will you persist in bringing things that are unreasonable to the touchstone of reason? I don't know, I don't care how absurd what I am saying may sound; it is true, true, Laurence Alsager,—as sure as death is true, or any love that ever was more bitter. Yes, it is true:

now think your worst, and say your worst of me; still you must see that I am far more wretched than she is. What had I to endure? What had she? I won her husband from her. If I did, was he a prize, do you think? A selfish, sensual, brainless fool; a man without taste, or manners, or mind; a man who is a living contradiction to the theories of rage and education; a man of whom she must have sickened in a year, if she had ever gained sense enough to find him out. She is not very clever, you know, and she might have taken longer for the discovery, if the habitual society of men who are gentlemen had not enlightened her. But she had a more sure and rapid teacher, who brought her consolation too." There was a world of malevolent meaning in the tone in which she said this.

"What do you, what can you mean?" he asked.

"Ah, you are getting interested now, Sir Laurence, when my discourse turns on her. Wait a little, and I will explain. I asked you what did she lose; I need not ask you what did I gain; the one includes the other."

"He was her husband," said Laurence.

"Her husband!" repeated Laura, with intense scorn. "You have caught the cant of the proprieties' school, have you? Her husband! And what were you? My lover, Laurence. Ay, you may forget, you may deny it; but you were, the day you landed in England,—I should have only needed opportunity to win you back again. Her husband!" (with a bold hard laugh)—"she might have taken mine, and welcome!"

Sir Laurence looked at her in growing disgust. Lord Dollamore was quite right; there was a strong dash of vulgarity about Laura Hammond, and it appeared whenever she lost her temper.

"Yes," she went on, more and more angrily; "think of her, and think of me. She suffered the tortures of jealousy, did she? of lawful legitimate jealousy, for which good people would give her pity, if she were not too proud to take it. She suffer! What did I suffer? I tell you, Laurence Alsager, she *could not* suffer what I suffer; it is not in her, any more than she could love as I love. She is a handsome, cold, egotistical woman, who thinks of her *rights*. Her husband belonged to her, and I took him, and she didn't like it. She felt it much as she would have felt my stealing her pearls or her Dresden china, I daresay; but *suffer!* Why, she's what is called a *good* woman; and if I chose to break with Mitford, he would probably now return to her, for he likes her rather; and she would receive his apologies, and all would be right again. Yes, she'd stoop to this stupid meanness, because he's her *husband,* you know; and matrimony is such a remarkably sacred institution, that a man may do anything he pleases. And you talk to me of a woman like *her* suffering!"

Sir Laurence made no answer. He was thinking how truly, from her own debased point of view, Laura Hammond read the character of the woman she had injured so deeply.

"You don't answer. Tell me, don't you know she would be reconciled with Mitford to-morrow, if he asked her?"

"I cannot tell you, indeed," he said coldly; "you had better 'break with Mitford,' as you phrase it, and find out."

"Will you not at least acknowledge that I had to suffer? The time of my bondage was short, but she deprived my freedom of all its value. She has won you, Laurence; and what is it all to me? I don't believe, in all her well-regulated life, she ever experienced such a pang as I felt when I saw her indifferent to Mitford's brutal neglect, and to my insolence, one morning, because she had just had a letter from you; a commonplace letter enough, Sir Laurence—she told us all about it—but I can never forget or forgive the serenity of her face; it seemed as if she had been removed into a world apart from us all."

How little she dreamed—how far, in her blind furious anger and self-abandonment, she was from dreaming of the secret stealthy delight with which the listener heard her words!

"You impute to Lady Mitford your own ideas, your own indifference to right, Mrs. Hammond; she is a woman who is incapable of wronging her husband, even in thought, though that husband be no worthier than Mitford. She rules her life by principles, and in her estimate of marriage regards the obligation rather than the individual."

"Indeed! That's a very pretty sentence, Sir Laurence, and you have learned your lesson like a very docile little boy. But hadn't you better reserve it for repetition elsewhere? for really sentiments of such grandeur are quite thrown away on me."

She was exasperated to the highest pitch by his perfect coolness, and tears of rage stood in her eyes. He had preserved an imperturbable composure; neither her passion nor her sarcasm moved him. Desperately she caught at the one hope that remained. She came towards him suddenly, dropped upon her knees by his side, and hid her face, covered with her hands, on his arm, while he sat astonished and confused.

"Laurence!" she sobbed, "listen to me. Do you not know that all the wicked things I say are said because I am miserable; because the love of you and the loss of you have turned me into something that I dread to think of and to look into? Have some compassion on me! I wronged you, I know; but can you not forgive me? Do you think the prize I won brought me any peace? Be merciful to a woman's vanity and weakness. Am I the only woman who is weak and vain? You did love me once; you could love me now, if you would only put aside your pride, if you would only try to be merciful to the errors which I have so bitterly repented. Laurence, this woman, who has been the cause of all—whose wrongs are upon her own head—what can she ever be to you? You know she is, according to your own account, *too good* to be tempted from her duty, while I—I am free; there is no barrier between us now—and I love you."

She raised her drooping head, she let her hands fall, and she looked at him. The time had been when such a look would have brought Laurence Alsager to her feet; but now, he had said truly, "that time was dead and buried."

He rose with an air of stern determination. She had risen from her knees, and had resumed her chair She was deadly pale; her eyes were wild and haggard; and she caught her breath with a sort of gasping sob, which threatened a burst of hysterical passion. Laurence spoke low and sadly:

"When you come to think over what you have just said, you will be angry with yourself for having uttered, and with me for having heard, such words. I will not dwell upon them, nor will I voluntarily remember them. If you had never caused me more than the pang which your first faithlessness to myself made me suffer, I might indeed have pardoned it, for the sake of the old glamour, and made myself miserable by marrying a woman whom I could not respect, because I had once loved her. But that the woman who jilted me for Percy Hammond's rupees, then betrayed Hammond for Sir Charles Mitford, and would now discard Mitford for me—by the way, I am a much richer man than Hammond was; barring the widowhood, your speculation has been defective—should dream, in the wildest paroxysms of a woman's unreasonableness, that I could be cajoled, or bribed, through my interest in another, to put her in my honoured mother's place, is beyond my comprehension."

She looked at him, still with wild haggard eyes, and still she sobbed, but shed no tears.

"Farewell, Mrs. Hammond," said Sir Laurence, as he took his hat, and turned towards the door; "you and I are not likely to meet again. I hope the remembrance of this interview will induce you to consider whether it might not be better for you to endeavour to imitate the woman whom you have not only injured, but vainly endeavoured to traduce."

"Curse her!" hissed Laura, in a tone that was no more like a woman's than were her words. "Let her look to it! I will punish you, Laurence Alsager, through her."

"No, you won't," he said; "for the first move you make in that direction, I will write to Mitford (I shall never be without information), and inform him that you did me the honour to propose to break with him in my favour."

"He would not believe you," she said, in a voice hardly audible from the intensity of her passion.

"O yes, he would; Mitford is not a fool on every point; and rumour says he's jealous, which is likely to quicken his intellects. At all events, I advise you to let Lady Mitford alone."

"Let her look to it," said Laura; "I owe this to her, and I will pay it."

He smiled, bowed, and left the room. She started from her chair, and listened, with her hands clasped upon her temples, till she heard the half-door shut; then she knew that he was gone—then she knew that her bold game was lost—and she felt that she should never see him more, who was the only man she had ever loved, even after her own cold and shallow fashion. She gave way to no passion now; she smoothed her hair, glanced at the glass, and rang the bell. When it was answered, she directed that Mademoiselle Marcelline should be sent to her.

Demure, quiet, and respectful as ever, Mademoiselle Marcelline entered the room.

"Marcelline," said Laura (she addressed her maid by her name now), "I am going to my room. Come to me in half an hour; I want to talk to you about something."

"A letter came for madame this evening," said mademoiselle; "but I took it from the *valet de chambre*, as I thought madame did not care to be disturbed."

Mrs. Hammond opened the letter. It was from her solicitor, and informed her that the final decision of the court, on her application for the guardianship of her stepdaughter, had been given that day against her. She frowned, then threw the letter down, with a short laugh.

"Everything is against me, I think. However, it is rather fortunate for Alice."

At the same hour on the following evening Sir Laurence Alsager was writing his letter to Helen Manningtree from Dover.

CHAPTER XXX.

NATURE AND ART.

Lady Mitford's composure had been shaken by her interview with Sir Laurence Alsager more rudely than by any of the events which had succeeded each other with such rapidity in the course of the short but troublous time since her marriage. She had reckoned upon his friendship to support and his society to cheer her, and now they must be relinquished. There could be no doubt, no hesitation about that; and she did not doubt or hesitate, but she suffered, as such keenly sensitive and highly-principled natures can suffer, whose only possible course is to do the right thing, and pay, without having counted, the cost.

All the loneliness, all the dreariness of her lot came on her foreboding spirit, as she sat alone in her dressing-room, two days after her parting interview with Sir Laurence. She had been thinking of the day at Redmoor when their first confidence had been interchanged; she had been remembering his counsel, and taking herself to task for having neglected it, or, at any rate, for not having tried more earnestly and more persistently to follow it.

"I must have been to blame in some degree," she thought; "I ought to have tried to please him more; but—" and then she sighed—"I had been used to please him without trying, and it is hard to realize the change; and before one does realize it, it is too late. I wonder if there is any case in which it would not be too late from the first; I wonder if any woman in the world ever yet succeeded in retaining or recovering the heart of any man when it had once in the least strayed from her. I don't grieve for myself now,—I cannot; but I blame myself. I might have tried—no doubt I should have failed; but still I might have tried. I might have asserted myself from the moment that they met at Redmoor, and I saw her clasp his hand as she did. But what is the use of asserting oneself, of putting one's position, one's conventional rights, against the perverted strength of a man's will? No, no; there is no security where the question is one of feeling; in the insecure holding of love we are but tenants-at-will."

She thought thus mournfully of her own lot, and condemned herself for faults she had not committed; she thought of Alsager, and took herself to task because she could not repress or deny the keen and compensating joy which the knowledge that he loved her gave; she thought of her husband with infinite compassion, with apprehension, and with hopelessness. The downward course had been run with awful rapidity by Sir Charles Mitford. Since he had discarded the gentle influence of Georgie, the benignant restraint, the touch of higher aspiration, and purer tastes had vanished, and he had returned to all the low habits and coarse vices of his earlier career. Georgie knew this vaguely, and she experienced all the horror and disgust which were natural to such a mind as hers. At first, when she recognized in the fullest extent the fact of her husband's infatuation with Mrs. Hammond, she could not understand why he should not be restrained by that passion, as he had been by his evanescent love for herself, from coarse and debasing pleasures. But she soon found out, by the light of her clear perceptions and the aid of her intuitive refinement of mind, how widely different were the sentiments which she had ignorantly compared; and learned that while there is no temporal salvation for a man so powerful as love, there is no swifter or surer curse and ruin than an illicit passion. When Georgie came to understand this fully, her apprehensions concerning her husband reached a height of intensity which would have been unreasonable, had she not possessed the painful knowledge of what his former career had been. She had hardly understood it at the time indeed, and her father had softened matters down very much, partly through the invincible amiability of his own disposition, and partly because he believed, in simple sincerity, that all "Charley's" misbehaviour had been caused by want of money alone; and that once rich, and holding a responsible position, he would not again be assailed by temptations to disreputable conduct. Whence it is presumable that the good parson knew a great deal more of the next world than he knew of this.

Lady Mitford's dreary reverie was interrupted by the entrance of her maid, who handed her a letter from Alsager. As she took it in her hand, she saw that it had been sealed with the ring which she had given him, and she broke it open with mingled joy and fear. The letter was brief, kind, and earnest. Sir Laurence told her that he was leaving England, and wished, before doing so, to place within her reach a source of consolation which he felt she might to surely need. Then, in a few words, he told her of his letter to Helen Manningtree; and besought her in any emergency, in any unpleasantness, if she were ill, or even if she were only lonely,—as he knew she had cultivated no intimacies in her own circle,—to send for Helen. He had not waited for Helen's reply; he knew so well how warm and sincere an acquiescence in his request it would convey. He told her of the attachment existing between Helen and the curate, and said, "Had there been no other reason for my rejecting your advice, I knew she was, at the time of my father's death, virtually affianced to Cuthbert Farleigh."

Lady Mitford paused in her perusal of the letter at this point.

"Cuthbert Farleigh!" she repeated; "surely it must be the same—it must be poor papa's old pupil; how very odd, if it should be! If he had ever mentioned me before him at Knockholt, he would have remembered me."

Her thoughts strayed back to her childhood and her old home, and she sat absorbed in a reverie.

"How thoughtful he is for me!" she said to herself softly; "how truly considerate! I will obey him in this and in everything. I will make this young lady's acquaintance-not just yet, but later, when I am more composed."

And then she thought how delightful it would be to talk with Helen about Laurence; to hear from her all the particulars of his life at Knockholt; to make all those researches and studies which have such an ineffable attraction for loving hearts. There could be nothing wrong in this; men and angels might scrutinize her feelings towards Laurence Alsager, and find nothing to blame.

There was little more in the letter, which concluded with an expression of the warmest regard.

Lady Mitford felt happier for the receipt of this parting note from Sir Laurence. It seemed to decrease her loneliness—to surround her with an atmosphere of protection. Georgie had never associated much with women in her father's secluded parish. The inhabitants had been chiefly of the lower classes; and since she had emerged from the gushing schoolroom period, she had had none of those intimacies which make up so great a part of the happiness of young womanhood. Perhaps she had concentrated her affections in the object who had proved so unworthy all the more obstinately, and had lavished them upon him all the more unrestrainedly, because she had none of the lesser claimants for them.

She looked forward now with almost girlish pleasure to making Helen's acquaintance and winning her affections, as she determined she would try to do; and she was surprised at herself as she felt her spirits rising, and recognized in herself more energy and hopefulness than she had felt for a long time.

Time slipped away, weighted though it was with care, and brought no change in Sir Charles Mitford's evil life. The husband and wife rarely met now; and when they did, their casual association was distressing to Lady Mitford, and embarrassing to him. Their wealth, the magnitude and style of their establishment, and the routine of life among persons in their position, afforded them facilities for a complete and tacit estrangement, such as the pressure of narrow circumstances would have rendered impossible. They went their separate ways, and were more strange and distant to each other than the merest surface acquaintances. Lady Mitford was, as it was natural to suppose she would be, the last person to hear particulars of her husband's conduct; but she watched him as closely as her limited opportunities permitted. For some time she had observed that he seemed restless and unhappy, and that the moroseness and discontent, which had been early indications of his relapse from his improved condition, were trying to the household, and, on rare occasions when she had to encounter them, distressing to her. He had no air of triumph now; he had no assured complacency of manner; these were gone, and in their place were the symptoms of suffering, of incertitude, of disappointment.

"I suppose she is treating him unkindly," Lady Mitford thought. "It must be something concerning her which is distressing him; he does not care about anything else. He is so infatuated with her now, that I verily believe, when he drinks to the frightful excess he sometimes does, it is to stupify himself between the time he leaves her and the time he sees her again. Poor fellow! poor Charley!"

She pitied him now with her good and generous heart. Perhaps the time that she had foreseen was near—the time which she had once hoped for, and now dreaded, though prepared to meet it with all the dutifulness of her nature—the time when the wicked woman who had taken him from her, who had laid the fabric of her happiness low, would tire of him and discard him; and he would seek forgiveness from the wife he had so cruelly wronged.

The moodiness and moroseness, the restlessness and irritability of Sir Charles had been peculiarly noticeable for some time after Lady Mitford had received Sir Laurence's letter, and they had not failed to receive the imprecations of the servants'- hall. Lady Mitford had been aware that much information might have been obtained through that fruitful medium, but she would not at any time have deigned to have recourse to it; and would have shrunk from doing so with additional distaste just now, as she could not avoid perceiving that she was the subject of closer observation than usual on the part of the domestics, especially her own maid and Mr. Banks.

One day, when Lady Mitford returned from her solitary drive, and having alighted from her carriage, was passing through the hall, she was encountered by Captain Bligh, coming quickly from the library. She saluted him courteously, and was about to pass on, when he begged to be permitted to speak with her. She acquiesced, and they went upstairs and into the long drawing-room.

She knew in a moment that he had come to tell her bad news, and she nerved herself to bear it, whatever it might be, by a strong effort. He waited until she had seated herself, and then said:

"I fear, Lady Mitford, I can hardly escape some share of your displeasure, incurred by my having undertaken the mission which has brought me here to-day."

She looked at him, and turned very pale, but she remained quite silent and still.

"You look frightened, Lady Mitford. Pray don't fear anything. There is much to grieve you, but no cause for alarm."

"Sir Charles—" she stammered.

"Sir Charles is well; there is nothing of that sort the matter. But I have a painful task to fulfil. Lady Mitford, are you aware that Sir Charles has left London?"

She fell back in her seat, and deathlike cold crept through her. She did not faint, but a momentary sensation like fainting passed over her. Her eyes closed, and her hands grew cold and damp. It had come, then, the catastrophe! She was deserted; he had left England with that woman; and it was all over! She was to be alone, and he was utterly ruined; there was no hope, no rescue for him now!

Captain Bligh was not a person adapted to act with discretion in a crisis of this kind. He did not understand women's ways, as he was accustomed to proclaim. He had a kind heart, however, and it supplied the deficiencies of his judgment. He merely handed Lady Mitford a scent-bottle, and waited until she had recovered herself. After a few moments she sat upright and opened her eyes.

"That's right!" said the honest Captain encouragingly; "I knew you would bear it well; I knew you had such pluck. By Jove, I haven't forgotten the ponies!"

"Tell me what you came to say, Captain Bligh," said Lady Mitford. "I am quite strong now;" and she looked so.

"Well, the truth is, Lady Mitford, things have gone too far, and Sir Charles is conscious of the fact. I would not have done such a thing for any one in the world but him. He and I have always been good friends, though he has done many things I could hardly stand. You mustn't mind my not being polished,—I don't mean to be rude; but I have such unpleasant things to say, that, by Jove, I can't manage to say them pleasantly!" He floundered very much in his speech, and fidgeted distractingly; but she sat quite still and listened to him. At last he blurted out desperately, "The truth is, that she-devil Laura Hammond has driven him mad! She has snubbed him, and tried to throw him over, and gone off to Baden without letting him know."

"Without letting him know! Then they are not gone together? I thank God!" said Georgie emphatically.

"Gone together! No; she never would be such a fool as that, whatever he might be. I beg your pardon, Lady Mitford. She has gone, as he believes, with the intention of throwing him off entirely, and trying it on with Tchernigow the Russian, you know; and Mitford would not stand it, and he has gone. He heard something last night which exasperated him, and he came to my rooms this morning—only a small portmanteau with him—and told me he was going. He told me to come down here, and send Banks off to-night with his things. I said everything I could think of, but it was no use,—he was simply desperate. Then, Lady Mitford"—and here Captain Bligh lowered his voice, and spoke with great gentleness-"then I asked him if he remembered the consequences of this to you."

"To me, Captain Bligh! What worse consequences can come to me than have come already?"

"Many, Lady Mitford, and much worse. You cannot live any longer under the same roof with Sir Charles; the scandal is too open and too great. He will disgrace himself, and make himself ridiculous at Baden, if much more serious mischief does not ensue; and you must keep aloof from the scandal."

"I am as much aloof from it as I can be here, I think, Captain Bligh," said poor Georgie; "and I will not leave my husband's house until he bids me. He may find that his going to Baden is useless; if she is resolved to discard him, she will do so as resolutely and as effectually there as here. No, Captain Bligh; this is my home, and here I will remain until I see the end of this matter. I will not forsake him, as he has forsaken me, at the beginning of it; I will not heap additional disgrace upon him, and give this story additional publicity, by leaving his house, unless he has told me, through you, to do so."

"No, no, Lady Mitford," said Bligh; "he has not done that. He begged of me to come to you, and tell you that he had gone. He would not try to deceive you, he said; if he could induce her to allow him to remain with her, he would, and never return to England. Yes, indeed,—so far had his madness driven him: but at all events he would never ask you to see him again; and whatever arrangements you might choose to make, he would be quite prepared to carry into effect. He said he supposed you would not remain here."

"He was mistaken," she said, very quietly and sadly; "I will remain here. Tell me what more passed between you, Captain Bligh."

"Indeed, not much, dear Lady Mitford. He was dreadfully excited and wretched, and looked fearfully ill,—he had been drinking deeply last night, I am sure,—and his manner was agitated and incoherent. He talked of his persecutions and his miseries, as every man who has the best blessings of life at his command and throws them away does talk; and his lamentations about this cursed infatuation of his were mixed up with self-reproaches on your account, and imprecations on the men who have tabooed him, and especially because he was rejected at the Maecenas."

"Poor Charles!" said Lady Mitford musingly; "all the enemies he has ever had could have done him little harm, had he not doubled in his own person the strength of his enemies to injure him. He began ill; and when he made an effort to do well, some gloomy recollection, some haunting fear, always seemed to keep him back. There was some evil power over him, Captain Bligh, before this woman laid her spells upon him—a power which made him moody and wretched and reckless. This was a subject upon which it was impossible for me to speak to him; and I accounted for it easily enough, and I have no doubt with tolerable correctness. You know, and I know, that the early years of Sir Charles's life were full of dark days and questionable associations. He was unfortunate at least as much as guilty; and not the smallest of the misfortunes of such a career is the power it gives to miscreants of every kind to embitter one's future and tarnish one's fame, to blight the hopes and the efforts with which one endeavours to rise above the mud-deposit of follies and sins repented and abandoned. There has never been a case, I am sure, in which a man who had gone extensively wrong, and who then tried to go right, and got a good chance of doing it, was not pursued and persecuted by harpies of the old brood, whose talons perpetually branded him, and whose inexorable pursuit kept him constantly depressed and miserable. Then he will be driven to excitement, to dissipation, to anything—which will enable him to forget the torture; but this very necessity deprives all his efforts of vigour, and renders him hopeless of success. I am confident that some such merciless grinding misery lay hidden in Sir Charles's life. I saw it very shortly after we came to town; and I had reason to suspect that he met with some annoyance of the same kind down at Redmoor. But he never told me, and there is no good in our speculating upon any matter of this kind. I can hardly consider myself entitled now to inquire into any affair of his. Did he give you any instructions, Captain Bligh? did he give you any address?"

"No," replied the good-natured Captain, quite saddened and distressed to witness her misery, and moved at the same time to great simple admiration by her composure and firmness, which the Captain denominated "pluck." "He did not say many words to me. He told me to come here and tell you what I have told you, and he said he would write. Let me leave you now, dear Lady Mitford, and let me return to-morrow and take your commands."

"Thank you," she said simply; and then he left her; and perhaps in the whole course of his chequered existence, and among his numerous and varied experiences, he had never felt so much pure and deep respect for any woman as for the deserted wife to whom he had had to disclose the full measure of her sorrow.

The days passed, and no tidings of Sir Charles Mitford came. Georgie had seen Banks, and had given him some directions relative to the things which Sir Charles required him to take to Baden, in an unconcerned and dignified manner, which had impressed that functionary as much as her conduct of the previous day had affected Captain Bligh.

"She's a deal too good for Mitford, and always was, even before he took to brandy and that ere Laurer 'Ammond," soliloquized Mr. Banks; "and I hope, for my part, he'll never come back."

Mr. Banks left town early in the morning of the day which succeeded the interview between Lady Mitford and Captain Bligh, and Georgie remained in her own rooms the entire day. An agitated restlessness was upon her, a feeling of suspense and apprehension, which deprived her of the power of thinking consecutively, and distracted her sorrow by changing its character. She expected to see Captain Bligh, and in her confused state of mind she had forgotten to say that no other visitors were to be admitted. At three in the afternoon, as she was sitting in her boudoir, striving, quite ineffectually, to fix her attention on some piece of feminine industry, a servant announced,

"Miss Gillespie."

Lady Mitford heard the name with unbounded astonishment. At first she associated no idea whatever with it; she felt certain she had never known any one so designated. But before the bearer of the name entered the room, she had remembered the handsome young woman whose superb singing and sudden disappearance had occasioned so much wonder and discussion at Redmoor. The association of ideas was not pleasant; and it was with a heightened colour, and something in her manner different from its customary graceful sweetness, that she rose to receive her unlooked-for visitor.

Miss Gillespie was looking very handsome; and the agitation under which she was evidently labouring had not the usual effect of destroying ease and gracefulness. She had always been quiet, and to a certain extent ladylike in her manners. Even in the Lizzie-Ponsford days she had not degenerated into the coarseness which might have been supposed to be an inevitable attendant or result of such a career. The ease and rapidity with which she had mastered the high-comedy style of performance, the finish of her acting, and the perfect appreciation of the refinement and repose which mark the demeanour of the true *grande dame*, afforded ample proof of Miss Gillespie's tact and readiness. She had needed only the accessories, and now she had procured them; and as she walked slowly and gracefully up to the spot where Lady Mitford stood to receive her, her rich and elegant but studiously-simple dress, her courteous gesture of salutation, and her nicely-modulated voice were all perfect.

"I daresay you have forgotten me, Lady Mitford," said she, "though you were very kind indeed to me when I accompanied my employers to your house at Redmoor; and your kindness made my position very different from what it had ever been before under similar circumstances."

"Pray be seated, Miss Gillespie," said Lady Mitford, softened by her respectful and graceful manner; "I am very glad to know that you have any pleasant recollections of your visit to Redmoor."

"But you are at a loss to account for my seeking you here, Lady Mitford, and venturing to call upon you without having first asked and obtained your permission."

Georgie's nature was so truthful that even the little every-day conventional matter-of-course falsehoods of society refused to come trippingly from her tongue. She was surprised at Miss Gillespie's visit, and she had let it appear that she was.

"If I am at a loss to account for your visit," she said, in her own sweet persuasive manner, "do not therefore suppose that it is not agreeable to me. I am very glad to see you, Miss Gillespie; and I hope it was not any unhappy circumstance which obliged you to leave Redmoor so abruptly at that time."

"One of the objects of my visit to you to-day, Lady Mitford, is to explain my conduct on that occasion. I am sure you will be infinitely surprised to learn that you were nearly, though unconsciously, concerned in it."

"I, Miss Gillespie! Surely I had not done anything—nothing had occurred at Redmoor—"

"No, no; you mistake my meaning, which, indeed, I must explain, if you will permit me to do so, by telling you a long story. Have I your permission, Lady Mitford?"

Georgie's astonishment was increasing. She marked the earnest gaze her strange visitor fixed upon her. She saw how her face softened and glowed as she looked at her. She knew that this young woman had a kindly feeling towards her; and she was so lonely, so deserted, that she felt grateful for that, though the person who bestowed it upon her was only a humble governess. She stretched out her hand by a sudden impulse, and Miss Gillespie caught and kissed it with intense fervour.

"You shall stay with me as long as you please, and tell me all your story, Miss Gillespie. I have done nothing to deserve the interest I see you feel in me; but I thank you for it."

Her visitor did not immediately reply: she sat looking at Georgie's face, more beautiful in its expression of grief and courage than when it was at its brightest, as though she were learning the features by heart. Lady Mitford blushed a little under the scrutiny, and smiled, as she said:

"You look at me very earnestly, Miss Gillespie. What is there in my face to fix your attention?"

"There is everything that I once did not believe in, while I longed to see it. There is beauty, Lady Mitford—well, I have seen enough of that; but there is truth and gentleness, sweet self-forgetfulness, and an impulse of kindness to everything that lives and feels and can suffer. The first time I saw that face I thought of the common saying about the face of an angel; but I soon ceased to think it was like that. Angels are in heaven, where their sinless and sorrowless sphere lies. Such women as you are on earth, to teach those who, standing far off, see them, to hope, and believe, and take comfort, because they exist and have their part in the same troubled world with themselves, but always bringing the image and the ideal of a better nearer, and making it real."

Her voice trembled, and tears stood in her eyes. Georgie wondered more and more.

"When I have told you my story, Lady Mitford," she went on, "you will be able to understand in a degree—you never could quite comprehend it—the effect that such a woman as you produces upon such a woman as I; for I studied you more closely than you could have suspected in that brief time at Redmoor; and I hold a clue to your history, of whose existence you were ignorant."

"Do not tell me anything that it will pain you to repeat, Miss Gillespie," said Georgie, seeing that she hesitated and changed colour.

"In that case I should tell you nothing, Lady Mitford; for there is little in my life that has not been painful. I daresay you would find it difficult to realize, if I could put it before you in the plainest words; and I am sure, even if you did realize it, you would judge it mercifully—you would remember the difficulties and the dangers of such an existence, and suffer them to have their weight as against its sins and sorrows. You know what it is to be motherless, Lady Mitford; but yours was a guarded childhood, hedged about with pious care and fatherly love,—they told me all about you down at Redmoor. Mine was a motherless childhood; and my father was a thief, and the companion of thieves. This is the simple English of the matter. You would not understand the refinements and distinctions by which the dishonest classes describe their different ranks in the army of thieves; you could not comprehend the scenes and the influences among which my childhood was passed; and I will not try to explain them, because they have no bearing upon what it concerns you to hear."

She had rested her arm upon a table beside her chair, and supported her head on her hand.

"My wretched childhood had passed by, and my more wretched girlhood had reached its prime, when I was brought in contact with Sir Charles Mitford."

Georgie recoiled, turned very red, and uttered an exclamation.

"I was associated at that time with some men who made their livelihood in a number of dishonest ways; and one of them had in his possession a document, by means of which he had maintained a hold over Mitford, then a young man of small means and very indirect expectations. The man I speak of died, and accident placed me in possession of the document. It was a forged bill!"

Lady Mitford covered her face with her hands; and as Miss Gillespie continued, the slow tears began to force their way through the slender fingers.

"Others knew of the existence of this bill, Lady Mitford, and I have no doubt whatever that they traded upon their knowledge. Every effort, direct and indirect, was made to get the bill out of my possession; but I resolved to keep it, and every effort failed. Perhaps I might have used it for my own purposes against Sir Charles some day, if I had never seen or known you. It is certain that I should have given it to him, and set him free for ever from an apprehension which constantly beset and tortured him, had I not known how unworthily he was treating you, how completely all the hard lessons of his life of poverty and shifts had failed to correct his low instincts and his utter untrustworthiness. Don't cry, dear Lady Mitford,—your tears pain me keenly; I must draw them forth a little while, and then I trust to dry them.

"I saw Sir Charles when he first visited Mrs. Hammond at Torquay. By that time I had drifted to land somehow, and I had contrived to get my wandering feet within the confines of respectability. I was quiet, even happy, in Mrs. Hammond's employment, though I soon perceived her to be the most worthless of her sex. That, however, troubled me little; and when Sir Charles came to the house and recognized me, and I said a few words to him which were not pleasant to hear, and I saw that he was in the toils, as—he had so often been before, I did not much care either. I disliked and despised him, and I liked to think of the hidden weapon in my possession, and to picture his amazement if he knew that not only was I Lizzie Ponsford,—acquainted with all his doings and all his disreputable associates,—but that I actually held in my possession the document for which he would have given so large a price, and which would have ruined him at any moment. I liked to know that my presence made him uncomfortable, and I suffered him to experience that discomfort to the fullest extent.

"You are shocked, Lady Mitford; such feelings are incomprehensible to you but I tell you simply and plainly that they were mine, because I am coming to the portion of lay story which concerns you. I went to Redmoor with Mrs. Hammond, and on the first evening of our visit I saw that you were suspicious and uneasy. I saw you, Lady Mitford; I observed you closely, and I loved you; not so much as I did afterwards, when every day brought some gift, some grace, some beauty of your mind and disposition freshly before me; not so much as I did when your sweet gentleness, your kindly courtesy, your unfailing consideration filled me with sentiments which I had never known before, when for the first time I learned what it was to be cared for as an individual. Do you remember the day you took me to your dressing-room, Lady Mitford, and lent me some of your favourite books, and talked with me of what kind of reading I liked, and showed an interest in me, as if I had been a lady and one of your most considered guests? No, you do not remember it, but I do. Then I determined to use the power I had over him on your behalf. I knew it would not avail long; I knew if even he were rescued from her, he never could realize your hopes, never could be worthy of you; but at least I could control him for the time. I tried and succeeded. I threatened him with exposure if he did not desist. I cannot tell you exactly the course of subsequent events; I have never been able to make that out to my own satisfaction; but I have a theory which I think is a right one. A few days after I had the interview I have mentioned with Sir Charles, a man appeared who had been mixed up in many of the transactions of the time past to which I had been a party. He met me, und told me a story which I did not believe, but which altered my position completely. He had come down to get me away; and whether he came as Sir Charles's *employé* or on his own account, I have never been certain. I believe the latter to be the more likely. He had two alternatives at his command: he might expose me if I refused to leave Redmoor quietly, and destroy all my hopes of attaining respectability in future, or he might take the bill from me by force or fraud, if I yielded to his threats. I did neither; I temporized; I made an appointment with him for two o'clock on the following day, and I left Redmoor, without clue by which I could be tracked, at daybreak. Let who would be the author of Mr. Effingham's proceeding (he called himself Effingham), I had balked their scheme, and I turned my back on Redmoor with one bitter pang of regret mingled with my triumph. I should see your face, Lady Mitford, no more, and I could no longer interfere to prevent the deadly wrong which was being done by your faithless husband and your false friend.

"All such regrets were, however, utterly vain. The imminent risk of exposure left me no choice. At least I would punish Sir Charles so far: he should never have the bill—he should never have the satisfaction of feeling that that ghost was laid. So I left the only place in which I had ever tasted happiness, and set my face to the hard world again. But before I stole away from your house that morning, I wrote a line to Colonel Alsager, and told him to take up the watch I had been obliged to relinquish. You are astonished, Lady Mitford; and well you may be. I had never exchanged more than a dozen sentences with Colonel Alsager; but I knew that the interest he felt in you was in no way inferior to mine; while his opportunities of exhibiting it were infinitely greater, and so I wrote to him."

"What did you do, Miss Gillespie, when you left Redmoor? I fear you had very little money. Forgive me if I offend you, but I gathered that from something Mrs. Hammond said."

"You are right, Lady Mitford; and it is like you to think of a need which you have never known. I *had* very little money; but I had a friend who put me in the way of earning some—how, I will tell you when I have finished the portion of my story in which you are interested."

The gentle look of forbearance and compassion in Georgie's face seemed to touch Miss Gillespie very deeply. Once more she took her hand and kissed it. Then she continued:

"I went to America, and for a long time I heard nothing of you, though I longed most ardently to do so. The echoes of the great world did not reach me in the distant sphere of my toil, and I longed to know how the only person with whom I had ever felt true human sympathy was wearing through her day. This may seem to you an unnatural and overstrained sentiment; and so it would be in the mind of any one who had any natural ties, or who was less desolate than I; but you must be able to comprehend my life before you could understand these inconsistencies. Let me leave this, then, unexplained, and tell you that I came back to England, and that I have heard all that has befallen you since I went away. I have never felt anything that has happened to myself in my vagabond life so much. Incidents I heard, but no one could tell me anything of you individually,—of how you were bearing your trials, of what face you showed the world, which would coldly criticise you—a creature as far beyond its comprehension as any angel in the heaven far beyond their sphere."

She spoke with intense feeling, and her fine face glowed with the depth of her sympathy and admiration.

"At last I caught sight of Colonel Alsager."

Georgie blushed, but her visitor did not appear to observe her emotion.

"I knew he could tell me what I thirsted to know, and I went to his hotel on the following day, but failed to see him; and when I sent a note, asking him to let me speak a few words with him, it was returned. Colonel Alsager had left town. I learned that his father was dead, and he, of course, a baronet now; but I heard nothing further—no one could tell me if his absence were likely to be prolonged. I had the strongest, the most insatiable desire to see you, Lady Mitford. I wanted to see the face that I had never forgotten, and find it as beautiful, as good as ever."

Georgie smiled sadly "Ah, Miss Gillespie, I have suffered much, and am greatly changed."

"Only for the better," she said eagerly; "only for the better. Every line in your face is lighted up with spiritual light now. When I saw it last, the girlish softness had not left the features and given the expression fair play."

Her enthusiasm—her feeling—were so real, and there was such a strong dash of the artist in her remarks, that it would have been impossible to resent them. Lady Mitford once more smiled sadly.

"I knew there was no chance that I should see you in any public place—your deep mourning precluded that possibility—and so I resolved to come here and present myself boldly before you. In the ordinary sense of society, between you and me there is a gulf fixed; but I thought your gentleness would span it. It has done so. You have permitted me to speak to you face to face; you have gratified the wish which another might have resented as mere insolent curiosity."

"Why do you speak thus, Miss Gillespie? Why should there be a gulf between you and me? I am not aware of any reason. I do not despise you because you are a governess, because you use the talents and the education you possess to earn an honourable livelihood. Why do you speak thus?"

Miss Gillespie looked at her, and an expression of deep suffering crossed her face.

"I will explain my meaning presently," she said; "but now I have something else to say. Is it true that Sir Charles Mitford has followed this woman to Baden? They say so at the clubs, and I heard it this morning. Pardon me, and tell me. I don't ask the question for my own sake, or out of idle curiosity. I have a serious, a most serious meaning."

"Yes, it is too true," said Lady Mitford.

"Then listen. He must be brought back: he is only gone to mortification and ridicule. I know a great many queer people, and I hear a great many strange things; and I heard this to-day: Mrs. Hammond is going to marry the Russian Prince

Tchernigow, a man who is a violent, jealous, brutal wretch,—I know all about him,—a man whose cruelty and vindictiveness are not to be surpassed; her punishment is in safe hands Dear Lady Mitford, I understand that look. You don't wish her to be punished, I am sure—quite sure of that; but if she marries Tchernigow, she must be. But it is not with that we are concerned: it is to bring *him* home—to rescue him from danger and disgrace and ridicule, for your sake; and you can do it—you, and you only."

Georgie was breathless with astonishment. Miss Gillespie rose and caught her by both hands. Then she went on speaking with great rapidity:

"Yes, I say you can do it. Write to him to-day—now, this very hour-and tell him Lizzie Ponsford has been with you; that *she* holds the bill which he employed that poor wretch Effingham to get for him; that Effingham cheated him from first to last—from the time of the Albatross till the day he went to the bottom of the sea with the Pocahontas. Tell him he shall have it placed in his hands on the day he returns to London. Your letter will reach him when he has learned the faithlessness of the woman for whom he has betrayed you. Do you not think it will touch him, written as you will write it,—with the gentleness, the pity, the pardon it will convey? At the moment of his greatest exasperation, in the full tide of his bitterness, a way of escape from one constant, overhanging, torturing cause of uneasiness will be removed; and by whose hands? Yours!"

She paused, breathless in her excitement, and took from her bosom a paper, which she laid on the table before Lady Mitford, who looked at it pale and trembling.

"You will do as I say, dear Lady Mitford—you will do it for his sake, and your own, and for mine? Let me have the satisfaction of knowing that I have been able to do this service for you—the only service I have ever done any one; the only one. I fear, I have ever wished to do."

"O no, don't say that," said Lady Mitford. "You misjudge yourself; I am sure you do, dear Miss Gillespie, or why should you have felt so much for me, and done me such a service? Do not write hard things against yourself. I will do this—it may succeed; but whether it succeeds or not, I shall ever be grateful to you, ever bless you for this act; and you will let me serve you in turn—you will tell me your wishes, and let me try to carry them out. You said you would tell me how you have been engaged since you left Redmoor."

"Thank you, dear Lady Mitford," said Miss Gillespie, in a low deep tone; "but you cannot serve me. I told you there was a gulf fixed between you, the patrician lady, and me. I am an actress, and my stage-name is Constance Greenwood."

Lady Mitford wrote the letter to Sir Charles, as her strange visitor had counselled her to do. She suffered much in writing it; she hoped much from its effect. Time rolled on, and she knew that Sir Charles must have received the letter; then she counted the days which must elapse before the answer could arrive, and, arming herself with patience, she waited.

CHAPTER XXXI.

AMONG THE SPRINGS.

It was the month of September, and the little town of Baden was full. It is now the big town of Baden, and is still, during its season, filled to overflowing; but the company is by no means so select, so pleasant, so agreeable as it used to be. The *vor-eisenbahn* Baden was as superior to the present excursionists' resort as was the ante-railway Ascot Meeting to what now is merely a succession of Derby-days in Bucks. Then, when you posted in from Strasburg, or arrived in the *eilwagen*, from deadly-lively Carlsruhe, you found Mr. Rheinboldt, the landlord of the Badischer Hof, attended by the stoutest, the best-tempered, and the stupidest even of German porters, coming forward to meet you with the pleasantest of greetings. You had written on beforehand if you were a wise man, and your old room was ready—one of that little row of snug dormitories set apart for bachelors, and looking on to the trim garden. You had a wash, with more water than you had met with since you left home (they were beginning to understand the English mania for soap-and-water at the Badischer Hof even so long ago), and you made your toilette and came down to the five-o'clock *table-d'hôte*, where you found most of the people who had been there the previous season, and many of their friends whom they had induced to come. Most of the people knew each other or of each other, and there was a sociability among them which the railway has utterly annihilated. Now London sends her bagmen and Paris her *lorettes*; but in those days, if "our Mr. Johnson" got as far as Parry by way of Cally or Bolong, he was looked upon as an intrepid voyager, while very few Parisian ladies, save those of the best class, came into the Grand Duke's territory.

It was hot in England in that September, but it was hotter at Baden. With the earliest dawn came thick vapours rolling down from the Black Forest, encompassing the little town with a white and misty shroud, which invariably presaged a sultry day, and invariably kept its promise. All day long the big red-faced sun glared down upon the denizens of the pleasantest corner of Vanity Fair; glared in the early morning upon the water-drinkers sipping the nauseous fluid in the thick and heavy glass tumblers, and tendering their kreutzers to the attendant maidens at the Brunnen; glared upon them as they took the prescribed constitutional walk, and returned to the hotel to breakfast; glared upon the fevered gamblers, who, with last night's excitement only half slept off, with bleared eyes and shaking hands and parched throats, took their places round the gaming-table as the clock struck noon, and eyed the stolid-faced croupiers as intently as though the chances of the game were to be gleamed from a perusal of their fishy eyes or pursed mouths. The revellers who were starting off for picnics to the Black Forest, or excursions to the Favourite or Eberstein-Schloss, glanced up with terror at the scorching red ball in the sky, and bade courteous Mr. Rheinboldt, the landlord of the Badischer Hof, to see that plenty of ice was packed with the sparkling Moselle, and to let Karl and Fritz take care that an unlimited supply of umbrellas was placed in the carriage. The Englishmen, whom M. Benazet, the proprietor of the gaming-tables, grateful for their patronage, had provided with shooting, or who had received invitations to the *triebjagd* of some neighbouring landowner, looked with comic wonder, not unmixed with horror, at the green jerkins, fantastic game-bags, *couteaux de chasse* or hunting-knives (worn in the belt), and general appearance of their foreign friends; and then when lunch-time arrived, and they saw each German eating his own sausage and drinking from his own particular flask, which he never dreamed of passing, they recollected with dismay the luncheons at similar parties in England, the snowy cloth laid under the shade of the hedge, the luscious game-pie, the cooling claret-cup, the glancing eyes and natty ankles of those who had accompanied the luncheon. Hot! It was no word for it. It was blazing, tearing, drying, baking, scorching heat, and it was hotter at Baden than anywhere else.

So they said at least, and as they were from almost every part of the civilized world, they ought to have known. There were English people, swells, peers and peeresses, bankers and bankeresses, a neat little legal set,—Sir Nisey and Lady Prious, Mr. Tocsin, Q.C., Mr. Serjeant Stentor, and some of the junior members of the bar,— a select assortment of the Stock-Exchange, and some eligible young men from the West-end government offices. There were joyous Russians, whose names all ended in "vitch" and "gorod," and were otherwise utterly unpronounceable, who spoke all European languages with equal fluency and facility, and who put down *rouleaux* of Napoleons on the roulette-table where other people staked thalers or florins. There were a few Frenchmen and French ladies; here was an Austrian gross-herzog or grand-duke, there some Prussian cavalry subalterns who could not play at the table because they had spent the half-crown of their daily allowance in roast veal, Bairisch beer, and a horrible compound called "grogs an rhum," which they drank at night, "after," as they said to themselves, "the English fashion."

It had been hotter than ever during the day, but the day was happily past and over, and the moon was streaming on the broad gravelled Platz in front of the Conversationshaus, and the band, stationed in the little oil-lamp-illumined kiosk, were rattling away at Strauss's waltzes and Labitskey's galops. The gamblers were already thronging the *roulette* and *trente-et-quarante* tables; and of the non-gamblers all such as had ladies with them were promenading and listening to the music, while the others were seated, drinking and smoking. It was a splendid evening; the diners at the late *tables-d'hôte* were wending their way from their hotels to the promenade; the consumers of the German *mittagsessen*, were listening to the band in delicious anticipation of the *reh-braten* and the *haring-salad* and the *bok-bier*, or the Ahrbleichart, at which another half-hour would see them hard at work; the clamouring for coffee was incessant, and the head-waiter, Joseph, who was so like Bouffé, was almost driven out of his wits by the Babel of voices. They chattered, those tall occupants of the little wooden round-tables—how they chattered! They turned round and stared at the promenaders, and made their comments on them after they had passed. They had something to say, some remark, either complimentary or disparaging, to make upon all the ladies. But there was only one man who seemed to attract any special attention, and that was the Russian Prince Tchernigow.

A man of middle height, with brown-black hair, a perfectly bloodless complexion, stern deeply sunken eyes, a stiff moustache bristling over a determined mouth. A man with small hands and feet, and apparently but little muscular development, but strong, brave, and vindictive. A man whose face Lavater might have studied for months without getting beyond the merest rudiments of his science—impassive, unaltering, statuesque. He never played but with rouleaux of napoleons—twenty in a rouleau; and though the space in front of him was shining with gold at one moment, or laid bare by the sweeping rake of the croupier,—winning or losing, his expression would not change for an instant. He had been to Baden for two or three seasons running, and was beginning to be looked upon as an *habitué*; the croupiers acknowledged his taking his seat, intending to do battle, by a slight grave bow; he had broken the bank more than once, and was a lion among the visitors, and notably amongst the English. Tchernigow's horses and carriages, his bold play, his good shooting, the wonderful way in which he spoke our language, his love of solitude, his taciturnity, his singular physique, were all freely discussed at the late *tables-d'hôte* of hotels at which the prince was not staving. His reputation of *beau joueur* caused him to be followed as soon as he was seen going into the rooms, and his play was watched and humbly imitated by scores. He seldom attended the balls, and very rarely danced, though he valsed to perfection; and all the women in the room were eager for his selection. His appearance on the promenade always excited attention, but he never gave the smallest sign of having observed it.

Among those who looked up as Prince Tchernigow passed was Lord Dollamore, who was seated at one of the tables, with no companion save his invariable one—his stick. Dollamore generally came to Baden every year. The place amused him; it was a grand field for the display of the worst passions of human nature,—a study which always afforded him infinite delight. He never played, but he was constantly hovering round the tables; and there was scarcely an incident which happened in the seething crowd, scarcely a change which swept across the faces of the leading actors, that passed unnoticed by him. He did not dance; he would have been prevented by his lameness from indulging in such a pastime, even had his taste impelled him to it; but he was a constant attendant at the balls which M. Benazet provided for the amusement of his patrons; and looking on at the actual life before him as he might have looked on the mimic life of a theatrical representation, he had innumerable conferences with his stick on all he saw and heard, and on the arguments which he deduced therefrom. He immensely enjoyed being seated, as he was then, in the calm autumnal moonlit evening, with a cup of excellent coffee by his side, a cigar in his mouth, and the ever-shifting panorama of human faces passing before him.

"That Tchernigow is really delicious!" he said to himself—or to his stick—as he looked after the Russian, and marked the excitement which he created; "there's a savage insolence about him which is positively refreshing in these days of bowing and scraping and preposterous politeness. How they chatter, and gape, and nudge each other with their elbows about him! and what a supreme indifference he affects to it all! Affects? Yes, *mon prince*, it is accepted as the real thing by these good people, but we are not to be taken in by veneer, *nous autres*! It would require a very small scratch indeed to pick off the Petersburg-cum-Paris polish, and to arrive at the genuine Calmuck substratum. Only to look at you to tell that Nature's handwriting never lies; and if ever there were a more delightfully truculent, ruffianly, bloodthirsty savage than yourself, *mon prince*, I am very much out in my ideas. God help the woman on whom you ever get a legitimate hold! Ah, that reminds me—what has become of the widow? There is no doubt that Tchernigow was badly hit in London. The only man received at her house, the only man permitted to assuage her grief, to wipe away those tears which doubtless flowed so constantly for poor Percy Hammond! What an audacious little devil it is! How pluckily she fought that business of guardianship to the child; and how gracefully she retired from the contest when she saw that she had no chance, and that defeat was inevitable! She's the cleverest woman, in a certain way, that I've ever met with; and I'd take my oath she's playing some long-headed, far-sighted game now, and that Tchernigow is the stake. No more flirtation and coquetry—for the present—*les eaux sont bases*; the widow is hard up, and means to *recoup* herself by a rich marriage. That's why that infatuated cad Mitford was snubbed so severely. I think she comprehends that Tchernigow will stand no nonsense, and as he is the *parti* at present in view, his will is law. She can't have given up the chase; but how on earth is she working it?"

A smart natty-looking little man in evening-dress, with smoothly-brushed hair and elaborately-trimmed whiskers, faint pink coral studs, little jean boots with glazed tips, irreproachable gloves, and a Gibus hat—a little man who looked as if he had just stepped out of a bandbox—stopped at Lord Dollamore's table, and with a bow, half-deferential, half-familiar, glided into the vacant chair.

"Ah, how do you do, Mr. Aldermaston?" said Lord Dollamore, looking up,—"how do you do? and what is the latest news in this Inferno?"

Every one who knew Mr. Aldermaston made a point of asking him the news, well knowing that they could apply to no better source for the latest gossip and tittle-tattle. Mr. Aldermaston nominally was private secretary to Lord Waterhouse, the First Commissioner at the Inland, Irrigation Office, and he had been selected for that onerous post for his distinguished personal appearance and his obsequious toadyism. It was not a situation involving a great deal of work, though any one noticing the regularity with which a large leather despatch-box, bearing a gilt crown, and "Charles Aldermaston, Esq., P.S., I.I.O.," was deposited for him by an official messenger in the hall of the Alfred Club, might have thought otherwise. The inferior portion of the duty was performed by a clerk, and Mr. Aldermaston contented himself with taking Lord Waterhouse's signature to a few papers occasionally, and receiving a select few of the most distinguished persons who wished for personal interviews. This left him plenty of leisure to pursue his more amusing occupation of purveyor of gossip and inventor and retailer of scandal. In these capacities he was without a rival. He always knew everything; and if he did not know it, he invented it, which in some respects was better, as it enabled him to flavour his anecdotes with a piquancy which was perhaps wanting in the original. He found occupation for his ears and tongue in a variety of topics; the heaviest subjects were not excluded, the lightest obtained a place in his *répertoire*. The rumour of the approaching change in the premiership, while passing through the Aldermaston crucible, encountered the report of Mademoiselle de la Normandie's refusal to dance her *pas seul* before Madame Rivière; the report of Lady Propagand's conversion to Romanism did not prevent Mr. Aldermaston's giving proper additional publicity to the whisper of Miss de Toddler's flight with the milkman.

There were not many people who liked Mr. Aldermaston, though there were a great many who feared him; but Lord Dollamore was among the former class. "He is a *blagueur*," Dollamore used to say; "and a *blagueur* is a detestable beast; but necessary to society; and Aldermaston is certainly clean. He knows how to behave himself, and is in fact an Ananias of polite society. Besides, he amuses me, and there are very few people in the world who amuse me."

So Lord Dollamore always spoke to Mr. Aldermaston at the club, and encouraged him to tell his anecdotes; and when he found him at Baden, he looked upon him as one of the resources of the place,-a purveyor of news infinitely fresher, more piquant, and more amusing than was to be found in the week-old *Times* or three-days-old *Galignani*, which he found at Misses Marx's library.

So he again repeated, "And what's the latest news in this Inferno, Mr. Aldermaston?"

"Well, there's very little news here, my lord, very little indeed; except that young Lord Plaidington is gone—sent away this morning."

"Sent away?"

"Yes; his mother, Lady Macabaw, wouldn't stand it any longer. Last night Lord Plaidington took too much again, and began throwing the empty champagne-bottles out of the window of the Angleterre; so Lady Macabaw sent him off this morning with his tutor, the Rev. Sandford Merton, and they've gone to Strasburg, on the way to Italy."

"Serve him right, the young cub. I went away early last night—any heavy play late?"

"Yes; a Frenchman whom no one had ever seen before won a hatful at roulette, and some Englishman whom no one seemed to know backed him and stood in. They looked like breaking the bank at one time, but they didn't."

"Was Tchernigow at the tables?"

"No; the Prince did not show up at all,—has not been there for the last three nights."

"So much the worse for Benazet; but what does it mean?"

"Well, I've a notion about that that I won't broach to any one but your Lordship. I think I've found the clue to that story."

"What story? what clue?"

"Prince Tchernigow's sudden cessation from play. You know what a mania it was with him. It must have been something special to make him give it up."

"And what is the something special?"

"A woman."

"Ah!" said Lord Dollamore, warming a once into interest; "*malheureux en jeu, heureux en amour,*—the converse of the ordinarily-received motto. Has Mademoiselle Féodor arrived from the Gaieté? or who is the siren that charms our Prince from the tables?"

"Mademoiselle Féodor has not arrived, but some one else has. A much more dangerous person than Mademoiselle Féodor, and with much more lasting hopes in view."

Lord Dollamore looked keenly at his companion, and said, "I begin to find the scent warming; but I make it a rule never to guess. Tell your story, Mr. Aldermaston, please."

"Well, you know, Lord Dollamore, I'm staying at the Russie, and I've made myself so agreeable to Malmedie, the landlord there, by little bits of civility, that he generally comes up to my room in the morning and lets me know all that is going on. He showed me a letter that he had about a week ago, written in French, saying that a lady wanted rooms reserved for herself and maid; that she would not dine at the *table-d'hôte*, being an invalid, and coming only for the benefit of the air and springs, but should require dinner and all her meals served in her own rooms. The French of the letter was excellent, but the idea of retirement looked essentially English. I never knew a Frenchwoman, in however bad a state of health, who could resist the attractions of society; so, though I said nothing to Malmedie, I guessed at once the lady was English; and as there seemed a mystery, I determined to penetrate it."

Lord Dollamore smiled, and whispered something to his stick; something of which the French word "*chiffonnier*" and the English word "garbage" were component parts; but Mr. Aldermaston did not hear the sentence, and only marking the smile, proceeded:

"They were expected on Wednesday afternoon, and I took care to be about. They came in the *eilwagen* from Carlsruhe,—a deuced fine-looking woman, with her face hidden in a thick black veil, and a very neat trim little French waiting-maid. The servant was French, but the boxes were English,—I'd take my oath of that. There was a substantial solidity about their make, a certainty about their locks and hinges, such as never yet was seen on a French box, I'll stake my existence."

"You have wonderful powers of observation, Mr. Aldermaston," said Dollamore, still grinning.

"Your lordship flatters me. I have a pair of eyes, and I think I can use them. I kept them pretty tightly fixed on the movements of the new-comers. Dinner was sent up to their rooms, but before it went up the lady's-maid went out. I was strolling about myself, with nothing to do just at that time, so I strolled after her. She went into the Angleterre, and in a few minutes came tripping out again. She went back to the Russie, and so did I. I had nothing to do, and sat down in the porch, behind one of those tubs with the orange-trees, to smoke a cigar. While I was smoking it, who should come up but Prince Tchernigow?"

"Prince Tchernigow!" cried Lord Dollamore. "*Connu!* I'm in full cry now, Mr. Aldermaston. But continue your story."

"Prince Tchernigow," continued Mr. Aldermaston, "and no one else. He asked for Madame Poitevin, in which name the rooms had been taken, and he was shown upstairs. He came the next day twice, twice yesterday; he was there this morning; and just now, as I came away from the *table-d'hôte*, I met him on the steps going in."

"Mr. Aldermaston, you are *impayable!*" said Dollamore. "I must pay a compliment to your perspicacity, even at the risk of forestalling the conclusion of your narrative. But you have told it so admirably, that no man with a grain of sense in his head could avoid seeing that Madame Poitevin is Mrs. Hammond."

"Exactly,—I have not a doubt of it," said the little man; "and if so, I think you and I, my lord, know some one whose state of mind must be awful."

"Yes," said Lord Dollamore, rising from his chair; "I see what you mean, and you are doubtless right. Poor Percy Hammond's relatives must feel it acutely. Goodnight, Mr. Aldermaston;" and he bowed and moved off.

"I'm not going to let that little cad indulge in any speculations about the Mitfords," said he to his stick. "That woman's far too good to be discussed by such vermin as that;" by which we may judge that Lord Dollamore's opinion of Lady Mitford had altered as his acquaintance with her had progressed.

The deductions which Mr. Aldermaston had made from this last experiment in espionage were tolerably correct. Laura Hammond was in Baden under the name of Madame Poitevin, and accompanied by the never-failing Marcelline.

She had hurried away from London for two reasons. The first, and by far the most important, was to perfect the conquest of Tchernigow; to clinch home that iron band which for the last two months she had been fitting round the Russian's neck; to bring him to make the offer of his hand at once. The short time passed in London since her husband's death had been spent in looking her future boldly in the face, and calculating within herself how she should mould it for the best. Lord Dollamore was right in one of his conjectures about her: she had made up her mind that the course of her life must henceforth be entirely altered. She knew well enough that even the short time she had been away from London and its world was sufficient to render her name almost forgotten; and she determined that when it was next mentioned it should be in a very different tone from that formerly adopted towards it. Respectability—that state so often sneered at and ridiculed by her—she now held in the highest veneration, and determined to attain to. She had her work to do; to restore herself in the world's good opinion, and to make, as soon as decency would permit, a good marriage. The last position gained, the first would necessarily follow. All she had to do, she thought, was to keep herself in seclusion and choose her intended victim.

She thought of Sir Laurence Alsager at once. She had yet for him a remnant of what she imagined was love, but what was really thwarted passion. Her feelings were stronger for him than for any other man; and he had large wealth, and a good old family title, and the good opinion of the world. When, after his interview with her, she saw the utter futility of her plans so far as he was concerned, she was enraged, but by no means defeated. The cast must be made in another direction, and at once. Prince Tchernigow was in town; she knew it, for she had had more than one note from him during her seclusion in the country, and she knew that Tchernigow was hanging on in town on the chance of seeing her. This flashed across her the moment Laurence had quitted her, and her heart gave a great leap. That was the man! He was a prince; he was three times as rich as Alsager, and was known in the best society of every capital in Europe. Life with him as his wife would not be spent buried two-thirds of the year in a great gaunt country-place, where interest in the Sunday-schools and the old women and the clergyman's charities were the excitements; life with him would be one round of gaiety, in which she would not be a follower, but a leader. He had been madly in love with her two years before; and from what she knew of his nature, she believed the passion still remained there. That could be easily ascertained. She would write him a note, bidding him to come and see her.

Tchernigow came at once. He had not been with Laura ten minutes before her sharp eyes had looked into his heart and read its secrets so far as she was concerned. He was chafing under a latent passion, a thwarted wish. When, just at the close of their companionship at Baden two years ago, he had ventured to make open protestation of his devotion to her, and she had turned on him with great dignity and snubbed him mercilessly, he had bowed and left her, cool and collected indeed in his manner, but inwardly raging like a volcano. He had never met with similar treatment. With him it was a question of throwing the handkerchief, to the delight of Nourmahal or whoever might be the lucky one towards whom his highness tossed it. The ladies of the *corps dramatique* of the different Parisian theatres were wild with delight when they heard that Tchernigow had arrived in Paris, and the will of *mon Cosaque*, as he was called by more than one, was supreme and indisputable among them. This was quite a new thing. Not merely to have his proffered love rejected, but to be soundly rated for having dared to proffer it, was to him almost inexplicable. It lashed him to fury. For the next season he kept away from London, determined to avoid the siren who held him in her toils, yet despised his suit. Then, hearing of her widowhood and her absence from London, he came to England with a half-formed determination in regard to her. He saw her, and almost instantaneously the smouldering fires of his passion were revivified, and blazed up more fiercely than ever.

He had more encouragement now, but even now not very much. He was permitted to declare his devotion to her, to rave in his odd wild way about her beauty, to kiss her hand on his arrival and departure—nothing more. Trust Laura Hammond for knowing exactly how to treat a man of Tchernigow's temperament. He came daily;

he sat feasting his eyes on her beauty, and listening—sometimes in wonder, but always in admiration—to her conversation, which was now sparkling with wit and fun, now brimming over with sentiment and pathos. Day by day he became more and more hopelessly entangled by her fascinations, but as yet he had breathed no word about marriage; and to that end, and that alone, was Laura Hammond leading him on. But when Parliament was dissolved, and town rapidly thinning; when Laura's solicitor had written urgently to her, stating that "the other side" was pressing for a final settlement of affairs—which meant her abdicating her state and taking up her lowered position on her lessened income—Tchernigow called upon her, and while telling her that he was going to Baden, seemed to do more than hint that her hopes would be fulfilled, if she would consent to meet him there so soon as her business was accomplished.

This was the principal motive which had induced her to start for the pretty little Inferno on the border of the Black Forest. But the other was scarcely less cogent. The fact was, that Laura was wearying rapidly of the attentions of Sir Charles Mitford. Her *caprice* for him was over. He had never had the power of amusing her; and since she knew that Laurence Alsager had left England, she saw that she could no longer wreak her vengeance on him by punishing Lady Mitford through the faithlessness of Sir Charles. Mitford saw that she was growing weary of him—marked it in a thousand different ways, and raged against it. Occasionally his manner to her would change from what she now called maudlin tenderness to savage ferocity; he would threaten her vaguely, he would watch her narrowly. It required all Laura's natural genius for intrigue, supplemented by Madlle. Marcelline's adroitness, to prevent his knowing of Tchernigow's visits. In his blind infatuation he was rapidly forgetting the decencies of life, the *convenances* of society; he was getting himself more and more talked about; what was worse, he was getting her talked about again, just at the time when she wanted to be forgotten by all men—save one. Mitford had followed her into the country, and only quitted her on her expressed determination never to speak to him again unless he returned to London at once, and saved her from the gossip of the neighbourhood. She knew he would insist on seeing her constantly when she returned to town. Hence her flight with only one hour's stoppage in London—and under a feigned name—to Baden.

"'I pray you come at once,'" said Dollamore, three days after his conversation with Mr. Aldermaston, reading to his stick the contents of a dainty little note which he had just received;—"'I pray you come at once.—Yours sincerely, Laura Hammond.' Very much yours sincerely, Laura Hammond, I should think. What the deuce does she want with me? Is she going to drive us three abreast, like the horses in the diligence? and does she think I should like to trot along between Mitford and Tchernigow? Not she! She knows me too well to think anything of that sort. But then what on earth does she want with me? 'I pray you come at once.' Egad, I must go, I suppose, and ask for Madame Poitevin, as she tells me."

He lounged up to the Hôtel de Russie, asked for Madame Poitevin, and was shown into a room where Laura was seated with Marcelline reading to her. Dollamore recollected Marcelline at once; he had an eye for beauty in every class, and had taken not an unfavourable notice of the trim little *soubrette* during his stay at Redmoor. He wondered now what had caused this sudden elevation of her social status, and did not ascribe it to any good source. But he had little time to wonder about Marcelline, for she rose at once, and passing him with a slight bow, left the room as Mrs. Hammond advanced with outstretched hand. She looked splendidly handsome; her eyes were bright, her cheeks flushed, her step elastic. Dollamore thought he had scarcely ever seen her to such advantage.

"You are surprised at my having sent to you, Lord Dollamore?" said she as soon as they were seated.

"No, indeed, Mrs. Hammond; I'm never surprised at anything. A man who has turned forty and suffers himself to be surprised is an idiot."

"Turned forty! Well, when you reach that age you shall tell me whether there is truth in that axiom." ("Flattering me!" said Dollamore to his stick; "wants to borrow money.") "But at all events you don't know why I asked you to come."

"I have not the remotest idea."

"How should you have? Three hours ago I myself had no anticipation of the occurrence of circumstances which have induced me to ask you to share a confidence."

"Hallo!" said Dollamore to his stick; "I share a confidence! She ought to have sent for Aldermaston." But he said aloud, "If I can be of any help to you—"

"You can be of the very greatest assistance. You may have heard how I have been left by my husband; how Mr. Hammond's relatives, by their cruel and secret machinations, so worked upon him in his enfeebled state as to induce him to make a most shameful will, by which I was robbed of all that ought to have been mine, and left with a beggarly income!" She had not forgotten that will, and any recurrence to it made her cheek flame in earnest.

Dollamore bowed. He ought to have expressed some pity or some astonishment; but he had never during his life been guilty of any conventionality.

"In this strait," she continued, "I have received succour from a totally unexpected quarter. In the most generous and delicate manner Prince Tchernigow has this day made me an offer of his hand." (Dollamore said he was never surprised, but if the stick was on the alert it must have heard him whistle.) "We are to be married at once!"

"Very satisfactory indeed," said Dollamore. "Fancy being a princess, with 'vassals and serfs by your side'!—Very delicious indeed."

"Oh, I'm so happy!" cried Laura, with that feigned ecstasy of joy which she had so often indulged in; "the Prince is so charming!"

"Is he indeed?" said Dollamore. "Yes; some people require to be known thoroughly before they're appreciated. But what will a friend of ours say to this? I mean Sir Charles Mitford."

"Ah!" said Laura, who turned pale at the name; "that is exactly the subject in which I require your assistance."

"Mine! How can I help you? Suppose he were to come here—"

"It is that I am dreading. I took every precaution to hide my destination. I came here under a feigned name; I have lived in the strictest retirement, having seen no one but the Prince since I have been here; and yet I never hear a carriage dash up to the door of the hotel but I rush to the window, and concealing myself behind the curtains, look out in the full expectation of seeing him leap into the portico. If he were to come now, under present circumstances, what should I do?—good God, what should I do?"

"What should you do? Tell him to go back again. You are not his wife, for him to bully and curse and order about. You are not bound to give in to his cowardly whims, and need not endure his ruffianly insults."

"You don't know him now; you don't know how frightful his temper has become to any one who crosses him. No, no, no, we shall be married at once, and leave this place; and should he come here afterwards, I trust you to tell him nothing more than you can possibly help; above all, to keep silence as to our intended route."

"That will be easily managed, by your not telling me which way you intend going. I'll do what I can to help you, Mrs. Hammond; but I may as well say, that the less I am brought into contact with Sir Charles Mitford, the better I shall be pleased."

"At all events you will do as much as I have asked you?" she said.

"I will; and as that principally consists in holding my tongue, I shall have no difficulty in doing it. When are you to be married?"

"To-morrow morning, at Frankfort, where there are both Russian and English embassies; and whence we start to—"

"You forget; I was not to know your route."

"I had forgotten," she said with a smile. She seemed reassured; her colour came again, and as she held out her hand, she said, "I may rely on you?"

"Rigidly to do nothing," he said; and took her hand, and left her.

"She's a very wonderful woman, and she certainly has had a great run of luck," said Dollamore, as he walked back to his hotel. "To think of her getting hold of this Calmuck savage! By Jove! rich as he is, she'll try and find her way to the bottom of his sack of roubles. Tchernigow is wealthy, but his intendant will have to screw up the moujiks to the last copeck to provide for madame's splendid power of spending. She's evidently completely frightened of Mitford now. It must be sheer brutality that has done that, for he was no match for her in spirit, or anything else."

As he said this, he arrived at the Badischer Hof, before the door of which was standing a dust-covered carriage with two steaming horses; and in the hall Lord Dollamore saw a man, whose back was towards him, talking earnestly to Mr. Aldermaston. The man turned round at the sound of footsteps, and then Dollamore saw that it was Sir Charles Mitford.

290

CHAPTER XXXII.

REAPING THE WHIRLWIND.

Yes; Sir Charles Mitford had arrived at Baden. He had written several times to Mrs. Hammond in her country retreat, and, getting no reply, had called at her London house. The old charwoman there left in attendance was as vague as Mrs. Hammond could possibly have wished her to be about her mistress's movements. She had been there, Lor' bless me, yes, she had been there; but when was it?—We'nesday week, she thought, but won't be by no means certain. It was the day as she had had b'iled rabbit for dinner; she knew that, 'cos she was preparin' the onions when there come that thunderin' rat-tat at the door, which quite discomposed her and made her 'art jump into her mouth. What had happened then? Not much—a puttin' a few things together, which the missis and the Frenchwoman managed between them. And then she was sent out for a cab; and the cab came, and they all got into it, and the cab went off. Where? She couldn't say; leastways, they would not let her hear the direction—told the cabman to drive straight on, and they would tell him presently; that was all she knew—yes, that was all she knew, and all Mitford could get out of her by the closest cross-questioning. Laura Hammond had escaped him; but of her destination he was absolutely ignorant.

How could he hit upon her track? The old woman—the last person who had seen her—was exhausted and pumped out, and had told next to nothing. Was there no one who could help him in this strait?—no one who could make some suggestion as to the best mode of discovering the fugitive? Yes!—a sudden brilliant thought struck him— the man who had discovered him when, as he thought, he lay so closely hid,—the detective, Inspector Stellfox.

He had given a handsome present to the inspector when he came into his kingdom—how long ago it seemed!—and he had seen him several times since on public occasions,—at the Opera, at Chiswick Flower-shows, at the Derby, and similar popular resorts. He had the inspector's address somewhere,—at some police-station down in the City; and he went to his desk, and turned over a heterogeneous collection of papers, and found it. Then he sent Banks down to the station-house; and that evening Inspector Stellfox was shown into Sir Charles's study, and placed by him in possession of the facts.

The inspector went to work in his own special way. It was a peculiar job, he said, and not too easy to work out; but he had hopes. He went back to the station-house, and communicated as much as he chose to tell to two of his best men. Then all three went to work. They found out the cabman who had taken Mrs. Hammond to the South-Eastern Railway; they found the porter who had taken the boxes off the cab, and the luggage-labeller who had marked them; they found the tick-clerk who had registered them "in transit," and whose book showed not merely the number of pounds' weight, but the name in which they were entered. They were booked for Cologne,—one could not in those days register any farther,—and for Cologne Sir Charles started immediately. There he picked up the trace. Two French ladies had arrived by the Ostend train, and gone—not to any of the grand hotels bordering the Rhine, but to a second-rate house, yet quiet and thoroughly respectable for all that— the Brüsseler Hof, kept for the last thirty years by Anton Schumacher. Were they recollected there? Of course they were. Anton Schumacher's eldest son Franz had been rather fetched by the trim appearance of the younger lady, and had gone down with them to the boat, and seen them on board the Königin Victoria, and recommended them specially to the care of the *conducteur*, who was a great friend of his. Where did they take tickets for? Why, at his advice, they took them for Cassel, on the left bank of the river. They were going, as he understood, to Baden-Baden, and he had advised them to sleep at Barth's—a right clean comfortable hotel in Cassel—and then post on to Frankfurt, where they could spend the afternoon and the night, and so get on right pleasantly to Baden the next day.

To Baden! Sir Charles Mitford's heart sunk within him as he heard the words. Baden! That was where Laura had been so talked about for her desperate carrying on with Tchernigow nearly three years ago. And she was gone there now, and Tchernigow had disappeared from London!

Doubtless they had arranged it all between them, and he was thrown overboard and sold. His mind was at once made up: he would follow her there or to the end of the earth; what did it matter to him? He told Banks to pack a small travelling valise; he called at Bligh's on his way to the station and gave him certain instructions, and he was off. Not a word of farewell to Georgie; not a look of kindness; not a kiss of love for that poor child lying broad awake and listening to his footsteps as he stole through the house at early morning! What could he have said to her?—he, going in search of his paramour, who had thrown him over,—what could he have said to the wife whom he had so cruelly treated, so recklessly betrayed?

So Sir Charles Mitford, after long and tedious days of travel, arrived at Baden, as we have seen; and the first person he encountered, ere he had scarcely put foot in the hall of the Badischer Hof, was Mr. Aldermaston. He had known him in London, and was perfectly aware of his qualification for news. There was no reticence in Sir Charles Mitford now; no coming delicately to the subject; no beating about the bush: all that had vanished long since. Besides, if there had been any delicacy remaining, Mr. Aldermaston was scarcely the kind of man for whom it would have been employed. So Sir Charles said at once, and hurriedly:

"How do, Aldermaston? Been here long?"

"Ah, Sir Charles, how do you do? Just arrived, I see. Yes; I've been here—O, three weeks about."

"Then can you tell me? Is Mrs. Hammond here?"

"There's no such name in the *Fremdenblatt*—the *Gazette des Étrangers*, you know." His little eyes twinkled so, that even Mitford's dull comprehension was aroused.

"But for all that, she's here. Tell me, for God's sake!"

"Well, there's a French lady here—says she's French that's to say,—called Madame Poitevin, who might be Mrs. Hammond's twin sister."

"Ah!" Mitford gave a long sigh of relief. "I suppose she's attracted the usual amount of attention among all the people here, eh?"

"She would have, doubtless, had she ever courted it. But the truth is, she has never left her hotel."

"Never left her hotel!" echoed Mitford, obviously delighted. "Which is her hotel? where is she staying?"

"At the Russie, lower down the town."

"Here under a feigned name, and never leaving her rooms,—that's strange," said Mitford.

"Yes; must be dull for her," said little Aldermaston, looking up to see the effect his words had on his companion; "lives in strict seclusion."

"Does she indeed? Poor girl! poor Laura!"

"Yes,—only one person permitted to see her; only one who is allowed to mingle his tears with hers."

"One person! and who is that?"

"A friend of hers,—Prince Tchernigow."

"Damnation!" screamed Mitford; "is he here? That cursed Russian with his sallow face has always been hanging about her; and is he here now?"

"O yes, he's here now; has been here for the last month, and has seen her twice every day since she arrived. I happen to know that," said Mr. Aldermaston, "from private sources of information."

"He has, has he? Curse him!" said Mitford, white with rage.

"O yes, he has; and curse him if you like to me," said Mr. Aldermaston. "He's no friend of mine; and if he were, I don't know that I've any right to object because a gentleman curses him. But I don't think I'd curse him too strongly to Mrs. Hammond when you see her."

"Why not?"

"Well, simply because he's going to be married to her to-morrow morning."

"To be married to her! You lie, sir!—you lie!"

"I say, look here, Mr.—Sir Charles Mitford; there is a point which must not be passed;—thus far shalt thou go, you know, and that sort of thing;—and you must not tell a gentleman he lies—'pon my soul you mustn't!"

"I beg your pardon; I scarcely know what I'm saying. To be married to-morrow morning!—to be married!"

"O yes; it's all right; it's not what you said, you know, but as true as possible. I know it for a fact, because I was at the post-office just now, and I saw letters addressed to the Russian ambassador, and to Mr. Koch, our consul at Frankfurt; and Malmedie told me that the prince's man has been over here to order a carriage and relays for the morning."

"What did you say the name was under which she was passing?"

"Madame Poitevin. But why?"

"Nothing-no matter; now the Hôtel de Russie!—all right;" and he started off up the street.

"*C'est lui! mon, Dieu, madame! c'est lui!*" That was all Mademoiselle Marcelline had time to utter as she opened the door of Mrs. Hammond's rooms to a hasty knock, and a tall figure strode past her. Mademoiselle Marcelline, even in the fading evening light, recognized the well-known form of Sir Charles Mitford; but her exclamation caused Mrs. Hammond to think it was Prince Tchernigow of whom she spoke, and to impute Marcelline's evident terror to the fact that she had not then put the finishing touches to her toilette or her *coiffure*.

When she saw who was her visitor, she made up her mind instantaneously to the line of conduct to be pursued, and said:

"May I ask the meaning, Sir Charles Mitford, of this strange intrusion into a lady's private rooms?"

He stopped still, and winced under her cold words as though cut by a whip. When he regained his voice, he said:

"Laura! Laura! what does this mean?"

"That is what I call upon you to, explain. You come unannounced into my rooms, and then ask me what it means. You have been dining, Sir Charles Mitford!"

"Ah, I know what you're up to, then; but you're not right—I'll swear you're not right. Not one drop of anything have I had for God knows how many hours. But I'm faint, weary, and heart-broken. Tell me, tell me, you heartless devil, is this true that I've heard?" He alternated from maudlin sentimentality to fierce rage, and it was difficult to say under which aspect he was most detestable.

"Let go my hand," said she, trying to snatch her wrist from his clutch; "let go my hand, or I'll call for assistance! How can I tell whether what you've heard is true or not, when you've not had sense enough to tell me what it is?"

She spoke in a deadly cold metallic voice; and what she said roused him to a pitch of fury. Ever since she had first discovered that he occasionally resorted to the brandy-bottle, she had taunted him with covert allusions to his drinking, well aware that nothing rendered him so savage.

"Curse you!" he said, "that's your old taunt. Did you not hear me say that nothing had passed my lips for hours? Now, answer me one question, or rather first hear me speak. I know all."

"Do you?" said she with a sneer; "then you are a cleverer man than ever I imagined you to be!"

"Prince Tchernigow is in Baden."

"And what of that?"

"He visits you daily—twice a day."

"And what of that? Why should he not? What is that to you?"

"Oh, Laura!—Oh, my darling Laura! What is it to me, she asks? I, who worship her shadow, who would put my neck down for her to tread upon!—Then he does visit you?"

"He does visit me. Does that answer content you? You deny that you have been drinking, Sir Charles Mitford, and yet you go on with this senseless rodomontade!"

"Then let him look out for himself, Laura Hammond!—that's all I have to say;—let him look out for himself."

"He is perfectly able to do that, if there were occasion. But there is no occasion now!" She took her cue from Dollamore's hint. "I'm not your wife, Sir Charles Mitford, for you to bully and threaten. You have no hold over me. And if you had, I am not a puny white-faced snivelling school-girl, to be put down by big words and black looks!"

"You are not my wife!" he repeated. "No, God knows you speak truth in that, at all events! You are not my wife."

His voice fell, and the tone in which he uttered these words was very low. Did a thought come over him of the "white-faced snivelling school-girl" who was his wife, and whom he had quitted without one word of adieu? Did the white face rise up in judgment before him then, as it would rise up in judgment on a certain grand day? He passed his hand across his eyes and sat silent.

"No, I am not your wife," she continued, "thank God! I never would have been your wife. And now listen, for this is the last time you and I will ever be alone together; yes—I swear it—the last time! What we have been to each other—the nature of the tie between us—you know as well as I. But what prompted me to permit the establishment of such a tie, you do *not* know, and so I will tell you. Revenge, Sir Charles Mitford, revenge!—that was the sole spur that urged me on to allow my name to be coupled with yours—to allow you to think that you had a hold over me, body and soul. You imagined I cared for you! That poor piece of propriety in England was jealous of me!—jealous of my having robbed her of her pet-lamb, her innocent Southdown! I cared for you then as much as I care for you now—no, I wrong you, I eared for you a little more then, just a little more, because you were useful to me. Now my need for such a tool is ended, and—I cast you off!"

She stood up as ho said these words, and made a motion with her hand, corresponding to the speech, as though throwing him away. He looked at her in astonishment—then his face darkened, and he said:

"Do you dare to tell me this?"

"I dare anything," she replied, "as you might have learnt ere this. Do you recollect the night in the fir-plantation, when your friend Captain Bligh came out in search of you, and we stood together within an arm's length of him? What did I dare then?"

"Not so much as you dare now, if you did but know!" said Mitford. "You knew then that, had the worst come to the worst, you had a man at your feet who was prepared to brave all for you; who would have scorned the world and all that the world could say; who would have taken you far away out of the chance of its venom and the breath of its scandal, and devoted his life to securing your happiness. Your reputation was even then beginning to be tainted; your name had even then been buzzed about, and you would have gained—ay, gained—rather than lost by the fortunate accident which would have made one man your slave for ever!"

"I had no idea you had such a talent for eloquence," said she calmly. "Even in your maddest access of passion—for you are, I suppose, the 'one man' who was prepared to do such mighty things—you never warmed up to say so many sensible words consecutively! But suppose you are arguing on wrong premises? Suppose there is a man who is prepared to do all that that hypothetical 'one man' would have dared? Prepared—ay, and able—to do more! More, for that 'one man' was married, and could only have placed me virtuously in the eyes of the world after long and tedious legal ceremonies. Suppose that there is now a man able and willing—nay more, dying—to make me his wife, what then?"

"Then," said Sir Charles, "I go back to what I said before—let him look to himself—let him look to himself!"

"He is perfectly ready to do so, Sir Charles Mitford," said a low deep voice.

Both turned, and both saw Prince Tchernigow standing in the doorway. Laura gave a great start, and rushed to his side. He put his arm calmly round her, and said:

"Do not disturb yourself, Laura; there is no occasion for fright."

"Ah!" said Mitford, with a deep inhalation of his breath, "I have found you at last, have I? You are here, Prince Tchernigow! So much the better! Let me tell you, sir, that—"

"Even Sir Charles Mitford will recollect," said Tchernigow, "that one chooses one's language in the presence of ladies!" Then, in a lower tones "I shall be at the rooms in half an hour."

Mitford nodded sulkily and took up his hat. Then, with a low bow to Mrs. Hammond, he left the room.

An hour had passed, and the space in front of the Kürsaal was thronged as usual. At a table by himself sat Sir Charles Mitford, drinking brandy-and-water, and ever and anon casting eager glances round him. His eyes were bloodshot, his hand shook as he conveyed the glass to his lips, and his whole face was puckered and livid. The aspect of his face brightened as he saw Prince Tchernigow approaching him. Tchernigow was alone, and was making his way with the utmost deliberation to the table at which he saw Mitford seated. He came up, took off his hat with a grave bow, and remained standing. Mitford swallowed what remained of his drink, and stood up beside him.

"You were waiting for me, M. Mitford?" said Tchernigow. "I am sorry to have detained you; but it was unavoidable. You used words just now—in a moment of anger doubtless—which you are already probably sorry for."

"They were words which I used intentionally and with deliberation," said Mitford. "I spoke of some man—then to me unnamed—who had come between me and Mrs. Hammond—"

"I scarcely understand the meaning of the phrase 'come between,' M. Mitford. It is doubtless my ignorance of your language to which I must ascribe it. But how could any one 'come between' a married man and a widow—granting, of course, that the married man is a man of honour?"

Mitford ground his teeth, but was silent.

"And supposing always," continued Tchernigow, "that there was some one sufficiently interested in the widow to object to any 'coming between'?—some one who had proposed himself in marriage to her, and who intended to make her his wife?"

The truth flashed across Mitford in an instant. He was beaten on all sides; but there was yet a chance of revenge.

"And suppose there were such a fool," he said,—"which, I very much doubt,—the words I used I would use again, and if need were, I would cram them down his throat!"

"*Eh bien, M. Mitford!*" said Tchernigow, changing his language, but ever keeping his quiet tone,—"*eh bien! M. Mitford, décidément vous êtes un lâche!*"

A crash, a gathering of a little crowd, and the waiter-who was so like Bouffé—raised Prince Tchernigow from the ground, with a little blood oozing from a spot beneath his temple. "He had stumbled over a chair," he said; "but it was nothing."

In deep consultation with his stick, Lord Dollamore was lounging round the outer ring at the roulette-table, when Sir Charles Mitford, with a flushed face and dishevelled hair, with rumpled wristbands and shirt-collar awry, made his way to him, and begged for a few minutes' conversation apart.

Shrugging his shoulders, and obviously unwilling, Dollamore stepped aside with him into an embrasure of the window, and then Mitford said:

"I am in a mess, and I want your help."

"In what way?"

"I have had a row with Tchernigow—you can guess about what; he insulted me, and I struck him. He'll have me out of course, and I want you to act for me."

Lord Dollamore paused for an instant, and took the stick's advice. Then he said:

"Look here, Si Charles Mitford: in the least offensive way possible, I want to tell you that I can't do this."

"You refuse me?

"I do. We were acquaintances years ago, when you were quite a boy; and when you came to your title you renewed the acquaintance. I did not object then; and had things continued as they were then, I would willingly have stood by you now. But they are not as they were then; they are entirely changed, and all for the worse. You have been going to the bad rapidly for the last twelve months; and, in short, have compromised yourself in a manner which renders it impossible for me to be mixed up in any affair of yours."

"I understand you perfectly, Lord Dollamore," said Mitford, in a voice hoarse with rage, "The next request I make to you—and it shall be very shortly too—will be that you will stand not by me, but before me!"

"In that case," said Dollamore, with a bow,—"in that case, Sir Charles Mitford, you will not have to complain of a refusal on my part."

Mitford said nothing, but he was cut to the quick. He had noticed—he could not, even with his blunted feelings and defiant temper, avoid noticing—that men's manners towards him had lately much changed; that acquaintances plunged up by-streets as they saw him coming, or buried themselves in the sheets of newspapers when he entered the club-room; but he had never been directly insulted before. He would revenge himself on Dollamore before he left Baden; meanwhile there was business on hand, and who should he ask to be his second? Mr. Aldermaston, of course; and he sought him at once. Mr. Aldermaston was only too delighted. To be second to a baronet in a duel with a prince, and then to have the story to tell afterwards, particularly if one of them killed the other—he didn't much care which— would set him up for life. Mr. Aldermaston agreed at once, and was put in communication with Prince Tchernigow's friend; and the meeting was arranged for sunrise in the Black Forest, just above the entrance to the Murgthal.

Prince Tchernigow called on Laura late in the afternoon on which these preliminaries were arranged. It is needless to say that he did not hint at them to her; indeed such care had he taken, that Laura had no idea Sir Charles Mitford had met the Prince since their first interview in Baden, though probably Mademoiselle Marcelline might have been better informed. But Tchernigow said on reflection it appeared to him better that she should go to Frankfurt that evening,—it would put a stop to any chance of talk, he said, and he would join her there at the Romischer Kaiser the next morning. Laura agreed, as she would have agreed to anything he might have proposed—so happy was she just then; and while the visitors were engaged at the late *table-d'hôte*, a carriage drew up at the side-door of the Hôtel de Russie, and Mrs. Hammond and Mademoiselle Marcelline started for Frankfurt.

Lord Dollamore was in the habit of breakfasting late and substantially. The tables were generally laid for the first *table-d'hôte* before the easy-going Englishman came lounging into the *salle-à-manger* about ten o'clock, and sat down to his *bifteck aux pommes* and his half-bottle of Léoville. He was not a minute earlier than usual on the morning after he had refused to act for Mitford, though he felt certain the meeting had taken place. But he thought very little of it; he had seen so many duels amongst foreigners which never came to anything beyond an interchange of pistol-shots, or which were put an end to after the drawing of first blood by a sabre-scratch. It was not until the door was flung open, and Mr. Aldermaston, with his face ashy pale, with his travelling-clothes on and his courier's bag slung round him, rushed into the room, that Lord Dollamore felt that something really serious had happened, and said, "Good God, Aldermaston! what has gone wrong? Speak, man!"

"The worst!" said Aldermaston, whose voice had lost its crisp little society-tone, and who spoke in a hoarse low whisper,—"the worst! Mitford's hit!"

"Killed?"

"No, he's alive still; was at least when I left. We got him into a woodcutter's hut close at hand, and there's a German doctor with him; but, from all I can make out, there's no hope. I must be off over the frontier, or I shall get in a mess myself. Send me a line to the Grand Laboureur at Antwerp, and let me know all, will you? Goodbye."

The scene which he had witnessed seemed to have had the effect of causing Aldermaston to age visibly. His whiskers were lank, his hair dishevelled, the hand which clasped Dollamore's was cold and clammy; and as he hurried from the room it would have been difficult to recognize in him the usual bright chirpy little news-purveyor.

As soon as he was gone Lord Dollamore ordered a carriage to be got ready, and sent round to the Hôtel d'Angleterre to Mr. Keene, the eminent London surgeon, who had arrived two days before, and who, on hearing what had happened, at once consented to accompany Dollamore to where the wounded man was lying. As they proceeded in the carriage, they exchanged very few remarks. Mr. Keene whiled away the time by the perusal of the new number of the *Lancet*, which had reached him by that morning's post, and which contained some delightfully-interesting descriptions of difficult operations; and Dollamore was immersed in reflections suggested by the nature of the errand on which he was then journeying. He had always had a poor opinion of life in general; and what he had witnessed lately had not tended to raise it. His prophecies regarding Mitford had been more speedily and more entirely fulfilled than he had expected. Mitford had gone to the bad utterly and speedily; and Lady Mitford had had to run the gauntlet in the fullest acceptation of the phrase,—had afforded a topic for the blasting tongues of all the scandal-mongers in London, from no fault of her own, poor child, but from the baseness and brutality of her husband.

These thoughts occupied him till the carriage arrived at a Point beyond which it was impossible for it to proceed further. The man who had driven Mitford and Aldermaston over in the morning, and who had accompanied Dollamore's carriage as guide to the spot, preceded Lord Dollamore and Mr. Keene over rough ruts and among intertwining trees, until at length they reached the hut. Dollamore pushed the door open and looked in, and saw a figure half-dressed, and with the front of its shirt soaked with blood, lying on a heap of straw in one corner of the wretched hovel; a peasant woman standing in the other corner, with two children huddled round her knees; and by the prostrate figure knelt a placid-looking man in black clothes,—a German doctor. He held up his hand in warning, as the door creaked; but Mitford's eyes, turned that way, had fallen on Dollamore, and he tried to beckon him to approach. Dollamore entered, and knelt down beside him. Mitford lips were moving rapidly; but Dollamore could distinguish not a word. The dying man evidently comprehended this. With the last remnant of strength he raised himself until his mouth touched Dollamore's ear, and whispered:

"Georgie—forgive—" and fell back dead.

CHAPTER XXXIII.

LAST WORDS.

The equipage and the establishment, the diamonds and the dress, of the Princess Tchernigow, furnished the gay inhabitants of the gayest and most gossiping city in the world with a subject for almost inexhaustible discussion. There was no sameness about them, but an ever-varying change; so that curiosity was never sated, and the last select few who had met the Princess, and told their story of her magnificence, had materials afforded them for a version of the princely splendours which differed materially from the version given by the select few of the immediately preceding occasion. With the proverbial impenetrability of the French to English social facts and customs, the Parisian *beau monde* could not be made to understand that there was "anything against" the Princess. They knew and cared nothing about the date at which the former husband of that fortunate lady had departed this life, and that at which he had been replaced by the Prince. Many good-natured and strictly moral English people endeavoured to instruct the Parisian mind on this point, and to make it understand that the Princess would have some difficulty with "society" in her own country. But these *idées insulaires* had no success.

Tchernigow had been popular in Paris before he had gratified it by bringing a new princess to sparkle and glitter, by her beauty and her splendour, in the Bois, at the Opera, at the balls, and at the Court. Paris admired the Calmuck; first because he was so immensely rich because there was nothing in the place, which contains everything in the world worth having, that he could not buy; and secondly because he was odd, so *bizarre*; because his character was as much out of the common as his wealth, and his eccentricities afforded them an increasing source of remark and speculation. He was the most polished Russian that had ever appeared in Parisian society—the most widely removed from the train-oil-drinking and no-shirt-wearing tradition of the Muscovites.

And the Princess? She had not been by any means unknown to fame in Paris. She had visited that city during her first bridal tour, and she had had a great success. The freshness and perfection of her beauty, which owed nothing to artificial means, but could bear any kind or degree of light; the piquancy of her manner, her first-rate seat on horseback, her dancing,—all these things had captivated the Parisians. Then, was she not so interesting, this beautiful little English lady, whose husband was so far from young? It was so charming to see them together, because one knew that in England marriages of reason had no place; and this fair creature must have reposed her affections in the feeble elderly gentleman, to whom she was so delightfully devoted, and who was so proud of her. She had had a train of admirers then, naturally; but it was early days, and there was nothing very *prononcé*.

Mrs. Hammond had been in Paris again and again after that first successful appearance; and if her devotion to the feeble elderly gentleman had been less conspicuous, her beauty and her vivacity had been more so. Of course she was "talked about;" but that mysterious and terrible word has one signification and effect in London, and quite another in Paris; and Mrs. Hammond's reign was undimmed.

When the Prince and Princess Tchernigow made their appearance on the scene in their attractive character of bride and bridegroom, considerable curiosity had been excited about them, quite apart from the legitimate interest to which they were entitled on their separate merits, and to which their union added vigour and intensity. The Baden story had of course got about, with more or less correctness of time, place, and circumstances; and the combination of a duel, involving the death of his adversary, with a wedding, in which the bride had been *affichée* to the slain man, was an irresistibly piquant anecdote,—and "so like" Tchernigow.

The Princess came off remarkably well in the innumerable discussions to which the affair gave rise. In the first place Mitford was dead, which was a great point; and in the second, the catalogue of the Prince's luxuries including some useful and devoted toadies, who made it their business to spread abroad a report which gained ample credence, that the unfortunate Englishman was a violent fellow, who had no manners, and who had assumed a tone towards Mrs. Hammond wholly unjustified by their antecedents; in fact, had persecuted that lady, and been *excessivement brutale*.

So it was all plain sailing with the Prince and Princess, and even the women took the liveliest interest in the latter. Poor dear creature, they said, how very sad, but how charmingly romantic it was! To think that she had been quite ignorant of the duel, and had not had the least idea that her bridegroom had shot a man just before he had married her! When she discovered it, how strange she must have felt! They wondered if it made her experience for a moment a very little of repulsion. But no, probably not,—the Prince was really such a gentleman; and the other deplorable person it was impossible to pity.

Prince Tchernigow possessed a mansion in the Champs Elysées; and thither, a short time after the arrival of the pair, all Paris (presentable Paris, of course) flocked to pay their respects, and inspect the magnificence of the possessions in the midst of which Tchernigow had installed his bride—doubtless the most precious of them all. Then came brilliant entertainments, and the Princess achieved at one stroke the almost incredible eminence of being declared by common consent the best-dressed woman in Europe—Paris meaning that continent, of course.

It was at the second of these entertainments that Madame de Soubise remarked to Madame de Somme, in a pregnant little sentence, beginning with the invariable "*dites-donc, chère Adèle,*" that Madame la Princesse seemed a little *distraite*, and had begun to wear rouge like the rest of the world. Madame de Somme acquiesced in her friend's remark, and further added on her own account, that the English complexions, undeniably charming, were very evanescent, and that really the Princess had no longer the appearance of being young. It was on the same occasion that several of the company had asked who was the "*petite dame*," so beautifully dressed, so quiet, and yet so *spirituelle*, to whom the Princess was so caressing, and the "best" men were invariably presented. The "*petite dame*" was small and slight, pale-faced, and rather plain, perhaps, than pretty. Her features had nothing remarkable about them, and her figure was redeemed from insignificance only by the taste and richness of her dress. But she was eminently attractive; and before long rumours circulated about the *salons* to the effect that the little lady—the close, the inseparable friend of the Princess; a charming Irish widow, who spoke French remarkably well, but with perhaps the slightest defect in the accent (it is so difficult to be certain that one is taught by persons who are *comme il faut*)—was as witty, as brilliant, as her friend was beautiful. She was so completely at her ease, and she enjoyed herself so much; and how delightful it was to see the affection which subsisted between the little lady and the Princess! Did one hint to the former that the Princess looked a little fatigued, she would be all concern and agitation; she would fly to her cherished Laura, and ask her in fervent tones if the pleasures, the delights of this evening of Paradise had been too much for her; and the two women would form the prettiest tableau in the world.

Did any of the worshippers at Laura's *canapé*, beside which the Prince, most attentive of bridegrooms, most devoted of men, kept his place steadily all the evening, admire the vivacity, the wit, the grace of the little lady, the Princess would reply warmly, that her dear Lucy was fortunate in possessing such a charming flow of spirits; and Tchernigow would remark that Madame Seymour was indeed a captivating islander, but that he understood the Irish ladies resembled the French in wit and vivacity.

When the season in Paris approached its termination, the *beau monde* was distressed to learn that the health of the Princess was not in so satisfactory a condition as the host of friends who were desolated by the intelligence could have desired. She was as much seen as ever; she was the gayest of the gay, the richest of the rich, the most brilliant of the brilliant; but she was not as beautiful at the close of the season as she had been at the beginning; and it was not to be denied that Lady Walford and Mrs. Fane—the last new brides and beauties from the English capital—had as many admirers, if not more.

The Princess still dressed better than any woman in Europe, conventionally defined; and her diamonds at least were unapproachable, though there might possibly be brighter eyes to be now seen under the Paris moonlight and waxlight.

"Going to St. Petersburg, are they?" said Lord Dollamore to his bosom-friend the Malacca cane, as he retreated gracefully from the side of the Princess's carriage, after a brief conversation with her. "Going to St. Petersburg, are they? She does not look enchanted; on the contrary, rather frightened, I thought. And that little devil Marcelline, doing her beloved compatriots with such perfect composure and success! I would not have lost seeing that for a good deal. Gad, the bow she bestowed upon me when the Princess introduced me would have done credit to a duchess! Madame Seymour, hey?—and Irish! By Jove, I have not enjoyed anything so much for an age!"

Lord Dollamore walked on chuckling and tapping his ear in his old manner. After a little his face grew graver and his confidences with his cane were resumed in a different tone.

"What the deuce has come over her, I wonder?" he said. "I see a change; but I don't know where it is. Is it in her face? is it in her manner? She's very handsome—she's wonderfully handsome still, though she rouges; but that's of course here-every one does it; though it's not a case of painting the lily, so far as the Parisiennes are concerned. Stop, though: there's such a thing as an orange-lily—forgot that. It's something in the expression, I fancy—something which gives one an impression that she's thinking of one thing and talking of another, which was never *la belle* Laura's way: she knew her *monde* better than to shock their self-love by anything of that kind. Yes: that's it, by Jove!" and Lord Dollamore struck himself quite a sharp little blow on the ear; "I've hit it: the expression in her face is fear!"

When Lord Dollamore had stepped back from the side of her carriage, and the horses were once more whirling it along, to the admiration of the multitude, the Princess sank back upon the luxurious cushions with a deep sigh. Madame Seymour looked at her with steady composure and not a little contempt.

"Agitated, are you?" she said; "and quite upset by old memories and all that sort of thing? What a weak fool you are! you are thinking of the last time you and that very estimable nobleman met, I daresay, and feeling quite sentimental. If you would remember, in addition, what you intended to do when that interesting interview took place (I remember it: I thought I never saw anything cooler or cleverer than his polite unconsciousness of the identity of your *dame de compagnie*; he used to walk with me in the shrubberies at Redmoor, and I've given him a kiss occasionally for a guinea),—if you would remember what you intended to do, and how completely you have done it, it would be more to the purpose."

The Princess turned towards her companion, and said in a hurried broken voice:

"You are wrong, Marcelline,—you are quite wrong; I was not thinking of anything of the kind. I was only thinking of this horrible journey to Russia. It terrifies me."

"Yes; but everything terrifies you, you know. How odd that Madame la Princesse should not be *enthousiasmé* at the prospect of beholding the ancestral home of Monsieur le Prince, of being presented to the gracious and urbane monarch who rules the Russias and the Russians! They are a little difficult to rule as individuals, I fear; but as a nation, no doubt, charming. I should have thought madame would have seized the occasion with transport."

"Marcelline," pleaded Laura, "don't laugh at me; I am in deadly terror of this journey. You can save me from it if you will. Do, do, Marcelline! It is all dreadful enough even here, where I have some protection—where at least he dares not kill me. But if I am taken there, to his dreadful country, I shall be quite helpless in his hands. He might kill me there, and none would interfere—no one would even know, perhaps."

"How ignorant she is!" thought Mademoiselle Marcelline, "and how cowardly! He has impressed himself upon her tolerably effectually, this lacquered savage, and she has succumbed. These Englishwomen are very shallow after all, no matter how bad they may be."

The Princess still pleaded, and Mademoiselle Marcelline, having derived sufficient amusement just then from her companion's weakness, and being somewhat fatigued by her importunity, told her at length, and shortly, that she desired to enjoy the drive, and therefore intended to change the subject. For her part, she did not particularly care about going to Russia; she understood that travelling in that empire had not been sufficiently systematized on that scale of comfort indispensable to persons of condition; and, on the whole, she rather thought they were not likely to go to Russia just then.

Madame Seymour's apartments in the Hôtel Tchernigow were among the most luxurious and elegant which that palatial edifice contained. They were inferior to those of the Princess in size alone; in every detail of comfort and sybarite ease they equalled hers. A tiny and delicious little boudoir made one of the *suite*; and this beautiful retreat was the scene that same evening of a rather remarkable conversation. The speakers were the mistress of the gem-like apartment and Prince Tchernigow. The former-dressed in the most tasteful and becoming evening dress it was possible for human milliners to concoct, and adorned with jewels, which also differed from those worn by the Princess chiefly by their size-and the latter, in his usual faultless attire, had met in the boudoir previous to accompanying the Princess to the very last entertainment at which they intended to appear.

"Well, Marcelline," said the Prince, "you did me the honour to summon me. What is it? Merely that I should tell you that you never looked so charming?"

"For nothing of the sort," said she, putting aside the compliment as beneath her notice and beside the question; "I sent for you to tell you that the Princess does not wish to go to St. Petersburg. She is nervous, I believe, and has some strange notions of the impunity of Russian princes on their own versts. At all events, she does not wish to go."

"I am perfectly aware of that fact, Madame Seymour," said the Prince, with a peculiar smile; "but we are going to St. Petersburg, *quand même.*"

"Very well," said Marcelline; and she held her wrist towards the Prince as a tacit intimation that he was to button her dainty glove. "Then we shall not meet for some time, for I have not the most remote intention of going to St. Petersburg."

"What!" said the Prince, with an angry start; "you will not come? You are not serious, Marcelline?"

"I am perfectly serious, Prince Tchernigow. I have no intention whatever of going to St. Petersburg at present, and I beg I may hear no more on the subject. Have the goodness to ascertain if the Princess is ready!" She sat down and turned over the leaves of a book.

The Prince walked two or three times up and down the little apartment, and swore a Cossack oath or two under his breath. Then he stopped opposite to her and said:

"Where will you consent to go then, Marcelline?"

"H-m!" She paused, with an exasperating air of indecision. "I don't exactly know; I think I shouldn't mind the Mediterranean."

As she took her place beside the Princess, whose beauty was less brilliant than ever that evening, and whose depression her attendants had not failed to mark, she said, "Don't look so wretchedly subdued and terrified, Madame la Princesse; you are not going to behold your princely spouse in the cradle of his race and the midst of a grateful peasantry. You are going to the Mediterranean instead."

And then she said to herself, "Poor wretch! I am glad I saved her from that for the present. I really object to torturing her, when there's nothing to gain."

Another season, and another, and the Hôtel Tchernigow opened its hospitable doors, and maintained its reputation for splendour, profusion, and fashion. But the health of the Princess afforded more and more reason for solicitude to the hosts of friends who were desolated by the intelligence that she was indisposed; and the beauty of the Princess began to require that adornment from dress which it had hitherto bestowed upon the utmost resources of decoration. Ugly rumours regarding the princely *ménage* had begun to circulate; and a few, a very few, of those in high places had abated the alacrity with which they had been wont to welcome the appearance of the Muscovite magnate in their *salons*. French society does not tolerate overt brutality; and there had been a story about a fall, and a broken arm; and though no doubt both circumstances were purely accidental, and indeed the fullest particulars were given to the numerous callers who were so anxious to hear of the dear Princess's progress towards recovery, the matter left an unpleasant impression, which all the efforts made by the Princess to convince the world that she was not only the richest, but the happiest, woman in Paris did not succeed in removing.

What efforts they were! How she rouged, and dressed, and danced, and talked! How she drove out with the Prince, and talked to him, and smiled at him! How she playfully wore the injured arm in a very conspicuous sling, and lamented that she was obliged to let "Alexis" drive her darling ponies for her, until her tiresome arm should be quite well, and how he perfectly ruined them! How she talked about the polished *parquets* as being so charming, but then so dangerous,—"witness my poor arm, you know,"—and held the beautiful limb out for pity and admiration! How she complained that she could not ride any more that season, the injury having been inflicted on the "bridle-arm;" and exulted in the promise of "Alexis" that if she would only take good care of herself, and get quite well, she should hunt in Leicestershire next season!

It was all very clever, but it did not do; and Tchernigow knew that it did not; and the Princess knew it also and better.

One night, at the Italiens, an Englishman who had known the Princess in former days saw her in her box, sitting radiantly in the front, while Madame Seymour occupied a less prominent position, and a couple of the most fashionable dandies of the day occupied the background. This gentleman had left a party of ladies in the boxes, and gone down to the stalls, and he now remarked to his companion:

"How awfully she is altered! I never saw such a wreck in so short a time. And surely that lady with her is some one I have seen before. Do you know who she is, Dollamore?"

"Yes, I do, of course. That lady is Madame Seymour, an Irish lady, a widow of large fortune, who is devotedly attached to the Princess Tchernigow. She lives with her,—for her, it almost appears; and she speaks French so like a native, that it is difficult to distinguish any difference."

"Ah, then, I am wrong; and we don't know her," said the gentleman, still looking curiously at the party.

"Well, perhaps you don't exactly know her," said Dollamore; "but you are right in thinking you had seen her. Madame Seymour used to be known at Redmoor as Mademoiselle Marcelline, and she was Mrs. Hammond's maid."

His hearer's exclamation of astonishment was checked by a sudden commotion in the Princess's box. She had recognized the English party at the moment when his companion addressed his last question to Lord Dollamore. She had fought hard for a moment against her overwhelming emotion; but the days of Laura's strength and self-mastery were over, and she fell fainting from her chair.

Very shortly after this occurrence the paternal yearnings of the Czar to behold Prince Tchernigow once more in the land of his birth proved too strong for his resistance. The Prince and Princess left France for Holy Russia; and that was the last that was seen of them in Paris.

Miss Constance Greenwood, Miss Gillespie, Lizzie Ponsford,—which you will— never saw Lady Mitford after that memorable occasion on which she yielded up possession of the forged bill. A considerable time afterwards Lady Mitford wrote to her a long and sweet letter, in which she reiterated her thanks for the great service which Miss Gillespie—so she still called her—had intended doing her; but she said, "even had the talisman which you left with me possessed the powers which you wished to invest it with, it was useless—it was too late." Lady Mitford added, that she had not forgotten the name under which Miss Gillespie had told her she was pursuing a theatrical career; that she had made inquiries, and found that "Miss Constance Greenwood" was spoken of in the highest terms, not merely for her transcendent abilities, but for the rectitude of her conduct. In conclusion, Lady Mitford invited her correspondent to come and stay with her when she would, and not to fail to apply immediately and directly to her when she was in strait or difficulty of any kind.

People had said that Miss Constance Greenwood's stage-tears were the most natural throughout the profession. They were not nearly so natural as those which welled up hot and blinding into her eyes as she perused Lady Mitford's letter, and which showered down thick and heavy on to the paper as she pressed it to her lips. That letter is yellow with age now; but, all stained and tear-blurred as it is, it is the choicest object in that delicate little desk in which Miss Constance Greenwood keeps all her treasures.

Not that she was Miss Constance Greenwood very long after the receipt of that letter. She had risen to the very height of popularity with the public, and had drawn a large amount of money into Mr. Wuff's treasury, when Mr. Wuff sent for her one day to his room, and told her in confidence that Mr. Frank Likely was going to give up the Parthenium next week and go into the Queen's Bench, where he would remain until he was "whitewashed;" after undergoing which process he and Mrs. Likely would undertake an engagement at the Hatton-Garden Theatre. "And the worst of it is," said Mr. Wuff,—"the worst of it is, my dear, that Mrs. Likely says she won't have any better-looking woman than herself playing leading business in the theatre. That's a compliment to you, my dear; but it seems that you must go; and as I've made an engagement with the Likelys, I am afraid you and I must part at the end of the season."

Miss Greenwood shrugged her shoulders and bowed her head. She knew that with her present *prestige* any manager in London would be glad to engage her. She was in no hurry, therefore, to seek for work. The Parthenium closed; Mr. Frank Likely's body was seized by the myrmidons of the sheriff; Mr. Wuff's season came to an end; and still Miss Greenwood had not looked after another engagement, though she had innumerable offers of terms.

How did Sir Laurence Alsager, so far away from England, keep au courant with London theatrical matters? Just as Miss Greenwood was weighing two offers in her mind, doubtful which to accept, she had a visit from an old gentleman, who announced himself as Sir Laurence Alsager's solicitor, and handed her a letter—a letter which said that the writer had never forgotten her intended kindness to a certain person; that he had heard of her theatrical success, and desired to serve her. Would she not like to be the lessee of the Parthenium—then, as he understood, vacant? If so, his lawyer had instructions to act in any way she wished; to draw what money she required, and to carry through the arrangement for her. Miss Greenwood gave a little cry of delight; her old love of fun sprung up in her. How glorious it would be to beat the Likelys with their own weapons and in their own den! She accepted Sir Laurence Alsager's kind proposition, she said; and while the lawyer went to work at his business, she went to work at hers. She set the eminent Spofforth to work on a new piece; she engaged Dacre Pontifex, who was as distasteful to Mr. Frank Likely as was Miss Greenwood to his wife. She got together a capital stock-company, and took the town by storm. Everything prospered with her, and at the end of each season she found large gains. She has long since repaid Sir Laurence Alsager's advance; and she has now great wealth, and some one to share it with her. Dacre Pontifex, who had so long made love to her on the stage, at length made love to her in earnest; and as he had always proved himself a thoroughly good fellow, she accepted him, And there is no happier couple in England. They have almost given up acting now; but they still retain the theatre, and are thought highly of by all who know them.

And Lord Dollamore? Lord Dollamore still lives, as well as, and in some respects better than, ever. He superintended all the arrangements for sending Sir Charles Mitford's body to England under the charge of Banks—a duty which that functionary performed with the greatest reluctance, declaring that he had not been engaged to "wait upon corpses;" and then Dollamore had a long and serious consultation with his stick, the subject of which was whether it would be expedient for him to make any change in his mode of life. The idea of marriage had never entered his head; but now that he knew Lady Mitford was free, he began to experience a curious sensation at his heart, which caused him at first the wildest astonishment, and then a considerable amount of trouble. He had watched Georgie through all her trials and temptations, and the sight had impressed him deeply. For the first time since manhood he confessed (to himself) a belief in virtue, bravery, and selflessness; for the first time in his life he felt an irrepressible yearning towards the possessor of these qualities; and he thought how the companionship of such a woman would illumine the decline of his aimless, purposeless life.

He was for some days in doubt whether he should not return at once to England, and after a decent interval proceed tentatively to see whether an offer of his hand to Lady Mitford would be likely to be successful; but he finally decided otherwise. He was no longer young, his manner of life was formed; and he doubted whether he should have strength to keep to all his good resolutions—in which case, and in the event of his marriage with Georgie, her old troubles would be renewed when she had less strength to bear them.

There is no doubt, however, that the mere fact of his indulging in such thoughts proved that he was to a certain extent an altered man. His tongue is much less bitter, his manner much less rough, his thoughts much less cynical than they were. The person who suffers most from him now is the *chef* of the Maecenas, when Dollamore rules the House-Committee. When that unfortunate Frenchman hears from the house-steward that Lord Dollamore has been seen whispering to his stick about an *entrée* or an omelette, he knows what to expect the next day.

When Lady Mitford was told by Captain Bligh, who executed his task with great feeling, if not with profound skill, that her waiting was all in vain,—that her letter had never reached her unfortunate husband, but had been carefully enclosed with the effects of the deceased, and consigned to the custody of Mr. Banks, she was not so completely overwhelmed as might have been expected. She listened patiently to all the details which it was considered necessary to give her, and bore herself with a gentle fortitude which surprised all who saw her.

The remains of the unfortunate Baronet arrived in due time; the funeral was "performed;" and Sir Charles Mitford rested in the family burial-place—the most unfortunate of a race who had been generally rather uninterestingly prosperous.

Lady Mitford found herself very rich. Not only did she come into possession of an ample jointure, but the entire sum destined for a provision for younger children was bequeathed to her, in case of the non-existence or death of such children. She was very much surprised to find that Sir Charles had made a will, not many months prior to his death, by which he had left her considerable personal property also; so that her position was an enviable one, as far as pecuniary affairs were concerned. How far that was, she had yet to learn. She had courage, resignation, and patience; and she had the good gift of common sense, enabling her to lay plans and make arrangements with judgment and foresight; but she was not cold-hearted, nor callous, and the time lay yet a good way distant at which she could reckon her riches and feel her freedom.

The next heir to the title and entailed estates was a boy named Edward Mitford, whom Lady Mitford had never seen, and who, with his widowed mother, lived in an obscure village in Warwickshire, where the heir to so much wealth and position picked up a very indifferent education at a school of fourth-rate pretensions and sixth-rate performances. No mention of this youth had been made by Sir Charles, who had, very naturally, bestowed no thought upon the distant contingency of his succession. The house in London had been rented by Sir Charles for a term of years; and Lady Mitford determined to retain it in her own possession. Having formed this resolution, and ascertained all that was necessary relative to her position, Lady Mitford wrote to the Reverend Cuthbert Farleigh. She recalled herself to his recollection, and appealed to his kindness. She was very friendless, she said, and wanted advice. Sir Laurence Alsager had told her that the kindness of heart which had been so distinguishing a characteristic of Cuthbert Farleigh in his boyhood was no less conspicuous in his more advanced and responsible years, and she asked him to come to her. She did not make any mention of Helen in the letter; she would defer that until they could talk it over, she thought; and then he would perhaps make her an offer of Helen's society, which she would gladly accept.

The Reverend Cuthbert answered the letter in person; and the meeting between the former friends and companions under such altered circumstances could hardly have failed to be affecting. Georgie thanked him with all her heart, and felt less lonely and desolate that evening than she had felt since the day on which Sir Laurence Alsager had left her. He had arrived late; and they agreed to postpone the discussion of the serious matters on which Georgie desired his advice until the following day.

As Lady Mitford sat alone that night before the bright fire in her dressing-room, she passed her life before her in mental review. She questioned herself concerning the grief which she felt so keenly, and yet blamed herself for not feeling with still greater acuteness. The oppression, the vague gloom of a great change, of a tremendous shock, from whose first effects she had not suffered so much as from that which succeeded, were on her. The dreadful death of her husband appalled her; less because it was *he* who had been killed, and because he had been killed in so awful manner, than because it seemed to set the seal of the curse upon their marriage. She saw that marriage now as it was,—a mistake first; then a disaster; finally a catastrophe;—and she recoiled with horror from the awful lesson of life thus opened out before her.

"Swift and sure," she thought, "punishment has followed wrong in *his* case. It seems hard, too; he was not the only man beguiled by a wanton woman, not the only man who betrayed and deserted his wife. Little as I have seen of the world, I have seen instances of the same thing; but these men, who had as little conscience, had more self-control, more judgment, more self-respect, and did not expose themselves to the risks which he dared, and which have been fatal to him. Poor fellow! poor Charley!"

Her reveries always ended thus, in sweet womanly compassion and forgiveness. She did not deceive herself; she did not lament for Sir Charles with the intense and passionate grief of bereavement; she did not make any false estimate of her loss, or give way to any sentiment in which the perfect truth did not abide; but she shrank appalled and miserable from the contemplation of so total a wreck as her wretched husband's life had been, from the possibilities of sin and suffering which it revealed to her.

Lord Dollamore had written to her,—Banks had brought the letter; and so she learned that the last thought of the dying man had been of her, the last word he had spoken had been her name. Georgie did not attach greater importance to this fact than it deserved. She knew how to discriminate between remorse and repentance too well to make a mistake; but she was very thankful for the message, very thankful that her husband had been permitted to utter it. She knew that in the future, as long as she should live, those words would be a comforting recollection to her; and she fully comprehended how much harder it would all have been to endure, had the silence which had subsisted between her and Sir Charles for several days before he left town never been broken, even by those two gasping, hardly-articulate sounds.

Cuthbert Farleigh and Lady Mitford held a long consultation, as they had agreed to do; and during its progress the curate learned that she was acquainted with the fact of his engagement to Helen Manningtree; and Lady Mitford imparted to him the permission and counsel Sir Laurence Alsager had given her to ask Helen to come to her in any time of need.

"You have had more than one such time of need, dear Lady Mitford," said Cuthbert, "since Sir Laurence wrote to you and to Helen; and why have you never made a sign, why have you never asked Helen to come to you?"

"Because I could not think it right, Cuthbert. The trouble I was in was of a peculiar kind,—my sorrow was the result of another's sin; and I don't think it would have been right to have brought a young girl like Helen in contact with it. When I think of my own girlhood, when I remember how far I was from the mere knowledge of such perversities in human relations being possible, I am sure I was right."

Cuthbert Farleigh remembered his own words to Helen,—"You are better without the confidence of an unhappy wife,"—and admired the directness with which the instinct and the principle of this woman had guided her to a similar conclusion.

"But now," she said, "that is all over. When you and I come to the end of our conversation, let the days which preceded the dark and terrible one of his death"—she paused for a moment to command her voice,-"let them be consigned to oblivion. There are no faults in the grave; all is so trifling, so small, so contemptible in the presence of that great mystery. I think it is a happy thing, Cuthbert, that the death of a person who has ever been beloved blots out not only anger, but dulls remembrance. I know this is the truth, that many and many a day I sat brooding over small offences, little slights, trifling but significant departures from the courtesies and the graces of love; and oh how miserable such brooding made me! Well, I forget them all now; every trace of bitterness has disappeared,—I remember only all the good there was in my poor Charley, Yes, Cuthbert, he is mine again now; he had ceased to be hers before he was slain; now he is mine again, and I am not going to dwell on his faults."

Cuthbert Farleigh was privately of opinion that Lady Mitford proposed to herself an exceedingly limited sphere of contemplation in respect to her late estimable lord; but he admired, he reverenced, as every man with the heart of a gentleman must, the simple, beautiful, unreasoning instinct of womanly tenderness.

"So now," she went on, "there can be no harm in Helen's coming to me. I am a widow so much sadder and more pitiable than other widows, that I cannot talk of him whom I have lost with that free outspoken pride which is so instinctive in other women, and which must be so sweet and so bitter too, so precious and so terrible. I am truly widowed; for life robbed me of my husband before death came to hide him from my eyes. The world will cease to talk about him soon, and it will forget me when it does not see me. There will be nothing objectionable in the quiet life which I shall ask Helen to share with me until you ask her to leave my home for yours."

Helen Manningtree obeyed Lady Mitford's summons; and from the first hours of their mutual association Sir Laurence Alsager's hopes and expectations were fulfilled. They "suited each other" exactly, and their companionship was beneficial to both.

Helen Manningtree and Mrs. Chisholm corresponded with great regularity with Sir Laurence, now travelling somewhere in the East, and furnishing the most inscrutable addresses for their letters, the attempt to decipher which they ordinarily gave up in despair and pasted them bodily on the envelopes. Their letters were written from London and from Knockholt respectively, and furnished the recipient with the fullest particulars respecting their writers, and the most accurate details of the few events which marked the first year of Lady Mitford's widowhood.

Thus from Helen Sir Laurence learned that the young Sir Edward and his mother had come to town on Lady Mitford's invitation, and that Georgie and the quiet little lady from the country soon became great friends; that the young baronet was a promising boy enough, but given to idleness, the avoidance of soap-and-water, and the pursuit of useless amusements, such as cricket and fishing, as contra-distinguished from classical and useful learning; that his mother and Lady Mitford having duly consulted the family advisers, and received from them the simple counsel that they had better manage the boy as they thought proper, had considered that the very best way of managing him would be to establish him comfortably under the charge of a private tutor of unusually desirable attainments.

When Ellen next wrote she informed Sir Laurence that the private tutor of unusually desirable attainments had been found in the person of Cuthbert Farleigh, who had, moreover, been provided with a very comfortable living not very far distant from Knockholt, by virtue of a mysterious arrangement whereby somebody gave up this piece of preferment at the present, in consideration of some other "good thing" of a similar kind which would be at the young baronet's disposal in the future. Helen did not understand the arrangement very clearly, but she had a perfect appreciation of its results; and though her account of the transaction, as written "out" to Sir Laurence (who, though he wrote vaguely of coming soon, was still beyond the reach of civilization and spelling), was remarkably confused, two facts appeared with unmistakable clearness. The one was that the family lawyers were satisfied with the arrangements ("There's no simony in it, then, or bedevilment of that kind," thought Sir Laurence, relieved when he ascertained this first fact); the second was that Helen's marriage could not take place so early as she and Cuthbert had hoped, because since Cuthbert had ceased to be a curate, the cares of property and position had fallen upon him, involving the repairing and altering of his parsonage-house, new furnishing, &c., &c. "So now, as it is so far off, dear Laurence," wrote Helen, "you really must come home in time for my wedding. I think we should have put the event off, at all events, in order to admit of Lady Mitford's being present; and now, as her year's deep mourning will have more than expired, she has promised to come. Indeed, I rather think our marriage will take place here. You would be much surprised, if you could see her, at her cheerfulness. I am sure it must arise from her perfect forgetfulness of self. She lives entirely for others, and her serenity and sweetness tell that peace is the result. Sir Edward is greatly attached to her; he and Cuthbert also get on very well together. As usual, Lady Mitford sends her kindest regards."

From Mrs. Chisholm Sir Laurence received good tidings of affairs at Knockholt Park. That excellent lady prided herself upon her letter-writing, fondly flattering herself, at times, that she turned her sentences in something of the same manner in which her gifted Augustine had rounded those flowing periods which had been so effective when the departed curate occupied the pulpit at St. Parable's. She liked writing letters, and especially to Sir Laurence; and though she furnished him with plentiful details concerning individuals of whose identity he had the most vague and confused ideas; and though she was very pathetic indeed on the theme of Cuthbert's removal "to a sphere of, I trust, greatly extended usefulness, but that usefulness to others to be purchased at the price of a relapse into spiritual destitution here very sad to contemplate,"—Sir Laurence liked receiving her letters.

The truth was, his heart yearned towards England And home. He had imposed upon himself a fixed term of absence, and nothing would have induced him to abridge that period; but all his resolution did not check his imagination, did not arrest his fancy, did not quell his longing for its expiration. The smallest details which reached him from the distant households in which he was held in such affectionate remembrance had ineffable charm for him. He found himself, under the most unpropitious circumstances and in the most unheard-of places, writing lengthy epistles to Mrs. Chisholm—letters full of almost feminine inquisitiveness, and enjoining the immediate despatch of voluminous replies. He rejoiced the good lady's heart by the sympathy which he expressed in all the local matters which she detailed; and he soothed her sorrows concerning the departure of Cuthbert by so dexterous an argument in favour of the almost inevitable eligibility of the curate destined to succeed him, that Mrs. Chisholm actually prepared to receive him with a gracious and hopeful welcome. Sir Laurence was right; only a young man of exemplary piety and conscientious intentions in the direction of parish-work would be at all likely to accept so poor a provision as the curacy at Laneham,—no doubt all would be well; and she hoped dear Cuthbert would not be led away by his preferment. It was, however, melancholy to observe how great a contrast sometimes existed between the lowly and hard-working curate and the proud, lazy, and worldly-minded rector. She trusted such a contrast might never exist in the case of dear Cuthbert.

The simple-minded lady was thinking, as she thus expressed her guileless hopes and fears, of one curate to whom preferment never came, and whom it never could have spoiled. She had a strong conviction that if there should prove to be any celestial institution at all resembling a bench of bishops in a future state, she should find her Augustine occupying a very prominent place among its occupants.

So the time passed on, and the period appointed for Helen's marriage drew near. The wedding was to be a very quiet one, as Lady Mitford had insisted on its taking place at her house, and the first year of her widowhood would have expired only a few weeks before the time for the marriage.

Mrs. Chisholm, Mrs. Mitford, the young baronet, and the Reverend Cuthbert Farleigh (rector of Everingham and principal on this auspicious occasion), Helen, and her hostess, were assembled at Lady Mitford's house on the last evening but one before the event. They were all together in the drawing-room, and were engaged in discussing the chances for and against the arrival of Sir Laurence Alsager in time for the wedding.

"I am afraid he has made a mistake," said Cuthbert, "about a steamer to Trieste. I can find no announcement of one for a week to come."

"No, no," said Helen; "Laurence said he would come, and Laurence will be here. I would not give him up if we were all in the church."

"What do you think, Lady Mitford?" asked Sir Edward; "I'm awfully anxious to see this Sir Laurence you and Helen are for ever jawing about,—I'm sure he's awfully jolly, though I suppose he's no end of a swell."

The Reverend Cuthbert Farleigh considered it his duty to correct the young gentleman's vernacular at this juncture, and Lady Mitford did not appear to have heard the question. At all events she allowed it to remain unanswered.

At this moment a servant brought Helen a note. "Come by hand from the Clarendon, ma'am," he explained.

Helen exclaimed rapturously:

"It's from Laurence! He's in London! We shall see him to-morrow! There, Cuthbert, you incredulous person, will you ever doubt Laurence's promise or dispute my opinion again?"

"Certainly not, after the day after to-morrow, Nelly," replied Cuthbert.

There was a small enclosure in Sir Laurence's note to Helen, which she had slipped into her pocket unperceived. It bore Lady Mitford's name; but Helen waited until she was about to take leave of her, as usual, for the night at the door of her own room before she handed it to her. When she was alone Georgie opened the note. It was very brief; it contained only three words. They were:

"FORTITER—FIDELITER—FELICITER?"

Georgie's reply to this query was perfectly satisfactory to Sir Laurence Alsager.

THE END.

CPSIA information can be obtained
at www.ICGtesting.com
Printed in the USA
BVHW071923260619
552031BV00001B/16/P